I0584570

The Guest

From Johannesburg

By

Donald McPhail

Also by Donald McPhail:
The Millionaires Cruise: Sailing Toward
Black Tuesday

Published by Plain Style Press
Copyright © 2019 Donald McPhail

Illustrations, Michelle Imbach Walters
Back Cover photo, Jack Wade Mellberg

*All rights reserved. Without limiting the rights
under copyright reserved above, no part of this
publication may be reproduced, stored in or introduced into a retrieval system, or transmitted,
in any form, or by any means (electronic, mechanical, photocopying, recording, or otherwise)
without the prior written permission of both
the copyright owner and the above publisher of
this book.*

ISBN-13: 978-0-578-46099-4

FIC014000 FICTION/Historical / General
FIC000000 FICTION/General
FIC043000 FICTION/Coming of Age

The Guest

From Johannesburg

Dedication

Dedicated to peacemakers who have been so important in my era: Martin Luther King, Nelson Mandela, Frederik Willem de Klerk, Mikhail Gorbachev, Mahatma Gandhi, Ira Sandperl and Joan Baez.

Through their examples and thoughts, they brought hope to troubled generations. In their individual ways, they have made the world a more beautiful place.

At this time, when certain people enjoy un-paralleled wealth and reek with selfish in-dulgences, we need hope and compassion more than ever. In a time when chaos, an-tagonism and artifice reign in America and around the world, we need truth, clarity and generosity more than ever.

My thanks to an old friend and classmate for the use of her prescient statement on my book's cover. Her words come to the heart of my story.

I have hope in people, in individuals. Because you don't know what's going to rise from the ruins. — Joan Baez

The Guest

From Johannesburg

CHAPTER ONE
Toward The Sunlight

The sparkling blue waters off of the island have turned black, as nightfall saturates the rough channel. Keali'i left shore an hour ago, easily maneuvering his board through the chop and was early for his pickup. But Kimo is late, the water is rough and Ke' is tiring. He's running out of time.

The channel is usually difficult, and it gets violent as the weather changes. Ke' struggles against the strong currents, arm-paddling to stay where Kimo might see him. He's tired now, and his big board is puny on this rough channel. "Got to get here, brah!"

As he waits, he knows something is wrong. Not just Kimo and the boat being late. It is this island, Kaho'olawe. Over the months and years, the explosive shells that pounded into its soft earth and burst against its coarse volcanic crust had taken their toll. The powerful urge of war is here, everywhere around. Great god Lono can help him. Or is he saying to go away?

Ke' watches the fast-fading daylight filter through the shadowy feathers of an owl circling above. "You, *pueo*." He admires this solitary, stolid creature, his beloved *aumukua*, *his chosen guardian since childhood. So powerful, gliding against the wind. Graceful, too, up so high, in his smooth and endless arc above this lone waterman.*

Ke' wishes he were up there and not on this rough water. "Take me away with you, aumakua," he shouts, realizing he is lost. Then to himself he murmurs, "Take me to the sunlight."

Cebo edges along the river, wary of the snags where ingwenya, *the crocodile, might be, or the muddy banks where* limvubu, *the hippos, travel after soaking in the cooling waters. He needs to reach the border by dark. All around the air is sweet with the light rains that signal a new season. Just now it is beautiful, and Cebo would feel the joy he felt as a boy here, if he weren't running for his life.*

He probably shouldn't have come, sneaking into South Africa so soon again. He heard that the police knew about his last visit, where he planned the march on Pietermaritzburg. But this time it was for his mother, Funeka, and he would not miss her funeral.

The ceremony was brief, as she had asked. It was good to see uncle Mandla and Mama's many sisters, though he barely knew them. He and his mother had lived a very long time in Johannesburg, serving the Malones and living on their property.

Funeka had become a christian when mother Malone insisted, after bas *Theo died. Then she returned home to KwaZulu to die in the tribal way, to be placed with her parents and their ancestors. He regretted he had to stay away for so many years. He had not seen Mama since he left her with mother Malone in Johannesburg. Living on the run was necessary for an activist, and not so dangerous for him as life in this country would be, an educated black man who believed in a better life.*

Life is difficult everywhere in Africa, but Cebo knows there is welcome for him and his political friends in Tanganyika and Mozambique, and further north. The money from his old friend Duff had helped. Though it had long since run out, the money Cebo had brought to the ANC cause has been noted and respected. And as an architect, he knows how structures are built, and how they can be toppled with a properly placed explosive.

He wants peace in South Africa, but the rulers have guns and tanks and jails. And their laws give him no peace. They would not have peace until after the liberation. Perhaps Kliptown would change this. There is hope still, that the Congress of The People will bring change. We shall see. We have hope for change and peace. But if this is not possible, I am prepared for war.

Keali'i's Hawaiian spirits and gods are different from the ones that Cebo knows, twelve thousand miles away in KwaZulu. Ke's gods are welcoming and hopeful, while Cebo's warn of the dangers all around, trying to guide him through.

Ke' knows that Lono was the creator, and a god of peace, and pueo the owl, is his friend and personal guide. Cebo knows that his ancestors watch over him, and now his mother is with them. They are always around him, warning against evil spirits, helping to navigate this life among the dangerous animals and the white police.

Ke' is just eighteen and already he knows his life is limited. It was foreseen, and he is prepared. Cebo knows his early life was unfair, because he was a black child who was born in South Africa. Though peace is his preference, the presence of white police all around him, with truncheons and pistols in their hands, makes him want to live a better life. He is not yet prepared to join his ancestors.

Donald McPhail

CHAPTER TWO

Marcus de Villiers

Duff Malone's story began for me in 1970 at the Outrigger Canoe Club in Honolulu, a comfortable and elegant place located on a beautiful stretch of beach near Waikiki. I was asked to attend a retirement tribute for Mr. Duff Malone, the legendary division manager for Pan American World Airways. As a writer, I was assigned to develop an article about him — sort of a puff-piece — for Pan Am's *Clipper* inflight magazine.

For thirty-five years he had held the position of Manager for the Pacific division. That's a long time in one job, in a complex region that was filled with conflict and change throughout his tenure.

My own background was part of the reason I got the job. I had been a journalist in South Africa, recently relocated to the United States. When I lobbied for the assignment, I emphasized that Mr. Malone — Duff — is also originally from South Africa and there would be a certain synergy, with insights that the two of us would share. There was another private reason I wanted the job, but that will come later.

Two unexpected things occurred that night. First, Duff suffered a heart attack just as the celebration began. Second, because of his illness I needed to rely on his wife Christy, as well as their children and friends, to provide background information for his story. That's how I met Masao and heard his story about Amache prison camp. I met others, as well, whose own wartime experiences led to an entirely different story, moving away from the initial theme and embracing more important matters, such as life and death, and the damages of war. Eventually, the Duff Malone article was overwhelmed by the powerful, painful memories presented by Duff and his family, and their close friends.

When I did meet Duff, I was not surprised to find that he and I believed in many of the same things, and for South Africans this means a great deal. For those of you who have always lived in America, relations between white people and others with different skin colors are not always spoken of openly. America is, of course, "The land of the free." You also proclaim, on the famous statue in New York's harbor, "Give me your tired, your poor, your huddled masses yearning to breathe free."

But recent events in the United States suggest that most white Americans picture the "tired and poor" as Anglo-Saxon people, or Celts, Mediterraneans, Slavs and others with pale skins. While this assertion may offend some of you, I come from a country that openly identifies races, scientifically and by category, in order to institutionalize the dominance of its white citizens. This is inhumane and wrong, but some might consider it less hypocritical

Donald McPhail

than the passage of laws that grant racial equality in this country, but are frequently ignored and unenforced.

As for America's racial divisions, I am stating a view that is likely held by people around the world. White people see America as a white country, but this is changing. Immigrants of all colors come here because it is a land of opportunity, and because of hope for better lives. Many of them also sense the underlying characteristics of honesty and good will that somehow continue here, despite barriers of greed and entitlement that often obscure these higher qualities, the way clouds often hide the sun.

I am writing from the United States in the seventies, and recent marches and civil actions illustrate the need for change here, and recent civil rights legislation demands it. While creating a law does not automatically modify behavior and attitudes, these laws can be used to bring them about. Without such laws, changes are unlikely to happen. A place like Hawaii, where much of this story is set, exemplifies how different races, cultures, ages and lifestyles can get along, even thrive. As you will hear, the Malones' home near Waikiki is a place where friends of different races and cultures often gather and share their surprising stories.

Duff Malone's own journey helps to examine cultures through the lens of nearly forty years of history. With many setbacks and challenges, his story brings discovery and rebirth for Duff. His experiences also clarify and shape his attitudes, where he embraces and appreciates the differences among cultures, as well as the inherent similarities of all people.

Between 1934 and 1970, Duff's time in Hawaii, there were explosive events that challenged and threatened the world, including three brutal American wars. These wars certainly influenced him and his airline's operation. They also revealed, yet again, that there are dangerous people in every race and culture, just as there are good ones. There were personal setbacks, too, including deaths of dear friends and loved ones. There had been a great deal of death throughout Duff's life, and it hurt him deeply.

Duff Malone's airline career began in 1934, when air travel was in its infancy and a man named Juan Trippe was obsessed with making Pan American World Airways into the world's greatest transportation company. On the advice of a colleague, Trippe hired Duff to manage Pan Am throughout Asia and the Pacific, and Trippe's ultimate goal was for his airline to be America's national airline, its flagship carrier.

The world was still emerging from the Great Depression in the thirties, but Trippe couldn't wait for better times. He had a plan, the people were in place and, somehow, financing was assured. One thing Trippe did not count on was the extent of Japan's military expansion across Asia and the Pacific. He was certainly aware of Japan's belligerence, but he believed their leaders would rein-in the military after their occupation of Manchuria. So he moved ahead.

Just how devastating these wars were was made clear to me when Duff and his friends described their personal experiences. I was not surprised at the brutality.

Donald McPhail

Even as a student in South Africa, I had read about Nanking and Shanghai in my studies. Nor was I surprised to hear of work camps in Japan, imprisoning captured Americans and their allies. But the degree of violence and inhumanity were beyond belief. First, Duff's close friend Werner Bergen described his imprisonment at Omori near Tokyo. Christy told me about Japan's attack at Pearl Harbor, as she reported to her morning nurse's shift and the planes suddenly screamed overhead.

Then there was Masao's story. Through his tragic experience, I learned of Amache and other internment camps in the United States where some 150,000 Japanese-Americans were imprisoned. These war camps may have been known to Americans, but I was not raised here, and I was astonished to hear about them.

The point is, brutality is worldwide, and not limited to certain races or cultures. There have been wars and prisons somewhere in our world, almost without letup, since the 1930s. Many of the wars were avoidable, and despite its claims to morality and justice, not even America was without blame.

Leading up to the second world war, Japan invaded countries throughout Asia, just as the Germans occupied their neighbors in Europe. Later, America launched its own brutal wars, in Korea, and currently in Vietnam, Laos and Cambodia. Many subtle lies have been told to justify these wars, and they were told by trusted government leaders and military men, in Germany and Japan, and also here in America.

What are the common threads? In the larger picture, the threads are political arrogance, economic expansion, and false statements to citizens and allies. Decisions to go to war were made by male elites in each and every country. They still are. Economic decisions were made by governments and supported by military leaders, and importantly, by capitalists who made money through the manufacture of arms and instruments of war. They were enacted by politicians whose public support could be built on scare tactics and lies, and their calculated calls for patriotism. This was true in Japan and Germany, and even here in America.

For Duff Malone, the common thread was a series of unexpected personal and professional challenges, including the loss of close friends and family members. But through all of these challenges, he persevered. This is a recurring theme in my story: his perseverance, and a transformation of sorts.

What I have just described — Pan Am's genesis as a world airline, personal experiences during difficult, often brutal times, and critical decisions made by political leaders whose motives were often not what they seemed — is the backdrop of Duff Malone's journey.

His life was not heroic, certainly not in the traditional sense. But looking at it in retrospect, we can see the arc of a heroic journey: the adventurous beginning, difficult conditions, lessons and adjustments, and the ultimate challenge that changed his life. His story began at his retirement party.

Donald McPhail

CHAPTER THREE

Retirement

"I think we should start with the sashimi!" Duff declared, in the confident tone he usually used with his office staff. He patted his wife's attractive knee with a hand that was tanned and weathered from many years in the Pacific sunlight. Then he leaned back, trying to take in the mellow music he recognized on the car's stereo. "Waikiki" was one of his favorites.

He loved the old songs and their gentle melodies. Not those current ones with all the noise, especially after a stressful week. He struggled to turn the business-thoughts off in his head.

Executive changes at Pan Am continued, and they affected him and his people. Harold Gray had succeeded Trippe in 1968, inheriting financial troubles caused by Trippe's overcommitment to the new 747. Then Gray was stricken with cancer and turned the company over to Najeeb Halaby late last year. Now Halaby was struggling.

The atmosphere was scattered, and that's what was making Duff's job more difficult. There seemed to be changes for the sake of change. He and his managers were constantly interrupted by newly appointed department heads in New York, many of them coming from outside the airline business. Their memos flew at him like swarms of insects, mandating time-consuming training courses for veteran ticket agents and ramp staff, and re-quiring all employees to dial-in to recorded messages filled with jargon intended to buck-up morale. Didn't they realize that you motivate people by getting to know them person-ally and listening well? Treat them fairly and show them they are appreciated, and they will be motivated and loyal.

But leadership was bent on change, and to Halaby this seemed to mean cutbacks in people and services. This seemed strange to Duff, because the new jumbo jets were supposed to put Pan Am far ahead of its competition everywhere in the world. Loading and flying the bigger planes requires more people, not fewer, and there's no way to save yourself into prosperity. Pushing his work from his mind, Duff held Christy's hand and tried to look calm, not noticing how concerned she was.

Christy still found him handsome, though his gray hair was sparse and his face carried the lines and creases of a man who had lived over sixty-five years. It was a proud face, with a younger man's eyes, alert and engaged, and a soft shade of brown. Six feet tall with broad shoul-ders, he had the build of a former athlete. Always trim and as graceful as a dancer, he was slowing noticeably, espe-cially the left ankle that had been fractured all those years ago.

Christy was worried about his stressful work, but also about his retirement. *He is so immersed in his job, his Pan Am family. What will he do without them?* While she loved Duff, sometimes she reflected on how he had changed, how his job had defined him. He is a successful executive for a major airline. This is good. But what will he do without it?

They sat comfortably in the rear seat of the hired sedan, passing familiar sights like the tennis courts, then the archery targets. In a moment, they will be adjacent to the Honolulu Zoo.

"That chap de Villiers will be meeting us. I hope we're not late."

"You worry too much, Duff. We'll be fine, and Mr. de Villiers will simply enjoy another drink while he waits. I'm glad you invited him. He sounded quite determined on the telephone. Is his article some sort of description of your Hawaii organization?"

"I'm not absolutely certain. He mentioned a profile for our *Clipper Magazine*."

"It's about you, then?"

"That's what he told me. De Villiers has written very nice articles about different executives, and the company felt the timing was good. He also has a South African background, and they thought we would get on well together."

"That sounds easy enough."

"It may be more than the single article, it seems. He said something about a bigger project, possibly a book about how Pan American started-up in Asia and the Pacific."

"That certainly is a larger story, he will find."

Duff smiled at the unexpected reminder. "As we found, didn't we?" The possibility of an interview had transported his thoughts back to those earliest days. "Good God," he exclaimed, "could it have been thirty-five years already?"

"Yes, that long," she said, "and look at the changes we've seen." Christy glanced over again, wondering where that eager young adventurer might have gone, replaced by this solid, successful company man.

They passed by wide green lawns, now filling with families at the barbecue grills and unfolding lawn mats and blankets. Youngsters were tossing frisbees, and aromas of teriyaki chicken reached them through open windows. Despite the eighty-degree weather, they both preferred fresh ocean air to the chill of air-conditioners.

Duff was in his favorite aloha-wear, a pale Hawaiian shirt and white slacks. When they moved to Hawaii, it had taken him at least two years before he felt comfortable without his formal cruise-director attire, the tropical suits and formal wear. Strange, he felt a little light-headed just now. Maybe it was the coffee after rushing through lunch. He should stick with his tea.

Christy reminded herself that this was his night, with all of the old friends waiting to surprise him. "Perhaps we should start with champagne."

"Fine idea," he agreed. "We are celebrating, after all."

"We celebrate every Friday. At the very same place. We're always finding something to celebrate. A birthday, a local holiday, a couple of birdies out at Oahu Country Club..." She often wondered if they could get away now that he was retiring, get out of the routine.

Donald McPhail

"It's been a few years since I birdied anything. But this is quite a different celebration, isn't it? I'm retired now. Officially. No more 'In the office a few hours a week' or 'Just a quick meeting in San Francisco.' I'm done with it."

"Of course, but I'll believe it when I see it."

"That's why I hired this car. To celebrate, and to save us the walk." Looking over at her, "You know, you have the bluest eyes. After all these years."

She was pleased that he still noticed. "It isn't a long walk," tilting her head toward the beach in the distance, off to her left. "And don't try to distract me with your blue-eyes maneuver."

There it was again, a little rocky, slightly out of breath. "They are amazingly blue. Crystalline." He came up short, intending to say something more glib, but held back.

"You are so full of it, Duff Malone." She leaned up and kissed him on the cheek. "You seem a little cold. Do you feel all right?"

"Of course." He gently moved his hand to brush away the question. It was Friday night, and they looked forward to their evenings at the club. And he knew how much they both enjoyed their banter, as they had since they left port in San Francisco over thirty years ago, on that *Malolo* cruise. Her radiance was what first struck him, and it continued to make everyone around her feel good. Not just the men, though she had always had a special way with them. It was clear that the wives respected Christy, as a a professional nurse, who raised two children while her husband was often away. She was also fun to be around, always first on the floor for those new disco dances. Duff knew that their own children adored her. Not every family could claim this.

"Remember when we met?" Duff smiled. "On that first cruise together. What an amazing journey that was. By the time we reached the first port-of-call, right here in Honolulu, we were attracted."

"We were, but for an adventurer, you were a little slow on the uptake. You could be so proper and formal, in those lovely tuxedos and white dinner jackets. And your elegant accent. There was something in the gentleness and the humor that attracted me, though, and something more. Especially when I saw you on the beach, in that swimsuit." She smiled with the memory. "It was just back there, remember?" She gestured again toward their favorite beach.

As they rode through Kapiolani Park, beneath the tall palms and craggy old banyans that framed the boulevard, Duff silently conceded that it would have been nearly as fast to walk the paved path along Kalakaua, the way they always did. Through the lawns, past the apartments and the familiar old Elks Club building, before reaching the club. It was just a fifteen minute stroll from their house. But tonight he wasn't feeling quite up to it. Good thing he ordered the sedan.

He tried to relax as the car crept through the Friday night dinner traffic, completing the triangular circuit around the popular grassy park, where nearly a century ago King Kalakaua himself had enthusiastically presided at his immense horse-racing track.

Donald McPhail

Duff tensed as they approached the club's entrance, as he spotted the red ginger in the garden. Christy had reacted, too. These vibrant scarlet blossoms still triggered the image of their daughter lying there among the succulents, drugged-out and injured from a surfing accident, as members had strolled in to dinner. She was twenty then, and struggling badly.

"She was so difficult," he murmured, stroking Christy's soft hand again, the way he did when he was agitated. "Thank God she's made her way."

Christy calmed his hand with hers. "She's a strong young woman now," nearly a whisper. She looked over at her husband. "Now all we have to worry about is Teo coming home safely from Vietnam."

"Our son and that damned war," Duff added. "Teo says he's fine, and we're not to worry so much. At least not tonight."

She smiled quietly and nodded.

He still loved to look at his wife. In many ways she was more beautiful than the day they met. "I was reflecting," he admitted as she raised her eyebrows.

"Yes, I could tell."

"About us. And a small prayer of thanks for Malia's progress, and another for Teo's safety."

She nodded, "She's doing well now, thanks to you. As for Teo, quite a large prayer, I should say."

"We do know his tour will be over soon, and he has told us he's been vetted for a some top jobs. Maybe the Pentagon. I wish he would get out and come fly for Pan Am."

"That would be the best news for me, Duff. If only he will consider it."

"Meantime, here's to us both. And to so many people, like old friend Bully, and those surfers and beachboys we see offshore when we sit at the club. And to your parents. Pete and Doris would be quite impressed with how our children turned out."

Christy was pleased that Duff still remembered those days. She had wondered. He was so immersed in that job of his. She knew how much her parents had loved Duff, and they doted on Malia, and grandson Teo, too. Christy missed their son, and she missed her parents. Pete and Doris were so proud when he graduated from Annapolis. Pete, especially, since he had been an enlisted sailor himself, and Academy officers were the gold-standard for him.

Malia's relationship with Pete and Doris was unique, starting in those two years when Christy had needed them most. Her parents raised Malia while Christy completed nursing school in San Francisco, after taking time off for nearly a year. She had never told them, or anyone else, who the father was. And she never would. Duff was Malia's father now, just as much as he was Teo's. She knew how much they loved him.

"You know Malia plans to stop by tonight?"

He relaxed and allowed himself a broader smile, "Yes. I spoke with her on the phone this morning, and she'll come by for a glass of wine. She works much too hard." Looking over, "But that's what nurses do, isn't it?"

"It wasn't always so with her, was it? We're very lucky."

"We are, indeed," and gave a soft squeeze.

The dark Mercedes glided to a stop at the entry and Malone was puzzled. "Where is everyone? And where are the dining room staff?" He released her hand as the driver opened the door. "Looks as if the restaurant is closed."

"Is it possible? Aren't they always open for dinner?"

"And where is Bully? He always greets us. Something is seriously wrong. Let me go see." Struggling out, he accepted the driver's arm for balance. Hips and ankles aching when he sat for more than a few minutes, he struggled off in the direction of the reception desk.

"Here, now. Duff. Wait for me." Christy slid across as the driver reached out to help her to step onto the walkway.

She caught up and took Duff's arm, but allowed him to lead. He was still strong, despite his occasional pains. He made his way along the empty path, turning left, with eyes fixed on the spacious dining room. The emptiness was puzzling.

As he passed the reception desk he wondered about the electricity. It seemed dim in there. Maybe a short circuit. At their board meetings, they talked about rewiring the old system. Surely, Bully or someone would be out here directing guests. With Christy next to him, he continued to slowly guide her along. Odd that he could detect savory dinner-smells.

He recoiled in an explosion of light and sound, pulling Christy with him toward the low lava-rock wall, scraping the side of his left hand as he reached out to keep balance. Then, embarrassed, he heard the lengthy shout, "Surprise!" and heard the ukuleles and guitars strike up a lively chord of welcome, then transition into his favorite song, "E Maliu Mai".

Then, when he saw the musicians who were playing in a corner over near the beach entrance, his skin tingled — "chicken-skin" the locals say — and he was moved to tears. It was Auntie Irmgard herself, the song's beloved author, playing alongside daughters Mihana and Aima and her niece Luana, the group she called *Puamana*. They wore traditional white dresses, and each was crowned with a lovely scarlet lei in their dark hair. What an honor!

Then he hesitated. *There it is again!* Duff needed to sit. His chest felt tight. Alarmed, as Duff slumped into the nearby chair, Christy immediately felt his pulse and her other hand went to his forehead. "Sit still. You're cold and clammy." Looking toward the lounge area, she called-out, "Bully. Bully, are you here!"

"Here Christy, over here. Behind the bar."

"Please call for an ambulance. Duff's having a heart attack!"

Donald McPhail

CHAPTER FOUR

Three Rascals

Cold...tubes...green walls...no goodbye. Duff closed his eyes.

Christy was startled when she saw the pale figure, tubes attached to a wrinkled arm. *Is this the wrong room?* The patient lay on his back, quite still. *Is he alive?* Then she saw Duff's faded blue shirt hanging in the open closet. Edging toward the bed, she recognized familiar lips puffing his irregular sleep-sound. A clear plastic bag hung from its metal stand, connected to an intravenous tube that looped downward and attached to the inside of his arm. *What will I do without him?*

Instinctively she inspected the connections and was satisfied they fit tight, with no kinks in the tube. After more than thirty years as a nurse at Tripler, she knew what to look for. She had volunteered three days a week at the old Fort Shafter location, then shifted to full-time after Pearl Harbor. From the beginning she had been drawn to Intensive Care, seeking out the most urgent jobs.

She watched the heart monitor as it pulsed on the nightstand beyond Duff, and was encouraged by the systolic and diastolic numbers, and with the regularity of the blips. This equipment is more modern than the bulky boxes they use in the Army hospital, but the screens are similar and they provide the same critical numbers.

Christy eased over to Duff's bedside. As she leaned toward him she saw one tired brown eye open, then another, accompanied by a wan smile.

"So you carried on without me, then? The party?" Duff rasped, using his elbows to push higher on the hospital bed, careful of the catheter.

She was heartened by his attempt at humor. "Well, I didn't, of course," she reached for his free hand. "All that secrecy and planning for your big surprise party, and I didn't even get to sip a glass of wine. You are very thoughtless, you know." She rubbed his forehead, hand lingering to sense his temperature.

"If I ring for the steward, will he bring us both some of that nice chablis?"

"Don't push your luck. More likely it will be a nurse, and she might bring you something a lot less soothing, like an enema. My professional advice is to leave that button alone. You'd find out how attentive the RNs here at Queens can be."

He leaned back into the pillow. "I would, wouldn't I? I've observed the very best! Prettiest, too!" He smiled again and squeezed her hand. "Now what do those doctors tell you? How am I doing?"

Christy sat on the bed, careful to avoid the intravenous connection. "It's serious, Duff. You had an angina attack, and your arteries need urgent attention."

"I knew I should have said something, but it didn't seem serious enough. I wasn't feeling quite right. No pain or anything. Just some tightness. Felt like I had walked up-hill. I didn't want to ruin our Friday night."

"Oh Duff, I wish you had said something. Your life is more important than some celebration." Rumpling his thin gray hair, "But you're alive, thank God. And you'll continue to be if we make some changes."

"What are the odds? With my father's history, I always felt I wouldn't get past fifty, and here I am heading toward seventy."

"Yes, here we both are. I want us to keep it this way."

"So tell me what is next."

"Let's not go into details just yet. For now, Dr. Kwan said that your heart is strong, and that's very good news. It's your clogged arteries. The blood isn't flowing properly, so your heart is working too hard."

"Can't that be fixed?"

"They've given you some medication, and they'll check later today to see if surgery is needed. Angioplasty is a possibility, a sort of balloon to expand the artery for blood flow, or it could take bypass surgery."

"That serious?"

"Yes, it could be that serious. No matter what they decide, we'll have to change our habits in your retirement. Healthier foods, no cocktails, more walking and less stress." She knew she was sounding too strict, and added, "If you are a very good boy, we can eventually enjoy a glass of wine with dinner."

"Only this one vice, my love? You won't like me much if I'm that perfect."

"You're about as perfect as I can bear, Malone. Now why don't you try to get some sleep? I'll stay on for a bit longer while you rest."

"You'll let Teo and Malia know what's happened?"

"I'll let them know you are recovering, and that you will work on getting stronger. I'll call Malia in a moment and write to Teo today, then find someone at Kaneohe to expedite it to him." She paused, then added, "I hesitate to tell you. Masao and Gio have been here, trying to get in to see you, but I made them go back to our their hotels until you're strong enough. And Bergen is getting testy. He wants me to drive him here as soon as you are receiving visitors. You and your rascal friends aren't making things easy."

Masao and Gio were two of their closest friends. Masao Tanaka was vice president of North America for Hawaiian Airlines, located in San Francisco, and Gio Sorvini was a dear friend from their first cruise together. Gio lived in Boston and flew over to attend Duff's party. He was staying for two weeks, to meet with fellow restaurateurs. Werner Bergen was more than a friend. He was like a father to Duff. They had worked together aboard ship for many years at American Express, and in recent years Bergen served in a dual role. He worked for Duff as a consultant throughout Asia, and he was also the generous landlord for their home near Diamond Head.

Duff fell asleep wondering when he would feel strong enough to see his old friends.

Donald McPhail

CHAPTER FIVE

Looking Inward

"Geez, Dad. Look at you." Malia kissed his cheek
before examining the tubes and checking the connections.
She was a striking girl, with pert sun-bleached hair and
shining blue eyes. Petite and tanned like her mother, she
was blessed with the same quick humor. Duff had watched
Malia as she entered the room, admiring her athleticism
and directness, and the energy in her step. She moved the
way she had as a little girl, sort of a bounce when she
stood and talked with him, up on her toes and moving her
hands to emphasize one thing or another.

"And hello to you, young lady," he chuckled. "You
and you-know-who are fixated on these tubes. She was
here this morning." He decided not to criticize her too-short
skirt.

"It's genetic, dad. We know you don't pay attention
to these things, so someone has to."

Like her mother, Malia was demonstrative with her
affection for Duff. And like Christy, she was a skilled nurse.
She was more outspoken than her mother. "Don't these

nurses check on you any more? Look, those sheets are untucked and your blanket is down around your knees."

"I couldn't comment on the sheet, but I put the blanket down there intentionally. I'm hot."

"A fever?"

"Not a fever, dear. Honolulu weather."

"Well, okay. Are they taking good care of you?"

"Yes, Malia. They are. And I know you're concerned about me." He patted the bed for her to sit next to him. "Has your mother given you a full report?"

"She has, and it sounds like they're considering surgery?"

"Some sort of bypass. That's one possibility, but the tests aren't all back yet. It could also be an angioplasty, or maybe just medication and better diet. Dr. Kwan thinks my heart is strong, and he believes in less invasive treatment."

"Less invasive is good, but you need to listen to him. Dr. Kwan is the best. If he says surgery, then you need to trust him." Then she adds, "Has mom talked with Teo? He would want to know."

"Not yet. Your mom is going to write him today. There's no way to phone, and a telegram would sound worse than it is."

"She'll have it under control, but it's important for him to know what's happening." Despite the heat, Malia shivered briefly, "It was a little eerie, getting off on this exact floor. You remember, dad?"

"I do," he responded, though he arrived under sedation and wasn't certain what floor they were currently on.

Donald McPhail

"Over in the other wing, wasn't it? Your recovery wasn't easy."

"It was the hardest thing I've ever been through. Obviously my broken rib was killing me. And I was mortified at what I must have looked like at the club." She hesitated, "Most of all I still couldn't get over losing Keali'i." Malia's eyes glistened. "He was my best friend, dad. I never had a best friend before. Then he was gone. It was so sudden." She went to the basin and grabbed a towel, holding it to her face as she sobbed.

Duff lay there connected to his tubes and watched, knowing he couldn't hold her, or offer anything other than quiet understanding. He couldn't bear to see her so unhappy.

Malia finished wiping her eyes and brought the towel with her as she came and sat at the foot of his bed. "But I did recover. It was hard, until I remembered the calming things that Ke' taught me through *Sati.* Sometimes I called it mindfulness and he would gently correct me. He preferred words like consciousness, recognition, looking inward. He believed in feeling and knowing, not just thinking. These were Ke's important lessons for me, understanding and sensing. I could live with different kinds of pain, go beyond it. He must have known what was coming."

Duff knew that Malia had struggled with much more than her rib fractures. The doctors cautioned them about depression, as well.

Malia had told her parents how unusual Keali'i was. He could be introspective and withdrawn, like a mystic. But then there was his mischievous side. When they first met he named her "Sunny", after the sunflower in a popular song that praised golden hair. That's when she started calling him Ke', short for Keali'i.

Malia was such a different girl after she met Ke'. She became patient with them, not so agitated about the tiny things that used to torment her as a little girl, like the style of her school clothes or doing simple chores. She repeated what Ke' had taught her, about participating, not ignoring; preventing, not reacting; preserving, not degrading. Then, from all of his calm new ways of looking at life, Ke' was suddenly gone. Like one of his gods, who appeared and then disappeared, he was lost somewhere out on the water he loved. Duff wished he had taken time to know Keal'i better. For a moment, Duff thought of his father, who was suddenly gone all those years ago for no reason at all.

Malia lost her direction when Ke' disappeared. She distanced herself from nearly everyone. Christy said it reminded her of how Malia had been as a little girl, when Christy came home from nursing school to see her after being away for several weeks. She would shut down and literally turn her back to Christy, then totter over to Grandpa Pete and Nana Doris.

After Ke's death, Malia hadn't exactly turned her back on Duff and Christy, but she was remote and remained closest to her friend Bully and her surfing pals, Mika and Stewie. Malia knew what to expect from them, and they gave her shelter. They had known Keali'i. She was with them just before she crashed on the rocks off Diamond Head. Since then, only Bully was there for her, and was strong enough to help.

"Dad," Malia smiled at him. "Where'd you go? I was talking about how my life changed here in the hospital. Then I lost you."

Duff looked up, realizing how far his mind had wandered. "Sorry, Malia. I was thinking about what you said about consciousness. You surprise me. I'm not sure how you worked through his loss, but so glad you did. You are a wonderful part of our lives."

She touched his cheek gently, "It helps that you support me, you and mom. As you drifted off, we were just talking about Ke' and his influence. It was right here that I decided to go to nursing school. That was because of Ke', too."

"I didn't know that. I always assumed it was because of your mother's example."

Malia walked to the window and looked out, "It was mom, for sure. But it was Ke' who helped me find the path. He was such a spiritual guy, Ke' was, so peaceful. He believed that our lives, all life, gets its spirit from the gods. Those ancient gods that he was always reading about. But he also believed in authenticity, not guesswork or made-up stories. He said that even the Bible is a human translation from Hebrew and Aramaic, and it must have been twisted by the many men who translated it over the centuries, into Greek and all the other languages."

Duff waited, not wanting to interrupt a line of thought he had never heard from his daughter. Then he was aware of her tears again. "I'm so sorry, Malia. Are you okay?"

"Yeah, dad. I'm all right. I cry when I think about him when I wasn't expecting to. It's nearly twenty years, and it still hurts."

"He was doing what he believed in, Malia. And he wasn't afraid. That was quite clear the one time your mom and I met him."

"No, Ke' was never afraid." She sniffed back her tears, "We were only in high school, and he already knew his life would be short." She straightened up and continued, "I struggled with them here in the hospital, my broken rib and my demons. I decided, since I'm not quite as spiritual as Ke' I could at least use his beliefs to heal people. Why not work with patients, the way mom does? But not in the military hospital. I needed to work in a public hospital, treating people from different cultures and incomes and ages." Then she laughed. "Ke' would have questioned my logic, I think. It's not a direct transition, going from his meditative thing and connecting it to traditional medicine. Some of it was mom's influence. But it seemed a logical extension to me."

"Did his gods teach about life and death, eternal life? I've been thinking about those things. As a nurse you deal with these beliefs."

"Yeah, dad. That was one of our earliest connections. He called me Sunny, in that sweet way of his, then he surprised me, talking about death and life, and why we're here."

Donald McPhail

"So Sunny, you believe in your God?"

"Why you ask?"

"My cousin Isaac, he goes to St. Louis High School, over near Kaimuki. They tell him about God." They sit on the old tree that had sprawled there since she could remember. He scuffles his flip-flops around, making little circles in the sandy dirt. "You believe?"

"I don't go to church, if that's what you're saying."

"Not so much church, but in a big God. Created life? Life after death?"

His clear dark eyes are noncommittal, but she knows he watches her closely, and responds, "You see that yellow hibiscus over there?" she motions to the bright flowers that divide the rough parking lot from the beach. "And you remember those fish we were watching over near the rocks, the red and black and green ones?"

"The a'awa. Of course."

"Do they look like accidents to you?"

"How do you mean?"

"An accident. Not so much that they are growing or swimming, but their colors. The shapes and patterns. So carefully painted onto those delicate petals. Painted onto those little fishes. Certain types of hibiscus look alike. Certain species of fish look just alike. Same pattern. Same colors, same markings as each other. Same with seaweed and coral."

"And so?"

"I read somewhere that the planets and stars and earth are all harmonious. They move around together. They actually send out sounds that are in perfect harmony.

People have heard them. How could that be? And what about smells?"

"What about smells?"

"You love the smell of garlic and ginger frying. So do I," she laughs, remembering the plate-lunch truck they both liked. "Who created us to love certain smells of things we cook, or sniff at in the garden. Or how we hate the smells of things bad for us?"

"I see that. So what are you saying?"

"Ke', these aren't an accident, or a gigantic coincidence. The harmony of sounds and smells. The fishes and flowers. I don't believe they came out of the ocean mud in some kind of million-year evolution, or accidentally showed the same color petals. Seems to me that they were put there. Put here on earth for a reason."

"You saying they were put here by God?"

"Sure. How else?"

He closes his eyes, thinking or resting, then slowly opens them and smiles gently, "My auntie tells stories about Pele, the goddess of fire, and of Kanaloa, god of the sea. Songs and ancient chants tell us how Lono created the land, and Pele made the volcanoes. Couldn't Lono be the one who painted the flowers and Kanaloa the sea creatures, and not this Christian God?"

"But we're taught that there is a single God, and he created the universe."

"But why not many gods? Some of them are like women, others like men, some like animals? And don't we *learn more about the sea creatures, like sharks and turtles, if we believe that they descended from Kamoho, who gave life and instincts to them? And Lono who painted those flowers and the forests, and gave them their purpose and individual ways?"*

Malia doesn't even pause, "Can't they be the same?"

"Is there more?" he urges.

"It's humans that seem to be confused, about 'Is it one God or many?' I doubt that the gods are confused. One or many, they themselves would know."

"And," he nods and silently whisks his hand across the ground, encouraging more from her.

She continues, "And what does it matter whether we call it one God or many? Same result, different interpretation. We have many languages. Why not many interpretations?"

Keali'i smiles and nods, "Akamai. Very wise. One God or many gods. There is no wrong answer."

"Only if someone thinks that their answer is the only one!"

Duff lay quietly after Malia said her goodbyes. He was tired and the medicine was working. As he drifted, his thoughts went to an isolated place near the water, that faded behind him as a boy paddled his board away from shore.

He awakened and turned onto his side, instinctively protecting the tubes in his arms. Malia knew Ke' set off for Maui on his surfboard, across the stormy channel. He never returned, and no-one ever found him. That's when she fell apart.

Donald McPhail

CHAPTER SIX

The Writer

They sat at an outside table at the Royal Hawaiian Hotel, just as she and Duff had done with Werner Bergen during their first visit some thirty-five years ago. Except now Duff was in the hospital, recovering from his heart attack.

The young man seated across from Christy, Marcus de Villiers, had held her chair and now waited patiently as she looked around. He was a tall man who appeared to be in his late forties, with a friendly expression and calm dark eyes. His neatly pressed white dress shirt and dark slacks set him apart from the other men around them, in their colorful aloha shirts and shorts.

"Thank you, Mr. de Villiers. This is a special place for Duff and me, the hotel and this particular spot. It's where a dear friend first brought us to lunch way back in the thirties. Naturally, the surroundings are completely different now, starting with that wide beach over there. Believe it or not, it used to be quite narrow.

"These gardens and palms were always lovely, but of course they are lush and fully grown now. The old Moana Hotel is still over there, with its famous Banyan tree. But look around us. We're surrounded by those massive cranes and high-rise hotels that dwarf everything. Thank God the noisy pile-drivers finally stopped."

Despite the construction around them, Waikiki beach was filled with sunbathers and swimmers, most of them young soldiers on R&R, away from the war. Mainly kids with short hair and wearing aviator glasses, they sported brightly patterned swim trunks in stark contrast to the drab khakis and camouflage fatigues they would wear on the flight back to Vietnam.

"It was kind of them to seat us here in this garden area, Mrs. Malone," he said gently, in an accent that was a more pronounced version of Duff's. "It seems very private." Looking directly at her with his dark eyes, he added, "I'm so sorry. I hope that Mr. Malone is all right."

"Thank you Mr. de Villiers. I saw him this morning, and he is improving, although his doctor is considering surgery to prevent another incident. And please call me Christy." She added, "You are a long way from South Africa. Duff said I would recognize your accent."

"I am, indeed. Another reason I'm honored to be writing about your husband. There are not that many South Africans who are prominent in the travel industry. And certainly, I will call you Christy, if you will call me Marcus." He. added, "I assume it is premature to inquire about visiting with your husband."

"Yes, a bit soon. Dr. Kwan will decide today or tomorrow about the next step."

"You were a nurse, I believe?"

A brief nod, "I was, Marcus. You have done some homework."

"Some, but I mention this because your profession makes you more aware, or realistic, than most people would be, of his condition."

"It does. And I know it is serious. But Dr. Kwan feels Duff is quite a healthy man for his age, except for the particular arteries. His heart is strong."

"As you are a nurse, and I hope you don't mind my being candid, I have a question. My editors need to make a decision today. I'm booked here for three weeks, to interview you and Mr. Malone for the article, and to research for a separate project. I would like to complete my interviews. At the same time, I don't wish to intrude on you or Mr. Malone if he is not feeling well. We could reschedule the article and I could make another trip here in a few months. But I must let my editors know."

Christy realized how honored Duff had felt to be singled out for the story. Though he seemed to prefer operating in the background, he was proud of Pan American and the key role he had played since the beginning. And she was proud of him. She was also worried about his health. "I should think he will be up to it in a week or so, Marcus. You say you blocked three weeks here. I suggest that you stay. Perhaps I can provide you with background or timing, whatever you need for context. Then, when Duff is stronger, you and he can concentrate on the personal side, his challenges and experiences."

"You think like a writer, Christy. That's helpful. As I indicated, I'm here for more than just the one story. I'm considering a book about Pan American's history, especially the expansion into the Pacific, beginning with the Flying

Clipper days. A lot of my research will be at headquarters in Manhattan. But I was planning to visit the Honolulu airport and Pan American's offices here, to work up a timeline. Maybe interview some of the senior employees. It seems quite straightforward. So, yes, I would appreciate the opportunity of visiting with you. Then when Mr. Malone feels stronger, he and I can explore his personal story." He paused. "You're smiling?"

"You used the word 'straightforward', that's what I'm smiling at. We once thought that, too. But based on our experiences, Duff's and mine, your book may be far less straightforward than you think. But you and Duff can talk about that."

He looked baffled, "I will take your caution to heart, and remain open to surprises. As to your interview, please, I'd like to know about your early days here in Hawaii, you and your family. And something about your own personal story. It helps to know about the people I'm featuring, even things that won't likely be in the final piece. It's research, and I'd like to know about where you were born, schooling, things like that. I'll just set this recorder near you, so it can pick up your voice clearly."

As de Villiers placed the black machine onto the table, he set the microphone into a small holder.

Glancing at the recorder, then back up, Christy spoke in a conversational tone. "Duff and I began here with Pan American in the thirties. Obviously, the world was different then, in ways that a young man like you could not know. The depression was more difficult than anyone could imagine these days. It affected everyone, even here in these beautiful islands. From what I recently read, the unemployment rate was twenty-five per cent throughout America then, and less than ten per cent in Hawaii. But that was still a lot. It seemed much worse when you saw lines of people waiting in line for food and begging on Bishop or Hotel streets downtown.

"Looking back, I wonder why anyone would attempt to create a new airline industry just then, considering all of the difficulties throughout the world. But there were independent men like Mr. Trippe, and more than a dozen more, all vying to be the first and the greatest.

"At first we thought it was just a handful of risk-takers competing with each other here in America. We soon learned that adventurous souls all around the world were starting their own airlines, in places like Britain, Holland, Germany, South America and Australia. This put pressure on Pan American.

"From the beginning, we knew that Juan Trippe was a leader, and a maverick. He was tough and smart, and some thought he shaved the rules a bit. He certainly made sure we concentrated on our goals. Listen to me, talking about 'we'. But from the beginning, all of us were fully immersed, husbands, wives, children. We were like a family, giving our time and emotions to help the company succeed. There were times we could have been accused of being some sort of cult. Our friends were from Pan American. They were the people we worked with, entertained, traveled with. But as the industry grew, our contacts extended beyond our own company. Maybe not as much as I would have liked, but we developed friendships at all of the airlines, and in many countries. We truly felt like citizens of the world. We had a common bond, you see. And we could fly almost anywhere, whenever we wanted.

"Mr. Trippe hired Duff away from American Express, where he had worked for almost ten years. Duff had always been a cruise man, from his early days back in South Africa. As a cruise director, he got to know most parts of the world, and he learned how to work with people in other cultures. His job involved more than just dancing with the single lady passengers, as some used to characterize it. It included negotiating with hotels, transport companies and shopkeepers for the shore excursions, in sophisticated places like London and Paris, as well as destinations less traveled by westerners, like Cairo and Mombasa. Those relationships were based on personal trust, which was more important than signed contracts. This would serve him well throughout Asia and the Pacific, where airlines were entirely new, and negotiations were often quite opaque.

"This background seemed to be what Mr. Trippe was looking for. Juan Trippe was a brave and adventurous man, and Duff admired this. My husband is quiet by nature, but he did have his own adventurous streak. Maybe Mr. Trippe saw some of himself in Duff," she chuckled, "though my husband is far easier to read and his motives have never been questioned the way Trippe's were.

"So Duff left American Express and the steamship industry, and we moved here to establish a Pacific headquarters for Pan Am. We eventually had two young children, Malia and Teo, and were in the same house that we live in now. You will be coming to dinner on Thursday, I hope. That's the way we do things in Hawaii. We share our homes and hospitality. You can meet Malia, who is a registered nurse and a supervisor at Queen's hospital. Teo isn't here, of course. He's a Marine pilot fighting in Vietnam. I'm so worried about him."

The writer nodded, "I'm not a parent, but I know I would be worried, too. It's a war, so he is at risk. South African troops have been engaged in bush wars for as long as I can remember. I know how I felt as a kid on the beach at Richards Bay, when our fighter jets thundered right over my head, attacking something in Mozambique. Scared the devil out of me!

"It is almost unreal that you and I watch these young men here, relaxing and sunning at the beach in front of us, knowing that in a day or two they will be flown back to Vietnam. I'm surprised that so many soldiers are black. I believe African-American is the term you prefer." Realizing that he was adding to Christy's worries, he quickly changed the subject, "You mentioned dinner on Thursday. Thank you, that is very thoughtful. I will be pleased to join you."

As they returned to more pleasant talk, she looked over at the waitress and signaled gently for iced tea. "We were talking about our early days here. Duff and I were young and naive, raising a family and helping to create an airline. Very quickly, Duff understood Mr. Trippe's plan, and he went flying off to remote islands and foreign countries.

But he and his people were doing things that had never been done before, and they faced immediate struggles.

"The first problem for Duff and me was time together. We were newly married, with a daughter, and we hated being away from each other. He was gone a lot, and that was difficult for all of us, especially Malia, and then when Teo was born. I learned to make the decisions, and to reassure the children. My parents helped with the reassurance part, naturally. And Duff worked hard to be a good father. I knew how much our family time meant to him. He wanted their childhood to be so much better than his had been. But travel was unavoidable, and he was drawn deeply into his work. I could see how it ate at him, being away from us.

"The next challenge was distances, and new operating bases. This is what you are probably more interested in. Mr. Trippe planned to establish the Flying Clippers from San Francisco to Honolulu, then to Midway, Wake Island and Guam, over to Manila and on to China. The schedule would begin with airmail contracts, that Pan American had already been awarded by our government. It would grow, with cargo and then passengers.

"Duff had to establish bases for refueling the planes. As he explained it to me many times, the first step was to create refueling stations straight across the Pacific. As you can imagine, the locations were determined by how far the airplanes could fly before needing to refuel, and whether some of the islands were even large enough to handle the process. There were already facilities in Honolulu, Manila and Hong Kong, with a limited station on

Guam. But nothing existed on Midway or Wake Island, two tiny atolls. The longest leg was the first one, from California to Honolulu. If they could make that, the airplanes could make it the rest of the way.

"Duff knew those refueling stations would be difficult, because the atolls were so small. But it was his job to make sure the bases were constructed on schedule, and that they were safe for water landings and takeoffs. If that weren't enough, they also had to be attractive enough for overnight visitors, and staffed to handle the flights.

"Then came the real complications, and they were enormous. While Duff and Pan Am were making their way west across the Pacific, the Japanese military was surging through Asia, taking Manchuria, then all of China, and moving across the ocean toward America. The second World War changed everything.

"Any story about Pan American's growth as an airline has to include the war, both in Europe and here in the Pacific. It affected everything we did. Pan Am's startup challenges on the atolls were modest compared with the military battles to come."

De Villiers nodded. "Yet they did establish the airline, despite these enormous barriers. It is likely impossible to separate the two stories, so I will have to tie them in somehow. I know something of Pan American's contributions to the war effort, in both Atlantic and Pacific. They flew more than 15,000 crossings, nearly 6,000 across the Pacific alone, delivering blood plasma, weapons, radio parts — carrying officers and politicians on more than 700 secret missions. Those photos of President Roosevelt aboard a Flying Clipper, for example, and flying over the hump in Asia."

She added, "Duff told us that they were heroic in a lot of less visible ways, too, like working with the Navy to build those Pacific bases. Later in Korea, they flew important cargo missions. That's when Duff got his battle training, and really became an expert on transporting in war zones, handling troops, weapons and logistics. I'm afraid they still are heroic, Marcus, in a different way," Christy shook her head. "You see Pan Am flying off from Honolulu to Vietnam nearly every day. They fly thousands of fighting men and women and medics into that terrible mess." She looked around at the young men lining the beach, "America seems to be in perpetual war, and it affects us all."

As he opened the recorder and switched-out his cassette de Villiers said, "As you have said, this is complicated history. Your company was restricted by these wars, when the government demanded concessions for the good of the country. But Pan Am proved itself, as well, and earned favorable status as political 'insiders' of sorts. When I met with your people in New York, they described how the war efforts earned special relationships with the government, and with foreign leaders.

"I need to explore this. In the meantime, let's return to your story. Maybe if you start in the beginning, with your family, where you were raised, school. How did you become a nurse?"

Donald McPhail

CHAPTER SEVEN
Christy Miller

Christy loved her life at the beach, because she loved her mom and dad. Pete looked after her during the day, when Doris was at work, and he usually took her to explore the cove with the sandy beach, and to swim. Rough as he looked, with graying stubble on his face and wearing his soiled work overalls after an overnight shift at the shipyard, Pete often picked her up gently and said he loved her. She would rub his whiskers, and he would carefully set her down, before changing into old shorts and an undershirt so they could go out exploring.

Some days, when he did decide to shave, Christy would sit on the hamper and watch him, holding her favorite stuffed friend Mousie and giggling at the soapy face in the mirror, then squealing when he quickly moved his hand and put a dab of shaving suds on her nose. Then they would clean up the mess and make their familiar way to the beach for another sunny adventure.

Doris loved her, too. Christy knew this, because Mom told her so each morning, as she went off to work at the hospital carrying a book and her sack lunch. She looked after Christy in the night time, after they had dinner together and Pete went off to work all night. Then Mom gave her a bath and they had story time together. At night Mom read with her, and talked about the places Pete had been when he was in the Navy. Way across the Pacific Ocean to the China Sea, to magical places like Shanghai and Hong Kong, Sasebo and Okinawa, Sydney and Brisbane. Doris hadn't traveled much herself, except to nearby places like Ventura and Santa Monica. So they both enjoyed these stories about Pete

They sat with Mousie and read library books and pored through atlases, so that Christy could see the cities, imagining how far they were from Long Beach. History books about Japan displayed photos of geishas dressed in exotic gowns, and holding little parasols as they posed before trees bursting with delicate blossoms. She wished she could see the colors. She thought the gowns would be light blue or yellow, and she was certain the blossoms were pink. She could almost smell their gentle fragrance.

During the day, Pete told her stories about his Navy life and the places they went. Compared to the huge battleships, his destroyer, the USS *Chauncey,* was not very big. He was a boatswain's mate, or "bosun" as Pete called it. He helped to steer the ship, and to tie it up to buoys or piers when they reached ports. When they were out on the ocean, Dad got to stand up on what he called "the flying bridge" and use binoculars to look far out at the ocean, in case another ship came too close or they got too near to an island or to something floating on the surface.

He told her how much he loved to watch the dolphins from far off. They would speed toward the ship, small schools of them, with fins slicing white streaks along the water. Suddenly they would disappear, then come out the other side, jumping and playing like it was a game. This is where Pete learned to love sea-creatures. Dolphins and gray whales were his favorites. Sharks were beautiful, too, but frightening for sailors, in case they were ever in trouble and had to use the life-boats. The different seabirds fascinated him, too — sea eagles and gulls, and giant albatrosses with ten-foot wingspans.

"What did you learn today, hon?" Dad would ask her as they made their way to their favorite sandy beach.

Yesterday she said, "We talked about stars today, and the moon. And how it pulls the ocean away from shore and sends it back again."

Today was different. "Daddy," she exclaimed, "today we read about nurses and hospitals, and how to be healthy."

"Is that right?" he chuckled. "So how do we stay healthy?"

"We need to keep everything clean. We boil things to clean them. And we use lots of alcohol."

"And who told you this?"

"Nurse Florence Nightingale wrote about it, and our teacher told us."

"You know that your Mom works at a hospital, don't you?"

"Of course, silly. I know that. I told everyone in my class how she helps all the doctors and nurses."

Christy carried the idea about nurses into her high school years. During summer vacations, Doris got her a temporary job in the office, helping with patient files and appointments. These experiences helped her decide to go to college, then on to nursing school when she graduated.

As her train approaches, she wonders if she's made the right decision. Dad was laid off from the shipyard and finds odd jobs now, but mom is still counted on at the hospital. Her parents assured her that they were saving carefully, and she needed to go to college. When Christy got the financial offer from Oregon Agricultural College, she eagerly accepted.

After living in Southern California, Christy expected Corvallis be more like the photos she had seen of nearby Portland. Changing trains in Albany, she knew she was almost there, yet there was still nothing but open, brown farmland dotted with barns and silos, next to a large river. And there were forested hills in the distance. No sign of a city. Actually, the surroundings are beautiful, in a peaceful way, but they feel isolated. Naturally, an agricultural college would be near farms, but where are the classrooms and buildings she envisioned?

Christy calms when she sees the attractive brick structures. Then she is impressed with the broad tree-lined streets and wide lawns that divide what look like classrooms, from the dormitories. She senses an energy here, as if she may have discovered a jewel hidden within the dusty fields of the Willamette Valley.

Checking in is surprisingly easy. She finds that her dormitory is within walking distance of all her classes, and she has been assigned a roommate named Eleanor. Eleanor is smart and attractive, and eager to accept the

*immediate invitations to campus parties. Parties aren't
Christy's style, and she knows she needs to earn money to
keep herself in school.*

*With her interest in medicine and nursing, she ap-
plies for a job at a veterinary clinic not far from campus.
She is surprised to be hired on the spot, then asked to answer the phones immediately, while her new employer, Dr.
Kissel, dashes from the office on an urgent calf-birthing call
out in Philomath. His wife Helen usually covers the office,
but she is home with a fever.*

*For two years, Christy divides her time between the
classroom, the dorm and her job. She rides her bicycle
everywhere, including to and from the clinic, where she
works four afternoons a week and all day on Saturday. On
stormy days, she walks with an umbrella, knowing where
the awnings are located if the rain gets really heavy. Sun-
days she is usually on call, in case of emergencies that
require an extra helper.*

*She begins as the receptionist, making appoint-
ments and collecting payments for Dr. Kissel. After her first
thirty days, he asks her to help Helen in the surgery.
Christy's pay is soon doubled from twenty-five to fifty-cents
an hour.*

*The Kissels are quiet, observant people, who al-
most never speak during surgery. As a team, Helen anticipates which instruments or procedures he needs, and he
nods approvingly at her decisions. After observing for two
surgeries, Christy senses the process, and is able to assist
Helen during complicated procedures.*

When he is out on the farms for his daily calls, Helen and Christy maintain the office, and handle minor tasks like medications, cleaning out small wounds, and counseling pet owners about parasites and grooming.

A generous woman, Helen also helps Christy to adjust to college life. Though twenty years older, she is about the same petite size as Christy. Quite a contemporary dresser, she frequently suggests different hair fashions, like the softer new styles and longer hair, and they discuss the latest mid-calf dresses and silky blouses. Though Christy has no time for dating or fashion, she always pays close attention to Helen's ideas. She is quietly saving up to buy a new dress and one of those elegant hats to wear with Eleanor one day, up in Portland.

For the rest of her time in Corvallis, Christy works with the Kissels. They both encourage her interest in a nursing career, suggesting she apply to an excellent training school in San Francisco, called St. Luke's.

Carefully saving her money, she visits Portland twice during her senior year, but feels uncomfortable tagging along with Eleanor and her friends. Instead, she takes the train by herself, and satisfies her curiosity by walking around different neighborhoods. She is impressed by the Norton Hotel downtown, where her guided tour of the city begins, and she longs for the day when she can afford to spoil herself by staying there, or at The Oregon or The Multnomah. These are stately buildings, catering to well-dressed customers.

From time to time, the Kissels treat her to overnights with them at the coast, in Newport or Florence,

Donald McPhail

and Christy loves being back among the smells and sounds of the ocean. They are traveling in their Packard over the Coast Range, and Christy has chills as she glimpses the ocean when they descend. The remarkable jagged coastline, with massive rock formations standing offshore, is far different from Long Beach.

When they walk along the sandy beach, Christy removes her shoes and tests the water, leaping quickly back. The ocean is freezing compared with California, and the air temperatures are colder, but they are invigorating. The seabird sounds and the salty ocean air are even more refreshing than she remembers.

These visits to the coast remind Christy of her love for the sea, and of how much she misses the quiet, sunny days with Pete and Doris down in Long Beach. But she is stimulated by all that she has seen of the ruggedness of Oregon — its dense forests, and wild rivers that twist and turn down to the ocean.

As her school-year ends, Christy is well prepared for each of her final exams, and quietly graduates at the top of her class. She has committed herself to a nurse's career, and is determined to succeed.

She knows that her parents can't spend the money on train tickets to Oregon for graduation. But the Kissels will be there for her, and Pete and Doris can attend the bigger graduation in three years, at St. Luke's.

Her mind is already on her next adventure. The train ticket is in her purse, and she is searching the San Francisco newspapers for information about weather, and apartments, and possible part-time jobs.

Excited as she is, the day of departure is a sad one for Christy and her Oregon-parents. There is little conversation as Dr. Kissel drives the three of them to the Albany train station, where Christy will board the Cascade to Oakland. Through tears, they tell her how proud they are, and insist that she accept "a little pocket money" for the trip. Then they smile and hug her close. They are all smiling bravely, but they can feel the sadness as the train pulls away.

Oakland is the next stop. She will stay in a hotel in Berkeley tomorrow night, then she can ferry across the bay to locate St. Luke's and to register.

Christy knows dormitory life from her time in Corvallis, and decides it is the best way to save money, as well as make friends and get to know the school routine. There are thirty-three girls in her class, all from California except for five girls from Honolulu. She rooms with Esther Chung, one of the Hawaii girls, and one from San Francisco, Marie Wilson.

Christy has never met an oriental before. Wondering if she practices exotic rituals or eats strange foods, she soon learns that Esther was born and raised in Honolulu and is a practicing Catholic. She loves sausages and hamburgers, and she introduces Christy and Marie to Chinese food in small restaurants out on Geary Street, and around San Francisco. Esther's strangest food craving seems to be for a gooey mixture called poi, which arrives in carefully wrapped packages. The other Hawaii girls always come to their room to share with each other. Somehow, poi is hard to find in San Francisco.

Donald McPhail

Eating, studying and exploring old neighborhoods together, Christy, Esther and Marie become closest friends, helping each other through the stresses of finals, and the austerity of dorm living.

From time to time, Christy allows herself to join other nurses when they go to Whitney's at the Beach, called "Playland" by her friends, or ride the trolleys around the city. She carefully avoids the young doctors, as her parents had cautioned her.

For two years, Christy studies hard, and she earns top marks for her work in the wards. Patients seem to brighten when she comes into their rooms, with her distinctive nurse's cap and reassuring ways, even the most serious cases. And the doctors, who at first found her to be a bit too reserved, as she stood toward the back during rounds, realize that she is a most observant pupil. They see her nod slightly when another nurse responds correctly to the procedure under discussion, and gets it right. Though she suppresses any negative responses, they can see that she is aware when a young nurse's answer is incorrect. Each time they call on her for a patient assessment, she speaks with confidence, and she is invariably right.

Just turning twenty-one, she will graduate in one more year, and considers applying for a full time position at St. Luke's itself, because San Francisco has now become her home. Most jobs are still hard to find, but nurses remain in great demand. At the same time, Christy feels the need to look further, to explore the world the way Florence

Nightingale had, and despite economic conditions, she chooses not to settle down yet.

Then she meets Dr. James Fordyce.

James, as he prefers to be called — "not Jim" — is an enthusiastic intern from Stanford Medical School, specializing in orthopedics. His booming voice and large gestures, and his unmistakable tendency to tease the nurses, sets him apart from the more reserved young medics. Marie has mentioned Fordyce to her, calling him, "a real knockout." She seems to have assumed first-rights on the handsome intern. Tall, with sandy hair and broad shoulders and an outgoing personality, he was a top swimmer at Stanford, an Olympic candidate at one time.

Marie was quite open about the afternoon they spent at Maverick's beach last week. "James surfed while I waited on the towel for him to finish. It was wonderful."

Raised in Piedmont across the bay, and always a top scholar, Fordyce is known as quite a ladies' man. He frequents the best restaurants in the city, and Marie anticipates a dinner invitation to Tadich Grill or Alioto's. He has a red Model T Speedster, and is often observed darting out of the hospital parking area in his flashy racing car.

James and Christy meet during a break in the cafeteria, after a long and difficult surgery. Fordyce had assisted on a fractured patella, and Christy was a last-minute substitute, mainly standing in reserve should another nurse require a break.

"That was you, wasn't it, Nurse Miller? Standing there by the exit."

Donald McPhail

"It was Dr. Fordyce, but I'm surprised you recognized me. The masks make us all look quite alike."

"You got me," he admits. "Actually, I saw you across the room a few days ago, and wanted to meet you. We pass in the wards, but I don't think we've been introduced yet."

He invites Christy to join him for dinner, possibly the next week. "Why not?" she decides, though she worries what Marie will think.

One Saturday, they drive north for a picnic in Sonoma, at a popular old winery; then on Sunday, to Monterey for lunch at newly rebuilt Del Monte Lodge. The next weekend, they take a picnic to San Gregorio, near Santa Cruz, and he rides the surf while she reads a novel, then studies for a test. They are falling into a comfortable and wonderful routine. And Marie has all but stopped talking to her.

The pattern continues, and their time together is increasingly affectionate, occasionally holding hands when they walk along the beach. Then two weeks pass and on the way to Napa, he confuses her, "It's your eyes."

"What on earth do you mean?"

"I recognized your eyes, even above your surgical mask."

"Oh that," she exclaims. "You are a real flatterer, I believe." She adds, with a note of seriousness that catches him off guard, "But can I trust you?"

He swallows, then replies, "You can always trust me, Christy." His own hazel eyes are clear and sincere, and his candid statement encourages her.

She hadn't known many boys in her tranquil life in Long Beach. Pete and Doris were her trusted support system, and they had guided her away from the eager young high school suitors. They warned her about boys, and what they were after. James isn't like this. She feels he is both kind and trustworthy.

"We're nearly married, you know." Then he adds, "At least that's the way I feel."

She blushes, "How can you say that, James?"

"We see each other nearly every day at the hospital, and we spend what little free time we have on these excursions. We're exploring wonderful places around the Bay Area. We're also exploring each other."

While it shocks her to hear this, Christy can't deny his logic. And she can't deny the tingle she feels when he mentions exploring each other. "I hadn't thought of it like that. I hope you're serious, and not teasing me."

"I'm absolutely serious. And I wouldn't tease you about something so important. In fact, I wish you wouldn't tease me, young lady. Or at least it sometimes feels that way."

"What do you mean, tease you?"

"This is the 1930s. Look around us. There is swing music. Sensual new styles. Prohibition is ended. And people feel there's nothing to lose. There is free will, as well. People are taking chances, going with their instincts."

"And our instincts are?"

"To run away next year, after you graduate, and when I'm settled into a full-time practice. To buy a ring, find a little house, and get married."

Donald McPhail

"Why that's crazy."

"Not so crazy if you think about it. I'm twenty-five, and about to get a major position. You're nearly twenty-one and will take on a new life in another year. We can start an exciting life together. How about it?"

Caught up in the joy of this picture, painted by a brilliant and handsome man. "I'll do it, James. I love the sound of this future. When can we meet your parents? When can you meet mine?"

"You're wonderful, my girl. I love your spirit, and I love you. I'll invite us over next weekend, to my parents' house and we'll tell them." Then he looks serious, and sounds strangely intense. "And no more teasing from you. We do need to explore, dearest. Stay with me tonight in Sausalito. We'll have a quiet dinner, and spend the night together. We will celebrate our future."

With two classes and a routine test on Monday, Christy hasn't seen James since their special night. Where is he? She feels guilty and a little frightened, for giving in so willingly. She is still sore down there, and isn't certain if it was from the rough beginning, when they nearly tore each other's clothes off and frantically explored each other's bodies, or his harsh entry. He seemed hypnotized, almost cruel. But she realizes that she has never done this before and maybe this is normal. But she will learn. They will marry soon, and they will learn from each other.

Christy arrives early to work on Tuesday, and it seems as if Marie is waiting for her. "Why didn't you tell us, Christy?" Marie gushes, "It's all over St. Luke's."

"Tell you what?" Christy is cautious.

"It's your boyfriend, James Fordyce. You tell us." Marie challenges. "At least, he was."

"I'm not at all sure of what you're saying," Christy's stomach tightens and she feels light-headed. She wonders what he might have said about her.

"Dr. Fordyce, James, departed yesterday after-noon, in full glory. He told us he got a great position at Johns Hopkins in Baltimore, and is already driving his way across country." She looks at Christy's reaction, and ex-claims. "My God, Christy. He must have known weeks ago. Didn't you know?"

Shaking her head, Christy dashes to the lavatory and locks the door. "He's gone? How could he be gone?" She gets to the toilet just in time, as her body gives way and she loses everything.

The remaining weeks are a blur. Barely able to fo-cus, she attends classes and does her rounds with the doctors, carefully avoiding Marie, but she worries about the physical changes. She recognizes the symptoms, of course, the cramping up and soreness of her breasts. Then she finds that one of the older doctors is available, Dr. Newfield. He isn't a teacher and she had never seen him with Fordyce, so she approaches him about an exami-nation.

Like Christy, Dr. Newfield immediately identifies the pregnancy and instead of lecturing, he patiently screens her blood-work and checks for other potential health risks. As her school term ends, she begins to see visible signs, and that's when she calls her parents, confirming that she

Donald McPhail

will be coming home in a few days, and that she would not be returning to school.

She will love her baby, she tells herself, but she will never forgive Dr. James Fordyce.

Donald McPhail

CHAPTER EIGHT
Christy & Mary & Duff

Christy returned to St. Luke's nearly a year after Mary was born, and she quietly resumed her final year of studies. It was agonizing to leave her daughter. As a nurse and new mother, she knew how serious these early absences could be for Mary. She also knew that if she didn't finish nursing school now, she never would. Then how could she support them?

Christy knew that Mary would be safe and adored by Grandpa Pete and Nana Doris. They had become Christy's own closest friends years ago. Now Doris adored her new granddaughter, and was home all day, able to be with Mary. With Grandpa Pete's help, Doris felt strong enough to look after her.

When she returned to her routine at St. Luke's, Christy's earlier classmates had graduated and many new students had transferred in from other schools, so she enjoyed a certain amount of anonymity. As for the teaching doctors, unless you knew them socially, they paid little attention to the nursing students. It was the interns you looked out for, and Christy knew she would take care of herself.

She rented a small room near the hospital and lived a private life. She studied diligently and was dependable on her daily nursing shift, though she no longer wished to work in the operating room during surgeries. Since she had earned enough surgery credits, Christy was granted an exemption to float among departments, and was assigned a different unit or floor each week. If a department was short-handed, as Intensive Care often was, she might remain there for a month at a time.

Shortly into the spring term, she saw an article in the morning *Chronicle*, describing a special sailing of Matson's luxury liner, *SS Malolo,* that would depart in late September. There were temporary positions for social directors and ship's nurses. The sailing followed her graduation, and would allow her to visit Mary before the two month assignment.

Anticipating a higher salary for the brief tour, Christy was quick to apply, taking a chance on showing up in person at the Matson office. She was elated to get the job, and while it would take her away for an extra two months, she knew the income would help her and her parents.

The cruise changed her life, nearly as much as her daughter had. Against all of her intentions, she was drawn to a man who was working on the ship. It began innocently enough, before they left port in San Francisco.

Wearing her official Matson nurse's whites, Christy is seated near the hatchway and listening to the ship's doctor as he briefs the new medical staff. This is her second

Donald McPhail

day aboard the Malolo, *and her new boss, Dr. Stanley, is filling it with lectures. At the moment, he is describing experiments on prisoners, that he performed during his regular assignment as head of surgery at San Quentin prison. The experiments sound a bit grim, and she asks herself what this might have to do with shipboard emergencies.*

"Excuse me, Miss," whispers a calm voice. She raises her eyes to see a serious young man in a black sweater, leaning toward her. He whispers again, and presents a small card. "Would you ask Doctor Stanley to contact me when he is free?"

Is that a British accent? *she wonders, as she watches him quietly exit through the hatchway. Then she looks at the card. "Duff Malone, Cruise Director, American Express Company."*

As she returns her attention to Dr. Stanley and his experiments, she places the business card into her pocket.

Christy wants to finish her letter to Mary. She is going to be late for dinner, but she isn't worried about the delay. She was invited to Captain Christian's table for the second night in a row and he seems a stickler, but he can wait. He should know how Dr. Stanley's lectures tend to run long, and just now she prefers to talk with her daughter.

At least it feels like talking. She can tell Mary how she misses her, and describe the work she is doing. Ship's nurse on the glamorous Malolo *is a special job, and Nana Doris will add little touches to the story to make Christy sound like Cinderella.*

Since reporting aboard ship two days ago, Christy has met many of the crew members, and seen some the early passengers as they were escorted to their staterooms. One of the crew was more interesting than the others, although he might not even be a crew member. His business card said "Cruise Director, American Express Company". She wants nothing to do with men, but there is something about him that draws her interest.

Christy doesn't want to miss tonight's mail pickup, since they will sail for Hawaii early in the morning. She has already changed into her newest evening dress, and she can limit her makeup and run a brush though her hair before dashing for the main dining room. She might make it.

Captain Christian smiles brightly as she approaches. Everyone else is already seated and engrossed in conversation. She sees the Captain gesture the steward away, as he stands to hold her chair himself.

He's a tall man, with broad shoulders and a pleasant face. He seems slightly overweight, a likely consequence of this life aboard a luxury ship. His dominant voice is abrupt, with a slight accent, Danish perhaps. He sounds quite cheerful when he addresses her, although yesterday she heard him speak sharply to two of his officers in the lounge, and it was definitely not pleasant. So far he is positive with her.

And there is that Englishman again, *she observes,* seated just across from me.

"Nurse Miller," says the Captain when she is seated and he is in his chair, *"please meet our cruise director, Mr. Malone."*

Donald McPhail

Malone stands briefly and nods, smiling in recognition. "Nurse Miller. I believe we met earlier today."

The Captain observes Malone's response, then introduces her to the officers and two attractive women who complete their table, as Christy tries to retain their names and faces. It seems that the ladies are passengers who boarded early, whose husbands will arrive in the morning. But her attention is divided, between thoughts of her daughter and wanting to ward off the attention of these two men.

Christy is especially wary of the Captain. Something doesn't seem right. This is the second time she has been seated next to him, and it doesn't feel like a coincidence. Last night was comfortable enough. There were times when he ignored her, talking shop with younger officers who nodded and agreed with whatever he said. Tonight he is devoting his attention to her, and he's a bit familiar. Maybe he's sending a warning to Mr. Malone.

Though the Captain is polite and gracious in a formal way, he presumes a closeness that is out of place. There, he touched my arm and just called me, "my dear", though we only just met.

Mr. Malone is observant, and seems to recognize the Captain's attitude. He has turned his conversations to the young woman next to him.

I certainly don't want to alienate the Captain. We'll be working together on the ship for two whole months. And he's done nothing to make me angry. But his strong personality is too much like the horrible Dr. James Fordyce.

After this, Christy felt she should shield herself in the company of other people during the cruise, and after being around him for three days, she felt that Duff Malone seemed a safe haven. He was calm and reasonable, and not especially interested in her.

Honolulu was the first port of call, and the Captain would not be with the passengers until the final evening ashore. As everyone disembarked in Honolulu, Christy heard a familiar voice, "Excuse me miss, are you looking for company?"

"Why Mr. Malone. Of course. Are you going ashore now?" Then she saw a dapper little man next to him, someone who wasn't from the ship. She smiled at the stranger, "If your friend doesn't object?"

Malone introduced them, "This is my colleague, Werner Bergen. Werner, Nurse Miller."

Christy decided to have some fun at Malone's expense. "I'm Christy, Mr. Bergen, and I have the honor of working with Mr. Malone. I'm a ship's nurse."

"Friends call me Bergen-san," he said, "so please indulge me. And in what capacity does this healthy young men require a nurse, may I inquire?"

She sensed a kindred spirit, and enjoyed seeing Malone blush so easily, "What a remarkable question, Bergen-san. I often ask myself that." She took Bergen's arm and sauntered down the gangway, chatting and flirting with this enchanting older man.

"Don't listen to her, Bergen," she heard Malone say, trailing behind. "I believe she is exaggerating."

From this comfortable beginning, the three of them became close friends. She was delighted when Bergen informed her that he was joining the *Malolo* and assisting Duff for the remainder of the tour. He was the American Express expert on shore excursions, and would supervise all of the shoreside activities.

As they sailed from Honolulu en route to Yokohama, Christy felt safe and at ease. Bergen was older, and a sincere type of man, and she wasn't sure he was attracted to women.

Malone appeared to like women, but for someone of his travel experience he seemed naive and uncertain around them. He was quite a charming man, but totally unaware of the obvious next-steps in a relationship. A man like this could surely be a safe friend.

Christy couldn't know that two violent acts would bring them closer together, and an injury would tell her how much her friend Malone meant to her.

These shocks led Christy to recognize that Duff was a responsible and compassionate man. More important to her, he was kind and he seemed to understand how they brought out good things in each other. Following Duff's serious accident outside of Shanghai, she realized, "Each time I see him, it's as if a light goes on in my heart. I can't explain it, and I don't want it to happen. But there it is. More than safety, more than trust. I love him."

Once they recognized they had fallen in love, the next part of their lives became clear. They would be married, and raise Mary together. Duff would accept the offer from Pan American, to help create this new airline industry.

As the Malolo carefully makes its way out of Tutuila
harbor, past Whale Rock and through Breakers Point, Duff
and Christy are different people. They still have their shipboard responsibilities, but they can no longer ignore each
other as they had before. They had said "I love you" there
on the beach, after fearing their relationship was over.
They had made a promise, and a commitment. Bergen
was their witness.

As the ship makes its way along the twelve-day day
journey back to San Francisco, it is difficult to concentrate.
Christy continues her daily dispensary duties, but those are
limited to standard ailments like sunburn or upset stom-
achs. Dr. Stanley is there for illnesses, or anything major.

By now, Duff's daytime responsibilities are limited
to organizing occasional celebrations like birthdays, or
crossing the equator. In the evening, his social duties are
not required, since the passengers have long-since formed
their own friendships and routines. He is free to circulate
around the ship, then excuse himself.

At dinner with the passengers, they complete the
obligatory chats, then make excuses to leave after the
dancing begins. Captain Christian must have noticed the
change in Christy, because his dinner invitations stopped,
and he no longer insists on the first dance of the evening.
Word has gotten around.

It's the first night underway and they have made
their separate excuses, and left the others with apologies.
Bergen and Gio will cover for them. Christy and Duff meet
on the promenade. It is near Duff's stateroom, and they
aren't likely to see any other passengers.

Donald McPhail

"Dearest," she whispers, "are you safe with this? You are still a ship's official."

"It will be fine," he says quietly. "This isn't some sort of fling. Besides, our passengers are not interested in us, or what we do. They're just anxious to get home."

The sun is just rising off to starboard as Duff wakens. Christy is sitting up, and he finds her the most beautiful person he has ever seen. As he moves his hand to touch her shoulder, he realizes she has been crying.

"What is it? Are you all right? Have I hurt you?"

"No. No, my love. You haven't hurt me. It is just so beautiful."

"And there is more?" He asks gently.

"I am just so completely happy, Duff. With us. With our love. But you're right. There are things we need to talk about." A sad smile.

"Go on," he places his hands over hers.

"Duff, there is no other way to say this. Yesterday at the beach you mentioned having a family. I already have a child…a little girl." She stops to watch his reaction.

His eyes and mouth relax and he gently says, "Tell me more."

"I have a daughter, named Mary. She's two years old now, and lives with mom and dad down in Long Beach. She loves them very much." She blinks away sudden emotion, and continues. "I was in my third year at St. Luke's, and I met this intern. He was from Stanford and we met in surgery. We dated for weeks, then he said he would marry me when he finished his internship. One day I found out he *was gone. I never heard from him again. And I was pregnant."*

Duff was quiet for a moment, then asked quietly, "How did you get through it? School? The pregnancy? Life?"

"Mom and dad are wonderful. I dropped out for one term and stayed with them at home. Mary was born in January, and I went back to school in September. It wasn't easy on them, or on me -- or on Mary. But we made it work, and I got my nurses degree."

"And her father? Does he know about Mary?"

"No," she pauses, "I couldn't bring myself to tell him. He didn't care about me. He didn't deserve this baby."

Duff touches her cheek, "I'm glad you told me. Glad you're here."

"You're glad?"

"Of course. I love you. Anyone who is part of you, I will love. You are quite a brave woman. Will you tell me more about Mary? Is she smart and energetic, like her mother?"

"Smarter and very beautiful. She's a lively, energetic girl. And she loves her grandparents!"

"I can't wait to meet her. I don't know much about children, but I know I'll love her."

Christy is silent again, gathering her thoughts. Then, in a whisper, "You surprise me. In a good way, of course. Of the many reactions I thought about, this is one I never considered."

Donald McPhail

Reentering Mary's world would not be easy for Christy. Already, her little girl preferred being with Doris and Pete, and who wouldn't? Christy realized it would take time together to earn Mary's trust, and to regain her role as a mother.

Christy and Duff returned to San Francisco filled with conflicting emotions. She was overwhelmed with joy, and filled with a keen sense of adventure. She also felt nervous. They were both overjoyed that she and Duff were in love and would be married within days. They were excited at the prospect of Duff's new job with Pan American Airways, and a home in Honolulu. But she was apprehensive about two important things: that Mary might not give Duff a chance, and that Duff's job would keep him absent for long periods.

Christy counted on the joy and adventure to sustain her, as she rode the train down to Long Beach to see Mary and her parents after the brief marriage ceremony in front of the Justice of the Peace. Duff had to attend a final American Express meeting in San Francisco, and this allowed Christy time to get to know her daughter again.

Naturally, Mary was excited to see her mother after so many months, but she was surprisingly withdrawn, frequently turning away. She was moody, and hesitant to let go of Pete and Doris. They were her family, and she didn't want to leave them.

Christy spent mornings with Mary, reading favorite books to her and sitting quietly with her in the front yard, or walking along the beach together. They talked about their nice home in Long Beach, and about another one, a big house on the beach in Hawaii. That beach had lovely, smooth sand and the water was always warm for swimming. Slowly Mary came around, and when Christy explained that Nana and Grandpa would bring her to Hawaii on a ship, and come and live with them, she reluctantly agreed.

Mary was confused, both about moving into a new house and traveling far away to a different part of the world. These were big changes. But Christy assured her they would all be together, and she always added, "We will live right on the beach."

One day Christy said, "There is a nice man named Duff, that I want you to meet in Hawaii. I hope you like him. Mama likes him very much."

Knowing that Nana and Grandpa would be with her had been the clincher. She barely heard the name "Duff." She was excited to be taking a ship with Nana and Grandpa in a few months, and would get to swim in the ship's swimming pool and sit at a dinner table with all of the adults. "Can I bring Mousie?" she asked, and Christy laughed out loud to learn that her Mary was playing with the same stuffed toy that she had loved as a little girl.

Mary moved to Honolulu without a fuss. It helped that she got to have a pretty new Hawaiian name for Mary, that Hawaiians pronounced *Mah-lee-ah*. She said she would miss the tidal pools where she and Pete explored each day, but when she heard of tide-pools in Hawaii, she was persuaded. She loved that Nana and Grandpa would live in the cottage behind her house.

Donald McPhail

CHAPTER NINE

Water Girl

Christy knelt down to pull a tiny green shoot from her rose garden and toss it expertly into the tin pail next to the hose. She was always vigilant about weeds among her favorite plants, determined that her few roses would remain even stronger, healthier and prettier than those in the nearby park gardens. De Villiers sat calmly in Duff's favorite chair, impressed with the variety of colors and delicate aromas around him. "What extraordinary gardens, Christy. You obviously put a great deal of work into them."

"I love my flowers, Marcus. There are so many lovely varieties here in the islands. I always take special care with my roses."

"How did you decide to settle here, below Diamond Head?"

"Duff and I loved this location, even before the adjacent houses were built," she said. "These houses are part of our airline story, as you will hear." While she had shared her own history, she carefully omitted some of the details, especially the part about St. Luke's and her daughter Mary. She did describe enough about growing up in Long Beach that he understood her love of the ocean, as well as her closeness to Malia, Doris and Pete.

"You said the your parents helped you and Duff raise your children, so you were able to have your own careers," said de Villiers. "Please tell me about that."

"They helped in so many ways. Duff and I tried hard to live normal lives, even though he was asked to travel so much at first, and manage a sizable operation later on. But in our line of work, nothing was ever quite normal. We had to operate a lot without him here, very much like the military families that we know. As a married couple, you recognize that he will be away for long periods of time. So you concentrate on your family, loving each other when you are together, and living your own lives when you are apart. But the distance has its consequences."

She went into the kitchen to rinse off the dirt and brought back glasses of lemonade, then sat facing him, looking serious. "I have to admit, Duff's time away from home strained our relationship, in ways he didn't ever realize. I missed him and our life together. I wanted him here with me, with us, and it hurt. But then I was able to travel with him on some of his longer trips, out to Shanghai and down to Australia and New Zealand. We would take the children with us over to Kauai or Hawaii island. Those times together helped us to get back on track as a family."

Calmer now, she continued. "It was a blessing that Pete and Doris were here with us. In the earliest years, this allowed me to do my nurse's work. They were here when Malia got home from school, and later on Theo, who we named after Duff's father. Here in Hawaii, that turned into 'Teo'.

Donald McPhail

"I got off my shift in mid-afternoon. After the Japanese attack, nurses were badly needed, so I got home very late. There were just so many injured men and women who needed help."

"What a frightening and chaotic time that must have been," he said, leading to his next question. "That's one of the primary themes, and I'm not sure that either of us is ready for your Pearl Harbor experiences just now. I'd prefer to save that conversation for a longer day, if you don't mind."

She nodded, and he turned several pages, "Could you go back to your arrival here, in the thirties?"

She sat back and closed her eyes for a moment, then looked at him, "I had studied hard, and my profession was important to me. I wanted to work, but my first love was my daughter. Our son Teo came five years later.

"As often happens, Malia and Teo had entirely different personalities. Malia was spunky and energetic, and though Teo was just a baby, you could see that he was quieter and quite an observer. As they got older, he was always building things, and Malia was always knocking them down." She smiled, "We did make her help to rebuild them.

"Duff would drive me crazy sometimes, calmly working with Teo, saying things that a child would not yet understand, 'No need need to worry, little man. We can always build it again.' It was surprising, though, by the time Teo turned four, he would knock them down himself, just to beat her to it. Then he would look at her in a certain way, and quietly rebuild."

De Villiers continued, with an understanding smile, "After speaking with Duff's airport colleagues, then his office staff, it sounds as if Duff and Teo are quite alike in some respects. Duff sounds like a calm sort of leader at the office. I wonder if he ever gets upset."

"You're absolutely right, they are alike. Duff seldom gets upset, and when he does it's pretty frightening. But your comment reminds me of something else Duff used to do, beginning when Teo was around eight. Duff always treats children like little adults, sometimes providing too much information for a youngster. Yet I'm sure now, that both of our children absorbed more than I realized.

"We were in the den and Teo was fussing over something, nearly in tears. It was a wooden airplane model that wouldn't quite fit together. Malia was over in her chair, reading.

"Duff sat down on the floor next to him, and I could see Malia listening and watching. 'What's going on, son?' Duff asked.

"Teo stayed silent, but had tears in his eyes. Then he said, 'I am so angry!'

" 'Are you angry at that airplane?'

" 'Angry, daddy,' and more tears.

" 'Have we talked about frustration? Do you know this word?'

"Obviously, Teo wasn't in the mood for conversation, 'I am angry. Leave me alone.'

" 'I just hate to see you waste all that anger on that airplane. You may need it some time.'

"This confused Teo, the idea of needing his anger."
Donald McPhail

" 'Sometimes, son, we mix the two things up, anger and frustration. They're both important feelings, and we don't want to waste our anger, if we're only frustrated.'

"This distracted Teo enough, that he began calming down, so Duff went on.

" 'You have every right to be angry, when something really unfair or bad is happening. But don't waste it on something that is only frustrating, like when that propeller won't fit right.'

"He knew Teo was not going to listen much longer.

" 'You know, when we expect one thing and get another, we all get frustrated. Adults too. You want that propeller to go onto the plane, and it doesn't. That's something we can fix. Frustrations can be figured out. But that's not important enough to get angry about. We save getting angry for when things are actually wrong, or very unfair.'

"I know Teo heard him. After that, he seemed to deal with his frustrations and not lash out. All these years later, I'm sure that Teo has his own conflicts in the military, that must be very hard. It must be difficult to go to war, against a country you don't even know or hate. I hear frustration in his letters. I hope it doesn't turn to anger."

De Villiers watched and made notes, but didn't interrupt.

"I think about this, too, when I see Malia, sorting through her issues. Some of her life has been quite difficult, even unfair. Some was frustration, from always competing with boys as a surfer, or in school. Some experiences could have caused anger, since they couldn't be fixed. Like someone betraying a friendship, or someone close dying unexpectedly. She finds ways to work through difficult things. She learned so much from her friend, Ke'. And maybe she remembers what Duff said all those years ago."

"Malia sounds interesting," de Villiers prompted. "Can you tell me about her?"

"You just try to stop me! She's a fabulous young lady. She was not easy to raise, but what a wonderful adult.

"It was clear from the beginning that she loved the water. When she was old enough, my dad got her a small surf board, sized for a six-year-old. He started her off in the waters near Waikiki, with three-footers over there at Queens beach. She quickly developed her confidence, and ventured into the low surf by herself, staying close-in as Grandpa Pete kept a sharp eye on her from shore, or a nearby rock. As she got older, she edged farther out. This worried me a little, but I knew how careful Dad had always been with me as a child, so I trusted him.

"Malia was fully at home in the water, and by the time she was ten she was out surfing early-mornings and late in the afternoon. She came home exhausted, and full of stories about the sights and sounds out on the ocean. She was so aware, coming home and describing little things, like the salty sea-smell mixed with the waxy-vanilla of her board, and the surprising scent of plumeria as it drifted out from somebody's distant garden. Usually she would come home famished, after smelling the spices and grilled meats from lunch preparation over at the Royal.

Donald McPhail

"She was seldom really alone out there, since there were always boys with her looking for decent waves. And Pete was watching from a distance.

"There is a clear pecking-order here in Hawaii, and the local surfers and beachboys respect it. There are help-ful 'uncles', those older beachboys like our friend Bully over at the club, and the rougher young men I refer to as beach-bums. Bully and his friends referred to them as 'Tavern Boys', for some reason.

"Since she was the only girl, most of the younger surfers gave her a difficult time at first, though they treated her with more respect as she got older. As for me, I didn't like her being the only girl, and I certainly didn't like it once they began noticing her figure. But I had always trusted Malia. I believed she was honest with me, so when she assured me there was no problem with the boys, I felt I needed to believe her. I knew that Bully and his pals were out there. Their rules were even more strict than mine. These men were older than the ones I refer to as beach-bums, and during the day they were in charge of every-thing that went on along the beach and the ocean, begin-ning over there in front of the Moana.

"Bully was also a paid beach supervisor and full-time host at the Outrigger Canoe Club. In fact, you must have met him that night at Duff's party over at the club.

"Beachboys like Bully and his generation are local treasures. They are true watermen, so they know the ocean better than anyone . Many of them earned their liv-ing back then, teaching visitors to surf the waves or to paddle those outrigger canoes. They were teachers and paddlers, and much more. Nearly all of them were colorful story tellers, musicians, singers, dancers — even companions for lonely lady-tourists, according to local legend. For Malia, they were surfing pals and loyal guardians.

If it was too rough to surf, they got their fishing poles and perched on the rocks waiting for strikes. Too calm, and they paddled their outriggers over to where smaller fish had gathered. I think Malia learned patience from them. They showed our children how to respect the sea and all that is in it. This was far more important for Malia. Teo never had much interest in the ocean or surfing. He concentrated on team sports on grassy fields, like football and baseball.

"But Malia was at home in the water, and they adopted her completely. The beachboys treated her like their own daughter and protected her from the *poi dog* beach-bums. As you may have guessed, 'poi dog' means something like 'mongrel' here in Hawaii.

"Bully and his friends have a club of their own, *Hui Nalu*, that regularly defeats the Outrigger Club in direct sports competition. The contests are friendly, but they are a deep matter of pride. As I said, the men of Hui Nalu adopted Malia, which is quite a tribute. Their membership has always been invitation-only, all men, mostly Hawaiian heritage, and closely guarded. The Hui Nalu members use the large men's changing-room at the Moana as their clubhouse. They are as proud of their club as the members of the Outrigger Club. Our friend Bully may work at the Outrigger, but he's a dues paying member of Hui Nalu.

Donald McPhail

"The surfing part was tougher. She had to create her own territory out on the water, waiting in the lineup for her wave. She got no help from the beach-bums. They jumped her spots in line and never helped when they cut her off, or she wiped out. They mostly smirked and looked the other way. No acknowledgement or apology with their hands, the way the guys acknowledged each other. But she kept at it.

"Since Malia refused to go away, even the beach-bums finally got used to her after a while, and actually called her *sistah*. As her surfing skills improved, she developed a style that impressed the regulars, so they helped her to learn the more complicated moves. When the surface was too calm for any excitement, they sat on their boards and traded stories with her. She learned the unique language, with words like "brah" and "tita" and "lolo" as part of her rough vocabulary. And we knew she could swear like any other local kid.

"During the school year, she attended Punahou, the private school near Manoa, though most of her young surfing pals went to public high schools like Farrington and Nanakuli. The older Hui Nalu beachboys were long done with school. Paid surfing and paddling lessons was their full-time day-job, and their night-time hours were devoted to playing music and courting the more attractive and well-to-do lady clients.

"When she turned fifteen, Malia felt she knew as much about life as any of her classmates. She had proven herself among the surfer crowd, almost as good as most men and far ahead of any boy. She was also good at keeping aggressive boys away. Hui Nalu men made sure that nobody messed with her when they were around. Not those beach-bums. Not the tough surfers from Waianae or Waimanalo. Not the occasional tourist kids who wandered over from in front of the Royal and the Moana.

"Malia knew Waikiki and Diamond Head intimately, because she had surfed there every day for half of her life. And she had seen the North Shore, where the massive waves ran.

"Meantime, she had to navigate life with me, and with Duff and her grandparents. Malia was trying to break away, and it was hard on everyone. We still saw her as a little girl. But we knew that many of her classmates at Punahou were often on their own, too. Not everyone was wealthy and caucasian. There were kids on scholarship, some of them living on homestead land with uncles and aunties, and many of them had worked jobs since they were twelve, or earlier.

"As I said, her surfing friends weren't at Punahou. Two particular boys, Mika and Stewie, were the ones she hung-out with the most, when she wasn't with Bully and the Hui Nalu watermen. Both boys had occasional jobs. Mika was a laborer I think, working for his uncle in construction. Stewie ran errands for a grocery store.

"She told us that Mika was an okay kid. She had no idea if he liked girls any more than he liked the mongrels that lived with Uncle. He was hesitant when he was out with other kids, sometimes too aggressive, other times a total follower. Those dogs were a lot like Mika. No-one really knew who his father was, and his mother had gone away, over to Kailua on the Big Island. Poor Mika needed to find a better place.

"Stewie was her friend, but he troubled her, too. She told me about him, after her accident.

"He was easy-going, with long hair and an easy way about him. He was mostly fun to be around, but she used to say there was a look in his eye that she didn't trust. She didn't want to tell me why she thought that, then admitted that once in a while he would touch her in ways that didn't seem right. Nothing serious. But sometimes he rubbed her shoulder, then slid his hand away. Or he sat closer to her in the car than he needed to. Or he would pat her knee, slapping at first, then hit harder until she made him stop.

"Other boys kept their distance, and that was fine with Malia. Some of the girls, too. At the beginning of every school year, we could see that there was friction between some of the *haole* kids and the locals. Punahou was known as a school for privileged white kids, since the student population was mainly caucasian — though many of them had been born and raised in Hawaii and so had their parents. But some were far from privileged. They were there on scholarships, just like many of the *kanaka*, or locals.

The early disagreements between the caucasians and the locals were triggered mostly by assumptions, I think. The brown-skinned kids often thought the white kids were stuck-up and spoiled. The caucasians thought the darker ones were surly, and superior about having Polynesian blood somewhere in their background. These were common expectations, and often incorrect. After a few weeks, unless something flared up, the students realized that they were just teenagers who came from different backgrounds, and they became friendlier. They lived different individual lives, which was usually interesting to learn about from each other, and their common enemies were usually called 'parents'.

"Of course, school was only part of their day. Malia and her classmates spent most of their time hanging out at a shave-ice stand with kids with Filipino, Hawaiian, Japanese, Samoan, Irish, Portuguese, Chinese, Indonesian, German, Italian and undetermined heritage. When they described certain culture traits, they were usually proud or self-deprecatory, often in the purest *pidgin* lingo. 'That's my *lolo potagui* side,' they would boast, meaning 'crazy Portuguese'. Or their *pake*, *katonk*, or *pilipino* side, meaning Chinese, Japanese or Filipino.

"Hawaii was not colorblind, nor completely tolerant. But Malia knew she was growing up in a place where friendships came in many different shapes and sizes and colors. These were basic lessons that helped her to navigate through school years, but she wanted to know more about these islands, about the Hawaiian culture. That was when Keali'i came into her life."

Donald McPhail

CHAPTER TEN

Keali'i

It was a drizzly Sunday at Waikiki, so Malia traveled out to the North Shore with Stewie in his ratty old Jeepster convertible. Like Malia, Stewie was a junior and eager to be done with school. He frustrated her because he was undependable. Sometimes he hit the books and made good scores on tests. Other times he skipped to go surfing and accepted zeros. She thought she could trust him, then he would do something strange, like take her lunch money, or hide her books, or grab her knee and make some sorry excuse. He didn't know what he would do after high school. Maybe flip burgers somewhere until he was old enough to be a bartender. Part-time work would give him enough money to survive while he lived at his uncle's house and surfed.

Mika was supposed to meet them at Haleiwa for shave-ice, but didn't show. Probably another job for his own uncle, over at Kaneohe. They stopped at a local grocery to call him.

"Howzit, Ke'," Stewie said to a slim local boy with dark hair and a soft smile, strolling out of the store with a bag of chips. "You see Mika around?"

"No, brah. Saw him last night at Gold Coin, but not today." He smiled again, raising his eyebrows at Malia. "Hey you, Sunny girl."

She was surprised he thought he knew her. "Hey, yourself. But my name isn't Sunny. It's Malia, yeah?" She gave him a tight smile.

"Maybe it isn't. Could be, though."

"Why would you say that, brah? I don't know you, even." She was edgy, but interested.

Stewie nodded at Malia, "Ke', what you talking about?"

"You hear C&K? That new tune…Sunflower?."

"Heard it, but I don't know the words."

He sang a few words describing a sunflower, and actually sounded like a singer.

"Ah, I get it. My blue eyes."

"Your bright blue eyes and sunny blonde hair. Just seems to fit. Stewie, meet Sunny!"

Remembering how Duff described her mom's eyes, she paused, then responded with a grin, "OK, brah! For you I can be Sunny! You, too Stewie."

"Right Ke', Sunny it is." Then, "Any good surf here, Ke'? Maybe you can show us some of your places."

"Nothing today, but I'll hang with you guys. Maybe grab a plate lunch. I got the hungries!"

Over the months, Malia was intrigued. The more she was around Keali'i, the more she wanted to know. She couldn't believe he was a year ahead of her at Punahou, and she hadn't seen him.

Donald McPhail

Sometimes she would go to a party with Stewie and Mika, but she would leave early and walk or hitch to Keal-i'i's loft. It was rough built, high in his auntie's old Manoa house. His parents still lived on Molokai, but sent him to Punahou for school. At his place in Manoa, the outside stairs creaked but you could make it silently up the steps if you knew which parts to walk on.

Ke', as Malia now called him, frequently squatted with a couple of pals near Haleiwa, where they could crash after a long day of surfing. Ke' didn't surf Waikiki. He preferred the monster waves off the north shore. She was surprised when he told her one day, "When I'm out there, those waves are like mountains tumbling around me. But all peaceful inside, Sunny. No lie. Comforting. You ever think about before you were born? Must have been like this. I read somewhere that the little baby inside can hear sounds, even outside sounds. Must be noisy to that little *keiki* inside of mama, all the fluids moving and churning around that teensy body, carrying the power of life. So powerful, like when I'm inside those mountains."

When Ke' talked like this, Sunny could understand only parts of it. The mama and the baby held her interest. She learned to listen, and to sort through the far-out ideas.

She knew that surfing wasn't just for sport, riding just for speed or for thrills. It was way more. With Ke's guidance, when Malia finally took on the massive surf off of Haleiwa and Laniakea, she was frightened, but got through that, then sensed the peace that he talked about. Moments of peace and solitude and home.

Unlike Stewie and the other surfers, he wasn't much interested in girls. He was too busy reading and learning from local elders he called *kupuna*, or surfing or playing music. Ke' was serious, always studying about early Hawaii and the monarchy, and saying he wished he was back on Molokai, on his parents' Kalama'ula homestead ranch, working beside his best friend, Kimo. They loved raising horses and tending the honeybees, and fishing in the old style. Ke' missed hearing the stories his father told him about the ancient Hawaiian gods.

He was a young man of conflicts. In his heart, he knew he was a waterman, though he knew his guardian spirit, his *a'umakua*, was an owl, *pueo* in Hawaiian. His sweet sense of humor made Malia laugh, though he was serious much of the time. And serious as he often was, he could play all the current local songs on his guitar — hang-loose rascals like Cecilio & Kapono, where he got Malia's new name, and other innovators like Sunday Manoa, or slack key master Gabby Pahinui.

As a storyteller, Ke' created poetic fantasies about where the ancient gods lived. He loved these spirit worlds. His stories went far beyond Hawaii and the Pacific islands. He described complex visions of parallel universes drawn from his learned *ha'ole* mentors, Yeats and Rilke, whose work he came across in a faded book at the second-hand book store in Haleiwa. He was fascinated by their visions of ghosts and borderlines between the worlds, just like Hawaiian mythology. Yeats' use of sea gods, and his references to shadowy waters and the sea of life were eerily similar to Hawaiian lore. Sometimes Ke' wrote down stories for Sunny, but he preferred the spoken word, or songs he memorized.

And what songs! He knew the old *mele* chants and the beloved Hawaiian hula songs. He sang with an incredible range, his mellow baritone sliding smoothly into heavenly falsetto, interpreting songs like "Molokai Waltz", with its inspiring refrain. His range was supernatural, from perfect low notes to spine-tingling highs. Ke' was no ordinary being.

He told Malia things that he had learned from his spiritual guides. Their wise and patient insights taught Ke' about the old ways, what they called Hawaiian consciousness. And he carefully respected special song-poems that came from individual families, that should not be sung to outsiders without the owners' permission.

He learned about the island of Kaho'olawe from a different source. A university group called "Kaho'olawe Imua" invited Ke' to bless their meeting at a church near campus. They had heard him sing and talk-story at a busy coffee house in Manoa, and they recognized his special gifts. As he read their faded flyer stapled to a communal wall, he learned that the group and the coffee house owners were dedicated to protecting the *aina* and *ma kai*, the land and the oceanside. Their total focus was on capturing and protecting the military-run island of Kaho'olawe, that was currently used for torpedo practice by Navy ships. Soon, although he was never a violent person, this island became his own private cause.

"I need to visit this place," he said to Malia after the first meeting. "I can't have a sense of these things if I don't know the land and water they want to protect."

"But it's a target for explosives, Ke', run by the military. How are you going to do that?"

He had already mapped-out his plan. "My best friend lives on Maui now, works with tourists. We can take his fishing boat over from Ma'alea, going around to the west shore of Kaho'olawe. Then ride my board in."

"That's dangerous, Ke'. Can't you go all the way in on the boat?"

"Only if I want them to see me, then kick me off the island," he laughed. "We'll go most of the way on his boat. Then I need to go in quietly, and I hear the west side is the best approach."

"You call this a fishing boat, Kimo?" said Ke', as he stepped onto the wide mahogany deck and set his board down across the cushioned seat. "You never told me you had a cruise ship."

Kimo was still wiry, and a real Maui-boy now, with sleek black pony-tail and a quick smile. Dressed in faded denim shorts and a Primo t-shirt, he knew his way around boat engines and deepwater fish. His uncle Moon hired him right out of high school, to help operate his tourist-boat business. Running out of Ma'alea, they attracted visitors staying over at Kaanapali and Lahaina, and from the increasing condominium resorts in Kihei. The boat was big enough for four fishermen and their gear, including big coolers for beer and sandwiches. The custom 350 horsepower Chrysler engine provided plenty of power for the large craft.

Kimo said he would transport Ke' to Kaho'olawe if he paid for gas. Laughing at the cruise ship comment, "Hey, brah. It's what Maui tourists expect. Big boat, all the gear. We can do this, I think, but you never told me you wanted to leave this late. Maybe three hours of daylight left."

"I thought you would have night-navigation."

"No stuff like that. Nighttime I go by moonlight, track from houses with lights on."

"No lights on Kaho'olawe, brah."

"Should be all right, Ke'. Not that far. I know the way across the channel. You have a half hour ashore and can paddle back out where I pick you up. Maybe dark after that, but always some lights at Makena and Kihei, leading us to Ma'alea."

Sitting at the back, Ke' and his surfboard warded off the spray from wakes of incoming boats as they low-geared out of the harbor. Further out it was calmer and Kimo revved up the big engine, speeding across the chop.

Ke' relaxed, thinking through his plan. They should be able to release close enough to shore for him to arm-paddle until he found waves to carry him to the beach. Fifteen or twenty minutes on the island should be enough time to get a feel, and see the kind of harm the bombs and shells had caused. Then he could scoot back out for Kimo to pick up and make their way back to Maui.

The trip into shore was easy enough. Ke' found a clear opening to a small beach and stashed his board up behind some thorny kiawe. He didn't need to see the actual navy shells or damaged land. He wanted to find ground high enough to look over the shoreline and out toward the channel. He needed to stand on natural rock and walk down along the sandy beach, to sense whether there was still enough tranquility beneath the surface to salvage this troubled island.

When he had seen enough, Ke' knifed his board back into the surf and slid down on it, digging heavy strokes into the chill, pushing himself out to the channel. He knew where they agreed to meet, and felt good he was ahead of schedule. And he felt good about Kaho'olawe. He could circle out there for a half hour if he had to, if Kimo ran late.

After a time, he heard an unexpected sound, "Is that you Pueo? He laughed aloud. There it was, an owl circling high overhead. Then waved, "I see you."

It was an hour or more, with no sign of Kimo's boat. Ke' was tired, and he knew how cold it would get. The channel was choppy enough on a calm day, but a night-storm could overwhelm him and his board. "Are you circling below, as well, Kamoho, you god of sharks? Perhaps I will see you soon."

No way I can see Kimo's boat at night. If I did, could never see me. Better start paddling and hope someone is out here. Kanaloa will look after me.

Keali'i never made it across the channel, and no one ever found a sign of him or his board.

Donald McPhail

CHAPTER ELEVEN

Malia's Fall

The waves pounded against the reef as their boards glided out of Rice Bowl over to Tonggs. A tricky crosscurrent pulled them toward the jagged rocks, and created funky surf off San Souci over to Graveyards. Lying flat on her board, Malia rested-up after fighting the rips for the past two hours. It was hard to get back on the water after Ke' disappeared. She wouldn't go back to the North Shore without him.

Stewie and Mika were off to the right and Bully was up front, riding that big rhino of his. Thank God for Bully. He was her guardian. He knew the ocean like a dolphin, and he kept her away from trouble — and kept her from thinking too much about Ke'. Bully was kind and a bit of a rascal, and *akamai*, very savvy. If it weren't for Bully, she wouldn't have gone back in the ocean.

She was exhausted, but also energized here with them, away from the automobile horns and tourists that everyone over on shore has to deal with. You could hear the traffic offshore, but the noise was doused by sea-sounds and the green, briny smell of the ocean. Two or three more sets and they'd be done for the day. It was challenging and electric. Not the absolute best-ever, but definitely up there.

Malia remembered back when she just started surfing -- *he'e nalu*, the surfers said, for "sliding on the waves" -- some of the boys, *blalahs* they like to call themselves, were impossible. They referred to her as Betty Kook, which was worse than being simply a Betty, the term for surfergirls. Kooks got no respect, because they ruined everyone's day with their foolishness and poor decisions. Plus, she was a haole girl, and that was never a good thing out on the water.

She was one of the regulars now. Just then, she sensed a change in the currents and used hand strokes to correct. "Stewie, we're too far over, close toward Diamond Head."

"No sweat Sunny. We can shoot in. Follow me. Mika went already."

Malia didn't like the onshore, or the feel of the waves, and what about Bully? "Stewie, where's Bully?"

"Gone back a while ago. Had to work early. Yelled over, but you must not have heard."

Stewie should have told her. She didn't feel right. Then the squall hit.

"Shit, Stewie. Sure to be rough water."

"You right, but no place to land. Too many scabs. Way close to Leahi Beach."

The rain hammered them and they could barely see, as they were dragged into the rocks. It could pass quickly or be there for another hour. If Stewie went in, so could she, but now she lost track of him.

"Ach," she rammed into a big rock and it hurt like hell. "My ribs, Stewie. And my head. Where's my board?"

Donald McPhail

When she woke she was on the sand and Stewie on top of her. "Stewie. Shit. What the hell you doing?"

"Nothing, baby. Just keeping you warm."

"Stewie. Shit! Get the hell off me! My rib's broken. Man it hurts."

Rolling off, "Didn't know. You didn't say nothing. Dragged you over here off the rocks, bleeding. Up there." He pointed to her shoulder, "and down there."

"You took my top off."

"I didn't. Was already torn, partway off."

"You bastard. You took it off."

"Just to help clean you up." Then mumbling, "We're stuck here, you know."

"How stuck?"

"This little beach has rocks on both sides. Can't get up the overhang."

Malia covered herself with the tattered top, "Ow. The damned ribs are broken maybe."

"How 'bout a hit?"

"What?"

"Here," he held up a plastic bag with something in it. "Always got my waterproof baggie! *Pakalolo*. Good stuff. Help with the pain."

"You know I don't do pakalolo. We talked about this."

"Yeah. Sure. But it might help stop the hurt."

"I feel like shit. I'll try anything right now."

Lighting up, Stewie passed it over. Malia sucked in, like she saw others do, then coughed and writhed in pain. "Jesus, Stewie. That's worse. No wonder I don't smoke."

"Try it again. Slower. Just a little and you'll feel better."

Again, Malia took the joint and inhaled, slowly this time. "Little better."

"See. So it's not too bad, huh baby?"

"Maybe better. But why you calling me baby? That's really weird."

"It's just...while we're here...I thought." He got that look he gets.

"I'm in fucking pain here, Stewie. My ribs are broken. And you're coming on?"

"Okay. Okay. Just, while we wait this storm out..."

"That's it, Stewie. You got to find a way out. You got it? Now. It hurts so bad, I need a doctor."

The air was fresh and clean after the storm, and Christy gestured at the park as they walked along the path, "See how quickly people get here with their picnic things. The rain barely ended, and there are families already at the barbecues."

"Such a popular place, people hurry to get a spot." Then pointing past the group, Duff said, "See over there, around those tables? It's where that fitness guru meets every Sunday morning with his group. Remember when I went on one of his long runs?"

"That didn't last long, did it?"

"Well, no it didn't. The talk about healthy living was quite good, but I expected a lighter workout. Something I could do. That was for serious marathoners."

Donald McPhail

As they approached the club, Christy noticed a small group of people gathered around the garden. "Scrappy, what's going on?"

"Oh, Christy! Bully's trying to call you. I just got here, but I think you should come quick."

"My God, it's Malia." Waving at Duff, "Quick, Duff, get a doctor or an ambulance." "She's wrapped in an old blanket. Let's not move her," Christy warned. "She could be badly injured. Maybe internal, or concussed. I'll get Bully to call emergency."

"It's all right folks," Duff gestured to the other guests, obviously shaken. "We'll take care of her. Please, go on into dinner." He wiped his face, then leaned down and felt her forehead, careful of the scratches and perplexed by the sweet smoky smell.

Donald McPhail

CHAPTER TWELVE
Not A Delicate Blossom

Duff felt stronger. He was grateful to be home from the hospital, able to stroll in the garden. He always loved sitting in the corner of the yard, underneath Bergen's favorite trees. He communed with the avocados, watching them slowly grow and eventually become ripe enough to pick. Not a difficult job, sitting and waiting, but it required patience. As he stood to prepare himself for their guest, the arthritic aches were still there, but those seemed far less important since his heart attack.

He was grateful that surgery wasn't needed, but Dr. Kwan told him he had to change his diet and stick to his new medications. And he had to get out and walk every day. "No more tension about your job now. You're retired," he had advised, with a rare smile. "But push yourself physically. You are not a delicate blossom."

Earlier, Duff had walked for forty minutes in Kapiolani Park. Now he rested back on the lanai in his favorite chair. He wore his usual small smile. Simply a habit, this smile served him well in business and diplomatic meetings throughout the world. To some, it conveyed good nature and a welcoming conversation. Others saw it as a sign of wisdom, that he may know something that has so far eluded them. Still others saw it as a sign of confidence and a test of their own nature.

Duff heard Christy greet de Villiers and escort him onto the lanai. He rose as their young guest presented his hand in greeting. "Duff," Christy said warmly, "meet Marcus de Villiers. I've told you about my nice conversations with him." She set a coffee mug next to the writer, and as she left she added, "You two boys have a lot to talk about."

"Marcus De Villiers, Mr. Malone. I'm honored to meet you. You must be glad to be home."

The accent was quite familiar, though Duff had not heard the true inflections since his last visit to South Africa.

"I'm very glad to meet you, Mr. de Villiers." He gestured toward the rattan chairs, that were placed to admire the peaceful garden and the ocean beyond. "May I call you Marcus?" Malone watched closely, as the young reporter removed his suit coat and placed it onto an empty cushion.

"Of course, Mr. Malone."

"Then you must call me Duff, young man. No need to be formal. So what brings you so far from Jo'berg, Marcus? It's quite a journey."

"I hear it is twenty-eight hours via Sydney," he laughed. "Much too long. Fortunately, I originated in New York. Not bad at all."

"I'll say. Quite an improvement over the ten-day journey we used to have. Thanks to companies like mine, I'm sure, travelers are accustomed to speed, so even twenty-eight hours must seem a long time." Duff sipped his tea and carefully set it down, "We occasionally get visitors from there. And they're surprised to find very familiar scenery here."

"Like that bougainvillea over there in your garden?"

"You have a sharp eye. Yes, that, and protea and ginger, and what we used to call the crane flower. They're called bird of paradise here." Duff pointed toward the side yard, "Of course, the avocados and mangos over there. And see that lovely jacaranda? A small touch of Pretoria. All of it growing in the same kind of red earth that I knew so well as a boy." He turned toward his guest, "But enough of plants and flowers. You came to talk about the airlines?"

De Villiers reached into his right rear pocket and removed a small notebook, then patted his shirt before reaching over to his jacket for his pen. "I'm doing a story on you, as you may know," and nodded toward his open page. "I hope you don't mind. It's for your company's *Clipper Magazine*. It's a tribute to your many years with Pan American, and the editors felt a South African slant would be nice."

"A South African slant you say?" Malone continued to smile, and drew out the words as if he were mulling them over. This seemed a bit odd, since South Africa had been ostracized by most nations for many years because of its despicable *apartheid* laws. In fact, Duff had read that the United Nations just issued another sanction against the South African government.

"Sorry, Duff. I know how our country is viewed. Let's say 'a proud home country's point of view', if that is more reasonable. It isn't intended as political in any way. Just a bit of a twist about your early years, and your many successes so far away from where you began. You opened a lot of doors for Pan American in Asia, commercially and diplomatically. Around the world, as well. Your achievements in China before and after the Pacific war, and your innovations during the Korean War, are quite widely known."

"You have done your homework, I see."

"I have tried, and I believe that you are are a man of contrasts, in what I consider positive ways. You often acknowledge your South African heritage, and you speak positively about people you have known there, of different races. More recently, you and your company provide essential services in what you have referred to as 'America's inhumane war in Vietnam'. Despite your own critical views of the war, you help Pan American to transport supplies and American military and medical staff over there."

"I'm a bit amazed, Marcus. You have certainly identified some of my personal views. And as for Vietnam, I learned some things about wartime operations during the Korean War. I help manage our Vietnam flights because our troops need our assistance, and we are bringing many of them home alive. Much as I despise the war, a lot of men and women are serving there, including my son."

"With Christy's help, I learned something about her background, and about Teo and Malia, and Christy's parents. I have also learned quite a lot about your early years here in Hawaii."

"And your newspaper allows you to spend so much time on this obscure story?"

Donald McPhail

"Sorry, I didn't clarify. Though I used to be with the *Star* newspaper, I'm not any more. I resigned six months ago, and I no longer live in South Africa."

"Go on," exclaimed Malone. "Why is this?"

"My own story *is* political Duff. I just wasn't willing to live there any more. And I wouldn't write the things they assigned me to." Standing, he paced behind the chair, possibly hesitant to continue.

"Better said, I would no longer sit quietly when they refused to print the stories I submitted. They said the government wouldn't take kindly to my pieces about young Biko and other so-called revolutionaries in SASO and other student organizations." Again, he hesitated. "Off the record, would you be willing to talk about your friend Cebo Msimangu?"

Startled, "Cebo, you say? Why Cebo?"

"Duff, are you aware that he is in prison with Mandela?"

Stunned, "On Robben Island? Tell me about this. Please."

"He was arrested with Mandela in Rivonia, in 1963. He is there with a life sentence."

Duff paled, "I am so sorry for him. I knew of Mandela, of course, but have lost track of him. They are still alive?"

"My contacts tell me that they are. The authorities are afraid to harm Mandela, for fear of what millions of black Africans would do. Twenty-five or thirty million non-whites could overwhelm twelve million whites, no matter how many policemen there are."

"And you think Cebo might be safe, as well?"

"Under Vorster, black people are never really safe in South Africa, especially in their prisons, but he appears to be for now." Tucking his pad back into his pocket, "My friends tell me that one day Mandela will be freed. He is talked about as the leader of black South Africans, even in prison. He is like a religious figure. Msimangu is respected as an elder for him, and he will go where Mandela goes."

"I can't imagine a peaceful end to all this, Marcus."

"And I can't imagine what a violent ending would be like in our country, Duff. That's why I'm working to help from the outside.

"It would be easier to walk away safely, so I respect you for working for the cause. But where do you live. How do you survive?"

"Freelance, Duff. And I'm pretty much living out of a suitcase right now."

"And are people interested in your stories?"

De Villiers chuckled and returned to his chair, shaking his head slowly, "That's why I'm here working on your story, Duff. Almost no-one outside of South Africa, except for a few academics or politicians, knows or cares about South African politics. There is a major revolution about to explode, and most people simply don't care."

"Well, then, this is quite interesting. I'll talk about my old friend when you are ready. Meantime, fire away."

Again, he drew his notebook. "So this is a feature story about your travel career. I should also warn you, I'm working on a larger story, which could become a book about Pan American's history, from earliest days through your current global status."

"You have your hands full, I should say, and our airline's history is quite a fascinating story. Mine should be considerably easier."

De Villiers riffled through his notes. "Here we are. You were born in Scotland but raised in Johannesburg, attended Jeppe High and were an ace footballer. After graduation, went into the cruise business with Thomas Cook and Sons, then hired away to New York by American Express. You've had an exciting career. Our readers want to hear how you got to America, and now Hawaii."

"Basically correct. As for football, if it hadn't been for my cracked ankle my last year at Jeppe, I would have been a professional rugger, as they say in America. That was my dream, to play for the Springboks."

DeVilliers raised his eyebrows, then scribbled into his little book. "I never heard that, Duff. About your Springbok aspirations."

"There is no way you would have heard. That was almost fifty years ago. I was set to try out but I was hit when my foot planted, and fractured my left ankle. It didn't heal properly, so I had to make a choice when I graduated. I could go into the family coal business, or accept a job on Eloff Street with Cooks."

"You mentioned your family. Are they still in Jo'berg?"

Duff's face hardened for a moment, then he relaxed again and spoke softly. "No, Marcus. There is no family left in South Africa." Duff chose not to share those confused and sad days after his father died. His parents were both young, in their forties when his father's heart gave out, struggling with a fire in one of the sheds. His mother was devastated, and soon her depression turned to angry, solitary drinking, finding Duff and Sandy guilty of being alive, while her husband was not. Duff would not talk of his guilt and sadness when she hissed her bitter accusations, or how he escaped to boarding school, and never went back.

Confused by Malone's momentary silence, he hesitated before responding, "I'm not sure I understand, Duff. Your family moved from Scotland, I believe, in the late eighteen-hundreds. Are they all gone now? Let me know if this is too personal."

Malone proceeded calmly, "I was six when I left home for boarding school, graduating from Jeppe High School. I was twenty when I left South Africa for New York, joining American Express, which was the world's premier travel company. Back then they provided fully trained cruise directors for all the major steamship tours. I returned to South Africa only once, just a few years ago.

"Commodore Walter Patterson, a wonderful man, was my boss and mentor at American Express from the beginning. He hired me. The Commodore was a reserved man, and very old-school. When he believed in you, he was consistent and generous. He believed in me, from the moment I moved from an obscure career in South Africa to a worldwide stage at New York headquarters. I always wanted to please the Commodore, the way you want to please a gruff father who might not hug much or show outward signs of affection, but who shows he cares for you in you in important, subtle ways.

"To be honest, I was startled back in 1930, that he would encourage me to leave the company after nearly ten years. I knew he was a friend who respected my work. I felt highly regarded there, with one of the top jobs for a major travel company. Yet he suggested I accept this job with Pan American, and I respected his opinion.

"The Commodore told me I was capable of greater things. He cited my anticipation of changing situations, my ability to 'think on my feet' and adjust to new surroundings — to not always follow the rules. He felt I could calmly disarm volatile situations, and please excitable clients. He also sensed that the future of American Express, like that of the new travel industry, would be soon be linked to airline travel. He wanted someone on the aviation side who understood his travel business, and would see how American Express would be an ideal partner. So he recommended me to the most dynamic of the new airline men, his close friend Juan Trippe.

"Trippe was shrewd and well-connected, a savvy promotor and a ruthless competitor. As you no doubt know, his Pan American Airways venture was funded by New York money, from Rockefeller and Whitney families, and other fellow Yale alumni. For immediate visibility, Trippe had engaged the world's most famous hero, Charles Lindbergh, to promote air travel and Pan American Airways.

"Passenger travel would begin with airmail routes, where companies would prove their ability to maintain a schedule. With larger aircraft in the design stage, passenger flights would likely follow. Trippe identified Latin America as the place to build our credentials. There were small airlines there, and he aggressively formed partnerships. He convinced three companies to operate under his leadership, using the single name of Pan American. Then he purchased two more Latin American airlines and formed PANAGRA in partnership with Grace Lines, a powerful company in its own right.

"The Commodore had quietly observed Trippe's expansions through his own government contacts and colleagues in the travel industry. American Express held worldwide domination of the luxury cruise, rail, and sightseeing markets, and Commodore Patterson believed that airline travel was inevitable.

"Small airlines were popping up in countries like Germany, Denmark, France, Britain and Holland. Even China. Unlike America, most of these airlines were financed by their governments.

"Importantly, famous pilots like Lindbergh had created excitement for flying, among people all around the globe. Speeding through the air at unheard of speeds, 'Lucky Lindy' gave airplane travel an incredible *panache*.

"Determined adventurers like Trippe were setting the stage for this passenger service. When engineers could design aircraft that were large enough, fast enough and safe enough, it was simply a matter of time until passenger airlines would emerge.

"The Commodore also knew that airlines would expand into traditional destinations that had been the founda-

tion for steamship travel. With his blessing, I joined Pan
American in Honolulu."

Donald McPhail

CHAPTER THIRTEEN

Early Days

"Christy and I arrived in Honolulu late in 1934," Duff continued, speaking toward the tape recorder. "We arranged for our family— our daughter Malia, and Christy's parents — to follow when the new houses were finished. With no airplanes yet, and no clear strategy in hand, I was there to settle in, open an office, and make agreements with local administrators to operate our flights once the aircraft were delivered. I would eventually need to oversee construction of airports and refueling stations at strategic points across the Pacific.

"Christy and I were temporarily housed in that beautiful hotel, the Royal Hawaiian, where you interviewed Christy last week, I believe. These early days went well, with a few minor surprises.

" 'What an extraordinary place,' was my first impression from our hotel room. I was referring to both our luxurious accommodations and Hawaii itself. There were spectacular gardens below, exuding the enticing fragrances of plumeria and frangipani that you still enjoy at the Royal. Standing on the balcony, I could almost touch the tops of the nearby palm trees. I love music, and remember hearing a faint Jerome Kern tune from the dance band over in the ballroom." Duff smiled at the memory, "All the way here in these islands, Jerome Kern. It was magical.

"The surf was splashing nearby, just as you are hearing from our yard today, and I could see this very house under construction. The familiar silhouette of Diamond Head stood, distinct and prominent, a mile or so further on.

"Our friend Werner Bergen, whom you will meet, owned these two new houses, and he insisted on renting them both to us for just $100 a year. He wouldn't accept a penny more. In fact, he preferred we pay him nothing, but we insisted.

"I will always remember standing at the hotel and watching a ship edging slowly away from Honolulu, off in the usual Diamond Head direction. I knew that vision was a symbol of my old life in the cruise business, and very different from the tenuous new job I had just taken.

"Unlike that ship, this new airline business was completely uncharted. We had no airplanes yet, and my job had not existed before, so it was quite undefined. As director of the Pacific division, I would have to forge new friendships, and create airline offices where none had ever been. I would need to arrange business licenses and hire administrative staff, then we would have to confirm landing rights. I would need to learn all about the newest Sikorsky and Boeing aircraft, and Curtiss-Wright engines. Then I would have to convince travelers that airplanes were safe and comfortable, and that my company would speed them to major cities in one-tenth the time of a steamship.

Donald McPhail

"Could I really do this? Could anyone? But I also knew that business travelers wanted speed, and they couldn't get that from steamships or trains. We could move them ten times faster, and this meant savings in time and money.

"As I learned at American Express, we would not be doing it alone. Even visionaries like Juan Trippe couldn't create a new company without like-minded people around him. As I watched the ship disappear from sight, I felt better about our prospects. But I still had brief, nagging moments when I wondered if I had made the right decision.

"It was this new engineering, this combination of comfort and speed that drew me to the job. I liked the idea of pioneering a new industry. I had learned the travel business as a young man in ports like Cape Town, Mombasa and Port Said. Now I had to use my imagination and competitive instincts to help make Pan American a successful airline here in Honolulu, and in destinations like Tokyo, Manila, Sydney and Shanghai.

"I could certainly learn some things from Pan American's experiences in Latin America, and from other airlines that were starting up. It always began with government air mail contracts for regular income, then cargo to bring in additional revenue. Our ultimate goal was to carry paying passengers once aircraft were large enough to provide comfort and dependable enough to operate regularly.

A local company called Inter-Island Air Service, which became what we know now as Hawaiian Airlines, was flying to Kauai, Maui and the island of Hawaii. You will meet Masao at our home later this week. He's Hawaiian's vice president, and quite a guy. Another small airline called CNAC, for China National Air Corporation, was operating in China back in the thirties, with an American partner, those engine manufacturers, Curtiss-Wright. Christy and I were scheduled to dine with their man in Hawaii, Paul Chen, on that first night, because we needed China. Mr. Trippe was intent on replacing Curtiss-Wright as the major partner, in the same way he had formed partnerships in Pan American's earliest days in Latin America.

"From an operating standpoint, Chen would have start-up challenges similar to ours. They had just initiated internal flights from Shanghai to Hankow, Nanking and other key cities whose names were unfamiliar to me, and they had to be experiencing early growing pains. Maintenance, refueling, backup planes, qualified pilots, those sorts of things.

"As for my office operating from Hawaii, it was certainly isolated from North America. At the same time, my first assignments were out in the Pacific, and my Hawaii base made it easier to reach places like Midway, Wake Island and Guam, which we needed for refueling, if we were going to reach Asian destinations like Canton and Manila.

"Christy and I both felt fortunate to be in Honolulu. Considering the lingering depression, I was grateful to be employed at all. From what I read in the news and saw on my visits back to the mainland, millions of people were not so lucky. The depression was felt even here in the islands.

"While the the stock market crash itself hit only a few people directly -- the small number of who actually invested in the market -- the devastating after-effect lasted for many years. Banks shuttered, some of them permanently, and many companies had laid off their workers. This was a hell of a time to be taking risks, like starting an airline. Yet we forged ahead.

"As you can imagine, we needed income from customers. There was pressure on all of us to get our flights up and running. We knew there was demand, first from the government with those air mail contracts; then from air freight, and then passengers. Cargo ships were large and slow. And even the fastest passenger ships couldn't provide the kind of speed that politicians and businessmen wanted. As I said, our airline would change all this.

"As for Hawaii itself, the Hollywood crowd was certainly evident here at the Royal Hawaiian hotel. Douglas Fairbanks was leaving in a limousine as we checked in, and actress Gloria Swanson was due to arrive any moment. We could see the staff hovering at the front entrance. And there were beautiful women and handsome men everywhere we looked.

"Christy and I were excited to be back in Hawaii. Our own lives were very different from the last time. I was now an airline man, no longer a cruise director. Though I was division chief for Pan American Airways, quite a respected position, I had not even one airplane to fly.

Our guests are already seated, the handsome Asian man and his companion, an unusually beautiful caucasian woman. Her dark eyes and jet-black hair contrast sharply with pale skin that looks as if it has never seen sunlight.

"Ah, Mr. and Mrs. Malone. I am Paul Chen, and this is my friend Sonia. She is here from Shanghai for a few days."

"Sonia, Paul, we're glad to meet you both."

As I hold her chair, Christy says, "How beautiful, Sonia. I can't help but admire your necklace. It is quite stunning."

"Thank you," she replies, in an unusual accent. English, but with abrupt, eastern European tones. "My mother brought it with us when we left Russia. We moved to Shanghai in 1918."

"Ah, then you are Russian."

"I am a citizen of China now," she hesitates. "There are many Russians in Shanghai. Quite a lively community."

Chen smoothly joins the conversation, in an erudite American accent, "So Mr. and Mrs. Malone, you too have newly arrived in Honolulu?" He raises his whiskey tumbler in a small salute. "I believe we have something in common. Several things, perhaps."

"Please, call us Christy and Duff," Christy responds, lifting her champagne glass to each of them and sipping, quickly wrinkling her nose, "Sorry, the bubbles," she hesitates, then continues. "We did recently move here, though Duff and I first visited nearly a year ago. I will never forget it." She extends her flute to touch Duff's highball glass, then Sonia's, then Chen's.

"Nor I," I add, looking across at our guests. "I'm quite new to my job, as I believe you are, Paul. And our airlines are very new. I believe we can help each other become acclimated."

Donald McPhail

"I look forward to this. Perhaps over lunch."

I had seen his given family name, Wei Chen Min, in correspondence, and knew that among his English-speaking friends he preferred the anglicized 'Paul". Chen had earned his engineering degree from the University of Shanghai, then his MBA from New York University, graduating just two years ago.

This was when he came to Juan Trippe's attention. He was one of the few Asians at NYU, and his interest in American aviation distinguished him from his classmates. Knowing how important the Pacific would be for our company, Trippe wanted contacts at CNAC who knew America and American business. It helped that Chen was personally connected to two key Pan Am board members, Whitney and Harriman. They knew Chen's parents in China, and they had sponsored his NYU education. I could see how comfortable he was doing business in America. I also knew that China bred a different approach to business. Often not what we expect in this country.

An example was the CNAC partnership. It was complicated. Day-to-day management was in the hands of local Chinese businessmen and political leaders, reading the numbers and making policy decisions, while operating management was in the hands of Curtiss-Wright's Americans. They hired the workers and flew the airplanes. The partnership held air mail rights that our company needed for official access to China, so CNAC was the final piece for Pan American's Pacific strategy.

"I believe that we have other things in common," Chen continues, *"including new residences here. We are*

new to our jobs. In addition, like Sonia, you and I were not born in America. This must make Christy the only real citizen."

We all laugh, and I ask, "Did my South African accent give me away?"

"It did, indeed. Though I have never been to Southern Africa, I met diamond traders in Hong Kong as a young man. They were from Kimberley, working for Oppenheimer at Anglo-American."

I nod in recognition. "And I hold a British passport, to further complicate matters. I was born in Scotland, you see."

"I didn't know that, and it does provide an extra layer of complexity."

"And you, Paul," inquires Christy, "Your beautiful accent -- or lack of an accent. You sound like an American."

"Thank you, Christy. I take that as a great compliment. I grew up in international schools in China, and lived with an American family in New York. They sponsored me at NYU, where I got my business degree."

"And now you work for CNAC?"

"Those are far too many acronyms, are they not?" laughs Chen. "Actually, I work for the Chinese government," he notes, nodding across the table and patting Sonia's hand. "And I also have a working relationship with the Curtiss-Wright company. Does this make sense to you?"

I smile, "I have had the good fortune to do business in China, Paul. I must admit that not everything makes

Donald McPhail

sense to me. At the same time, I try not to be too sur-prised."

Chen replies easily, "Then let us simply say that I work for China National Air Corporation, and the rest is not so important."

Donald McPhail

CHAPTER FOURTEEN
Cultural Differences

Duff looked at de Villiers with an amused smile, as he began to describe his surprising lunch with Paul Chen.

"I hope you feel patient, Marcus. This next part may not make it into your book, but it should provide a good idea of how we had to adjust to doing business in different cultures. I firmly believe that all cultures have similarities — how we are motivated, the need for business plans and the like. But I learned quite a lesson about doing business in China from my new friend.

"Chen promptly followed-up with his lunch invitation, and I was looking forward to learning more about him. He seemed smart and positive, and he was on a direct path to success with CNAC, perhaps beyond, into Chinese political leadership. He would be a valuable contact for me.

" 'Duff, let's go to a little place I know across the street.' Chen suggested to me.

"I hadn't been aware of anything across the street from the Pan Am office, except some run-down stucco buildings with signs in Chinese. 'Chinese restaurant?' I inquired.

" 'Sort of, my friend. Perhaps a little surprise.' "

I am quite ill at ease as we enter the crowded restaurant. The lighting is subdued and the air is heavy with cigarette smoke. We're escorted to a corner booth by an attractive Asian woman, who obviously knows Chen and treats him with deference. The booth looks directly out of a New York speakeasy in 1925, all red leather with brass studs, and our table is covered with white linen, along with multiple sets of chopsticks, some black and some white in color. Looking across the dining room, I see business men in suits and ties, Asian, caucasian, local Hawaiians, along with a few sailors in uniform.

Femme Fatale is the name on the menu, with the black outline of a cat with little horns on it. Then I realize there are no women customers, only men.

"Here, let me do the ordering for us." Chen waves at the hostess and hands her the menus, then barks some orders in Chinese. She smiles carefully and nods, hastily walking away.

"I jump a bit at the sudden brash music. It seems to come from a victrola with a strong speaker, featuring bluesy brass, heavy on the drums, in a woozy swing I might have heard once in New Orleans. As the music continues, lights dim further and a spotlight plays on the small rectangular stage in the center of the room. I watch the male diners sitting nearby in semi-darkness, with their faces just above the stage level.

"It's that stage," I realize. "That's what's out of place. What's it doing among the dining tables?" Soon the spotlight is filled with a young girl in a pink gingham dress, with blonde plaits tied with two pink ribbons. "What a beautiful face," I think. "Quite an innocent look. Perhaps she is a singer.

"Suddenly the little dress is on the stage and she deftly kicks it onto a nearby table. There stands the girl without a stitch on her, except for a garter on her right thigh. 'My God,' I exclaim to Chen, but he can't hear me above the din.

" 'Very beautiful girl, wouldn't you say?' he states proudly."

"Before I can answer, I watch the girl walk deliberately around the edge of the stage, within inches of the nearby faces. She grinds to the music and shows off her body. She encourages customers to tuck dollar bills into the garter that circles her white thigh. I feel quite embarrassed. She cannot be more than eighteen, and she's in front of all these men. I notice that she has no hair on her body. 'My Lord, she's even shaved down there!' I realize. Then the light shifts and she's gone, replaced by a black-haired vixen with shining red lips, wearing a glossy yellow rain slicker.

" 'This should be good, my friend,' says Chen. 'She is one of mine. You will see.' Chen fails to notice my anger.

"As the vixen drops her slicker, she too is totally naked except for the garter. And her pubis is shaven into a black inverted triangle, almost like a heart. 'You see, Duff. That triangle is my idea! Our Shanghai girls all do this.'

"I object, 'You can't be serious. This is obscene.' But Chen still can't hear me.

"As I rise to leave, the girl exits the stage and approaches our table, winking at Chen and raising her leg so *that he can slip a large bill into her garter. It looks like a hundred. As she allows his hand to linger, I can see marks on her leg and small red dots. Then I slip out of the booth and leave, storming across the street to my office.*

"But that isn't all. Chen finds me behind my desk, 'Duff, my friend. I am so sorry. I didn't know you would react like this. My clients love it. And our colleagues in the hotels and steamships are often here for lunch.'

"Then he is surprisingly frank, 'I thought you would like this place. You're a man of the world, and it is set up like my brother's club in Shanghai. It's the rage, right in the French Concession. This one is classy. Not ugly, like some places you see over on Hotel Street.' Chen gestures toward downtown Honolulu. 'Our guests enjoy it, even some of the wives.'

" 'You thought I would love the show?' I ask, clearly upset. 'I wonder what their parents think. Those little girls that you parade around.'

" 'Duff, these girls have no parents, most of them. They ran away from home. That little girl, the first one, her father used to molest her over in Los Angeles. She came here to escape from him.'

" 'What of the marks, Chen? On your girl's leg? Did she come to escape from that?'

" 'Again, Duff, I apologize if this offends. Life in China is quite different from here in America. I'm one of the restaurant's owners, and I provide some of the girls. I get to know them. The girl with black hair is what we call a White Russian. There are thousands of White Russian immigrants now in Shanghai. They escaped from the Bol-

sheviks, the Reds, because the White Army supported the old government. The Reds can't have that. You met Sonia at dinner. She finds the girls, some are concubines. She trains them and sends them to us. Some do use drugs, opium mostly. But they earn many times what they would get in Shanghai. Plus, we feed them and have a place for them to live. They wouldn't have that in China. As I said, our culture is quite different from yours.'

"You trouble me, Paul. I don't think of myself as a prude. I know what women sometimes must do to stay alive. The Crazy Horse in Paris. Naked musical shows in Rio and Valparaiso, in nearly every port in the world. But I want you to know, I'm deeply offended. This is a side of you I couldn't have imagined. I never want to speak of that place again.

" 'I understand Duff. We are friends, and I do not want to lose that. I respect you and Christy. You will not be troubled in this way, ever again.' "

Donald McPhail

CHAPTER FIFTEEN
Where To Begin

As de Villiers smiled quietly at this unexpected introduction to CNAC and Paul Chen, Duff felt that some chronology might help describe the Pan American story. "Our China connection, that is, Pan Am's China connection, turned out to be a crucial piece of our strategic puzzle. This became surprisingly clear during a meeting with Mr. Trippe, back in New York."

"When was the meeting, Duff"

"It was in 1935, and Trippe called us in. We all expected to hear how he planned to initiate flights to London or Paris. Other airlines were starting up in England and France, all around Europe. Most of us assumed that China and Japan would follow a year or so later."

"Before we discuss the meeting, tell me generally, what had you been working on out in the Pacific?"

"For the past year I had carried Pan Am's story to government officials in Asia and the South Pacific, sailing on steamers and hopping small airlines, visiting potential destination cities and establishing personal relations for eventual flights. I met with local airport administrators in China, Japan, Australia, New Zealand and the Philippines."

De Villiers politely interceded, "And what gave China such an important role?"

"China already had a going operation out of Canton, as I mentioned, CNAC. We could win the Pacific airmail contract if we could link into China. If we got the airmail, we knew that passenger rights would follow. Trippe proved this in Latin America. And as he did there, he found ways to get into the marketplace by buying-out the Curtiss-Wright share of CNAC. Trippe purchased the 45% partnership, and our friend Chen was promoted from Hawaii to Canton, as president. He essentially reported to me, since we ran the airline, but he was controlled by a Chines government board, as well."

"And what was China like in 1935?"

"It was extremely complicated, with internal political struggles, and Japan was always a threat. Paul helped me sort out the latest rumors — of Japanese incursion, and the ongoing conflict between Chinese Nationalists and the Communists. Paul assured us that the internal battles would stop and the two Chinese political foes would unify, if Japan continued its military threats."

"So there was conflict in China. What about in America, and Europe? Things were not any simpler anywhere in the world."

"That's true. Everyone was dealing with the ongoing depression. Jobs had been lost. Most people faced daily struggles and uncertain futures.

"This was true all across the country, not just our big cities and financial centers, and not just from the depression. Heartland states like Oklahoma and Texas had been crushed by a devastating drought destroying thousands of farms and homes. Farmers were moving to western states like California and Nevada. America's basic structure was being transformed.

"Overseas, as in America, countries were struggling with more than the depression. In their case it centered on Germany. Germany had been soundly defeated, and severe post-war penalties were imposed against them. Fifteen years earlier, the harsh 'War Guilt Clause' in the Versailles Treaty punished Germany and imposed massive reparations payments.

"Now, nearly fifteen years later, it was clear that many Germans still considered the clause a humiliation. German newspapers referred to it as 'the war guilt lie', and there were rumors that the Great War had been provoked by French politicians, not the Germans. Then they elected Adolph Hitler to the new position of *Fuhrer*."

Shaking his head, de Villiers said, "We know what Germany did. Why didn't someone put a stop to them, and to Japan?"

"There were parallels, that's evident. The difference is, Japan recovered from the depression well before other countries, including America. As a result, their military was well supplied, and many of their politicians were influenced by wealthy manufacturers and militant military officers.

"Their finance minister, Takahasi, had guided Japan out of its depression by following a peaceful path, advocating Japanese investment in its industries, and cooperation with western countries for fuel and industrial material. At the same time, military leaders vehemently disagreed with

Takahashi. They sought greater expansion in China, and demanded recognition of Japan as a world power. The Japanese took Manchuria from China in 1931 and created their own independent state of Manchukuo. Then they wanted more.

"It was China's continuing internal struggles that invited Japan's invasion. Nationalist Chinese troops, the Kuomintang, were led by an unpredictable Chiang Kai-shek, who issued harsh proclamations one day, and backed away from conflict the next. The Communists were his internal enemy, led by young Mao Tse Tung. Working together they might have repelled Japan, but their fixation on each other created openings for Japanese invaders."

"Interesting stuff, that they didn't teach us in school," said de Villiers. "What more did you learn at that New York meeting?"

"As I said earlier, we knew that we needed China for us to establish a legitimate presence in the Pacific. The key pieces of this airmail puzzle were Honolulu, Manila and Canton. But we couldn't get there without enough fuel. We needed to refuel along the way. To do this, there were multiple tiny pieces scattered across the Pacific, and Trippe identified those tiny atolls called Midway and Wake Island.

"As for the meeting, I remember that we were seated around the large conference table on the fifty-eighth floor of the Chrysler Building. We knew this lofty location symbolized Trippe's intention to be America's flagship airline.

"I was certain that I looked as intimidated as the three other young regional directors. The four of us were

seated directly opposite our president and his key executives.

"Everyone in America knew Trippe's image, from
the recent *Time Magazine* cover — serious expression,
thin lips, dark hair and a prominent forehead, much like
mine.

"He was articulate in his opening remarks, and
quite animated when he presented his worldwide vision. I
wondered about his aloofness as the others made their
presentations. Trippe had moved his chair noticeably apart,
like an emperor of sorts. He was obviously orchestrating
the meeting in the background, while his officers spoke —
jotting notes and passing them to the speakers.

"Then Trippe spoke again, deftly summarizing key
points and presenting a passionate vision for this new airline. 'Gentlemen, Pan American World Airways is going to
help shape this country's destiny. Mail contracts, aircraft
and customers are our responsibility,' gesturing toward his
executive staff and the board members behind them. Then
he nodded toward me and my colleagues, 'Landing rights,
airport construction and even more customers are yours.' I
felt he was looking straight at me. 'Without those, we can't
even begin.'

"Trippe continued, still holding our attention. 'This
will require months of travel for each of you, often to places
that currently have no runways or flight facilities. Our service will begin with flying boats that carry airmail, *Flying
Clippers* we'll call them.' He paused, and seemed pleased
as we all nodded and smiled at the clever name for the aircraft. 'They can land and take-off on the water. With engi-

neering assistance from the government, we'll build an infrastructure. First, mooring and fueling for these Flying Clippers, and then proper lodging and dining for passengers. Then runways and maintenance facilities that can handle larger, faster land-based planes. And you division managers are our ambassadors. You'll speak for me, personally, when you meet with foreign leaders.'

"Pausing again, he said firmly, 'We are a new industry. All of this will be new to you, because it's new to the world.' Looking directly at each of us in turn. 'I know you can do it.'

"As the meeting was drawing to a close, I realized that Trippe was addressing me, personally.

" 'The latest information, gentlemen, and it may surprise you. Early next year we will receive three Sikorsky flying boats and three more Martins, and we will place them in the Pacific.' The room fell quiet as he paused. Even some of the stoic board members reacted with a raised eyebrow or a grim smile.

" 'We begin in the Pacific, not Europe.' I sensed a rustling, as directors turned to look at me.

" 'Mr. Malone, your next step is to complete construction at Hawaii, Midway, Wake Island, Guam and the Philippines by the end of the year. This will launch our airmail route, and eventually we will carry passengers. We already have the landing rights there. We also have a Navy contract and an airline partner in China. Now we need to prepare for commercial flights. Fueling stations, terminals, hotels, recreation. Everything. We are going to create a direct route across the Pacific, all eight thousand and seven hundred miles of it. You will launch airmail service in November, followed by passenger service in April.' "

Donald McPhail

CHAPTER SIXTEEN
1935: Atolls and Islands

As they relaxed on the lanai, Duff looked over at de Villiers, who was leafing through his notebook, looking for where they had left off. As usual, the tape recorder was on the nearby table.

"That was quite a challenge, Duff," he said. "And it cannot have been easy. Creating new airline operations in different countries and colonizing nondescript islands sounds very complicated."

"Well, some of it was basic engineering, and it helped to have assistance from our Navy contacts. I had help with this from headquarters, of course, and they consulted with government engineers.

"I needed to be a quick learner. We set up a detailed schedule of tasks and knocked them off, one by one. As for the surprises, we were adventurers at the time, weren't we? We were helping to create a new industry.

"Certainly, it was quite a risk when we visited those remote atolls, and those early flights scared the bejesus out of me! It took quite an imagination, and some bloody good designers to turn them into refueling and operating bases. It took skilled pilots and navigators to even locate them, and to land safely. And it took quite a good advertising message to paint them as romantic tourist destinations.

"The first steps in our grand plan were to explore and engineer Midway and Wake Island, then Guam and Manila. These refueling stations would allow us to continue to Canton and fulfill our airmail contract. The passenger flights would come nearly one year later."

De Villiers interrupted gently, "You mentioned the American Navy. I didn't realize they were so involved with Midway and Wake. I see that Subic Bay was already well established in Manila because of the Naval base there, and for the most part, so was Guam. But I didn't know of their involvement on those atolls."

"The Navy had done a survey of Midway and Wake a month earlier, and this helped us with our work. Our government knew there might be trouble with Japan, and they wanted a head start on those atolls, near to Asia. There were also Navy technicians working with our construction crew aboard the cargo ship *Northhaven*, that was to arrive shortly after our flight did. I traveled on our own survey flight in early May of 1935, with a construction crew fast on our heals. Some of the crew were active Navy men."

Our seaplane has been in the air nearly eight hours and I know we should see Midway soon. Captain Musick indicates we are right on schedule. The Northhaven *left Honolulu over a week ahead of us, scheduled to arrive at Midway shortly after we do. It carries enough material and heavy equipment to build our new air bases and guest hotels.*

Donald McPhail

We coordinated this survey flight to arrive two days before the ship, so we can assess the challenges before the others arrive. When the **Northhaven** gets here, we will brief the engineers traveling with the ship, and review the construction plan. All the materials were carefully loaded, so the heavy equipment can offload first, then be used to remove the remaining material without delay.

The ship carries over a hundred men and enough material for complete Pan Am stations at Midway and Wake. Within weeks they will construct airports and offices, and create new resort facilities. I'm still amazed that the ship could carry two entire forty-eight room prefabricated hotels, each with a porch and veranda -- even detailed in-room amenities like wall decorations, ash trays, lamps and fixtures.

This survey flight is also an important chance for me to get to know Pan Am's lead pilot, Captain Ed Musick, and his flight crew. He is already a legend, but I had not met him before.

As we began, Musick advised we would average 150 miles an hour westbound, though the eventual return trip would be against prevailing winds, and was likely to average just 130 miles an hour.

En route, the Captain has been talkative, and well informed about these "islands". He informed us, though I knew he was really talking to me as the only newcomer aboard, that they are not really islands, but atolls. "An island is surrounded by water, while an atoll contains another body of water inside. And atolls are made of coral."

Midway is located 3,200 miles from California, about halfway between California and Asia. This is 1,300 miles from Honolulu, and the Hawaii mileage is critical, because it is within the Clipper's flying range. Without this refueling post, Pan Am can't cross to the Philippines and China. Japan had already invaded northern China, and long since occupied Manchuria, so Tokyo is not in our plans. Australia is another challenge entirely, since Britain asks its former colony to refuse any U.S. landing rights until their own Imperial Airways is fully ready to compete.

Now we begin descent. I look down to see small rocky crags sticking up from the sea, and tiny islands encircling blue-green lagoons. They are far too small for habitation or landings. Then we spot two sizable islands, one significantly larger than the other, and the crew moves into landing mode.

"Let's take her around once, gentlemen, so we can see both parts of the atoll." Musick eases into a gentle circle. "That smaller one is called Eastern". He continues the turn. "We'll land off of Sand atoll. It's higher ground, and is the one the hotel will go on. That's what the brochures will call Midway."

As Musick banks the craft and turns into the wind, we descend smoothly over the reef that protects a large lagoon, and the plane bumps firmly down, bouncing to a stop on the glassy surface.

As a cruise man, I have visited spectacular atolls in the Indian Ocean, like the Seychelles and the Maldives, but Midway's uninteresting terrain seems desolate by comparison.

Donald McPhail

*We are camping out for two nights, and early the
second morning I see a big ship off in the distance. The
vessel can only be the* Northhaven. *There is quite a celebration when the ship arrives. Over a hundred men descend on Midway, coming in small boats and rafts. I knew
that some of the technicians were recently loaned to us
from the U.S. Navy. Most of the workers wear dungarees
and are shirtless in the heat. The men seem full of youthful
energy and are heavy with tools and supplies. Some are in
their thirties, engineers and specialists in electrical and
plumbing work, but most are younger, looking fit for construction and heavy labor. All seem proud to create an airline destination on this empty island.*

*We are using the entire crew to unload the cargo
for this place, then plan to leave twenty-three crew members here to complete the construction. The remaining
workers will depart in a day or two and continue to Wake
Island. There they will offload most of the remaining cargo
and leave forty-six men to complete that construction. The
ship will then continue to Guam and Manila for what little
remains to be done.*

*The following morning, as our small group boards
the China Clipper for the seven hour flight to Wake, I know
that this construction project is in good hands. We depart
just after seven in the morning, struggling off the water into
a dark sky. Though the clouds look ominous, we pass
smoothly through and find bright sunlight.*

*En route, Captain Musick comments on how much
the young men remind him of his college football team-*

mates, or top-notch soldiers just out of training camp. They are young, confident and eager for the task.

We fly for six and a half hours before spotting the u-shaped atoll ahead, completely surrounded by a prominent circle of coral. The water within is green and inviting. As the Clipper descends we recognize that these sandy islets will be quite challenging as a base.

Wake Island is empty and bleak. Only an adventurer or a hermit, or an aircraft in need of fuel will see much need to visit here. It is not even a solid island; merely an atoll comprised of three different islets. The entire group is surrounded by coral reef. But we descend and land smoothly in the peaceful bay.

The next morning, we depart for the twelve hour flight to Guam. There has been a U.S. Navy base here for some time, with water and electricity, and a sizable mess hall and barracks. It won't take much work to develop these into an acceptable passenger stop.

After a welcome shower and comfortable overnight at Guam, we fly another twelve hour leg to Manila and complete the inspection trip. I know the flight crew is far more exhausted than I am after this long journey. At the same time, everyone seems exhilarated by this promising start.

"I can't tell you, Marcus, how important that first inspection trip was for me, and for our trans-Pacific flights. First of all, I got to know Ed Musick, and he became one of the best friends I ever had. Second, this trip initiated suc-

Donald McPhail

cessful construction of the refueling stations that allowed us to launch airmail service."

De Villiers looked puzzled, "Duff, why was the timing so important? You had won the mail route. Why all the pressure on yourselves?"

"Actually, we had not won the routes. They were coming up for bid in October, and we were positioning ourselves to win. This was quite a risk on Trippe's part, to invest so much on building those stations, with no guarantee we would get to operate them. In the meantime, Musick and other pilots made additional survey flights, while Trippe cajoled and discouraged competitors from submitting bids."

"Cajoled?" asked the writer.

"Well, he disarmed one competing airline that was being organized by Donald Douglas, the aircraft man. Trippe bought-out the new airline and put Douglas on the Pan Am board of directors. The other potential bidder was Inter-Island Airways, which was owned by powerful Matson Navigation at the time. He used Pan Am stock and another board seat to discourage their bid."

"That's very bold, I'd say." De Villiers shook his head in admiration.

"I would too, Marcus. And it worked. In October, the Postmaster General approved Pan American's bid, the only one submitted, as it happened. So we were in business if we could successfully complete the inaugural flight.

"Just weeks later — it was November 22, 1935 — Ed Musick set off on the China Clipper out of Alameda, and most of America followed our progress on the radio. Hell, there were one hundred thousand people lining San Francisco Bay and the Marin headlands, to watch his flight lift off from the lagoon and soar into the Pacific. A few days later, Trippe told me the flight was so heavily-loaded with fuel and airmail that Ed decided to fly under the structure of the nearly-completed Oakland Bay Bridge, not over it, so all the accompanying small planes did the same thing. It must have been spectacular. I was in Honolulu with all the dignitaries, waiting to greet the Clipper when it arrived."

"Carrying airmail, not passengers, and it was that big an event?"

"We were breaking a huge barrier with this flight. It was the first trans-Pacific flight for any commercial airliner. Six days later, after nearly sixty hours of actual flying time, the Clipper landed in Manila. Everyone knew that passenger service would come next, as it did with great fanfare the following September. This airmail flight had changed the pace of world travel."

Donald McPhail

CHAPTER SEVENTEEN
Meditation

The conversations with de Villiers were good for
Duff. He found some old notes in his desk, that refreshed
his memory about the early years. Morning and evening
walks were building up his stamina. Pushing himself intel-
lectually was good, too. It kept him from stewing about his
health.

He needed to stick to Dr. Kwan's regimen. Walk
farther each day, and eat intelligently. Fruits, fish, fresh
vegetables and lean meat. This shouldn't be so hard, really, living here where fresh fish and fruit are so easy to get.
But it would take discipline to avoid his old habits, and he
knew that Christy would keep him on the straight and narrow.

The old photos and reports triggered unexpected,
random memories. Their very first trip to Honolulu, where
he and Christy were met by Bergen and two young ladies,
wahine, with flower leis. Those healthy young workers from
the *Northhaven*, shirts off and digging trenches on Midway.
The newspaper clipping of him and Ed Musick, smiling for
the young photographer in Manila. Waving at friends on
the steps of San Francisco City Hall, right after he and
Christy were married.

He remembered some of the difficult times, too. The loss of Ed Musick. Brother Sandy's brave battle with cancer, and their need to return to Johannesburg. Malia's depression and close call on the offshore rocks a half-mile away. That sad photo of him and Christy in their garden after the Pearl Harbor attack. Pete had insisted on taking it after Duff made his way back from New York and San Francisco, not realizing how strained Christy and he had become over his absences. Their escape from Shanghai was surreal, after Chen was killed while the Japanese invaded. Christy's determination to keep their marriage together had gotten them through plenty of challenges. He wished he'd been more aware. Perhaps the most difficult was after the Japanese hit Pearl Harbor, not knowing how his family was, or if he would be able to get there. He had no contact with Christy for nearly a week, and had no idea if she and Malia and Teo had survived. It affected her parents, too. They were nearly seventy then, and never quite got over the shock and fear.

Funny how your memory jumps around in time. Life's events don't fit into an orderly sequence. Thoughts bounce from Shanghai to Johannesburg to New York, yet they make sense as you look back and assess a lifetime.

His conversations with de Villiers stirred up these incidents, and Duff felt he needed to talk about them. De Villiers' article would be about Duff's role in Pan Am's expansion into the Pacific, but Duff's history felt like much more than that. The war years became the bigger story for Duff. Japan through China, Malaya, the Philippines. The horrors of Pearl Harbor. America's hard-fought victory.

Donald McPhail

Then the bitter Korean War. And now fears of the Cold War with the USSR and Communist China, and a wasteful, unconscionable war in Vietnam.

We've seen so many decisions from people in power, that have led directly to violence. By military leaders, presidential advisors, even by bureaucrats. In Chen's case, if those old rumors were true, even by an angry mother, Madame Chiang.

More than these acts, or the different wars, Duff knew his story was about the people who made up his life. *That's what makes our mind jump around and keeps the story from being simple. It's the different threads, about the people you love and the things that happen with them, that make a life. Christy, Teo, Malia, Doris, Pete. All of them have enriched my life. So is this my life passing before me before I die, that people talk about? It better not be. We have far too much to do yet, Christy and I.*

Colleagues were telling him he should take his time, to enjoy a full retirement life, whatever that might be. *Let's not be too gradual,* thought Duff. *Better to work a bit harder on recovery, and extend the timetable.*

For some reason, this made him think of Teo, and what he was doing in Vietnam. He hoped their son was all right. Recent letters were different, agitated. Up to now he tended to be brief, positive, describing what he and his pilot buddies were doing to help protect the South Vietnamese. In the early days, Teo described how he and other Marines were building schools in some of the nearby villages, for local kids. Now he was asking for newspaper clips about the war protesters. *What was this about?*

He looked out at the ocean. *People talk about meditation. I wonder if this is what they are referring to. You
can see movement out there. The clouds, or an airplane,
or a bird. Just like those ever-shifting tide-pools, there is
constant change. The picture is calm, but never the same.*

In the distance he saw the familiar steamship edge
toward Diamond Head, its distinctive white funnels just visible against a bright blue horizon. He knew that route well,
having sailed at least a fifty times on Matson ships, the
Malolo, Mariposa, Monterey and *Lurline*. Known as "the
White Ships", Duff had seen them at their peak, when they
sailed weekly to California or to far-off Pacific ports.

Early on, steamships were his only method of travel
to Pan Am meetings on the mainland, and to most of Asia.
Back then, he worked for an airline that didn't yet have
flights, but he had plenty to do. He had overseen construction of the hotels and refueling sites on Midway, Wake and
Guam. And Pan American was well on its way into China
and Auckland. But then the Japanese military threw everything into chaos.

Duff had heard American colleagues blame the Japanese people for the war, but he knew that wars were
started by governments, not citizens. Certain leaders were
driven by the desire for power, for territory and resources.
That's why Germany expanded into Poland and so much
of Europe, and that's why Japan expanded into Korea,
China and the Pacific. America is at war in Vietnam, but
what is the desire for power there? America's government
talks of stopping the expansion of Communism in the Pacific, some sort of "domino-theory". But this image seems

too simple, promoted by politicians, and repeated, even by educated Americans.

As Duff rested, he caught sight of the big airplanes as they slowly rose from the runway just fifteen miles to his right, arching east to the mainland or west toward Asia or Australia. He looked for Pan Am's blue globe on the tail. That symbol still moved him, though there were rumors that even this symbol might change soon. A lot has changed since Trippe retired.

What a time they had, Bergen, McAvoy, all those dedicated people, building this great airline! He still knew the departures by heart, and each different type of plane. He was proudest of the simple, elegant white-and-blue livery. *America's flagship,* he thought proudly.

There goes our newest 747 creeping ever so slowly aloft. When Duff first rode this massive plane, with its wide corridors and spacious interior, and that unusual bulge at the front, it felt as if it rolled forever down the long runway, trying to gather enough speed to struggle off the ground. The process was slow and steady, and of course they always made lift-off. *What a marvelous plane. Can it be Pan Am's salvation, or too big a financial risk?*

While he sat and played this aircraft recognition-game, Duff was deeply troubled by the number of military charters he knew were heading west to Vietnam each day. Some days Pan Am alone flew six Boeing 707s from Honolulu to Saigon, filled with soldiers -- kids far younger than Teo -- returning to fight this atrocious war. Delta, Braniff and United, and the non-scheds had their own chartered military flights. *What a massive, bloody waste of life this war is!*

The politicians who got us into this mess should see what we see. Anxious, empty-eyed kids all over Waikiki, in their short hair and aviator glasses, wearing newly-bought shorts and loud shirts they may never get to wear again, chasing girls and liquor and drugs, and listening to earsplitting music about ending the war.

The soldiers called themselves "the walking dead." Duff knew veteran Pan Am stewardesses who had made multiple flights in and out of Saigon and Danang, and their stories always ended in tears, from frustration and sadness over these kids returning to Vietnam to be killed.

Teo was over there, and every day he was in danger, flying who knows where and dropping who knows what. *I wish they would tell us more. But do I really want to know? We read about so much carnage in the daily papers, body-bags carefully counted and summarized. Justifying our latest success by weighing our dead against theirs. How could we come to this, in America of all places? Bloody awful! And why is Teo asking about the war protesters?*

Donald McPhail

CHAPTER EIGHTEEN

Bergen-san

"You look quite grim for a man who should be recuperating," the gentle voice came from his right, slightly out of breath but still firm for a man in his eighties.

"Ah, Bergen," Duff shifted, returning from the mists of his thoughts. He turned to greet his friend, who had completed his wheelchair trek across the yard, and along the path that paralleled the beach. "I must have been daydreaming."

Werner Bergen was like family to Duff, his oldest friend. Bergen's gentle helper, Yoriko, usually brought him out for his afternoon visit around now, but Duff had lost track of time. Now over sixty, Yoriko had watched after Bergen all these years, beginning in Yokohama. He looked stronger today. Peppy almost, in his yellow and white floral shirt.

Still able to maneuver his apparatus, Bergen sometimes convinced Yoriko to let him wheel himself out, like today. She knew it tired him, but she respected his small personal victory. Early on, Duff had seen her on her knees, using a trowel to smooth and tamp down the gravel pathway to make his trip easier.

Bergen's skinny arms were stronger than they looked, as he diligently rolled the well-oiled chair along. He had long-since transcended the many scars and the useless legs that were severely beaten nearly thirty years ago by the Japanese interrogators. Bergen refused to die or to ask for help then. Now he was proud of these small moments of independence.

He insisted on living, with Yoriko's assistance, in the adjacent cottage he designed himself when he constructed the main house back in 1934. She lived in her own little suite, near enough to hear if he should cry for help.

Bergen leased the beachfront land from Bishop Estate, one of Hawaii's major landholders, but he had never lived in the big house. Instead, he rented it to Duff and Christy for nearly nothing. He wanted them to have it as their home, but he didn't want them to pay for it. After much friendly haggling, they agreed upon a symbolic fee.

Bergen insisted on providing Mr. Ozawa, as well, who would stop by to tend and nurture the marvelous grounds during the week. The seaside garden included striking white and red crinum, or spider lily, blue ginger, and many types of orchids, in bright pinks, crimsons and delicate yellows. And, of course, Christy's roses. They were framed by hearty royal poinciana. Bergen also insisted on providing four special trees: two avocado and two mango. Over time, all four of them bore enough plump fruit to supply Ozawa's family, and Duff's, with buttery avocados from January through May, and juicy Mangos from June through September every year.

Donald McPhail

"Bergen-san, I told you about the writer, Marcus de Villiers. Do you remember?"

"Of course I remember," Bergen snorted, "Do you think I'm getting senile?"

"Of course not, old friend. You found your way down the path this morning, did you not? All the way to the lanai?"

"Don't be smart, young man," Bergen chortled. "It doesn't become you."

Duff patted him softly on his arm, "As I started to say, our writer friend will be here shortly to speak with both of us. I told him about our early days aboard ship, and now he would like to hear about the early airline days. Are you up to it?"

Bergen's white mustache moved upward in a kind smile and his tired eyes brightened slightly. "I think I'd like that today, Duff. There are stories within stories, and I would like someone to know them. Is he a patient sort?"

"Quite patient. And quite interested in our experiences."

After making sure that Bergen was comfortable in his wheelchair, having moved it close to the microphone, de Villiers settled into the chair next to Duff. "Mr. Bergen. That is, Bergen-san, thank you for speaking with me about your experiences. As you know, I am working on a larger book about Pan American in the Pacific, and that is the focus of today's conversation. I can draw information for Duff's article from the larger topic. Are you comfortable with this?"

"I am most comfortable, young Marcus, and quite honored to participate in your research. So please ask-away."

"Let us begin with some of your own background, here in Hawaii, or back to your steamship days. You set the pace, and I can adjust with questions later on."

"I live here now, with my friends Duff and Lady Christy, and my companion Yoriko. We moved here when I was evacuated to Honolulu from the prison camp. That was after the war ended, in 1945. Christy's blessed parents had been the first residents, and I was most grateful for their careful nurturing of my future home.

"I joined American Express as a young man of thirty, as their worldwide expert on steamships and shore excursions. Though I was born in Germany, I spent my school years in New York. After university, I joined North German Lloyd and learned my trade on passenger ships, large and small. I traveled the globe, picking up different languages and meeting people in our business.

"As I said, I joined American Express. Then, for nearly ten years I operated out of a wardrobe steamer trunk, on one ship or another. I didn't need an apartment or house, since I was usually aboard luxury liners or staying in hotels while I assessed them for our tour programs. My job was to work with hotels, restaurants and transportation companies, creating unique tours in major cities like London, Paris and Amsterdam for the European division; Hong Kong, Shanghai, and Yokohama in the Pacific. I also got to know lesser known Pacific gems like Java, Sumatra and Borneo.

Donald McPhail

"I heard about the new airline industry when Pan American approached Duff out in Pago Pago, of all places. Some friend of our boss put ideas into Duff's head, about a romantic new industry that traveled ten times faster than our steamships.

"This new airline industry intrigued me, and I felt that my knowledge and contacts would be helpful for Pan American. Naturally, I also liked the prospect of working with Duff again, introducing him to the many people I had come to know.

"So when an old friend in Yokohama invited me to stay with him and help complete a book he was writing, I convinced Duff to hire me as a sort of consultant for Asia on behalf of the airline. I could edit my friend's book, and work part of the time in this airline business.

"I knew of Trippe's adventurous plans to build a global empire, and I wanted to help. Duff was intrigued with my idea of moving to Asia, but he was a little concerned with my preference to live and work from Yokohama. Japan was not altogether stable then. As for me, I knew several Japanese dialects, and was actually quite impressed with their political leaders. I truly felt the military influence would diminish with time.

"Longtime Finance Minister Takahashi was a progressive leader who emphasized cooperation with western countries. In contrast, Japan's occupation of Korea and the recent invasion of Manchuria were deeply troubling.

"But I felt my relationships in Yokohama and Tokyo would keep me safe, and that Takahashi's guidance would maintain stability. He had brought them back from the 1929 depression in just over two years, far sooner than America and most other nations. At the same time, his emphasis on cooperation with other countries and reduced military spending was encouraging. Unfortunately, his policies alienated a number of Japanese nationalists, including military leaders.

"I knew Takahashi slightly, from my earlier work there. I felt his approach was sound, and that Japan's economic success would overcome the advocates for independence and authority. I also felt the military adventurism would be limited to China, which was a perpetual adversary.

"And so I accepted my friend Ariyoshi's hospitality. My plan was to first work with Duff to target key cities like Tokyo, Shanghai, Sydney and Manila. These were popular ports of call for the steamships, so they would be first on the airline's list.

"With its internal struggles, Japan would likely take longer to grant rights to a foreign company, so my personal presence there could be helpful. I was accepted there because I spoke the dialects and I had helped to provide aid to Yokohama following its massive earthquake. America's engineering support and a $100,000 American donation, were crucial to the recovery and reconstruction of this once-beautiful city. My friend Mr. Ariyoshi was the official who received our donation, and that is why he was so generous as to host me.

"Ariyoshi proposed to create an office and living space for me in his home, and to provide meals. In return, I would edit his journal about the rebuilding of Yokohama. I could continue my work for Pan American, and be closer to Duff's Asian contacts than I would be in Hawaii."

"When you arrived in Japan," asked de Villiers, "how did it seem to you? You had not been there for six or seven years."

"Perhaps I should begin with the house," Bergen shut his eyes to conjure up the vision of his old friend's home. "When I arrived, I remembered the lovely house from my earlier visit. That was when I introduced Duff to my dear friend. I can almost see the detail. The two-story structure, nearly three stories with its triangulated upper floor, was large for the neighborhood. Many sites were still empty. They had been leveled, and had not yet been built upon.

"Ariyoshi's original house was badly damaged in the quake, and this one was constructed in 1928. Built in a western style, the blue-gray exterior was elegant. It would have been quite at home in Hawaii or California. The narrow top floor was gabled and embellished with a small extravagance of deep red beneath the dark eves. It appeared to be an attic, perhaps a small bedroom.

"As the driver hoisted my steamer trunk up the walkway to the rear entry, I approached the front door, removing my shoes and placing them on the little stand. Knowing I was expected, I gently knocked and the heavy white door opened, with Ariyoshi and Yoriko standing together, beaming.

" 'Bergen-san,' he said, 'welcome to your Japanese home.'

" 'Ah, Ariyoshi-san, and lovely Yoriko,' I bowed, then reached out with two hands, grasping each of theirs in mine. I embraced them together, 'I am honored to be in your home.

" 'Bergen-san,' spoke Yoriko, in a dialect she knew was familiar to me, 'We are so pleased you have returned. We have missed you very much.'

" 'It has been seven years,' I responded, 'although now that I see you, it seems so recent.'

"As they escorted me through the house, I admired typical Japanese touches, with the use of movable walls and sliding screens that covered loft areas above the living room and den.

"Ariyoshi and I easily renewed our friendship, reverting to the familiar terms from the past, always referring to each another as 'Bergen-san' and 'Ariyoshi-san'. The house had been thoughtfully prepared to accommodate me, and he invited me to stay for as long as I liked. At the age of eighty-one, Ariyoshi realized that he needed to accelerate his writing pace, if his book was going to be completed. He had weakened noticeably since my last visit, in 1929. His sister died two years previous, and Yoriko remained, providing meals and personal care, still looking after him.

"Nearly thirty, Yoriko had a young brother, Koji, who lived with them in the house, helping to lift Ariyoshi and carry him from room to room, or to wheel him for outings to the nearby park. Koji was a thoughtful, athletic boy of eighteen, who made time to tend to the garden when he wasn't busy with Ariyoshi. There was a small central plot where

Donald McPhail

they got vegetables to grow, enough for two or three dinners each week during the summer.

"Recognizing his frailty, Ariyoshi was determined to complete his chronicle of Yokohama's rebirth. Entitled 'Ho-o, The Vermilion Bird', his work was nearly completed and I would provide the finishing touches, such as the design of the cover, and the interior layout.

"While I didn't officially work for Pan American, I was under contract to open doors for Duff and Pan Am management in key political offices. I carried letters that authorized me to discuss landing rights and facilities that the airline might require. Living there in Yokohama, I would travel by train to meet with Japanese government authorities in Tokyo, or travel by ship to Canton, Manila and other potential destinations.

"To outsiders, the prevailing Japanese culture seemed closed and distant, but I knew there was great Japanese interest in America. For example, just months before, the famous Babe Ruth had drawn thousands of Japanese fans to watch him and fellow major leaguers Lou Gehrig, Charlie Gehringer and Jimmy Foxx play a series of exhibition games against Japanese All-Stars. The games were very popular.

"Japanese citizens and politicians had visited America for decades, and many of them followed American clothing styles and practices, and watched our film stars. In contrast, America's 1924 Immigration Act had stunned the Japanese, abruptly halting immigration to America. This harsh act caused great resentment in Japan. America's

rejection had been painful and offensive, and it lingered
more than ten years later.

"Personally, I believed in the finance minister's
strength. I admired his emphasis on international cooperation, and his preference for withdrawal of Japanese troops
from China. It seemed as if his policies were strongly supported by the Prime Minister, and had been accepted
among elite Japanese, and if they prevailed I felt China
and Japan would be safer.

"I was troubled by persistent rumors of collusion
between activist military officers and rich industrialists, who
formed Japan's most conservative political party. This is
what had happened in Germany, you will recall. Then, in
February, 1936 Takahashi was assassinated. The military
quickly took over the government, and treaties that limited
Japanese military were fully disregarded. Takahashi's
death immediately weakened relations with America and
Britain, and pushed Japan into the Nazi sphere of influence.

"I knew I should have left Japan. I waited far too
long. My editing work was going well, and I was taken with
Ariyoshi's book. It was vivid and hopeful, because his own
compassion came through in his writing. Perhaps this
blinded me to the attitudes outside of our home.

"There were many admirable things that happened
following that massive earthquake about which he wrote so
passionately. They were truly inspiring traits among these
Japanese who were hit the hardest." Bergen was wander-
ing afield, but de Villiers quietly made notes, then moved
the microphone closer to Bergen.

Donald McPhail

"The earthquake was a total surprise. As Ariyoshi described it, a simple, tranquil day was first smashed by the massive jolt, throwing people out of buildings and off of piers into the sea. Then, half an hour later, a massive tsunami hit. Over forty feet high, it flowed inland for miles, then withdrew, sucking thousands of helpless people to their deaths. The inevitable fires followed, charring countless thousands of homes and people. In the end, the Great Kanto earthquake and its aftermath killed more than 140,000 people. It destroyed ninety percent of Yokohama and left over sixty percent of Tokyo's population homeless.

"I was so engulfed with his sad and touching stories, that I didn't pay enough attention to the changes in attitude toward me on the streets and as I rode the railway. Looking back, the atmosphere in Japan had become quite militant toward an Anglo, although I still felt safe.

"Clearly, the nationalist attitude was fueled by Japan's military successes in China. I was briefly encouraged when the new government was formed in 1937, led by Prince Konoe, who was not a military man. The economy flourished, but primarily because of military industries, especially arms production that was manufactured with natural resources taken from China. 1937 was also the year when the Japanese invaded Shanghai, after many months of threats and skirmishes. But Duff will tell you how he and Christy escaped from China on another day.

"I remained in Yokohama and was generally left alone by the authorities. I had decided to link my decision to leave Japan to whatever our embassy chose to do. If they left, I would leave. Then, in December of 1941, as I returned from an exhausting trip to Manila, I was walking to retrieve my luggage when I heard a loud voice calling my name. It was a soldier calling out to returning passengers, first in Japanese and then in English, 'An American, Mr. Werner Bergen. Please identify yourself.' I raised my hand toward the official, and was swiftly taken away with no explanation. Sudden as that, I was a prisoner of war."

"Mr. Bergen," said de Villiers, "You were actually arrested by the Japanese?"

Bergen was tired from speaking so long and reliving his experiences. His hands shook slightly as he rubbed his forehead. "Young man. This is becoming difficult. I am tired now. Perhaps another day?"

"Of course. Of course. I'm very sorry to tire you in this way."

"Don't apologize, please. I do want to continue, but not just now. Let us meet again in a day or so."

Donald McPhail

CHAPTER NINETEEN

Shanghai 1937

Duff and Christy were prepared to discuss Pan American's relationship with CNAC, and about their friend Paul Chen. China National Air Corporation had been a pivotal piece of the Asian puzzle, and a complicated one.

"We tend to work with our own cultural biases, don't we?" Duff began. "We seem to apply our own values to others, and working for Pan American, I tended to apply normal American business practices, even when I was in other countries. My managers and I eventually became better listeners and observers, and we adjusted our values to fit local customs. If the Chinese or Philippine administrators entertained in lavish surroundings, then so did we. If they made payments to local officials in order to overcome local objections, then we did, as well. The warlords in so many parts of China had their fiefdoms, regardless of who was the official Chinese leader. If you wanted to land an airplane to deliver mail in Szechuan province then you needed to pay a sort of ransom to Marshal Liu Hsiang, the local warlord. Listening and learning were valuable assets.

Our experience with Paul Chen was a painful example for Christy and me. Despite an ancient and accomplished culture, China was a primitive country on many levels. There were masses of people in the cities, and villages were often tucked into remote and mountainous areas. This often crowded, alway harsh environment led to a different regard for life than we have in America, a disregard, almost. It also led to a clear disregard for the lower classes. In the Settlement, business, bribery and nepotism were a regular way of life. It was even worse outside the walls. And everywhere, the abuse of women was deplorable."

Christy nodded, and injected, "At the same time, the educated Chinese we met were entirely civilized and sophisticated in the arts, and in their social rituals. The silks and tapestries, sculpture, jewelry, the centuries of art and music." She added, "But even highly sophisticated people could be quite brutal with each other."

"We learned a harsh lesson," Duff acknowledged. "After our initial dinner with Chen in Hawaii," Duff began, "we came came to know him quite well. He overcame our initial distrust by the way he operated day-to-day as an airline colleague, directly and earnestly. He also earned my respect as an analytical man, with a keen sense for scheduling and pricing. With CNAC operating entirely within China, he depended on relationships with other airlines and steamship companies, to bring passengers to him from other countries.

"As next-door neighbors in Waikiki, we became friends, and when Pan American purchased Curtiss-Wright's partnership with CNAC, I became Chen's manager of sorts. I was his official sounding board for decisions about flight schedules, pricing and customer solicitation.

Donald McPhail

Officially, he reported to his Chinese board of directors and to our American coordinator in China, William McEvoy. Mac had an admirable character and calming nature, and he seemed to thrive in China's complex environment.

"As for Chen, Christy and I enjoyed his quiet sense of humor, and I certainly respected his grasp of the airline industry. But we never lost sight of the man's anomalies, and the young girls who were under his control.

"Chen had been named managing director for CNAC the year before, and had relocated to the elegant Shanghai headquarters. Back in China, he naturally assumed his Chinese name, Wei Chen Min. He also revived his links to the Kuomintang and with Madame Chiang kaishek's family. At McEvoy's suggestion, Chen also established contact with certain key warlords, knowing CNAC flights would need alternate landing fields for emergencies.

"Chen told me that his rapid ascension had irritated certain old-line government leaders, two of whom were generals in the Chinese Air Force, and formed the Chinese board of directors. He worked to set them at ease, demonstrating his deep commitment to China, and introducing the generals to certain business connections in America. Despite their stated support, he remained wary of his position.

"While Chen oversaw the Chinese interests, the day to day company operation had been run for many years by McEvoy. Hired by Pan American but reporting to Chen, Mac had earned respect by clearly demonstrating it himself toward his Chinese colleagues. Foreigners, Americans in particular, often snubbed or ignored the Chinese, but Mac and his staff understood the importance of allowing local officials and workers to 'save face', and he always showed deference. Operating an airline in China was a group effort, involving pilots, maintenance men, fuelers and high-level executives of both races, and Mac made certain that they helped each other.

"When CNAC wired a formal invitation for us to attend a banquet in Chen's honor, Christy hesitantly agreed to accompany me to Shanghai. Knowing the importance of protocol, I felt that her presence would express greater respect than if I attended alone. The Pacific division was running well. We had even received a national award from President Roosevelt, and the timing was reasonable for this China trip.

"McEvoy, met our flight at Lunghwa airport, located just outside the French Concession. He picked us up in an elegant town car, sitting in front with the driver as we edged through the Concession, then entered the International Settlement during heavy mid-afternoon traffic. He had booked us into the Park Hotel adjacent to the race track, where we would have two days to adjust before the Saturday evening festivities. At Chen's request, we planned a private lunch meeting with him on Sunday at CNAC offices in the Astoria Building, in the French Bund. Then Christy and I would fly to Manila the following day.

"I can tell you, the Shanghai we found in 1937 was not at all like the one we had seen during our *Malolo* cruise. Within the walls of the International Settlement it didn't seem like China at all. We could have been in New York City or Paris during the Roaring Twenties. There were elegant bars and hot jazz places like the Little Club, the

Donald McPhail

Paramount and Saint Anna; private clubs, like the Del Monte and Majestic Cabaret, where it was common knowledge that CNAC pilots were accompanied by mysterious women who worked in sophisticated bordellos situated near the Russian consulate. They were White Russians, and they might have been displaced Romanov princesses or daughters of Russian tea merchants. There were elegant dance halls in our hotel, called the Venus Cafe and the Tower Club. All along The Bund, the attractive boutiques and cafes could easily have been in Paris, lining the Promenade des Anglais or the Champs Elysees.

"This part of Shanghai was certainly an enigma. Americans, Russians, French, Dutch and other mysterious foreigners lived in great comfort among wealthy Chinese. Everyone had servants and *amahs* for their children, socialized and dined in private clubs, and went to the race track for drinks and bets and camaraderie, even though rumors of imminent Japanese invasion persisted. 'Their targets are outside the walls,' was the attitude.

"As we rode along we could see genuine panic outside, in Hongkew and other shabby neighborhoods. Mac told us that the rumors of Japan's imminent invasion were everywhere. The laborers, beggars and the desperately poor lived in rough shacks or on the street, and were afraid to lose what little they had.

"As for the rumors about Japanese troops invading Shanghai, we knew that they had heavy anti-aircraft artillery atop their Consulate-General along the Whangpoo, just downriver from The Bund. We could see it from our hotel. We could also see the Japanese warship, *H.I.J.M.S.*

Odzumo moored at the wharf, just below the Consulate. Shanghai's mayor had publicly ordered the artillery removed, but it remained firmly and defiantly in place.

"Chen's banquet was scheduled for Friday night at the Cathay Hotel. The hotel dominated social events within the International Quarter. It was distinguished by its tower, topped by a unique blue tile roof in the shape of a small pyramid, and shared an opulent corner of Edward VII and Bund, with the Quarter's other luxe hotel, the Palace, with its own distinctive Pagoda style roof and wealthy clientele.

"McEvoy had made it clear that he avoided these formal Chinese banquets, where the women were often excluded and the men seemed determined to drink themselves into oblivion. But he knew this event would be different. Chen was a sophisticated man, a gentleman, and women had been invited.

"Friday night arrived, and our driver crept among the anxious transients that lined both sides of the street, some spilling out into traffic. The acclaimed waterfront now felt like a refugee zone. Thousands of poor Chinese had moved to the protection of the Settlement, many of them sitting or sleeping along Avenue Edward VII.

"Despite the chaos, Christy and I observed the stately buildings that faced a carefully designed quay, quite out of place now, with its expensive sailboats smartly moored to small wooden piers. Shuttered cafes, now closed in anticipation of an attack, suggested a place where the elite had recently gathered and socialized.

"Our touring car pulled into the *porte-cochère* and uniformed doormen swiftly opened the passenger doors and assisted Christy, as McEvoy and I easily stepped out on our own. We entered the spacious rotunda and admired the opaque leaded-glass ceiling two stories above, bordered with sleek greyhounds and brilliant lemon yellow panels. Within these magnificent Deco surroundings, we watched tuxedoed westerners sporting beautifully coiffed and gowned partners, mingling with Asian businessmen in tuxes or traditional *cheongsan*, and their wives in slimming Mandarin dresses or the latest Paris gowns. The white marble corridors were spectacular, punctuated by gigantic vases filled with rich red and violet cut flowers.

"Quite familiar with the Cathay, McEvoy showed us the way to the main ballroom. As I viewed the elite who came to pay homage to our friend, I couldn't help but think of the peasants who camped along The Bund.

"Chen was waiting for us as we entered, standing with tuxedoed airline colleagues whom I recognized as members of the CNAC board.

" 'Aloha, friends,' laughed Chen, hugging Christy and kissing both cheeks. Then as he shook my hand he pulled me into a Hawaiian-style hug, prompting quizzical looks from the board members and a smile from Mac.

"Chen shook McEvoy's hand and gestured to his associates, 'Mr. Loo, Mr. Tang, please meet my dear friends, Christy and Duff Malone, and, of course, you already know Mr. McEvoy.'

"As they nodded, Chen continued, 'Mac, would you mind entertaining Mr. Loo and Mr. Tang, while I introduce our friends to our other special guest?'

" 'Of course, Paul. I'll update them on the revised Hong Kong operation.'

" 'Christy,' Chen gently took her arm and nodded toward a corner of the room that had been cordoned off, like a throne room. Except, instead of a king on a throne there was an elderly man in a simple blue robe, seated on a plush red chair surrounded by what appeared to be courtiers.

" 'I am about to introduce you to Mr. Soong,' said Chen. 'He is very famous here in China. In part because of his age. Some say that he is over one hundred and five years old. He lived during the Qing dynasty, and fought against the British in the second Opium War, although he was educated in London. Later, he was an advisor for Dr. Sun Yat Sen, our leader at that time. Even now, he is quite observant and sound of mind. Like the two of you, he is my special guest tonight.'

" 'What an elegant man, Duff,' Christy commented, as we approached. 'He looks so aware, and calm. And see that unusual blue *cheongshan*, with the meticulous gold embroidery. The golden flowers tumbling out of the basket seem so delicate.'

" 'The eyes of a sage. Quite regal.'

" 'Good evening, Uncle,' said Chen, smiling gently.

" 'Good evening, Wei Chen Min,' Mr. Soong nodded, and held his gaze before looking over at Christy. 'You would be Mrs. Malone, I believe?'

" 'Yes, Mr. Soong. I'm honored to meet you.'

" 'And Mr. Malone,' he reached up to shake my hand.

Donald McPhail

" 'Mr. Soong. You have quite a strong grip.'

" 'Exercise, Mr. Malone. Qi Gong, and a daily walk.'

Chuckling, " 'Perhaps more than I do each day, sir. I am impressed.'

" 'And you are from Africa, I am told.'

" 'Originally from South Africa, though born in Scotland.'

" 'Many valuable things in South Africa, I believe. Diamonds, gold, many beautiful animals. There are traders here in China, with South African diamonds. And elephant tusks.'

" 'Yes, I believe there are. China, of course, is quite an international marketplace.'

" 'A place to purchase things, and to create fine designs. We have not yet learned how to harvest our own buried treasures, I am afraid.'

" 'Yes, many countries seek your natural resources. Japan, Britain.'

" 'Most of the countries in this International Settlement, Mr. Malone. And not just our iron ore. Opium, too.'

" 'Yes. I believe opium has been the cause of many battles and treaties.'

" 'So you know China, Mr. Malone? Mrs. Malone?' He watched us attentively.

"Christy responded, 'We know something of opium dens,' nodding at me.

" 'Not personally,' I added. 'Some years ago, two of our clients were foolish and were nearly lost not so far from here, near the French Concession.'

" 'Not unlike the Generalissimo's daughter, I should say.'

" 'Chiang kai-shek?' Duff was puzzled.

" 'I will tell you both, as I know you are also Wei Chen Min's friends. Madam Chiang is still quite upset.'

" 'I don't understand,' Christy responded.

" 'We will not be seated near Wei Chen Min this evening,' the old man explained. 'That has been changed. Madame Chiang has asked that he be seated with her and the Generalissimo. That, of course, must be honored.'

" 'What does it mean, Mr. Soong,' I asked.

" 'It is out of our hands, Mr. Malone. This means that Wei Chen Min's life is in danger. If he is allowed to live through the night, he will receive Madame's full protection, an envious position. Without her protection, we will see him no more.'

" 'How could this be. How could his life come down to this?'

" 'It is about Madame Chiang's daughter. Last year she did something foolish. She and a schoolmate ran off from their chaperones on a childish adventure. They used their status to hire a car, to take them to a kind of restaurant that offers theatrical training. Wei Chen Min and his brother own such a place, and did not realize who the girls were. They warned the girls, who would not go away. So, they asked the girls to remove their clothes, which they did not do, of course. This frightened them and they quickly returned home, but foolishly told her mother.' "

Donald McPhail

"The banquet was long and uneventful, and we were both grateful when the final course was served and the last toast raised. The extraordinary menu was complicated and occasionally mysterious. I was willing to try nearly every dish, but Christy wasn't as adventurous, carefully asking a British seat-mate about the likely contents of each one.

"She was able to enjoy several vegetable dishes, though the spicier ones were too hot for more than a nibble. Chicken and fish were artistically presented and tasted quite delicious. I discreetly asked Christy for certain of her portions.

"Toasts had been plentiful and spoken in Chinese, so we speculated quietly to each other about the subject matter. Of course, I participated for the first few rounds, then deferred for the remainder. With the assistance of an experienced French diplomat, Christy was able to arrange for fruit juice throughout the evening.

"Though we were worried for Chen's safety, there was no apparent threat to him during dinner. As the Generalissimo's preferred guest, he was fawned over and treated to each of the dishes, accompanied by ample rounds of the mysterious Chinese liquor that I was nursing.

"We were glad to see Chen so readily accepted, and wondered why Mr. Soong had been worried."

It is four on Saturday afternoon, as Duff and Christy stand awkwardly in cocktail attire, along with other guests, on the roof platform of the Park Hotel. They were invited to an impromptu cocktail party, quickly thrown together to

watch the war unfold. They had spent most of the day rest-
ing up after the banquet, preferring room service and read-
ing their books. Against their better judgment, they donned
formal wear and made their way to the rooftop.

Quite rested now, they feel both guilty and appre-
hensive. The stated purpose of this party is to observe the
war just a few miles away, outside the walls. They are safe
within the confines of the International Settlement, and
their vantage point presents an ideal site to observe.
Everyone knows that the Japanese have threatened to at-
tack Chinese troops along the Whangpoo River, and it
doesn't seem to affect the party.

The sky is dark with possible rain, and someone
speculates that the Japanese planes might be grounded.
Then, just after four-thirty, excitement builds when they see
anti-aircraft fire from the Odzumo, then feel the concussion
from distant explosions.

They recognize markings of Chinese bombers
emerging from the clouds amidst the shelling, trying to re-
taliate against the Japanese. As the Chinese planes ap-
proach, black dots of bombs are visible far from the Odzu-
mo, falling slowly and dropping harmlessly into the river.
Four more Chinese bombers attack from a different direc-
tion, and drop their loads. "But look!" someone gasps. "The
bombs are drifting toward the Settlement. Jesus, that's a
mile from their target!"

Christy holds tightly to Duff's hand and winces as
they see explosions along The Bund, over near the same
big hotels where they celebrated last night. They turn their

*backs and crouch slightly as winds from the blast reach
them.*

*"Duff," Christy points, "The flames and smoke.
Those poor people along the promenade."*

*"Good Lord, those are Chinese planes, bombing
their own people. Are they mad?"*

*They see fragments in the air, and realize that
among the fractured concrete and bits of buildings, those
must be bodies broken apart by the impact. Automobiles
are on fire, tossed through second floor windows that are
fully aflame. Then another bomber, too damaged to stay in
the air, is dumping its load as it falls toward the race track.*

*But the bombs find a large building near the
refugee shelter. "My God, it's the shelter!" someone
shreiks. "There must be thousands of people in there."*

Christy lay in bed, too stunned to sleep. She tried,
but visions of corpses and burning flesh invaded her
thoughts. "Wars don't happen to us," she thought, knowing
it wasn't true. She wept until no more tears came. Then
she lay still and breathed deeply, then listened to Duff's
own rough breathing and occasional dream-sounds.

An hour later, she sat in silence in their suite, tea
poured and the English-language newspaper open on the
end table. "This can't be, Duff." Christy slid the paper aside
to place her cup down. "Yesterday can't be real."

"Too real," he responded, awake and edging out of
bed. He slipped his feet into waiting slippers and came to
place a steadying arm around her shoulder, glancing down
at the *Evening Post*.

Christy read a moment, then, "The paper says we watched a tragedy. As if we were watching an opera, we stood safely in the audience while people killed each other. Nearly two thousand dead. Over a thousand at the promenade, and nearly a thousand in the Great World refugee building."

"It was surreal, just standing there, watching a war," Duff removed the suitcase from its closet storage space, and began packing clothes into it. "Let's get away from here as quickly as we can."

A harsh ringing sound, and Duff realized it was the room telephone. "Yes. Hello. Yes, this is Mr. Malone. You're connecting me to whom?"

"Duff, what's going on?" asked Christy

"Connecting to Mac." Turning away, "Mac, yes. What is happening."

Duff quietly listened, nodded and eventually grimaced. "What's that? He's dead you say? My God. Are you certain?" Nodding again, he placed the phone on its cradle.

"It's Paul, dearest." Duff hesitated, then continued quietly. "He's dead. He was found yesterday. Poisoned, perhaps. It is being investigated, Mac said. But he was skeptical."

"Oh, Duff. This just isn't right. No matter what Mr. Soong told us. He was doing so well here."

"Mac said he had enemies in the Kuomintang, and we know what that means. Madame Chiang. A celebration. Praised, and then killed."

Donald McPhail

"We must get out of here. Duff. I don't understand this place."

"I don't either. Mac says he'll drive us to a boat. The war is raging out there and CNAC isn't safe for flying. This fight is between the Chinese and the Japanese, and they better not harm an American vessel."

Donald McPhail

CHAPTER TWENTY

Homecoming, 1938

They felt comfortable with de Villiers, so Christy
and Duff invited him to their home for breakfast. De Villiers
would walk over from the Royal for coffee, half papaya, or
sliced mango, or chunks of pineapple. Duff, of course, preferred his tea, and was restricted to toast and fruit. While
Duff held back on the butter, he allowed himself a single
spoonful of jam, alternating flavors daily between guava
and passionfruit.

De Villiers accepted another coffee refill from
Christy, "How long had you been home from Shanghai,
Duff, before you were off to South Africa?"

"It was less than a year. So much was happening
then, Marcus. And so much of it was very painful for us. It
was eight months after Paul's death, when a letter arrived
from my brother. I had not heard from him for about a
month, though we usually wrote each other weekly. Christy
saw the letter, and knew that I would be gone for several
minutes reading it, and possibly responding.

"Five minutes later I appeared at the lanai, where
she was about to open her book.

" 'I'm sorry, love. We need to talk.' "

" 'Duff. What is it?' "

" 'It's Sandy.' I was weeping, as you can imagine. 'He's going to die.' "

" 'Duff, no. Oh, I'm so sorry. What is going on?' "

" 'It's a tumor. It must have been there for a few months.' I unfolded the letter, 'Sandy said that it is his kidney or pancreas. The pancreatitis diagnosis has become a cancerous tumor.' "

" 'You need to go see him. He will need help.' "

" 'He does want help. But it may require more time than we have. He's flying to South Africa in two days — he wrote this letter a week ago. He prefers to die there, near home. And he's asked me to meet him there as soon as possible. He doesn't know how long he has.' "

" 'Of course you must go. Mr. Trippe will understand, won't he? For your brother?'"

"Staring past her, somewhere into the sea, I couldn't respond. Then, 'Yes… Yes. I believe he will understand. He knows how well we are doing out here.'

"Sandy was my only family, and we had not seen each other for so many years, since I left for New York. Now living in Scotland, his letters brought us closer. Sandy understood what we had gone through as kids. He had shared those sad years in Johannesburg.

"Though he was more of a laboring man than I, growing up around the coal mines and loving that kind of work, he was also a direct and expressive correspondent. Wherever I traveled, I always looked for a letter awaiting me through a hotel manager in Hong Kong or Manila.

Donald McPhail

"Christy insisted on joining me. She knew that Sandy and I would need time together, and that I would rely on her, so I could concentrate on him.

"She knew, much more than I did, how difficult this journey would be for me. It wasn't just the distance, though back then, just getting to London from Hawaii was not easy. It would take ten days or so, whether we went via China and India, or across North America and through Europe."

"You told me earlier," de Villiers noted gently, attuned to Duff's emotions, "that you and Sandy were close. Yet you had not seen him in such a long while. Was there a particular reason?"

A reflective chuckle from Duff, "That's one of the Malone traits, I'm afraid. It's odd. We seem to prefer distance, somehow. We can be out of touch for weeks or months, then we write or telephone, and feel as if it were just a day or so between conversations." Patting her hand, "It certainly wasn't that way in your family, was it Christy?"

"Most certainly it was not," she laughed, "I loved being around my parents, and I love being with our children. That's why I'm so grateful that Malia lives nearby and stays in daily contact. And it is one of many reasons why I don't like Teo so very far away from me." She lifted Marcus's cup, "More coffee?"

"Thank you, Christy. Just a splash. So Duff, this journey was difficult on many levels, and quite emotional."

"It was the certainty that was so powerful for me. There had already been so much death in my life. Sandy was only thirty-eight, two years older than I, and he had always been fit. Four months before, he wrote me of some sort of stomach pain. Dietary, maybe. In his next letter, he had been diagnosed with a serious stomach ailment, possibly pancreatitis. Then his doctors suspected a tumor. Finally, they confirmed the tumor and it was inoperable. That's when his telegram advised, 'I'm flying home to Johannesburg, where I belong.' "

"So there we were, Christy and I, on a three-week pilgrimage to South Africa. We didn't know what to expect once we got there, except for that one given. We knew that Sandy was dying, and that we needed to say our good-byes.

"We left Malia and Teo in the care of their grandparents. They were little, and they already knew Nana Doris and Grandpa Pete would spoil them.

"It had been nearly twenty years since I left South Africa to work in New York. Through our letters, I had followed Sandy's life in Scotland, where he worked as an engineer for a large coal company near Elgin. So odd that we never met his wife June. She died ten years before and he had not remarried. They had no children, so Sandy was free to make his own decisions.

"A private man, Sandy was hard to read, not outwardly emotional. When he told me how determined he was to return to Jo'burg, I knew he would do just that. It was the place where our parents were buried, and that is where he wanted to be, together with them near our former home.

"Back in 1929 we agreed to sell the Johannesburg house, after mother died. Sandy wanted to move to Elgin,

Donald McPhail

where our family had originated, and where his wife's family still lived. Christy and I had just returned from our Pacific
cruise when I learned that mother was dying."

"It must have been a difficult time for you, Duff. Losing a parent is painful. And back then it was difficult to get
there for her funeral. Travel took such a long time."

Duff shook his head slowly and looked into the distance, "It was not so difficult, Marcus. You see, I had not
forgiven her yet, for all those terrible childhood terrors. The
threats and accusations. All these years later, I've finally
accepted how frightened she must have been when father
died. She was alone, raising two boys in a rugged and
changing country. She was depressed, she must have
been. She may not have realized how angry she got when
she drank brandy. She would awaken the next day, wondering why she felt sickly, and with no recollection of the
hateful things she said to us."

"I'm sorry, Duff, to have brought this up."

"No, Marcus, don't be sorry. I faced it when Sandy
died, and I can talk about it now. But when she died, I was
filled with hatred. I wanted no part of that house. Not any
contents or furniture, not even proceeds from the house or
mines. I asked Sandy to arrange for my share to be given
to our childhood friend, Cebo. He and his mother Funeka
were my shelter after our father died. Funeka had since
died, and I was never able to reach my old friend, but
Sandy's solicitor assured me that the money was placed
safely in his name. Perhaps unrealistically, I hoped to locate Cebo while Christy and I were there to say farewell to
Sandy."

The focus on his friend seemed to brighten Duff, and he was ready to continue. Pointing down at the recorder, "Does that thing ever need a new tape, Marcus? This next section could test its limits. I'm about to take you down the east coast of Africa."

Smiling at Duff's lighter comment, "It will give us about thirty more minutes, Duff. By then you may need a break, and I'll fix it. Please go on."

"Although I had escorted groups on many cruises between Durban and Southampton early in my career, I had had been away for a long time and forgot how massive a continent Africa is. As Christy and I flew from London, I had to remind myself to be patient. The Union Castle steamship would take more than two months to travel the same five thousand mile distance that our plane would fly in six days, and the steamship stopped in twenty ports.

"I had also forgotten how undeveloped some of the stopovers would be. After all, we were flying down the coast of Africa, not across the United States. The airports and fueling equipment were quite primitive in countries like Sudan, Uganda, Kenya and Tanganyika. We were lucky they had equipment at all. Plus, our pilots had to buzz some of the runways to clear them of giraffe or zebra or elephant.

"I must say, the Imperial Airlines flight crew were impeccable. Imperial is the company that operates these days as BOAC. The planes were spacious, with sleeping accommodations for twenty passengers, though only twelve were on our trip.

"The flights seemed long, especially flying all those hours over the Sahara. The full day over the desert encouraged reading and chatting with other passengers, until the captain pointed out clumps of forest and grassy areas, and sites along the Nile. The two hotel overnights en route encouraged a certain degree of camaraderie among the dozen travelers and our flight crew. But nothing like the friendships we used to make on those lengthy cruises.

The first few hours out of London pass quickly. I finish The Times *and wonder aloud about Teo and Malia.*

"By now," Christy laughs, "they will have convinced their grandparents to include guava jam and sweet bread!"

I nod in agreement and fold the newspaper, tucking it next to me. "And Pete will already be exhausted from the Natatorium visits, or hikes around the park!"

Though the reason for our journey is sad, we enjoy our time together, talking about things so easily neglected in daily routines at home.

"You know, my last flight with Musick surprised me. We were headed for Manila and he diverted over to some remote islands where there are tribes of people who have never actually seen outsiders. Much like some of the villages below us now, the ones more inland that are shielded from intruders."

"That's sad, Duff, don't you think?" Christy responds. "We shouldn't disturb people who may not want our kind of progress. Even the airplanes' engine sounds must frighten them."

"We saw some of that in Borneo, remember? On our last cruise?"

"Yes. That's what I mean. Those poor tribespeople were herded out to see us, and sell us trinkets. They barely wore clothes. Sadly, most of our fellow travelers hardly noticed them, and couldn't wait to sail on to Sydney and what they called, 'more civilized people'."

"I still admire the necklace that you have from Borneo, with the little shells. Which reminds me, Musick has invited us on a trip to Pago Pago next January, then on to Auckland. You and I can revisit our favorite little beach at Tutuila. And you've never been to New Zealand."

The crew chief joins us to identify key points, easily seen from flight altitude. The Nile River is clearly visible, flowing below like a bold, shiny ribbon. It is punctuated by dense foliage in places, and savannas where animals are visible. Then for miles the river creeps through arid deltas. We fly low enough to see the river banks and occasional views of elephant and rhino, but too high to distinguish where hippo heads and crocodile snouts lurk in the water.

After Sudan there are herds of animals at every fueling stop, first at Port Bell in Uganda, then Ksumu in Kenya and Mbeya in Tanganyika. All around the landing strip, we spot herds of elephant, rhino and giraffe, and literally millions of kudu, zebra, water buffalo and different varieties of deer.

Our flight path stays south, over the Blue Nile as it serpentines down to its head at Lake Victoria, the massive lake that is shared by Kenya, Tanganyika and Uganda. Then we know we are nearing Johannesburg.

Donald McPhail

It is mid afternoon when we finally land at Rand Airport in Johannesburg. We quickly pass through customs and locate our luggage. Government officials are cordial and smartly dressed, in their tropical white shorts, knee-length stockings and short-sleeved shirts. The pronounced accents are familiar, and they remind me how much my own inflection has changed during the years away. The Nie Blankes *signs in Afrikaans language were new for me, meaning "non-whites", advising which bathroom non-whites could use, or which water fountain.*

This reentry is quieter than I expected. There are small reminders of my early years, like the red earth that is also common in Hawaii, and the bougainvillea and jacaranda trees. I now feel much less like a returning South African, and more like an outsider who is just visiting.

As we say our goodbyes to the other passengers, it is clear that we are all beginning to focus on our next experiences, quickly hugging and wishing each other well and hoping to see each other again. While personal relationships were formed during our week together, I find it interesting how different these partings are from the sad goodbyes after lengthy cruise ship journeys. Lifelong friendships are unlikely to occur on an airplane.

Since Sandy arrived late last week, he is already under doctors' care at Rosebank Hospital, some fifteen minutes away by taxi.

We walk past the nurses station, looking at the numbers. I had learned from the receptionist that my brother had been moved into an intensive care area.

"You go on. You and Sandy will want time alone. You can let me know when you want me to join you."

"But you will be bored…"

"I'll be fine. I'm at home at hospitals. You just go ahead."

Seeing 1128 on a door, I walk quietly into the room and see sunken eyes that open slowly above a pale and unshaven face.

"Is that you, Duff?", croaks a tired voice. "It's me, Sandy. I'm here Duff."

I gasp, then try to smile, reaching over to touch his shoulder. I want to hug him, but I'm not sure what I can touch without causing harm. I hope he hasn't noticed my shocked expression.

"Duff! My brother." He swallows and continues, "Come here and hug me. I don't care about the pain. It has been far too long."

Good God. I barely recognize him. He feels so thin. His nose protrudes from darkened eye-sockets and hollow cheeks.

Sandy struggles, trying to sit up higher.

"Can I adjust this for you?" I reach over to move the handle that elevates the head portion of the bed, careful of the clear tubes running from his body into a medicine bag of some sort.

"Did they tell you I'm dying?"

Donald McPhail

"You're as gloomy as ever, Sandy. Always exaggerating," I try to chuckle, then place my hand on my brother's arm. It's skinny and wrinkled like an old man's. "No, they didn't tell me that," I continue quietly. "They said you were pretty damn sick, but nobody's talking about dying."

"Know what, Duff?" Sandy starts to speak, then seems to be drifting, as he shifts his eyes toward the empty doorway. "Is that someone?" He asked weakly, "…or is it someone…so Duff…I'm…"

I wait, thinking the medication is creating visions or dreams of some sort. "Shall I call a nurse, Sandy? Are you all right?"

"No…not just yet. No call. Just catching my breath a second…sometimes…the medicine gets me sometimes…"

"Can I get you something, Sandy?" I turn to the door, "Should I call your nurse?"

He looks up again and grins weakly, "It's better now…be OK for a little while…Duff. How are you doing? The airlines. You flew here on an airplane?"

I touch his arm again, "You're what's important, Sandy…what you're going through…"

"You know, Duff…It's really funny…odd, I mean. How much things change. How fast. We don't see each other…now it's late…" He smiles wanly and closes his eyes again, but continues his thought. "I was doing real well. Working…getting around in Elgin…with my dogs…"

"You said you retired. Your letter."

"Yes. I retired. Nearly ten years with the company," a sort of laugh, then a harsh cough. *"Sorry about that...."* Quiet again, eyes open. Looking someplace up in the distance. Remembering, maybe.

Sandy struggles to turn his head toward Duff without disrupting all the tubes. Sunken eyes momentarily very clear, *"I'm scared, Duff. I'm fuckin' scared."* Sudden tears roll down his cheeks.

"Why me?" he struggles with the words, and his whisper comes out like a scream, *"First June, my wife. Why me?...Why now?"*

He looks up for some kind of answer, and I want to bolt the room. Get away from this. Instead, I sit still and look back at my brother, tears running off my chin. Then I look away, out the window toward the roof of the next building. Somehow I say, calmly, clearly, *"I don't know, Sandy. I wish I knew."*

Christy waits outside in the corridor, listening and observing, and silently willing me the strength I need to get through these moments. *"Are you okay, Duff?"*

I manage a grim smile as I tiptoe out the door. *"Okay as I can be just now. He's drifted off. He wants to meet you, but not just now. He said..."*

She takes my hand with both of hers and soothes, *"Later is fine, Duff. Just fine. Let's go settle into our hotel. We'll freshen up, then come back to see him in the morning.*

Donald McPhail

"So you were a nurse, then Christy?" Sandy is cheery with his question this morning, and his face has taken on some color.

"I was and I am, Sandy. Duff allows me to continue my work, even though he spoils me terribly."

"You must know these fancy medications they're giving me?"

"I know something about them. Why, do you need some help, or something changed?"

"No. No. Not that," he chuckles. "It's just that they make me dream funny dreams."

"Ah, yes some of them will do that."

"Last night, after Duff left," he looks up and raises his thumb in triumph, "See, I remember you were here, brother."

"A good thing, Sandy. You still have your wits about you."

"Last night I dreamed of doves, for God's sake. Doves."

"And what were the doves doing?"

"That's just it. I was stuffing them into my mouth. Hundreds of 'em, like those fluffy marshmallows you get as a kid."

"Marshmallows?"

"I haven't eaten one for years, but suddenly all these doves, stuffing them like marshmallows. And I was laughing, tears rolling down my cheeks in this dream. They kept on strutting into my room, turning into marshmallow fluff."

"That's a good sign, Sandy," assures Christy. "A hallucination, some call it. And it means you're feeling better."

"You're teasing, of course. But it surely made me feel better, that's for certain. I haven't laughed like that in years!"

"The next day he was dead," Duff said, and de Villiers sat silent. "Christy and I were there with him at the end. 'I'm ready,' he said, quite firmly. 'And I'm not afraid now.' Before he closed his eyes, he added, 'I love you, Duff.'

" 'And I love you, Sandy,' I told him, with tears rolling down my cheeks.

"Christy and I watched silently as Sandy held our hands, then we both flinched as he strained and elevated his chin, made a last sigh and he was gone. We knew that Sandy's own calm, and the laughter we had shared, had calmed us as well. We were almost serene. I remember, Marcus, that those last few days were some the best I ever had with him. While we saw each other so seldom, we loved each other. No pretense. No false hope. No old troubles with our mom. Just love."

Donald McPhail

CHAPTER TWENTY-ONE

Cebo Msimangu

"Before we leave your South Africa trip, could you tell me something about your friend Cebo?" de Villiers asked. "He is quite a respected man, you know. I'll share some things about him in a moment. First, do you mind telling me what happened during your visit."

"This is quite a surprise, Marcus. I didn't realize that Cebo is well known, and want to hear more when you are ready. As for our visit with him, here is what I remember. Two days remained before our return flight, and I had given up any hope of locating Cebo. I suspected that Bantus, *kaffirs*, as many of the whites demeaned them, were often overlooked or cheated by officials, and I wanted to be certain that both Cebo and I had not been cheated by the bank.

"Christy and I were booked into the Carlton Hotel, that massive structure we both remember on Pritchard Street, near John Orr department store. The offices of Clement Wilson were located next door. Wilson was the expensive solicitor who had worked with Sandy in 1929, for the sale of our family's mines operation and the liquidation of our home.

" 'Yes, I see, Mr. Malone,' Wilson intoned, 'I should say that your wishes were carried out. In 1929, some ten thousand pounds was installed at the Standard Bank in the name of Mr. Cebo Msimangu. I might add, for what it is worth,' he peered over his eyeglasses in the manner of a pedantic professor or government official, 'that Mr. Msimangu is not traceable. As a Bantu, he has no local address and no-one appears to know of his tribal heritage.' "

" 'I see,' I responded as coldly as possible, almost mocking his own rudeness, though I did not truly see. 'What efforts were made to contact his family? I believe my brother stipulated that they lived in Mtubatuba or Mpangeni, an hour or so north of Durban.' "

"He continued in his superior tone, 'I didn't know that, Mr. Malone. You see, we were waiting for Mr. Msimangu to contact us.' "

"Christy and I made eye contact, and we both stood, 'Thank you Mr. Wilson. I believe we are done here. If you would provide me with the name of the manager at Standard Bank, I will speak with him later today.' "

"Surprised at the meeting's abrupt end, Wilson extended his hand to us and huffed, 'Of course. The manager is DeWeel. Marius DeWeel. I will tell him to expect you.' "

"As we returned to the hotel, Christy was aware of my frustration. I hoped that Wilson had found Cebo, and that the money had been delivered."

"Thirty minutes later, we were about to leave our room and walk to the bank when the telephone rang. I answered it, and am sure I looked puzzled, 'And you are?" I paused, 'Thank you Mr. Bonnett. Yes, we will see you in the lobby in five minutes.' "

"Christy couldn't know what the man had said, 'Duff, what is it?' "

" 'A fellow by the name of Bonnett says he has a family friend who would like to meet with us.' I replied."

" 'Do you know of any other family friends in Johannesburg?' "

" 'Only one. Cebo,' I laughed. 'While we were out looking for him, Cebo appears to have found us.' "

"I immediately recognized Bonnett from his description. He said he would be by the bell desk. 'Mr. Bonnett, is that you?' "

"The tan, slim man stood and offered his hand. He wore typical business attire, tan shorts and bush shirt, with matching calf-length stockings. He had an easy smile and thinning black hair, and was obviously quite anxious. 'It is, Mr. Malone. Mrs. Malone.' "

" 'And is your family friend named Cebo?' "

" 'He is, sir. And he asked if I could bring you to him.' "

" 'Can he not come here, perhaps dine with us?' "

" 'Mr. Malone,' he explained quietly, 'Cebo is a black man. He was banned by the government, so he is officially not welcome here in South Africa. He is an architect, and a member of the ANC, the African National Congress. It's a growing political organization, and he works with leadership on strategies. Because he assured me that you are to be trusted, I will add that most of the time he is in exile, so he lives in and out of the country. Sometimes Mozambique, sometimes in Rhodesia or Tanganyika.' "

" 'But I read in England that South Africa is progressing. Hertzog and Smuts are working together. Xhosa and Zulu and other tribal people are working, voting and owning property.' "

" 'That may be believed overseas, Mr. Malone. But it is not realistic. There are many restrictions about owning, buying and selling. And it is not just black people and whites. Coloureds and Asiatics are restricted, as well. And tribal chiefs control most of the small parcels allocated to black Africans. Ownership is always under study by the white government, and it is constantly being revised to reduce Bantu rights.' "

" 'And is the African Congress a real organization?' "

" 'The party began in 1912, and I assure you, it is quite real. People like me are helping them when we can.' "

" 'Then please, take us to Cebo. I have news for him, and I think he will be pleased.' "

"Bonnett drove us in his sturdy Alvis, to a shop in west Johannesburg, beyond Roodeport. A cautious driver, he watched the road carefully while he explained how the dominant points of view in South Africa conflicted. 'Some white politicians are for educating and employing the tribal population, many others demand exclusion from any rights at all, because they are not white. A number of white citizens consider blacks as no better than animals. The Bantu are often abused or ignored, and are a major source of cheap labor.' "

Donald McPhail

"He went on, 'Public attitudes are usually along ethnic lines. Liberal English-speaking South Africans tend to encourage education and limited sharing, while conservative Afrikaans-speakers want complete separation of races, under white control. Naturally, the ANC favors education, sharing and employment, though certain of their own members recognize how vast their numbers are, and simply want to kill the whites.' "

"From the kind of small and similar houses we were passing, it was clear that the outskirts of Johannesburg were in transition, where the gold mines and new residents intersected. Apparently, builders had been encouraged to rapidly construct basic houses to fit the needs of a growing population, and streets were laid out in repetitious grids.

" 'Here we are,' Bonnett informed us, as he turned into a run-down neighborhood. His car coasted in beside a small wood-framed house with abandoned automobiles settled on the dusty front yard. Two black men sat inside next to an opened doorway, and one of them waved to Bonnett, a sort of salute.

"Bonnett assisted Christy out of the back seat while I walked around the car. I followed them through the door, into a dimly lit room. Worn window shades were rolled down and a single light shone in the next room. Three black men were seated in low wooden chairs.'

" 'My friends, I'm pleased to present our guests, Mr. and Mrs. Malone, from America,' Bonnett announced."

"A well-groomed young man with quick, dark eyes and dressed in workman's faded coveralls, arose and strode to us, smiling broadly and extending his hand in greeting. He was about my age. 'Duff. Young Duff, is this you?' "

" 'It is, Cebo. It is your old friend, come to see you.' I wrapped my arms around him and pulled him into a long hug, then stepped back. 'And this is my wife, Christy. Please meet my oldest friend, Cebo.' "

"Though the black man hesitated, Christy reached forward and circled her arms around him, saying, 'Duff has been so eager to see you. I'm so proud to meet you.' "

"Standing across from them, I began, 'I cannot get over this, Cebo. How did you locate us? How could you know we are here?' "

"Speaking in an elegant British accent, the black man explained, 'First, I am so sorry to learn that our brother has died. I did not get to speak with him, but I did stop in his room after, and I paid homage. That is why I am dressed like this. To be ignored by hospital officials. As for finding you, I did not know, Duff. I was simply fortunate. You see, some weeks ago your brother sent a letter to an old employer of mine, who found me. That person told me that Sandy was ill, and he was returning home. I asked after him at the two main hospitals, and learned where he was. When I went to the hospital, I was fortunate to find friendly nurses' assistants. They said I just missed seeing you, but I could likely find you at The Carlton.' "

" 'How are you now, Cebo? And what is it you do? Are you safe here?' "

"He laughed gently, 'I am safe enough, Duff, for a black man inside this country. Thank you for your concern. I left South Africa for school in Nairobi, then in London. In fact, I spoke on the telephone with Sandy over in Scotland once. He told me of your career with the big ships, and now the airplanes. He said he had important news for me. But we were rushed, and we never discussed anything further. My degree is in architecture, but my profession and I are not now welcome in my country. I have also written things about voting, you see. And about fair wages.' "

" 'Mr. Bonnett said that you live elsewhere. Can you support yourself this way?' "

" 'I can, but it is not so easy. Without permanence, I can no longer present credentials for any important architectural jobs. So my political work expands.' "

" 'We have much to talk about, and I want you and Christy to be acquainted. I also know that you are rushed, so may I tell you something?' "

" 'I welcome your thoughts.' "

" 'You have a bank account in your name at the Standard Bank, here in the city. It is administered by our attorney, Mr. Clement Wilson. Be aware, Mr. Wilson is not a friend of yours, or anyone with dark skin. He made no attempt to locate you, though we instructed him to many years ago. At the same time, I meet with the bank manager tomorrow. If we can see you again, perhaps I can bring instructions about how you can gain access to your money. This could help you to survive for several years.' "

" 'I am honored and grateful, Duff, that your family remembers me. And that you are so generous.' "

" 'You know what our life was like back when we were boys, Cebo. The three of us were like brothers. After our father died, we did not know how my mother might act.

Every day was a mystery, sometimes very bitter for all of us. I got away from her anger and sickness by living at school. You and your mother could not go away, and had to look after Sandy, and after her. You are certainly one of our family. I'm sorry that Funeka is no longer here for me to thank, and to appreciate. She was a dear woman.' "

" 'Thank you, *bhuti*, my brother, if I may call you that. I have felt this way, and am so glad that you do, as well.' Cebo reached over and hugged me again, then Christy. " 'And so you are my sister now,' he smiled, dark eyes watching."

"Christy replied, 'We live in a place where hugs and family are part of everyones' lives. I am honored.' "

"Looking beyond her, toward the open door, Cebo said something rapidly in a foreign language and his two friends stood and removed the chairs, taking them to another room."

" 'I must go, Duff, Christy. I am no longer safe here. My transport has arrived and I must take leave. As for the money, there are ways to provide it. I would ask you to keep it for yourself, but our Congress is badly in need of help. And so I ask you to advise the bank that you are sponsoring a student in Nairobi. That you wish to set up a separate account in my sponsor's name, Mr. Bonnett, for that purpose. You can reach me through Mr. Bonnett.'"

"As we left South Africa, Marcus, I was torn in many directions. I had settled Sandy's affairs in Johannesburg and put him to rest in Rosebank, next to our mother and father. This was more orderly and calm than our dysfunctional life had been. At the same time, while we stood at Sandy's grave, I fully expected to be arrested at any moment. I was afraid that Wilson and the banker, DeWeel, had contacted the South African authorities about Cebo's account. Using a white man, Mr. Bonnett, as the signator on the account likely held them off.

"Then as we passed through Rand Airport I wondered when one of the authorities might pull me aside. But Christy and I got through the exit process and boarded our flight as scheduled. Ten days later we arrived in Honolulu and resumed our life, but not the same life we had left."

Donald McPhail

CHAPTER TWENTY-TWO

Aircraft Down

"That was a very sad period for the two of you," said de Villiers. "Your brother's death was quite tragic. Such a young man, and he must have suffered greatly. And while Paul Chen wasn't family, he was your friend. But there was more to come."

"I believe you are about to ask us about Captain Musick," said Duff. "whose death came the next January, on a flight that Christy and I were scheduled to be traveling on. Yes, those months were some of the most difficult in my life. In our lives.

"Ed Musick and I had hit it off, as they say. From our first trip together to explore Midway and Wake, we formed a bond. Musick had taught me about where to locate a landing strip, and how to coordinate ground crews. I had given Musick advice, how to tell his passengers about these little islands in terms that would excite them, and suggested that he encourage travelers to introduce themselves, get to know each other the way we did on ships, and to enjoy travel as a way to create friendships. These suggestions came from my early steamship days, when passengers traveled as much for the personal experiences as for the destinations.

"After the early trips to build facilities on Midway and Wake, I got to fly with Musick several times, to Manila, Canton and Sydney. Sometimes Christy came along. They always enjoyed each other's company.

"Ed and I were both quiet types, but our conversations were never dull. We had each spent our adult lives in travel, so we had many overseas adventures to share.

"Musick tended to explore structures like mountains, canals and castles, and places around them. He visited the Suez Canal as a young man, and could have crossed paths with me back in the twenties, when I was guiding a South African group to Cairo and Giza. We laughed at our different experiences at Giza, seeing the pyramids under quite different conditions.

"Musick was also intrigued by our links to China and CNAC, because he wanted to fly up the Yangtze river to its origin, as he had flown up the Amazon to Peru's Mt. Huagro, near Cuzco, and the Nile to both Ethiopia and Lake Victoria.

"I was drawn more to people than to the sites, enjoying personal contact and stimulating conversations. I must admit, I was slightly adventurous, too, since my South African heritage had provided access to experiences in the wilderness, for elephant and rhino sightings, and to visit tribal villages in Natal.

" 'But now you seem to rough-it aboard those fancy ships, or in cities with deluxe hotels,' Musick often chided me.

"I acknowledged that I might have gotten soft,

favoring destinations where comfortable hotels were present, along with decent dining and good wines. But Musick's stories of water landings off of Borneo and primitive encampments in New Guinea invariably captured my admiration.

"The January trip was on my calendar, as a way to travel together and to include Christy in the adventure, testing Kingman Reef and Pago Pago as refueling stops. Each of these small places required a difficult landing. Musick planned a dry-run in late December, then would repeat it with Christy and me in January.

His call came in December. "Duff. Ed here," I was pleased to hear Musick's calm voice, as I waved two airport supervisors out of the office with a thumbs-up that indicated they had accomplished what they wanted.

"Where are you today, Captain?"

"I'm actually in Honolulu, but heading out shortly for San Francisco. Just confirming our arrangements for January. I was making sure the missus could join us. Knew I'd better get to you before Christmas so you could arrange it. I seem to remember a story about the two of you getting together in Pago."

"I remember how guilty I felt. 'Ed, I'm really sorry. Christy and I would love to see Samoa again, but I just learned that we can't join you this time. I'm called to San Francisco for a meeting on January tenth. I need to cancel out of the trip. Can we get a rain-check, pal?'

" 'You know you can. Let's try again in March. We may have some new contacts over in Sydney by then.

Those Brits are playing hardball for their friends at Imperial, but I think something might break loose for us there. At least that's the scuttlebutt among the pilots.'

"I had a bad feeling about this San Francisco meeting. Maybe it was the disappointment of letting-down my friend, and missing out on a visit to a very special part of my courtship with Christy. That small paradise in Samoa had changed our lives.

"I went to the San Francisco meeting, awakening early and deciding to walk up Powell Street for breakfast at Sears. It was a Londonish kind of San Francisco morning — brisk and threatening to rain. Though newly opened, the small cafe was already a favorite for Pan Am staff.

"Still unsettled after breakfast, I walked down to Pan Am's office just off Union Square. I used the side-door on Maiden Lane and trudged up the familiar old stairway for a little exercise. As usual, I entered the conference room fifteen minutes early. But the room was surprisingly active, and I immediately sensed something was wrong."

" 'Jesus, Duff. Did you hear?'

" 'What Bruce? What are you talking about?' I set my jacket over the back of a chair."

" 'Musick. It's Ed. He's down in the water, out of Pago.'

" 'No, Bruce. That can't be right. We were supposed to be with him. He left there yesterday for Kingman Reef. My God. No, they're a day ahead of us. Christ almighty. It's today. Is he all right?'

" 'Duff, he's dead. They're all dead. Wings said they caught fire dumping fuel on the way back.'

Donald McPhail

" 'Oh, no. That wonderful, beautiful chap.'

"I don't remember what I did after that. I must have sat in the meeting room for an hour or so, then made my way back to the St. Francis for my luggage.

"For some reason, as I rode in the taxi to San Francisco International for the evening flight to Honolulu, I was in tears again, wondering, 'What do you do when you lose your brother, and another kind of brother in the space of two months? What kind of sense can you make of it?'

"I couldn't blame a war for Musick's death, or an insidious attack on his pancreas. It had been a mechanical failure on a clear and peaceful day in Pago Pago. He was following protocol, dumping fuel so he could land and have the engine repaired. It was so unfair. So many people would miss him and his crew-mates. I was surely at a loss."

De Villiers quietly turned the tape machine off and sat back in his chair, not speaking. Christy stood and walked over to stand behind me, placing her hands on my shoulders and hugging me against her. It was nearly forty years ago, and once again I was in tears.

Donald McPhail

CHAPTER TWENTY-THREE
Omori Camp

Bergen was late and they wondered if he was feeling well enough to continue. During his last interview, he had seemed determined tell his story about Omori Camp. Realizing it would not be a pleasant experience to relive, de Villiers had been sensitive to Bergen's limited stamina. Christy hoped that they were not trying to resume their conversation too soon.

She and Duff were in the kitchen when de Villiers arrived. Malia had called once, and was hoping to join them for dinner. She might be kept at work for a procedural meeting, and would let them know. Christy was quietly reading *The Advertiser* and enjoying her second cup of coffee, as Duff sat with his tea, going through his own notes. They offered de Villiers a place near the coffee pot, knowing by now that he was quite a caffeine addict.

Christy often placed a flower from their yard into a kitchen vase. Today she floated a yellow plumeria in a small lacquer bowl, with the blossom's lovely sweet scent adding to the pleasant sunshine. The three of them flinched when they heard a bump against the door, then relaxed when they saw Bergen's wheelchair pushing through.

"Lady Christy, Duff, de Villiers," he gasped. "I'm sorry for the clatter. It's this damned chair."

"Bergen-san, good morning. It's not like you to raise such a fuss." She moved to the door and leaned down to exchange kisses, as she touched his forehead, which felt normal. Then she wheeled him over close to the table. They saw each other every day, but always enjoyed their hugs and kisses, Hawaiian-style. She moved to the cabinet where his green tea and cup were stored.

"You're a noisy chap, in your old age," laughed Malone. "Are you licensed to drive that thing?"

"It isn't exactly the town car I had back when I first met Lady Christy," he chuckled, then looked over at de Villiers. "Back then, Waikiki was the Moana and the Royal, with an early incarnation of the Halekulani down the beach. The streetcar ran from downtown. Did you know there was once a streetcar?"

Duff responded, "Yes, old friend. We remember. You treated us to lunch outside at the Royal. Now the street car is gone, the old race track is gone. Life is changing here in the islands. I also remember it was on that trip when you decided to build this house for us."

"Not exactly 'for us', I'd say," objected Bergen. "You and Christy had only just met. The house was initially designed and constructed for me, in my old age. But instead you dragged me into that airline job and shipped me to Yokohama."

Enjoying their teasing, de Villiers brought his tape recorder out and placed it on the kitchen table. Christy rested her hands on Bergen's shoulders and kissed the top of his head. "You boys behave now. I know it's serious to-day, but please don't overdo."

Bergen looked over at her and responded, "Don't worry too much about us, Christy. I have sorted through this prison thing many times since then."

Curled on the cold bare earth and clinging to the man who is dying beside him, Bergen knows he has to act. Even if they kill him. As he shivers and clings, he returns what little warmth he can. For a thin and aching man of fifty-four, the music of death is audible here at Omori, and it is unmistakable in this fetid room. He can hear it. He is ready, but he still has much to do in this life, and he is damned if he will let these cruel bastards win.

Bergen understands the dialect spoken among the guards, but they don't know he knows. To them he is a gai-jin, a foreigner who knows nothing about their country. He has heard them ridicule their frail captive. Dysentery, and infections on his legs keep him off the job. He is worthless in their mines, and next to helpless as a ship loader. Now they slash his legs with canes, killing him off if they can. He has heard their savage intentions. He must act.

The ragged prisoners gag on maggoty fish, and rice contaminated with straw. Most are sick and all are starving, desperately guarding what little life remains. Information is precious, and they share it carefully at day's end as if it were bits of candied ginger. They share news about hair-trigger guards, or new inmates, or recent deaths.

That's how Bergen learned that Omori stockade is somewhere between Tokyo and Yokohama, on a man-

made spit of land connected by a single bridge. During brutal work days they encounter scores of other prisoners, as they struggle past with loads of military equipment or heavy cotton sacks filled with fresh vegetables and tinned goods, carrying them onto Japanese warships. Each night the prisoners are separated into small groups, clustering together, craving warmth.

Every day Bergen watches corpses carried away from an open area where the men are often made to exercise. "The grinder" the prisoners call it, referring to the tarmac where they used to drill and march at their U.S. bases. The term is a bitter one now, because that's where their captors grind them down, force them into humbling drills with rocks and heavy timbers, though they can barely stand.

Each day, Bergen notices that a panel truck drives onto the grinder, loading dead bodies and hauling them through the main gate. Just today he senses a wisp of humanity from the regular driver, a young man in an unmarked uniform, who carries no weapon. The armed guards ignore him, as if he has no status.

This day, as the young man places the bodies in the back of the truck, Bergen observes a small gesture, like a blessing, as the boy quietly pushes the rear door closed after placing the final body inside. Then he returns to the driver's seat, enters and drives away.

Bergen knows how prisoners who fall down are disposed of. If it is a slight stumble, they kick the body to see if there is any spirit left. If there is, the guard calls for the boy in the unmarked uniform. He will carry the prisoner back to quarters and leave him there to recover for a few hours and resume work. If there is no reaction, the same young man hauls the body away in his truck. Bergen needs to speak to him.

If he can get outside the walls and across the wooden bridge, Bergen might make his way down the road to Yokohama. The only way across is in the death truck, but he has to remain alive to do it.

Once across, a gaijin *on the move is totally exposed, but he knows there are some Japanese who do not believe in the war, who never wanted it. They might help. They watch their crazed and brutal soldiers and are ashamed. Many are aware of what their soldiers did in Nanking seven years earlier, raping, and killing babies, and what they are doing throughout China today. There are also many who will immediately turn him in. Bergen has to take his chances.*

But how to get outside the gates? Maybe he could die and come back to life? Or would he simply die?

Staggering across the grinder just after noon, Bergen falls hard, stifling his groan when he hits the pavement. As he lies there a guard comes over and kicks him sharply in the ribs, and Bergen wills himself not to cry out, lying still as a dead man. The guard raises his gun and removes the safety latch, then changes his mind and calls for the driver, striding away toward his other prisoners.

As the young driver leans down to lift him, Bergen whispers, choosing a dialect that local working people

*would know, "Do not react, young man. Please. Just an-
swer, do you understand me?"*

Stoic, the boy whispers, "Yes.

"Please, son. Place me in among the dead."
"Will you live, old man?"
"Yes."

*The boy gently places him among the bodies, shuts
the door and returns to his cab. As they ride away, Bergen
struggles to free his nose and mouth, trying to shut out the
moist stench of excrement and bile and death that perme-
ates the uniforms beneath him, and to concentrate on the
next step. He suspects that he is not the first prisoner to
plead for help, nor the first one saved by this young driver.*

*Bergen awakens in the dark, unable to identify
where he is. His back aches and his legs are numb. The
stench has been replaced by the scent of roses and laven-
der, and he is covered in a warm blanket. Voices around
him talk about the heroic boy in his unmarked uniform. He
has brought dozens of prisoners to this Buddhist temple. It
is a sanctuary where volunteers rescue foreign soldiers
and place them in local homes. Some of them recover and
some do not.*

*He wakes in pain, as he is lifted again and carried
out of the warm room, covered in a soft material, then settled onto the hard, chilling corner of a place that smells of
fish. A door slides shut.*

*Then the sound of an engine, and he feels move-
ment. The ache continues and the truck bounces wildly. He
can't protect his back with his arms confined in the wrap-*

Donald McPhail

ping. Then he slams again against the hard floor and passes out.

He wakens again when the transport stops and the engine dies. He hears a panel slide open, and becomes aware of a quiet voice. "Are you alive, sir?" in a familiar dialect.

He attempts to speak, but cannot. Clearing his throat, Bergen utters, "Yes. I am alive."

Quickly the cover is removed and again he begins to shiver. "Here, sir. I will carry you inside."

"My back, son. Careful of my back. Something is broken."

Once in his soft arms, he asks, "Where are we, young man?"

"Yokohama, sir. At your friend's house."

"Ariyoshi-san? How did you know?"

"We find out, sir. We have many friends."

"Will you take me to him?"

"Not to him, sir. He is no longer alive. I am so sorry." He lifts Bergen, carefully, and proceeds to the rear door of the house.

"Bergen-san," Yoriko's voice is urgent, and subdued. "It is you. Bring him in, quickly. Set him there, on the cushions."

As he is placed onto the softness, he realizes that his legs are numb. He looks up to ask a question of the young man, but he has vanished.

"Bergen-san. Our friend Ariyoshi-san is gone. He was very tired and preferred to join his wife in peace."

"Were you with him?"

"I was with him. We prayed together, and I felt his breath leave him. It was peaceful and very sweet. We spoke of you before he left us, and he wished to see you once again."

Bergen had been rescued, and he was hidden away in the attic above the third floor. The room panels were temporary, and allowed Yoriko to keep him clean and quiet as he recovered from his ordeal. But his legs remained numb.

Hidden away, Bergen ate the healing meals that she prepared for him. Broth, with ginger and bits of fish. Fresh carrots and beans from the garden. He slowly regained his strength. But his legs had given out. The beatings and forced exercises had fractured bones in his feet and destroyed the cartilage in his knees and ankles. He strengthened his upper body by rolling onto the wooden platform beside his mattress and repeatedly pushed up off the surface. Then turned over and held the sill above him, pulling himself up, and easing back down. Slowly his legs healed, but they were useless. On warm evenings, Yoriko helped him out into the garden, where he sat in the dark without fear of being observed.

He was still hiding at Ariyoshi's in August, 1945 when Yoriko saw unfamiliar soldiers marching in the street that fronted the house. Recognizing the non-Asian faces and foreign flag, she took a chance and ran toward them, not knowing how to draw their attention. From the long line of uniformed men, she approached and touched one on the shoulder, saying, "American?"

Donald McPhail

"No madam, Australian." The tall man stepped out of his group and smiled down at Yoriko, cupping his ear with his hand to ward off the surrounding din. The dirty uniform was neatly tucked, and he carried a pistol at his belt.

"I have an American, sir."

"You have an American, where, madam?" His dirty face looked confused, as he stood patiently.

"In our house, sir. He is hiding from Japanese soldiers."

Waving at the passing troops, "You, corporal, bring three of your mates. Come with me."

Quickly, the four uniformed men accompanied Yoriko to the back of the house and entered carefully.

"Up, sir. The stairway."

"Wait here, you two. Monte, come with me," edging up the stairway, pistol drawn.

A moment later, "All settled, then. Up here, men."

They hurried up the stairs and found Bergen sitting up, with the wall panel slid back to reveal his hidden spot.

"I heard. You are Aussies, I believe," said Bergen, using his English for the first time in months. "I'm safe, thanks to my friend Yoriko. Please be kind with her. She is not our enemy."

"Aussies we are, sir. And we'll be sure that miss Yoriko is looked after. We will bring her to you before you are shipped home."

"Sergeant, I would like her to travel with me, do you see? I no longer can walk, and she assists me. She is my foundation now. She is my family."

Smiling and shaking his head, "It may not be easy, sir. She is Japanese. But we'll do what we can. Will you tell her that she can stay here until we come for her?"

Following respectfully, but looking worried, Yoriko asked, "Bergen-san, will they look after you and keep you safe?"

"They will, Yoriko. Then they will come back for you. I told them I want to take you to America with me. You are my family."

Donald McPhail

CHAPTER TWENTY-FOUR
College Decisions

Christy realized that they had said very little to de Villiers about Teo, and felt that his accomplishments would add to his story about Duff. A noted local athlete and student, his mother felt that graduation from the Naval Academy and becoming a Marine aviator was quite an achievement, even if she was adamantly against the war he was fighting.

She didn't dislike the military. In fact, she had great affection for the soldiers in her care at Tripler, especially those who had been so badly injured in the Japanese attack at Pearl Harbor all those years ago.

The teachers and company officers that she and Duff met on their Annapolis visits were smart, cordial, and dedicated to their jobs. Teo's classmates were the brightest and most enthusiastic group of young men she had ever seen. She also respected the Army administrators with whom she still worked at Tripler. Many of them were personal friends. Overall, she liked the military men and women she had met.

She just disliked and disrespected the war in Vietnam. It made no sense to her, and it put military people like

Teo in genuine danger. With all of this talent and dedication, how could they waste it in a country as far away and disengaged from America as Vietnam? Was there oil to be had, or uranium that we needed to keep away from the Soviets or China? Were there strategic ports or air bases to protect? Many felt that America was entangled from its earlier support for the French, when the Vietnamese tried to escape from colonial rule. It is obvious that America's current intention is to block Chinese or Russian political influence in Vietnam. Was that enough to justify any of this killing?

It wasn't a good day to be the mother of a fighter pilot, especially one who seemed to be experiencing his own doubts about his assignment. When Marcus arrived, she sat with him and told her son's story.

"It seemed like Teo always had a plan. Since he was seven years old he wanted to be a pilot, that was clear. He was proud that his father worked for Pan American, and knew that our pilots were respected around the world.

"He also wanted to play professional football, and be a quarterback. Every day he read the sports pages and saw photos of the great college passers, with names like Babe Parilli and John Brodie. The Hawaii newspapers carried stories about professional players, too, like Otto Graham and Norm Van Brocklin, and he wanted to be like them. You wouldn't think I would remember those names, but guess who helped him paste their newspaper articles into his scrapbooks? Teo sometimes wondered if he could be both a pilot and a football player.

Donald McPhail

"He always worked hard. He loved to run and jump, and to throw the ball. No matter who he played with — neighbor kids, coaches, his dad — Teo ended up throwing the ball. He would come home with skinned knees and elbows, and never anything broken, thank God. But his arm never got sore, and you would never see him without his football.

"Eventually, he went to St. Louis High School, where they always had good players. At first the competition worried him. He came home and fretted about how these other quarterbacks were too good. He would never get to play. But one of his coaches, Bradford Kenau, sat him down and gave him some valuable advice. In fact, I sometimes apply it to my nursing job at Tripler, believe it or not. He said, 'Don't compete against another player. Compete for the position.'

"When coach Kenau explained it, it made good sense. He said, 'If you compete against someone else, you worry about their skills, their speed, their progress. Don't do it. It's a distraction. This keeps you from concentrating on your own skills. Listen to what your coach really wants from the position, and try, every play at every practice, to do these things better than anyone has ever done them. Try. You want to be the best who every played, not just best on the team. You do that, and you're going to play.'

"This clicked with Teo. He worked hard, and had this incredible focus. So much so, that after a game he would come home and he had not even heard the crowd noise, the chants and yells after he scored a touchdown. He only saw and heard what was happening on the field.

And he was always thinking one or two plays ahead, ready to call the next one.

"As a starter during his junior year, he received letters from two mainland colleges, Oregon and Colorado. He also got a letter from Eddie Erdelatz at Navy. They didn't exactly give scholarships to the Academy. Basically, everyone was on scholarship because you were officially in the military. But they did recruit you to play ball and sit at the training table. Then, like every other midshipman, you spent several years as a Navy officer.

"He worked out all summer in the Honolulu heat, running the bleachers with teammates at Honolulu Stadium, then on the beach in Kailua and in the shallow water just off shore. Every day he threw to Vince Cordeiro, his best receiver, and even ran patterns himself to get his legs in better shape.

"He was the Crusaders' offensive captain in his senior year, and made All-ILH. Teo scored well in the college aptitude tests, and weighed the benefits of living in Boulder or Eugene, but remained curious about Annapolis. Navy or Marine Air could be a great lead-in to the airlines, and without any actual wars going on, the military life looked pretty attractive. But there were Hawaii kids at both Oregon and Colorado who would make it more like home. He was quietly leaning toward Oregon, even if it rained a lot. Of course, there were girls in his life. No-one steady, but we knew one who seemed to attract his interest, named Lani. She was a good student and quite a successful dancer in a top hula club, we call it a *halau.* Lani was going to Georgetown to study law.

Donald McPhail

"When he discussed his college options with Duff and me, Teo was surprised that we both recommended Annapolis. We saw how well he would fit into the disciplined Academy system, and that a Navy pilot background would provide a military career, or added experience to join Pan Am. Teo wondered what exactly Navy and Marine pilots did in peacetime, since America hadn't been at war since Korea ended. Probably practice runs, to keep Russia from acting up.

"As for football, Navy was respected for its toughness and discipline, since they seldom had large athletes. Teo thought he had a chance to play there, and was encouraged by coach Erdelatz's recruiting letter. To an impressionable young athlete, this felt like a commitment. In addition to his application, letters of recommendation were required from teachers and local supporters. Teo was amazed and humbled, as were we, by the enthusiastic statements made by Dr. Yoshihara and coach Kenau, about him and about us, as parents. Their encouragement made Teo want to go to the Academy all the more.

He did extremely well on the SATs, but was disappointed to make only first-alternate for the congressional appointment. He got high scores, but someone tested slightly better. He knew how competitive the Academy process was and decided to give it one more go. When he received an offer to attend Menlo Junior College near San Francisco, and to play football there, he accepted. He knew that a few years back, another Hawaii athlete, Al Harrington, played running back at Menlo before qualifying for Stanford. Who knows, if he worked hard at Menlo, played for a season and tested again for the Academy, he might get in. If he didn't he'd have a choice between Oregon, or maybe even Stanford.

Donald McPhail

CHAPTER TWENTY-FIVE
Midshipman Malone

Mom and dad were visiting Menlo on parents' night. Teo had done well enough at quarterback, considering the stodgy fifties offense. When he enrolled at Menlo, Teo didn't realize that coach Strom was an old-school, grind-it-out man. He knew they played a wing-T, and assumed that included some downfield passes.

Teo was a traditional play-action pass type quarterback, using his running backs to pound for yardage, then working in a fake to the halfback and tossing it to the wide-open receiver on a flag route. He worked hard to adjust, but coach Strom wasn't flexible. He pounded, and then he pounded again, leaving little room for the wide-open part. In tackling drills, Strom loved to match smaller quarterbacks against massive fullbacks or linebackers, just to show the little guys how to take a hit. Toughen them up. Still, every day Teo worked hard and did the tackling drills. After practice, he stayed late and worked on his footwork and drops, always thinking about what he would call to overcome the defense that was stuffing all the runs.

Now it was spring in Atherton, and fruit trees were in blossom all around the fertile San Francisco peninsula. The Oaks had gone four wins and five losses, but the wins came against some talented teams from Hartnell and Contra Costa.

Once mostly farmland, Menlo Park, Palo Alto, Woodside and Atherton were now home to plenty of Stanford and Santa Clara alumni, who remained in the area and helped create wealthy and well-run communities. Menlo was just a junior college, but its graduates included wealthy entrepreneurs from Iran, Hong Kong and London, as well as all around the U.S. While at Menlo, Teo had taken the requisite college aptitude tests, and finally heard back from two schools, Oregon and Navy. The Navy response cinched it.

"Congratulations," it said, "we are pleased to inform you of your acceptance to the United States Naval Academy." Teo waved the letter at his parents, as he met them at Scotty Campbell's restaurant across from campus. "I've been accepted." Then he handed them a brown envelope with a brochure in it.

Catalogue of Information, U.S. Naval Academy
The United States Naval Academy is maintained by the Government, under the immediate supervision of the Bureau of Naval Personnel of the Navy Department, for the sole purpose of educating and training young men for careers in the Naval Service.

The Navy looks forward with confidence to passing on its leadership to the hands of young men imbued with the ideals expressed so aptly by John Paul Jones.

They had seen enough to be nearly as excited as their son, but he insisted they read the last paragraph. It meant more to him than they realized:

Donald McPhail

It is by no means enough that an officer of the Navy should be a capable mariner. He must be that, of course, but also a great deal more. He should be, as well, a gentleman of liberal education, refined manner, punctilious courtesy and the nicest sense of personal honor.

"Personal honor," he repeated. 'This is what appeals to me, no matter what else Navy offers. I may need to scrub decks or paint ships, but the idea of honor and loyalty is something I want."

Duff hugged his son and looked past him, at Christy. Duff knew they were both extremely proud, but he had no idea that honor and loyalty would change Teo's life ten years later.

Teo pulls on the white plastic helmet, his name inked onto white tape at the front so that the coaches can tell one player from another. His cleats clatter carefully across the concrete outside the new field house where the plebe team dresses for practice. They reach the grass and break into a swift trot, alongside other players in their new plain practice uniforms. "There must be more than a hundred of us," he thinks. "I wonder how many quarterbacks?"

He knows many players from Plebe Summer and this helps settle him down. The locker room had been crowded with other nervous athletes, and that made him even more anxious. He didn't think he would throw up, but he didn't feel so good.

Everything is designed for pressure, and you have to get used to it. But football is Teo's lifeline, it's what he thinks about and feels every day. He needs to succeed. So he calms his nerves and pushes himself.

First day of plebe practice is filled with new experiences, new coaches and new challenges. They reach the field, and he joins the others as everyone spreads out from the forty toward the goal line, where four young coaches in gym gear stand facing them, waving them into orderly lines.

He heads to the back of the line closest to him and faces front. Soon all the players stand silent, waiting for orders. Then the warmup exercises start, and the familiar rhythm of jumping-jacks settles him down, followed by windmills, then pushups and leg stretches. As they complete the warmups, coaches move to different parts of the field.

Someone calls for quarterbacks over in the far endzone, and he quickly sprints to the two coaches who are stationed there, sensing pressure from others running to the same place. They arrive in a cluster, breathing hard and casting glances at each other. Teo counts at least a dozen others in the group. Some of them are pretty big.

He reminds himself of what coach Kenau had told him. You don't compete against the other players. You compete against what the coach asks you to do. You try to be the best to ever do it, anywhere. The rest takes care of itself.

They pair off to warm up with brand new footballs that the coaches toss to them. He stands across from one of the taller players, more rangy than muscular. He has an easy stride when he throws, and even this first soft toss comes in with some zing on it. No-one talks, as they throw the balls back and forth, until Teo breaks the silence. "Hey, where you from?"

"Ohio," he responds and smiles slightly. "Where are you from?"

"Hawaii," smiling back.

"That's it men," shouts the older coach. Let's get together with the centers. We'll show you how we take the snap and make our drops."

The rest of practice sped by in rapid fire: snaps, ball position, quick-step drop-back technique, ball release. Then passing to receivers, using the precise steps and skills they had just learned.

Teo is panting, but not tired. He is elated with what he is doing. Nobody explained before, how to take that first long stride from center, "Quick now. Faster. Get back fast and you get the pass off. It's quickness, not speed."

The drills make sense and Teo finds he is hitting the out pattern right on time. As he waits his next turn he watches the others. Five or six are doing fine, but others are taking too many steps — six steps puts you on the wrong foot to throw. Some are holding the ball down low, gunslinging sidearm, getting frustrated, puffing from the constant running from drill to drill.

Finally, the long whistle to gather around Coach Doolen, our head coach. "Don't be last, men!" he shouts at the handful of players who gasp heavily as they arrive at the massive circle of tired teammates, some taking a knee.

"On your feet, men," he orders. "We aren't done yet. Before wind sprints, I just want to say, 'Good job.' This was a good first day. Now make four lines across the far

goal line. Offensive linemen in front, then defense, then backs and receivers, then quarterbacks. OK, go."

After wind sprints Teo stands outside the field house, shoes off and pounding them against the wall to get the dirt out of his cleats, and his friend from Ohio says, "Good job today, Hawaii."

"Thanks Ohio, you too."

"What do you think?"

"About what?"

The lanky quarterback asks, "Think we'll make the team?"

"What do you mean?"

"You saw all those other quarterbacks. Some of those guys are high school All Americans."

"I don't understand," responds Teo. "You threw the ball better than anyone. And you won all the sprints there at the end."

"Yeah, but there are some good athletes out here. We all need to work a little harder."

Donald McPhail

CHAPTER TWENTY-SIX
Light Snow In Georgetown

It's term break and we have a long weekend off. As a plebe, I wasn't allowed to spend the weekend away from Bancroft Hall, but as a second-year man, a youngster, we have some flexibility. I have my own civilian clothes, but just lightweight Hawaii stuff, so I borrowed some warmer clothes from Riley. I had hoped to be a little more stylish for maximum impression, but this isn't cutting it.

Lani is someone special. I think she likes me. We've known each other since second grade, and I've always been attracted to her. Who knows how interested she is? I've never been with a girl before, and I'd like the first time to be her. Does this mean I'm in love? Or am I just another horny guy in DC?

Riley's sport coat feels loose and strange. The jacket fits OK, an old tweed from his stash of civvies. But the dark pants are baggy, and the knit tie is pretty dull. After wearing plain academy uniforms, I need something more colorful.

I walk from the bus stop, to the address that Lani gave me, and it looks fancy. The front door is five steps up, and the place has two stories. I ring the bell and there she is, looking older than I expected, in a pink sweater and dark skirt. It's been three years since high school and she seems grown up, and a lot more serious. I feel like I'm star-ing.

"Hello Teo," she says, kissing me gently on the cheek and leaving a slight fragrance. "You're just in time."

"Hi Lani. Aloha," I stammer. "You look great!"

She looks down at my small gym bag and puts it in the hallway, then reaches for my hand and leads me into the living room. "Teo, I want you to meet my friend Ginnie. We're in school together at Georgetown. This is her apart-ment. I'm staying with her while we take a term off to work in the District."

"I'm pleased to meet you Teo," says Ginnie, smiling and looking me over.

I begin to sit, but Lani says, "Wait, we have a lunch reservation not far away. And I want to show you some places."

"Bye, Ginnie," says Lani over her shoulder. "If Michael calls, will you tell him around five tonight? Thank you."

So I follow her down K Street, first in one shop, then another, exploring her favorite boutiques. She talks about the old stone and brick buildings, and narrow houses that used to be slave quarters until this century, when they were upgraded into expensive homes. We continue over weathered brick streets, where she walks to and from work each day. I follow along, scuffing my plain navy shoes on the cracked sidewalk.

Donald McPhail

These expensive stores and wealthy people make me uncomfortable. Lani used to wear basic Hawaii clothes, shorts and tee-shirts with flip-flops. Now we're looking at fancy skirts and blouses. She darts into a tiny antique store and admires the colorful little jewel-boxes, picking them up to examine the workmanship. As I wait outside, I peer through the window and see a white-haired saleslady seated behind a magnificent old desk, and I move quickly aside before she can look up and spot me watching her. I'm not sure why I don't want her to see me.

I've known Lani since elementary school. She was the first girl I ever kissed, in the loft above her neighbor's garage. We were in the fourth grade by then, and playing a kind of spin-the-bottle. I had no idea she fixed it so she would win each time. I never forgot her choosing me. I wonder if she still remembers. Two weeks later, she moved on to another boy. But I never forgot her.

"I know we talked about it, Teo," Lani remembers, "But please remind me. Where are you staying tonight,"

Surprised, I fake it, "I'm not sure yet. Ah, probably the Manger-Annapolis hotel. They give us a special rate."

"Well, we have a big sofa. I think you saw it when you arrived."

My hopes soar, "If you and Ginnie don't mind…"

"Neat! Michael will be over for dinner, and I want you to meet him. He teaches at Brown."

"Is Michael a friend of Ginnie's?" I ask hopefully.

"No, Teo. He's my beau. I think I'm going to marry him when I finish my work here. His father is a rather famous composer."

I don't remember what we said over lunch, or how we got back to Ginnie's apartment. I quickly gathered my gym bag and left, apologizing for the sudden change in plans. I pass a couple of bus-stops, but don't feel like riding back to Annapolis just yet. It's getting dark, and I see big fluffs of snow dropping softly onto the old brick as I walk past the whitening houses, past tiny tailor shops and bookbinders that are now shut for the evening. The parked cars are no longer identifiable, Fords and Chevys whitening in snow. For a moment there is no sound, and I feel empty, like one of these old street-lamps with its flame gone out.

I turn, and looking back up L Street I see a hazy picture, like a Christmas card I once imagined. Rows of residences, glowing inside, warm and welcoming as the snow-mantled street narrows in the distance. I think I have never seen anything sadder, or so beautiful.

Donald McPhail

CHAPTER TWENTY-SEVEN
June Week: Class of 1965

"Teo. Hey, come on. We got beer waiting at the rooming house. And chicks."

He looked up to see his goofy roomie, Chuck Riley, wearing his summer whites and chomping at the bit. Teo had forgotten the day, forgotten the time. Still dressed in casual whites, he was engrossed in the next assignment, and his mind was already at flight school in Pensacola.

"You go, Chuckles. I'm finishing some forms, then I have to arrange to ship stuff home."

"It's Monday, man. We got a picnic scheduled on the boat, and sexy girls from Mary Washington waiting for us."

Monday. That meant another two days until June 9 graduation. Then programs for three more days. Musical performances, parade rehearsals, formal parade, parents' dinners. "Oh shit, parents' dinners. My folks are coming in from DC tonight. Chuck I can't go anywhere. I got to get ready."

"That's all arranged, Teo. Man, this isn't like you. You're way too attached to your next assignment. Your parents are staying with my folks over near St. John's.

Harwood House I think it's called. They know they can't see us tonight, so the four of them are going to dinner at one of the old taverns, for a little local history."

"I knew they were staying at Harwood, and weren't with us for dinner. I just let time get away from me. I need to get my gear ready for Monday's getaway and today's the day to do it. We're scheduled-up the rest of the week."

"I know you have the train ticket. You've packed your personal stuff for shipment home to Hawaii. We all have P-rade practice and graduation rehearsal. What else?"

"I'm just uptight Chuckles. Vietnam is really heating up and they need more pilots. I need to get over there, and I'm working on a faster track."

"Jesus. How fast can you go? You're at the top of the class here, near it anyway. You got flight school, and you're receiving an award tomorrow."

"All right. I'll slow it down for a few days, but I can't join you with the Mary Washington girls. I'm leaving town soon. I'll be sent to 'Nam. I'm not into one-night stands. So what's the point? My head is into the next step. I need to get to flight school. You hear what they're doing over there?"

Shaking his head, "You're already packing your bags for Vietnam? I know you're fixated again. Can't you just let it go until it actually happens? We worked our asses off to graduate. Can't you at least come and enjoy some of the fringe benefits?"

"No, Chuckles. You go. I'll catch it next time."

Donald McPhail

June was an erratic month in Annapolis. Temperatures could be in the low sixties or the low nineties, so your best girl had better bring a wrap to wear with her light formal gown at the graduation ball. You could also count on a rain shower of some sort, but there were plenty of gallant young men around to snap open an umbrella and offer the lady some protection.

And if you didn't have a best girl, you could show your parents around, then let them take you to dinner. Duff and Christy had visited several times before, so Teo had already taken them through the public areas in Bancroft Hall, the big dorm that housed all 3,800 midshipmen. And they had walked through the open area called Tecumseh Court, just outside the main entrance, snapping photos along with all the other families and tourists. This is where the Brigade gathered for noon muster, observed by busloads of curious visitors from all over the world. The Academy was popular on the main bus tour routes.

Middies got used to the tourists early in plebe year. It was startling at first, when middle-aged couples or little kids would walk right up within inches and stare, or interrupt your hasty walk to class and ask to have their photo taken with them. You didn't object, though, when a young girl in a revealing t-shirt linked her arm through yours and insisted on posing with you. And you were genuinely proud when an elderly man in a WWII veterans cap asked if you would stand with him while his wife took a picture. This was when you thanked them both and got another middie to wield the camera while you proudly posed with the two of them in front of the Tecumseh statue.

"What a delightful day, Teo," said Christy. She and Duff held hands as they turned off of College and strolled along Prince George Street. "Smell that daphne in the garden over there."

"That's Carvel Hall Hotel, mom. I thought of putting you there, but I thought you and dad would enjoy the St. John's campus area."

"We do," said Duff. "You surprised us. It is quite the opposite feel from your Academy."

"That was intentional, dad. I know you like reading the classics, and that's what St. John's teaches from. They're known for literature and philosophy."

"Different, indeed from your military school. Though I suspect that some of your officers have learned from the classics, as well. Or at least from recent classics, like mister Churchill's books."

"Back to those lovely aromas. Daphne, and I believe I see wisteria. Do you have any allergies, dear?"

"No, mom. I don't think they're allowed in the military."

"Don't be smart, Teo," she smiled patiently. "I just remember how wisteria always started me sneezing when I was growing up."

"We'll go over to Reynolds Tavern again, mom, dad, if that works for you."

"I always love that place for lunch. The quiche or fried oysters are wonderful," agreed Christy.

"Crab cakes for me," added Duff. "Lead on. We're in your hands, officer."

Donald McPhail

They sat at the back of the century-old tavern, where generations of graduates had taken their parents to lunch. "We're very proud of you, son," said Duff, as Christy nodded in agreement. "You took a difficult path, and you did it well. Look at you. Twenty-two now, and nearly an officer."

"Thanks, Dad. Mom. I probably wouldn't have come here without your encouragement, back when I was thinking of playing football in Oregon or Colorado. That was pretty much all I cared about."

"That's just the point, isn't it? You could have taken an easier path, and you would have gotten plenty more playing time at one of those places. You don't seem sorry about that."

"I'd be lying if I said I wasn't sorry about not playing more. But what can you say when you're stuck behind the best quarterback in college history?"

"Quite an honor, I should think."

"I didn't think so at first. I came here to compete. If he weren't a great guy -- funny, humble, smart enough to pass these engineering courses -- I wouldn't think it was much of an honor. But when your best player is also your hardest worker, it's special. Practicing with him every day, watching him throw the ball seventy yards downfield, or do something as unexciting as pulling away from all of us in wind-sprints, grunting and straining like a guy just trying to make the team. And to be one of his friends. Yeah. It's been an honor."

"What about your first assignment, Teo?" Christy asked. "We were hoping you would be based at Pearl Harbor, or something out of San Diego. Any chance of that? Could aviation training get you close to home?"

Laughing to himself, then looking serious, Teo said, "I wish it worked that way, mom. Stationed near home, I mean. We can get preferred assignments if we're ranked high in the class. But this is the military. We don't look for 'close to home'. We want a bigger challenge, or specialized education, or extra responsibility. There's more involved."

"That's what I meant. We hoped that would allow you to choose something nearer to home."

"I put in for Marine Air, mom. Remember those early plans to be a pilot? Those were solid. I'm heading to Pensacola for training next week. I told you this, remember?"

"Of course you did, Teo," Christy said, "But I'm just being a mother about things." There were tears forming. "We thought you would take some time off."

"Mom. Mom," patting her arm. Then putting his hand on her shoulder. "I would love to come home with you and Dad. See some friends. Even hang out with my surfing sister," he tried to get Christy to smile.

"But we're at war now. Vietnam is just building up, and I'm needed badly. Marine pilots are going to be a big part of this war, and I want to get over there as soon as I can."

"You want to get into battle?" Duff looked startled. "When you came here, there was no war in sight. America was at peace. What does Indo-China have to do with America, that we would go to war?"

Donald McPhail

"You remember when President Kennedy met us at football practice up in Rhode Island? When we were at Quonset Point in 1962? I wrote you about it."

"You did. You said you shook hands with the President."

"It was more than hero-worship, dad. I was inspired. I still am. President Kennedy is the only President I've had that seemed to understand what I care about. What young people are concerned about. All the others were like stern parents," holding up his hand as if to defend himself. "Kidding aside, they all seemed like old politicians who don't know how to talk to us. Truman, Eisenhower. They lectured, but President Kennedy gave us energy and hope."

Then he looked down, gathering himself, "He stopped by after afternoon practice. We were doing two-a-days in August, and he spent twenty minutes talking with us, he and his staff did. He looked us in the eyes, each of us, and told us how proud he was to meet us." Teo's face had changed, as if a mask had frozen in place, a look of determination. "And when he was killed, I've never been so angry in my life. And hurt. He was a hopeful man. A leader. And that son of a bitch killed him. The least I can do is go and win his war."

Lunch was half-eaten, and no-one felt like finishing. It was clear that the conversation had ended, at least the serious part. Duff left cash on the table and they thanked the bartender as they walked past. Duff hugged Teo as they got to the doorway.

Teo walked them back to St. John's and their lodging, holding Christy's hand. They talked about the busy June-week schedule, how they would see each other tomorrow, and try to have dinner together with Chuck and his parents. No more was said about home, or vacation, or the stunning colors and aromas in the Carvel Hall gardens. No more was said about flight school. This war in far-away Vietnam had already changed their relationship and Teo wasn't even there yet.

He was sorry about how his parents reacted. Dad worried about being in harm's way, and mom worried about nearly everything. Would he have enough to eat? When could he visit home after flight school? He knew she was just as worried about "harm's way" as his dad. He also realized they couldn't possibly understand his immersion in this war. Or his need to do something tangible to honor his late president. Teo had sat there on November 22nd, drawn to the mess hall with his classmates listening to the radio reports from Dallas. No-one could believe it. JFK shot dead by an assassin. The motorcade sped him to the hospital. He was alive, then he wasn't. This inspired, smiling man, who had touched Teo's life. He was dead, and America was in trouble.

Teo didn't care much about June Week, or the graduation ball, or graduation leave. He planned to skip all the pomp and prepare for advanced placement at flight school. He was due in Pensacola right after a two-week graduation leave, but he would skip that, too. He was taking the train to Florida, so he could arrive fully prepared for this next venture. Some of the new ensigns and second lieutenants would drive their shiny Corvettes down, many with their girlfriends. But Teo wasn't going to spend that kind of money on a flashy car, or a girlfriend. He wanted to get to the war, now.

Donald McPhail

CHAPTER TWENTY-EIGHT

Pearl Harbor

"If it works for you, we will move around in time again today," de Villiers began the conversation more formally than usual. "Today I'd like to go back a bit, to talk about the Japanese attack on Pearl Harbor." He knew it wouldn't be easy for Duff to limit himself, because he tended to take a little longer with his descriptions. He also realized how traumatic it must have been for Christy, and he wanted to help make it a little easier for her.

"We know that the Japanese attack suddenly brought America into the Second World War. I'm interested in your own personal experiences. How did that day unfold for you, and for your family?" He looked at each of them, "Are you all right with this?" He turned to the recorder to be sure it was on.

Duff began, "I wasn't here, Marcus, but I wish I had been. You can't imagine how frightening it is when your family is in danger, and you can do nothing about it. Not knowing if they were dead or alive is something that still comes into my thoughts at the strangest times."

De Villiers was unprepared for his response. He knew Duff had been in New York. "I'm not sure what you mean by 'strangest times'. Could you be more specific, Duff?"

"For months, maybe years after the attack, I used to think about it every time I arranged a trip," he said, slowly sorting out his thoughts. "I felt guilty. I was tempted to cancel whatever the meeting was and not go. This wasn't reasonable, of course, because of my line of work, and it was just a brief fear. Then I would realize, 'How can I support my family if I can't do my work?' And whenever I got on a plane. Always at takeoff. All that power and thrust, and fighting the laws of gravity. I was naturally afraid at takeoff. Now I was afraid I would never see Christy again. Never see Teo and Malia. Would they be safe while I was gone? What if someone attacked them again?"

De Villiers nodded and turned his notebook pages, allowing Duff to calm, then asked Christy, "Were you aware that Duff felt this way?"

He could see she was close to tears when she responded. "I never knew this, Duff. All those years ago, and I never knew."

Duff closed his eyes and nodded, then opened them. "I didn't want to tell you. I felt so guilty. You and our family went through so much together."

Gently, de Villiers asked Duff, "Could you describe where you were and what you were doing when the attack took place?"

"Of course. I was off in New York for a meeting when it happened. I was returning on a United flight, and I didn't know about the attack until I made a change of planes in Chicago. It was Sunday, nearly five o'clock in the evening there, and it was odd that a radio was playing loudly in the terminal. I recognized the voice of the news announcer, John Daly, reading a bulletin about an attack at Pearl Harbor. That was odd, too. I would normally shut out the noise, but I knew his voice. Daly was born in Johannesburg where I was raised and was well known in America.

"My heart fell, of course, when I realized what he was saying. It wasn't possible. A bombing at Pearl Harbor? Then I spotted one of United's managers and identified myself. He quickly updated me as we hurried to my San Francisco flight. There was so much that was not known. I was a mess. That trip to San Francisco is the longest flight I've ever been on. I didn't know if they were alive or dead. I was angry at myself, at Japan, at my job. It was indescribable."

"And how did you finally hear about your family?"

"Once I settled myself down, I wondered who I could contact when we landed in San Francisco, to obtain some facts. Could I contact Christy or Pete and Doris by phone, or would the lines be shut down? Then I wondered how Japan attacked, by ship or air? What was attacked? Where was the damage? How bad was it? Then I could reconstruct where the children would be, then Christy. Pete and Doris would have been at our home. Then I wondered, are our Pan Am people safe? How about our aircraft? You can imagine how frustrated I was. I had all these questions, but there was absolutely nothing I could do.

"It was about eight at night when I arrived in San Francisco. Our airport manager met me at plane-side, and briefed me as we walked to find a quiet spot in the terminal where we could talk. He had traded teletypes with the Honolulu operations people, and he detailed what they knew. Hundreds, maybe a thousand Japanese war planes hit us in two separate waves.

The first one started just before eight in the morning, Hawaii time; the next one an hour later. Most of the damage was at Pearl Harbor. Some damage was reported over in Waikiki, from our own anti-aircraft mortar shells that missed their targets and arched over to that side the island. That worried me, since our home was in that direction.

"More than fifteen hundred people had been killed at Pearl, and that number was rising as information came in. Over a thousand on the *USS Arizona* alone, which must have been the main target. My God, what a heartless, savage tragedy! Of course, no-one knew if another attack was coming, and Hawaii was now under martial law. All airline flights were halted, as well.

"We got to an office and I placed a call on his phone, but the operators were flooded with calls and I could not get through to our home number, or to my office. I was panicked, because I didn't know what was happening with my family.

"I stayed out near the airport, spending every waking hour at our terminal office. I finally got a message through to Christy via our San Francisco office. My staff people in Honolulu had spoken with her, and they assured me that she and our children were all right. Her parents, too. None of our staff was hurt, and our flights couldn't operate."

Turning to Christy, who had quietly waited for Duff to finish his description, de Villiers asked, "How could you manage it, Christy? Duff was away. You were in a war zone. It sounds like a nightmare."

"It was the worst day of my life. Nothing else is even close," she began. "Not knowing was the worst part for me. Where were Teo and Malia? My parents? How could I reach Duff, and as unfair as it sounds, I wondered why he wasn't there to help. I got over that, but first reactions aren't always kind. On reflection, as bad as it was for me, it must have been terrible for him.

"It was early Sunday morning and I was driving to Tripler hospital to sub for someone. That's about twenty minutes from here. I assumed the kids were still in bed. Mom and dad were always up and about by then, having coffee and enjoying the quiet early part of their day. Those days Tripler was at Fort Shafter and had four hundred and fifty beds, half the size it is now."

"I parked near the entrance and heard airplane engines, much louder than usual. Tripler is on a military base and you get used to them practicing, but this was much noisier, growing louder, and it had such an angry sound. I looked up and couldn't believe that the sky was dark with planes. There were hundreds of them directly overhead, going toward Pearl Harbor. At first I wondered why so many of our planes were flying this early on a Sunday morning, and why so low. But they weren't our planes.

They were marked with the red Japanese insignia. It didn't
seem real to me.

"They were past us, and the next moment I was
watching bombs dropping from the sky, the way I had
watched them falling on those buildings in Shanghai. I
could see them. Only they were bombing our ships and the
structures at Hickam, and destroying them. I heard explosions and could see flashes, and then one massive blast.
Later I learned it was the barracks for some 2,000 men.
Then I saw people running on the road and pointing. I
heard sirens and saw a dozen ambulances speeding out of
the parking lot.

"I rushed into the Emergency Room and joined the
ER staff as they prepared for casualties. It wasn't ten minutes later when the first two ambulances came back with
sailors and marines from Pearl, and at least one civilian
firefighter. Like all the nurses, I pitched in where I could,
bringing supplies and sterile instruments in preparation for
more injured. We were well trained, but not for something
of this magnitude.

"Soon I was wiping off wounded men, ferrying trash
containers outside, emptying bloody pans, and helping
surgeons to scrub up. By noon, nearly five hundred casualties had come in. Some went directly to surgery, others,
maybe four hundred, went into the wards for treatment.
More than one hundred patients died.

"We worked for twelve hours straight, most of us.
Some stayed longer. We used nearby Farrington high
school for overflow. Nurses worked and cleaned, and when

Donald McPhail

we could, we talked with the injured men, reassuring them and making them as comfortable as we could.

"I can't describe the courage I saw there, from the wounded men, of course. They were incredible. But also from the nursing staff and the doctors. God bless them, they kept at it until there were no more new patients. Then they stood and looked around for more to treat. A new shift had come in, and they insisted that we go home. So finally, after we cleaned ourselves and got ready to leave, many of us realized what we had gone through. We looked at each other and came together for a group hug. We stayed there for what must have been ten minutes, clinging to each other and weeping."

Donald McPhail

CHAPTER TWENTY-NINE
The Days That Followed

"With the horror and carnage, I had completely neglected my children and my parents. They would be frantic, and I now realized the danger wasn't only at Pearl Harbor. All day there had been reports of explosions in Waikiki and downtown, and rumors of Japanese submarines and possible invasion from the sea. Nothing was known.

"All over the island, phone lines were down and no-one knew where anyone was. As I drove home, I found that martial law was in place, and roads were closed and troops were positioned everywhere. I knew back streets, so when a main road was backed up I could turn around and cut through a neighborhood. Though everyone was advised to remain indoors, people were gathering out in the streets and asking each other what they knew. They were incredibly cooperative, stepping aside from their street-conversations and allowing my car to go through. Seeing my soiled nurse's uniform, several of them asked me to wait a moment, then handed me food. I hadn't eaten, so the *manapua*, pork buns, and *malasadas*, local fried pastry, were heavenly. And glasses of water.

"When I finally got home, it was nearly eleven o'clock and everyone was waiting for me. I was so happy to see my children and my parents. Our reunion was fueled by tears, gratitude, relief, exhaustion and the fear of another attack. The fear lasted for days. You know how frightening it is, when you wait and wait for something that never comes? And we had no idea where Duff was, except somewhere on the mainland.

"We knew we were in the first days of a war with Japan, and we had to adjust. None of us remembered the Great War, so we didn't really know what the local restrictions would be be. Could we venture out, or take our kids to school? When would the next attack come?

"Looking backward, of course it was logical that airlines and steamships would be shut down. Of course the schools would close, in case there was a follow up attack. When they reopened, students would carry gas masks and hide under their desks during air-raid drills. Barbed-wire barriers would line Waikiki Beach, to prevent an invasion from Japanese ships. And blackout curtains would be used in every home, with lights out after dark to prevent another invasion from the air. But there were limits on telephone calls, and scarcity of food, rationing of gasoline. These were all things we had to adjust to, and so we did. But where was Duff? Did he know we were all right?"

"So when did you make contact with Duff?" de Villiers asked.

"We finally reached each other two days later. Telephone use was highly restricted, because of the extreme volume. Finally he got through from his San Francisco of-

Donald McPhail

fice. He had attempted many times, but could never get connected.

"It was very emotional when we spoke. I broke down in tears, I remember, and then so did he. He was so happy to know we were okay and undamaged. After that, we knew we could wait until commercial flights were restored. If he could call me now and then and reassure me, that would be enough.

"Then he remembered the uniform that he had in his suitcase, Juan Trippe's dress uniform for Pan American executives. He wore it to official meetings, so why not now? There was an Army Air Corps office at San Francisco Airport, so Duff put on his uniform and marched over to ask for a lift to Honolulu. I suspect that he even offered a sharp salute when he walked in.

"The next time he telephoned it was six days after the attack. He was calling from Pan Am's desk at Honolulu Airport. Duff arrived on a military transport that morning, and they jeeped him over to the commercial terminal. Obviously, we were ecstatic. He was able to get a taxi home, and we continued with our lives, that were greatly changed by a world at war."

Donald McPhail

CHAPTER THIRTY

Internment Camps

"Duff, I asked Marcus to join us for lunch with Masao and Gio. Do you mind?"

"Of course I don't mind. If I did, what would you do?"

Laughing, "You don't need to be testy about it, just because you're in a weakened state."

"I'm not that weak, I'm happy to say. But I do agree that he would be a nice addition."

"I suggested that he bring extra tape, in case they decide to tell us some of their own stories."

Sorvini and Masao said they were stopping by for lunch, because Christy promised to make her famed prawn-avocado salad. But Duff knew they wanted to see if he was healthy. Sticking to his diet, Duff would have his prawns with herbs and fresh lemon, while everyone else would savor the spicy remoulade sauce that Christy created.

Masao visited Honolulu from San Francisco at least twice a month for company meetings, and frequently played golf with Duff, so they saw him often, but Sorvini's presence was a rare treat. He stopped by the hospital shortly after Duff was admitted, but visitors were not yet

allowed. So he and Masao got together and invited themselves for lunch.

Though Sorvini usually stayed with Duff and Christy
in the big house, this time he was the guest of some of his
business friends, who hosted him nearby at the New Otani
and scheduled him to visit with different chefs.

Early in the week Sorvini visited local restaurateurs,
contacts he had made at food industry shows around the
world. Hawaii had some talented chefs, and he was interested in the combinations of Asian and Mediterranean
dishes that were becoming popular. The highlight was a
private dinner with George Matsuoka, Christy's and Duff's
good friend over at Pearl City Tavern. George featured
platters of fresh seafood, both sashimi-style and sautéed
or broiled, and spicy *poke* in his special seasonings.
Everyone knew that Matsuoka was going to launch his own
restaurant out on Nimitz and it was a rare treat to sample
his creative dishes.

Local chefs always welcomed Sorvini to their
kitchens and traded ideas on preparations, ingredients,
cuts of meat, presentation, costs -- all those things that serious chefs care about.

Duff heard Christy welcoming them. They had
come in through the side door and went straight to the
kitchen, where they always hoped to see Christy. Enjoying
his rest, Duff remained on the lanai and listened to the affectionate teasing. He remembered the same *ho'omalimali*
when they introduced Masao to Sorvini back in 1960.

He considered joining them in the kitchen just as
Masao came out to the lanai. "Sit Duff. No need to get up

just for us." Masao leaned down and gave a gentle hug. "You're supposed to be resting. Gio will be out shortly."

Quietly handsome in his bright floral shirt and tan shorts, Masao Tanaka was an avid golfer who played at least once a week, at Oahu Country Club when he visited Honolulu, or at his favorite home courses, Olympic Club in San Francisco and Stanford golf course near Palo Alto. There were plenty of travel industry friends, not just in Hawaii, but in Japan, Scotland, Australia and all around the world. Masao could always find a friendly foursome even on short notice.

He was a natural story teller, alert with facts and always mindful of his listeners, making eye contact with everyone and drawing them into the conversation with his warmth. Duff also knew Masao as a dogged and decisive business man who was proud of the services provided by his small inter-island airline. Hawaiian was literally the first commercial airline in Hawaii, starting out in 1929 with Sikorski amphibian planes, and while they regularly upgraded to the latest aircraft, they had never expanded services beyond the short inter-island routes. But thanks to Masao, literally every major airline was aware of his company and welcomed him to their offices. And he was beloved by his customers. Now in his mid-thirties, he was extremely popular with the ladies in Pan American's reservations office and at the airport ticket counter.

Despite their age difference, Masao and Sorvini were instant friends, and they always arranged to visit with Duff and Christy when they came to the islands. They had looked forward to reuniting at Duff's surprise party.

Sorvini finally came out, holding Christy's hand and carrying an open bottle of pinot grigio by its neck. He remained trim and meticulous all these years later, in sharply pressed gray shirt and black trousers. "She coerced me into helping in the kitchen," he teased.

Duff stood to greet his old friend with a hug. "Gio, it's wonderful to see you. You look fit, for a man with my wife's lipstick on your cheek."

"Ah, Duff. I am still Italian, after all these years. How can she resist? As for my fitness, it is the healthy food and good wines."

Sorvini had fallen in love with Hawaii. Initially, on the *Malolo* cruise where he and Bergen encouraged the seagoing romance between Duff and Christy. "Remember, Christy, when the four of us — you and I, Bergen and Duff — spent a glorious day touring in that private car. The driver took us to Pearl Harbor, with a stop at the Pearl Harbor Yacht club."

"I do, Gio. Duff found that little sitting room with all the old photograph albums. Then we drove all the way to the North Shore. That was a long way. We should have taken the train, like most people. We must have followed the tracks for twenty miles or so."

"That's where we had lunch," interrupted Duff, at that charming Haleiwa Hotel. I still have a group photo of us at Haleiwa Bridge. It's over in the den."

Sorvini added, "The shoreline was breathtaking up there. Those massive waves were larger than any of us had ever seen. My personal highlight that day was our extraordinary dinner not far from here, at *The Willows*. What a special arrangement through Bergen's friend Moke at the Royal. The food was unique, of course. The baked pig was perfect, cooked all day underground, and fresh salmon, so moist wrapped in some sort of leaf. And the lovely music from the little ukulele band. But it was the friendliness we all felt, that sense of welcome. That was my lesson as a restaurant man, to always let guests know that they are special."

Their final guest found his way around the house, "I hope I'm not intruding."

"Marcus, welcome. Please meet our friends Masao and Gio. Of course we already warned you about them."

"I decided to join you despite the warning," said de Villiers as he shook hands and they all took their seats for lunch.

Christy had decorated the table with colorful place settings, and set each spot with her much-anticipated prawns. She passed a basket of baked bread and promised a light dessert. Then they raised their glasses and toasted, and continued the conversations.

Duff welcomed de Villiers, "We're glad you could join us Marcus. Can you relax with us for a few hours, without that infernal recording device?

"I have it with me, but I'll leave it off for now, to sort of cleanse the palate so to speak. Just some friendly con-versations, with no story lines or themes."

"You have come to the right place, Marcus. And speaking of cleansing the palate, this is a very nice wine, Gio," said Masao, as he tipped his glass toward Sorvini. "I enjoy Italian wines. We tasted some very nice ones in

Umbria. I visited just last year for the first time. It was a fascinating place."

"A very special place, indeed, Masao. I haven't been there for many years." Sorvini seemed to hold back whenever Italy was discussed. He had never talked about his younger days, even with Duff. And after he left Italy as a young adult, he seemed to have visited only once or twice.

"Were you raised in that region?" asked Masao.

"No, not in Umbria. Nearer to Lugano. A town called Bellagio. And you Masao," he teased gently, "please tell our new friend which island you are from."

"I'm from the island of Alameda, over in San Francisco Bay," knowing that his island heritage would get a laugh from his friends. "Marcus, I apologize for being sarcastic. Most of my customers assume I'm from Maui or Oahu, so my Alameda-island origin usually gets a laugh or two." Like Sorvini, Masao never said much about his childhood.

In response to a comment from Christy, about the popularity of Italian food, even in Hawaii, Sorvini said, "It was not always popular, my dear. There was a time when my Italian restaurants became very unpopular among certain patriotic Americans." Sorvini refilled Christy's glass, then Masao's and de Villiers's. He had brought three bottles of his favorite, and always made certain that Christy received special attention.

Sensing a story, de Villiers quietly adjourned to the lanai and returned with his recorder, turning it on. "If you don't mind, I do want to learn about your experiences."
Donald McPhail

"I have no objection." Sorvini's smile had become uncharacteristically sad. "I was nearly sent to prison, you see, for being an Italian. If it were not for our late friends Lloyd and Alita, and a certain senator from Massachusetts, I would have spent several years at a detention camp in Texas or New Mexico." Masao watched intently.

"It was 1942, and you remember that terrible time. Germany was taking over Europe and fought a bloody battle with Russia. German submarines were sinking Allied ships in the Atlantic, and were said to be patrolling America's eastern coast. And fascist Italy was aligned with nazi Germany. Of course even here, my friends, you were attacked by Japan."

Sorvini continued, glancing over at Masao in a kindly way, adding, "That was when President Roosevelt issued those three proclamations, 2525, 26 and 27, taking away the rights from Americans of Italian, German and Japanese descent. These were most shameful acts by a frightened government. I believe they did terrible things to you and your family, Masao, did they not?"

Masao nodded and spoke quietly, "Yes. Yes, they did terrible things." He lifted his own glass toward Sorvini, perhaps to acknowledge his statement, or to seek another refill. "I know something of Italian internment in America, which is what I believe you're leading up to. Germans, as well. Not just on the mainland. You know they interned Germans and Italians here in Hawaii? At Schofield and Kaneohe, and near to downtown, on Sand Island. Of course, Sand Island is where they imprisoned Japanese-Americans, too, beginning the day after Pearl Harbor.

There was another one, Honouliuli, located in a gulch over Central Oʻahu, near Ewa Town."

"No, I didn't realize that," Gio responded. "I didn't know about Sand Island and the other places. With such a large Japanese population here, so well known by families and teachers and friends, that makes no sense."

"It doesn't make sense," Masao agreed, "if you are rational. But there were many frightened and irrational people, as we learned. I would like to hear of your experience, Gio. Then I'll share my own story."

"I will finish quickly, my friend, since my incidents were simply frightening and disrespectful. I believe yours cut very deeply."

Masao nodded again, and remained silent.

"I mentioned the senator," Sorvini moved his hands, as he always did. "You know I have had restaurants in Boston, New York and Montreal for many years, that I visited regularly; and I occasionally traveled to Europe. Though I was technically a citizen of Italy at that time, I had filed the papers and studied. I was well on my way for American citizenship.

"And so, after a visit to our Montreal establishment, my flight landed on a typical hot and humid day in Boston, and I approached the customs desk. This was in July, 1942. When the customs agent asked me to show identification, I handed him my passport, which was Italian, something I had done many times without incident. However, this time the agent questioned me about some recent passport entries, of three months before, to London, Brussels, and Zurich. He asked, since I was in Switzerland, had

I been to Italy. And if so, why did it not show on my passport pages. I said that I had not been to Italy in fifteen years, and that my complete travel record was as shown.

"He called for a supervisor, and while I was standing there in front of many others, he called me a dago and a Mussolini sympathizer. I told him he had no reason to say such things, and appealed to his superior. Instead of cautioning his agent, the supervisor called over another officer and asked him to place handcuffs on my wrists, and that is what he did."

"Gio, you never told us this," Christy interjected. "What did you do?"

"I had little time, and thought about the only people I knew who might be able to assist me."

Duff nodded, "And you called Lloyd."

"I did. The officials put me in a small room at the airport, a filthy place adjacent to the men's toilet. When they finally allowed me a telephone call, I remembered that Lloyd had worked in government and I had his telephone number in my address book. He and Alita were not at their home, but an assistant asked me some questions and promised to contact them. I was in this room for over six hours, and was resigned to go wherever they planned to take me. I didn't know if my luggage was still with me, and had only a little cash. Then one of the officers returned and said that I was free to go on my way. That they would contact me again at my home in Boston."

"And did they contact you?"

"They did, on two occasions. The first was one week later, in a letter from the Department of Justice. They

stated that under Proclamation 2527 and the War Reloca-
tion Authority I was to report to their Boston facility on September 1, 1942, for transport to a prison camp in Fort Stan-
ton, New Mexico. I was to bring certain items with me, and
to make arrangements for the disposition of any property,
such as my home.”

"I can't believe it. How terrible.”

"I was powerless. But fortunately, that was not the
end of it. Two days later there was a knock on my door,
which I answered. It was a man, sort of a government-look-
ing person in a plain gray suit and brown hat. I knew he
represented some official organization by that formal way
he held himself. But then he removed his hat and asked to
come in for just a moment. My first reaction was fear, but
something told me to invite him in. Over coffee, he relaxed
a bit and told me that he was from Senator Connelly's office, and that my letter was a mistake. It should not have
been sent. Then he handed me a personal letter from the
Senator, that indicated a copy had also been sent to the
Justice Department. The senator apologized to me for my
inconvenience at the airport. He also acknowledged my
citizenship application, said that I was a resident of good
standing and that I would not be bothered again.”

"And were you?”

"No, dearest Christy. Not really. The matter disappeared, although I often felt I was being observed in my
Boston restaurant, or sometimes walking on the street. But
it made me cautious to travel, even to Canada.” Patting
Christy's arm, he added, "I have been in many dangerous
situations in my life, mostly when I was young in Italy. But I

have never felt as threatened as I did when those two customs agents captured me and took me into that little room.
I felt their hatred. I could almost smell it. And that they were
afraid of me. I also recognized that I was completely at
their mercy."

"Helplessness is a terrible and frightening feeling,"
asserts Masao.

"You have felt it, my friend. I can tell."

"Something else, Gio, that makes it difficult to describe. In the Japanese culture, we're taught not to talk
about ourselves. It's like bragging. Sometimes it is uncomfortable for me to describe what we went through, because
it was painful. Then there's this additional hesitation."

"Time has passed, Masao. You're here with friends.
If you are willing to share your memories, we are proud to
share them with you."

Leaning back in his chair and looking at us, one
after another, Masao openly shared the moisture in his
eyes, along with his story.

"The suspicion and insults began in December,
1941, at our home in Alameda. Right after Pearl Harbor
was attacked. That's when Proclamation 2525 made Japanese subject to arrest and detention. Then two months
later, on February 19, 1942, Executive Order 9066 took our
homes away and sent us to the internment camps. We
were helpless every day for three years, in our tiny allotted
space in Colorado."

Donald McPhail

CHAPTER THIRTY-ONE
Amache

Mama is not smiling and it makes him sad. It's morning, the time when she tries to make Masao laugh, because he has a hard time waking. This morning she is quiet.

At school, no-one is nice. Not his fourth grade friends, Ernest and Phillip, or even his teacher, Mrs. Pruitt. They look away and act like they are mad at him for something. Some say bad things to him. Pasted on Ronnie Wong's desk is a big piece of brown paper that his parents made, saying "I AM CHINESE" in big back letters.

Papa comes early to take him home. As they walk through the familiar neighborhood, he breaks into tears. "Papa, what is happening? Are you mad at me, too?"

"No, son. No," Papa stops and kneels, then wraps his arms around the boy. His soft jacket is warm and smells his kind smell. "I am not mad at you. Never think that."

Wiping his little face on papa's sleeve, Masao asks again, "What has happened?"

"Something very sad, Masao. We learned today that Japan did a terrible thing. Their airplanes dropped

bombs on a part of America, the Hawaiian islands, and our Navy ships. They hurt many people."

"Why did Japan drop bombs?"

"We do not know, Masao. But America is going to punish Japan."

"Papa," he says to his father, who sits in his usual chair at the kitchen table. "Papa," he repeats, then walks quietly into the kitchen as his mother looks down and con-tinues to fold the laundry.

"Yes, Masao," his eyes glisten as he looks at his son.

"The boys at school today, why didn't they talk to me? Even my friend Curtis. He called me a Jap." Masao turns in his chair, reaching up to fold his hands on the ta-ble, in the same way that way his father is holding his.

Papa stretches across and rubs the back of Masao's head, murmuring, "This is why I brought you home early today."

Masao recognizes other changes during the week. Papa no longer rides his bicycle to work. Instead, he walks with his son to school each morning and home again each afternoon, just when lunch period begins. Masao no longer attends afternoon class.

And Papa is dressed differently. He doesn't wear normal work clothes, with a necktie and jacket. And Mama doesn't smile. She is away all day, from early morning until dinner time. They don't go outside the house at night any more, to the Buddhist church where Papa always leads discussions. Now they stay away. Yesterday he heard

Donald McPhail

Papa say that Reverend Kono was arrested and taken somewhere.

He doesn't like school any more. The kids push him out of line during milk break, and always call him names. Masao is proud to be Japanese and he is an American. Why does "Jap" feel like such a bad word?

He sees a big black car parked in front of their house, under the Linden Street sign. He watches as Mama and Papa look at it from behind the curtains.

The next day, when he and Papa get home from school, Masao watches Mama put his clothes and books into a small suitcase. Papa looks sadder than ever. "We have to move now, Masao. We live too near to that Navy base, and they are making us move away. Here, put these on." He hands Masao his church clothes and a warm jacket.

Papa has his brown hat on, and they get a ride from Mr. Ita. He feels bad when they reach his small gray car and set their belongings into the trunk. Under her heavy overcoat, Mama is wearing her best dress with flowers on it. She is not smiling. He wants to run back to the house.

They have two suitcases filled with things, and a blue cloth bag full of clothes. It is crowded in the car, but Papa thanks Mr. Ita for this ride to the train station. When they drive along the streets of Oakland toward 16th street, there are many cars moving slowly in the same direction. All of them are full of people dressed in dark suits and overcoats, as if some are going to a wedding, others to a funeral. When they arrive at the station they see more Japanese families.

"We must board the Los Angeles train," Papa tells them. "It will take us to a town called Turlock." Then in a strange voice, "I don't understand." Masao has never seen his father cry before.

"They say we must assemble there. What does this mean? Then we are to move once more. To Colorado." He crumples the papers as if to toss them into the bin, then opens them again, smoothing them against his leg. "This is what our orders say."

The train is chilly and crowded, and the crinkled old seats smell dirty. There are children Masao's age, and younger ones. Very old people, too, and some Papa's and Mama's age. Most of the men wear their dress-up hats. People are friendly and sad. A girl in a pink and green plaid dress sits in front of him and offers a piece of hard candy, smiling shyly. Masao is glad that no-one is calling anyone bad names.

All the shades are drawn, and as the train rolls along it becomes warmer. He is sleepy and lies across Mama's lap, enjoying the good smell of her nicest dress.

When he wakes the train has slowed, and he straightens while Mama sits upright and stares straight ahead. Peeking between the shade and the corner of the window, he sees bright winter sunlight and open fields, like farms. And they are filled with green leafy plants. The metal wheels squeal to a stop and everyone is quiet. What will happen next?

Donald McPhail

Finally, an older man wearing a uniform comes into their car and shouts, "Everyone out. This is Turlock. Everybody out."

Waiting their turn, they move into the crowded aisle and help each other with suitcases and boxes and baskets. When he reaches the exit, Papa jumps down from the high bottom stair, stumbling on coarse gravel that smells of old grease and waste. He regains his balance and reaches up for Masao, setting him gently next to the suitcases and their basket. Then he reaches for Mama and carefully helps her down onto the track bed. Around them the ground radiates chill and dampness, and Masao wants to go home.

Three months later, Masao is perched next to his parents on another train. He is glad to leave Turlock, where it was cold and boring. They had to stay in tents at the fairground, sleeping on cots with their jackets on, and just waiting. There were kids to talk to but nothing fun to do. He and his parents walked together to a bigger tent to eat food he didn't like, like tinned vegetables, but they never had fresh fruit or ice cream. They got rice, too, but he didn't eat the other food.

For a few days Masao went to the tiny school where kids of all ages were crowded into a single small room. He was miserable. Then they were told to move again, to Merced, another farm town not far away, but they didn't stay there long. They slept in a big, dusty building where hundreds of other Japanese families sat on the dirt floor, or on their suitcases.

The Merced building smells like a place where horses or cows are kept. It's dusty, too, and there are spider webs. They need to stand in lines for everything. There aren't enough toilets and people have to go out into the cold fields or in the bushes nearby. They stand in line for food, plopped onto metal trays. Mama says nothing.

One morning everyone lines up again with all their belongings. Then they walk up a rickety wooden ramp and into a darkened train car.

Masao is glad to be back on the train. It might take them to a better place. And there are kids his age to play with. No-one knows how long the ride will be. Papa heard someone say they are going to Utah, and someone else said Colorado, and it could take three days.

They have to keep the windows covered, and no-one is allowed to raise the shades to look out. They talk and sleep, and conductors sometimes come and hand out pieces of bread and some apples and cups of water. Masao prefers something sweet, so he trades his bread to a boy for another piece of apple.

Some of the adults have packs of cards, and they ask if anyone wants to play. Others share old newspapers that they had in their suitcases, or books. Masao watches an older girl in a dotted blue dress playing with two shiny-white dolls that look Japanese, with cherry-red lips and black hair. They are dressed in colorful clothes, like the pictures of geishas that he used to see at home. Then her parents make her put the dolls back in the bag, quickly looking to be sure the conductor is not around to see.

Donald McPhail

Masao wonders how long three days will be on a train. His ears feel full, like they are expanding. And it is very cold. "We are in the mountains now," Papa says. "We will go only a little higher until the train will come down the other side, and our ears will feel better."

In a place called Denver, they get off and board another train, with older cars. This one looks like it hasn't been used for a long time. The leather seats are chilly and worn, with stains on them. "This will take us to our place," says Papa."

That was almost a whole day ago. Now Masao is hungry and he wants his own bed. Papa says, "Soon, now. Be patient." Mama looks straight ahead.

It is morning again and Masao watches out between the curtains, as they slowly pass a red brick building with a tall tower. "It says Pueblo," advises Papa. "We must be near." When Masao wakes once more, they are at a place they call Granada. He can see the wind whipping against the big weeds in the fields.

They wrap themselves in their warmest clothes against the sharp spring breeze. They have been away from home for nearly four months, now. Once again, they take their bags and get off the train, easing down onto the rocky rail bed just like everyone else. There are so many of them! It is chilly, like Turlock, but Masao is glad to be outdoors again. They all begin walking, carrying suitcases and bags, an endless line of tired travelers on a rough dirt road. It's the biggest crowd Masao has ever seen. All trudging quietly, patiently to the next place.

They move through the dust, and over rocks and bumps. Nothing is growing in the fields except for scraggly weeds. Finally they come to a fence with barbed wire on it, that has a sign.

"Amache," says papa.

"Ama chi? Is it Japanese?" Masao asks.

"Ama che," he repeats. "It is probably an Indian word."

Papa is quiet for a moment, looking at mama with a small smile. "Ama and chi are Japanese, but we don't use those words together. They are not polite." It is the first time Mama has smiled since they left Alameda. Masao doesn't ask what they mean.

They walk for a long time before they see the rows of low buildings that look like storage sheds elevated a lit-tle off the ground. "These must be for horses, Papa," said Masao.

They all look the same, hundreds of plain buildings with long, pointy roofs and small metal pipes sticking up. They have doors and windows along the sides, and are separated by dirt yards. Surrounding the buildings that lie off in the distance, there are more dusty dirt fields, with more dead weeds. No paved streets. No trees or gardens like at our house.

"No," says Papa quietly, "these are not for horses. This is our new home." He looks at Mama, then looks away.

Masao described his family's internment in detail, remembering the clothes that hung in his closet, the

Donald McPhail

crowded dining halls, and the dull teachers who assigned lessons in outdated schoolbooks. "Who would want to come to Amache, out in the middle of nowhere, to teach these Japanese children, the children of suspected spies? No matter that they are eager to learn and have been raised in American classrooms, pledging allegiance to the United States of America." Masao showed no anger or identifiable emotion, but his words were bitter. His own emotions were there, like surface scars covering old, deep wounds.

Christy quietly offered coffee or tea, as they moved out to the lanai, Masao, Gio, Marcus and Duff. It was nearly evening, with a slight breeze that felt good. Duff nudged Gio and offered a single malt that he had been saving. "It's a Tallisker, my friend. I think you'll like it."

"I was about to join you with tea," Masao smiled at Christy, "but Duff is very persuasive, you know. I think I'll join them in a wee dram."

"None for me, sorry to say," Duff asserted, "I'm on the mend. But I can still pour. How about you Gio, Marcus, Christy?"

Marcus nodded and remained quiet as he moved the recorder, observing Masao and Gio, clearly touched by Masao's experience. "You were describing the camp in Colorado," he prompted gently. "Amache, I believe you called it."

Masao tipped his tumbler toward Christy, then sipped. "Ah. That's very smooth. Beautiful, Duff." He continued his story, "Yes, Amache. In some respects, it wasn't so bad, believe it or not. During our two years there, we tried to make it like a home. All of us did. We had schools and sports teams. We planted vegetable gardens and flowers. There were church services, both Buddhist and Christian. We even had dances on the weekends, at the high school for us kids, and in the rec hall for adults."

Again, he raised his glass and looked each of us in the eyes, nodding. "But we all knew we were still in prison. We had American flags outside our school and the dining hall and library. Some of the families got visits from sons in U.S. Army uniforms, who had seen battle time in Europe. We were typical Americans. But we were still in prison."

Gio asked, "What was daily life like, at Amache?"

"It's late, but since you asked I will give a short version. We lived for over two years in tiny apartments, within single-story buildings. Each building had three families in separate units that were contained within long, low structures. They looked like Army barracks. There were drafty community bathrooms, with no doors or privacy. For meals, we had to wait in long lines outside a dining hall.

"We made it work, despite the close quarters, creating homes as much as we could. Flower gardens and yards out in the barren dirt. In open areas, we planted vegetable gardens, with enough squash, beans and fruit to provide decent meals in the mess halls, where we had convinced them to place our own Japanese cooks.

"My parents, all the parents, had the hardest part. Not just raising us kids. The American government excluded our parents from any of the community councils. They were first-generation Japanese, you see. Instead, they appointed us *nisei*, the second generation, to be the leaders,

even though we were so young. This distrust hurt our parents very much. They had lost their homes, lost their jobs,
lost their dignity, and now they lost their natural positions
as family leaders.

"My father withdrew after that, went very silent, like
my mother had. He found an outlet in woodworking and
wood sculpting, creating beautiful artwork from simple or-
ange crate containers, ones that were scrapped by the
kitchen staff. He removed the thick ends, and from those
he carved lovely birds and turtles in peaceful settings.
Quite beautiful. Now I have those in a special place, at
home in my living room.

"As for me, I did well enough in school, although
teachers were often not well prepared. As I said earlier,
they were not much motivated to inspire Japanese children
way out in a windswept corner of Colorado. So we taught
ourselves, through discussions and extra reading. There
were about thirty-five to a class. We studied, played sports,
flirted with the girls, went to church." He paused and
laughed, "Sometimes we flirted with the girls at the
church!" By lightening the mood, Masao seemed to gather
the energy to complete his story.

"We returned to Alameda in September, 1945, and I
went into junior high. Obviously, kids could see I was Japanese, and the nicer ones ignored me, or simply tolerated
me. There were others who were not so nice, who waited
every day outside the school exits, and chased me home.
If they caught me, they beat me up. Punched me in the
face, shoved me into the ground. They bruised me pretty

bad. Chipped a tooth. Each day I looked for new exits from the school building, and new routes home.

"As the year went along, things got a little better. But it took time. Remember, there were nearly two hundred thousand Japanese-Americans interned around the country. More families were able to return, so additional Japanese students came to our high school. Kids got used to us, and by the time I was in high school the bullying and chasing stopped. But I knew that the hatred stayed with some, and not just the boys. Girls can be pretty hateful too, you know," he winked at Christy.

"So to this day, I haven't forgotten the internment or the hatred, especially what it did to my mother and father. After that very first day, she never got over it. This happy woman never smiled again. I refused to let it make me bitter. In fact, I served in the U.S. Army for three years, right at the end of the Korean War. I was stationed in Okinawa as an MP, Military Police. We looked out for our soldiers over there, made sure they were safe, and that the Okinawans were safe from them. I tried to be fair with the soldiers, but also with the Okinawan civilians."

"Safe from our soldiers?" asked Christy. "I thought they were in Japan to keep the peace."

"Our base was in Okinawa, and the Japanese consider Okinawa to be different from Japan itself. Yes, they told us our assignment was to maintain peace," Masao nodded. "But if you know military men, you know they are like groups of men everywhere. Many of them get restless, drink a little too much sometimes. Some are very ignorant. Bullies. Not everyone in a uniform is a hero. There are many good men in our military, but there are thugs, too. Bad ones. That's why they needed MPs. Some of it was racial. Some of the white soldiers were openly disrespectful of the negroes, and of Japanese-Americans like me. And the Okinawans looked at me strangely, too. But Amache burned it into me. I never want to judge someone by what they look like. Here in Hawaii, there are lots of races and mostly people get along. They refer to their own *potagui* or *pake* or *haole* heritage, and poke fun at themselves. But it is not perfect here, either. People are sensitive. So I encourage tolerance whenever I can."

"Sometimes at the club," added Christy, "I hear people tease Bully about his *pake* way with money, though I think he's quick to claim he is mainly Samoan, with some Hawaiian."

Chuckling, Masao clarifies, "That's a compliment, Christy. Pake means Chinese, and people in Hawaii generally see the Chinese as thrifty, shrewd business people. Someone who refers to his pake-side is proud of his business sense." He shakes his head, "Though it can also mean stubborn or pig-headed. Not so complimentary. Nothing is just one way."

"And 'potagui'?"

"That's a jokester, sometimes. Good natured," he chuckles, thinking of his fun-loving airport manager on Maui. "There are lots of Portuguese in Hawaii, and they are often thought of as passionate or emotional, quick."

Duff chimes in, "You don't have to interpret *haole*, my friend. I've never heard it in a flattering way."

"That's probably true, Duff. Except when a white guy refers to himself as haole. Then it can be an admission of understanding, about the 'ugly American' types, who have often given caucasians a bad name."

"I wonder if my co-workers thought of me as a haole?"

Masao smiles broadly, "Duff, I know your people at Pan Am here in Hawaii. Pretty much all of them by name. I can tell you that none of them would ever look at you as a haole. They like you, and trust you. They know you're a fair man, and you've lived here for many years. So all of them look at you as 'Mr. Malone', or 'Duff', or 'that kanaka'. But I can tell you, they respect you as a leader, and most consider you a friend."

Donald McPhail

CHAPTER THIRTY-TWO

Peace

This will be a quiet Sunday, Duff told himself. Perhaps when Bergen is up and about, we can plan some sort of an adventure. Maybe Malia could come by and drive us out to Mokoleia or Waianae. Masao's story had saddened them all, and it nudged him toward introspection.

"What would it have been like," Duff asked himself questions he had been asking for nearly fifty years, "to grow up with a father? How would life have been different? Or to have a real mother, someone who hugged me." He had wrestled with these two issues for most of his long life. The absence of a father, and having a mother who was angry and bitter at her children, because they survived and her husband did not. Duff was gentle and understanding about nearly everything else. Why couldn't he let this go?

"Why did your father have to die?" she snapped at them, in the cold and angry voice she used when she drank brandy. Then the anger disappeared and she wept. They weren't even ten years old, for God's sake. Sandy was seven and Duff only five, and she told the boys it was their fault. Isn't that what she was saying, that they caused his death?

But she hadn't really said that. "He's dead and you're not," she said. It felt as if it were their fault. But maybe she meant, if she had a choice she would have preferred their dad. Maybe she didn't know what she was saying. Maybe she didn't realize how it felt when the two little boys heard her say these painful words.

Almost fifty years later, Duff started to loosen his grip on her. The hatred was subsiding. Most of his life had been good. He hated that early time, but he really wouldn't change anything, because the bad and the good had led him to this life with Christy, and Malia and Teo. He wouldn't change this life. Not for anything.

He realized now, his mother drank because she was afraid. She lost her husband, her deep and forever love. Likely she was in shock, some books suggested, or deeply depressed. He knew that she drank too much, because she had the illness that he had seen in so many people over the years. You could pick out the alcoholics in the airline business today, the ones who always enjoyed a martini with lunch, or who quietly slipped out in the warm mid-afternoon, for a bloody-mary or vodka over ice, over at the Moana bar.

As a cruise director, he always spotted the chronic drinkers early in the cruise. He knew they would require extra attention and care. And a few of them would create awkward scenes. With food and liquor flowing freely aboard ship, they found excuses to hang around the bar early in the day. Or they ordered two drinks at a time "to avoid inconveniencing the steward." Then gulped them down and ordered two more.

Donald McPhail

Some were simply gluttons, and may not have had the illness. But it was the personality change that identified true alcoholics. They ended-up arguing over trivial things, spouting gibberish instead of logic. Or instead of anger, they ended their evenings face down, snoring at their dinner places, until their companions asked a steward to help him back to their cabin. "Poor John is too tired from all the activity. Too much sun, I'm afraid."

Duff understood now that his mother was ill. How could a young woman not be depressed and afraid, suddenly left alone with two boys and a lonely, onerous life ahead? And he knew that alcohol was a depressant, that made a sad or frightened person even sadder or more afraid. But despite all that he knew, there were times when he still felt unworthy, even in his respected position with the airline, a little like that guilty, confused boy who might have caused his father's death.

Life was good now. Perhaps it was time to let mother go.

"Malone-san. Mr. Malone," he heard Yoriko's frightened voice from the outer edge of a daydream. "Would you and Mrs. Malone come please, to help me?"

"Christy! Are you in there?" he shouted to the kitchen window.

"Yes, Duff! Here! What's wrong? Are you okay?"

"I'm all right. Yes. It's Yoriko. Something must be wrong with Bergen."

"You stay still, Duff. Sit there." Christy dashed onto the path toward the cottage, while Duff stubbornly made his way along. When he arrived, Yoriko was at the door and her face was buried in Christy's shoulder, with the two strong women sobbing quietly against each other.

"Christy?"

"He didn't wake, Duff. He's gone. Thank God it was peaceful."

"Thank God."

"You will want to see him, Duff. He was such a friend."

"Malone-san, will you take this," she handed Duff a moist white face-cloth. "Please moisten his lips, in the traditional way. It is 'water of the last moment'."

"Yes," Duff was off slightly, seemed confused. Then he said, "Of course, Yoriko. I will do this." He approached his old friend and gently touched the cloth to his lips. Then he removed the cloth and leaned down to kiss him on the forehead, with a barely audible, "Farewell, old friend."

Christy gently took the cloth and handed it to Yoriko, then she kissed the cold forehead, as well.

For the next few minutes, Yoriko went about a ritual for which she was well prepared. First she brought a small table to the bedside. On it she placed a simple cluster of white pikake from their garden, accompanied by a bowl-sized hollow stone containing two or three pinches of fragrant incense, and a small white candle, like a votive.

They withdrew to just outside the door, so they would not disturb her.

"We need to let his doctor know, dear," Christy reminded him quietly, "or may I do that?"

"Please, you do it. I need to sit over there for a moment."

Donald McPhail

Yoriko approached as he started to walk away, and whispered, "Mr. Malone. What should I do, please? Will he be buried here? May I stay until the funeral?"

"Of course, Yoriko. Of course you can stay. You must continue to live here. We will place his ashes back there, in the yard. With a small stone."

"Thank you, Malone-san. He will like this. He loves this place."

Duff took her hand, "You can help us, my dear. First, let us talk about the exact spot."

"He spoke of this with me, some months ago when he was feeling much pain."

"How about right there? Over in the back, near the mango trees?"

"Yes, there I think. He loved this house. He loved you and Mrs. Christy so much."

"Good, then. This is a start, Yoriko. We will need your help deciding many things. But let us talk about that later. Make no mistake, we want you to remain here. This is your home."

Donald McPhail

CHAPTER THIRTY-THREE
Chu Lai To Laos and Back

"You know what napalm does when it hits the ground and splatters somebody?" Teo sounded combative.

"I told you, man. I just try to hit the target." Riley hated it when Teo got this way.

"You know what it's made of?"

"Christ, Teo. I'm trying to concentrate on my book here."

"It's jellied gasoline, with white phosphorus mixed in to keep it burning. You can't shake it off your hands or your body, and it sticks to you until it burns clear down to the bone."

"Why do you do this, man? We don't make the rules. We just carry them out."

"As for rules, doesn't it frustrate you, Riley, that the world knows we're at war in 'Nam, but nobody knows we're bombing the shit out of Cambodia and Laos?"

His lanky wingman, once his Academy roommate, nodded and wondered what had gotten up Teo's butt today. He'd been irritable for two weeks now. In fact, today was pretty mellow compared with the day before. He should never have taken those R&R days in Bangkok. "You get ahold of some more American newspapers, pal?"

Teo shook his head, "Care package came, with a book in it, about World War Two. My parents thought it would be good reading. Obviously, they hadn't read it first. Says we napalmed Tokyo five months before dropping the atom bombs on Hiroshima and Nagasaki. I don't think my folks have even heard of napalm."

"So what's your point?"

"It was 1945. We killed a hundred thousand Japanese, nearly all civilians. We incinerated them with napalm. You know how many we killed a month later, with the A-bombs?"

"Tell me."

"Those mothers-of-all-bombs killed 130,000, only thirty thousand more."

"And your point?"

"We never hear about the hundred thousand in Tokyo. Why not? Why didn't that end the war? It was just as deadly, and people were just as dead. Why create new atomic weapons, if we already knew how to obliterate people like this?"

"Jesus, Teo, this is killing me. You should have hired one of those cute guides on R&R, like Murphy and Koslo did. They were sweet chickies, and those guys came back a lot happier than you."

Calming down, "Bangkok was okay," Teo shook his head, "but not everyone has to get laid. It's a place to get caught up on the world."

Donald McPhail

"Depends on what you're interested in, I guess. Murph and Kos had been away from pussy way too long. That's what they were interested in."

"I know. I'm a prude, man. I don't see risking disease or screwing somebody I don't even know."

"An honorable man! Maybe you should write to my sister, then," laughed Riley. "She was hot for you during June week, after I set you up."

"Yeah, well I'm sorry that didn't work out. My head was already at flight school."

"I remember that. You were in a hurry to get to 'Nam. How's that look now? You sound like a guy who wants out."

"Just about. I hear this thing could be over soon, then we'll all get out. Meantime we're dropping tons of shit on those poor country people. And they're not even our enemies. We're doing to them what we did to those poor fucking civilians in Tokyo."

Since 1964, America's official war was in Vietnam, but it had edged over into the two neighboring countries. Teo saw the rumors in the newspapers, and denials by Nixon and Kissinger. It pissed him off that they were hiding their raids into Laos and Cambodia from the public. Give it a purpose. Either make it official, or stop the devastation. For Annapolis grads who were raised in the idealistic fifties and sixties, the Academy's honor code meant something, and these secret missions attacked their character. The pilots knew where they flew, and where they dropped their deadly loads. Maybe it was naive, but what about ethics and integrity? Obviously, the U.S. government isn't bound by the Academy honor code, but what about international law?

Teo prepared for his Vietnam assignment the same way he had prepared for the Academy, for football and for flight school. He studied the material. He knew America had been in Indo-China since the fifties, helping French troops maintain control of their Asian colonies. Hell, America had paid millions to back the French government. He also remembered what he'd read and heard during plebe year back in 1961, when the North Vietnamese Navy was playing chicken with American destroyers in the Gulf of Tonkin. Those incidents barely made headlines, but it laid the groundwork for the next game, and an excuse for war. What were we doing there? Why were they messing with us? They were just provoking us, and our government took the bait.

Teo and his Academy classmates grew up without wars. They were born in the early forties, and World War II was finished in 1945. Korea hadn't been talked about much in high school. There were stories about General MacArthur's "Old Soldiers Never Die" speech, and his tiff with President Truman. But that war was far away in Asia, and Teo and his classmates were only little boys then.

In 1961, Teo and his Annapolis analytical geometry teacher, a civilian named Davidson, were the only two people in the classroom regularly arguing against going to war in Southeast Asia. Predictably, patriotism and the feeling that a war would speed these future officers to higher

Donald McPhail

rank formed the main argument favoring immediate military action against the remote country. "We'll kick their ass and be out of there in six months!" was the popular boast.

Sure as hell, the war started officially in '64, the result of a more famous Bay of Tonkin confrontation. America was still there in '69, and our country has gone crazy.

The insanity started back when Kennedy was shot, and it's all gotten worse. The racists got Martin Luther King last April, and the world was shocked. We hoped that Bobby Kennedy would heal the country, make it fair. And get us the hell out of this war. Then he was assassinated by some kook, Sirhan-something, last June. And here in 'Nam it's weirder and crueler and more fucked-up than ever. Troops are still dying and U.S. bombs are destroying the people we're trying to save. And we're battering two non-combatants, Laos and Cambodia.

America had no official presence in either country, but the Ho Chi Minh Trail went through them both, providing a powerful path for the enemy -- North Vietnamese Army and Viet Cong -- to move supplies and troops into the official South Vietnam battle zones.

This trail was one of the enemy's greatest assets, named after their Communist leader, who had been a U.S. ally and once saw America as a beacon of freedom and liberty. During the Second World War he helped U.S. intelligence in the battle against Japan. Ho Chi Minh quoted Thomas Jefferson at a ceremony in Hanoi celebrating Vietnam's liberation from the French, while the band played the Star Spangled Banner. But we pushed him away out of fear of communism. In this world of broken

promises and political contradictions, his belief in land re-
form and socialistic views distanced him from American
political leaders and he was drawn to the Soviets.

Ho Chi Minh Trail was 1,000 miles long, and big
enough for bicycles and enemy troops. Hidden beneath
the trail's surface was an ingenious network of intercon-
necting tunnels, also nearly a thousand miles long. They
were meticulously dug over a period of years. The tunnels
housed radio and communications facilities, food,
weapons, medical aid stations and living areas. Tens of
thousands of enemy soldiers were hidden in those tunnels.

Our mission was to destroy them in a firestorm of
napalm, which was designed to ooze into the underground
channels as the intense heat sucked oxygen from any
open space, suffocating whoever was inside.

Teo's bombing session would last all day. Six different sections were assigned, of two planes each, with each
section flying in consecutive launches. Teo and Riley and
the other pilots killed time in a cramped house-trailer within
an easy sprint to their F-4's. Sweating in the grungy boxes,
they passed the time the same way Teo's Navy football
squad had in the locker room before their Saturday games,
with combatants pacing, sleeping, writing notes, crapping
or barfing until game time. Different players had different
waiting routines.

Though this was a more serious mission, the pilots'
wait lacked the pregame emotion of a big ballgame. Over
here it was a familiar routine, since Teo and his flying team
went through the sequence several times a week. At the

same time, the enemy was smart and unpredictable, and far more lethal than any team he had ever played against.

Teo flew F-4 Phantoms, a swift and precise fighter and attack jet, with a thousand mile range and top speed of fourteen-hundred miles an hour. His flight territory stretched from the top edge of South Vietnam to the Gulf of Tonkin at the north, and west into Laos and Cambodia. Assignments could range from troop cover to air support, to bombings of all kinds.

This was a quick and powerful plane, and they were targeting the Trail in Cambodia. Firepower included rockets, missiles, and high drag bombs up to 2,000 pounds. They also carried napalm. One aircraft in the section was loaded entirely with napalm cannisters.

The Ops phone rang and they darted from the small trailer to the F-4s, launching into stormy weather. They expected to be back in thirty minutes or so, start to finish. Teo knew he would incinerate hundreds of square miles of countryside that camouflaged a suspected tunnel entry point. Direct hits would collapse the tunnels, and the intense heat would smother and incinerate everyone in the vicinity.

Teo was the Section Lead for two F-4s, himself and Riley. They were first up to drop their loads on VC tunnels that were suspected of heavy traffic. They took off into heavy rain showers and low visibility, and it was crappy all the way to the target area. They needed to hook up with their Tactical Air Controller, TAC, who would fly a slower, lower propeller craft that would mark the target with black smoke, then adjust for subsequent runs. TACs were a unique breed. They were brave and resilient, and absolutely essential to the mission.

Ceiling was down to about fifteen-hundred feet, and the rains continued. The terrain was level in the immediate area, though Teo knew they needed to pull up quickly to avoid crashing into mountains after dropping their loads.

He was tense and alert, flowing with pregame adrenaline. He spotted the black smoke marker, so he dove to a thousand feet. He knew the TAC would draw fire, and so would he. In split-seconds he had to make flat dive angles and keep the pull-offs low, looking out for Riley and their TAC. Teo was sweating profusely as Riley dropped back to trail him in, allowing enough time for Teo's drop and pull-off.

He spotted the marker smoke about 150 yards from the target, and heard the TAC report a few hits from automatic weapons. He stayed with it, and got a good fix on his target. Then he darted in and dumped two cans of napalm, pulling off and maneuvering for another run. He had heard what could have been a couple of hits to his plane, but the F-4 was operating well as he completed the turns. Riley followed Teo and obliterated the TAC's smoke, and stayed behind him.

As he began his final run, Teo heard from the TAC that his first drop had been right on target. The weather had improved so he had a clearer run this time, and knew he would hit the next one cleanly. Again the TAC marked with smoke and Teo dropped the napalm, pulled off and reduced speed to reconnect with Riley. He was still sweating from the heat and the exertion, and he cringed as he returned to base with the thought of the burning enemy soldiers.

Teo and Riley got back to their hootch, tired and in need of hosing-down. As always, a primitive shower would have to do. Then they could cross the bridge and find a cold one, or maybe a dozen, at the O Club. Riley went out scrounging for soap, since the communal outdoor shower never had any.

As he peeled off his salty shirt, Teo saw the envelope on his bunk. Since mail and care packages rank higher than anything else, at least for him, he decided the beers could wait. He saw a fat brown envelope with a Cleveland address, from an old Academy teammate, Frank Wikman. Frank was a talented flanker-back, with a quick wit and liberal persuasion. Teo and Frank were mostly on the same side in the midshipmen political discussions, and he was just as crushed as Teo when President Kennedy was shot. They traded letters every November 22, reminding each other to "keep the faith". The deaths of King and Bobby Kennedy followed, and any tiny gleam of hope was obliterated. Pain. Disbelief. Anger. For Teo and Frank, it got stuck on anger.

Frank had opted for Supply Corps after graduation, and had done most of his time in San Diego. He hadn't been in battle. He hadn't fired a shot in anger. But he was still cynical and pissed. He just finished his Navy obligation, and was home in Cleveland, struggling. He was trying to find a civilian company that might actually understand how Supply Corps translates to budget analyst, financial planner, comptroller or any number of leadership jobs.

Civilians had little appreciation for military skills. That's why some of their classmates were starting their own companies, usually making weapons or military communications systems.

Duff's envelope was stuffed with a folded-up newspaper, Frank's home paper, the *Plain-Dealer*. Around the outside, likely in case the censors were checking, was a sports page from November 2, when the Browns beat the Cowboys 42-10, and Frank had circled the box score in red, scrolling on the margin, "Good News!! 1st year in NFL. Roger was 6 for 11 today!!" He referred to Staubach, who had also served his Navy active duty, and was working to find playing time with the Cowboys. They all tracked his progress, and were genuinely proud.

Hidden inside the sports page was another newspaper and folded pages torn from *Life Magazine*. These were recent articles about the war, and Frank had scrawled "Bad News!! More sickening truth! Happened 20 months ago. Published only now!!"

<u>My Lai Massacre: Cameraman Saw GIs Slay 100 Villagers</u>
By JOSEPH ESZTERHAS
(c) Thursday, Nov. 20, 1969, The Plain Dealer
U.S. Army troops "indiscriminately and wantonly mowed down" civilian residents of a tiny South Vietnamese hamlet on March 16, 1968, a former Army photographer has told The Plain Dealer. Along with his eye-witness account, the former photographer has made available to The Plain Dealer a set of photographs taken at the village. They are being reproduced today on two pages of The Plain Dealer. This is the first publication of the photos, which also are in the hands of U.S. Army authorities investigating the sensational accounts of the village deaths.

Donald McPhail

Teo unfolded the newspaper, and glossy photos fell out, from Life Magazine. They were horrifying. Dead bodies strewn along a dirt road, taken by an Army photographer. Piles of bodies in a field, mostly women and naked children, all dead. A caption described an old, exhausted woman in front of a young mother who held a baby in her arms. They were simply frightened people, desperately afraid for their lives. This was a grandmother who had defended her daughter against American soldiers who were going to rape her. The daughter was unbuttoning her blouse as ordered. Later, the women and their babies were shot dead, not by some foreign barbarians, but by our own American soldiers.

Mothers and daughters had been raped, and tiny babies shot and bayoneted, and it took twenty months for this horrific massacre to reach the public. How many more atrocities had Americans committed since then, attempting to save this forlorn country? The photos were graphic and disgusting. Teo went outside and threw up into the rocks.

Donald McPhail

CHAPTER THIRTY-FOUR

Bergen's Memorial

"The services could be held here in the yard," Christy gently led the conversation, knowing that Duff was far off balance since his friend's death. She knew how he would be, with his own mortality seriously threatened by the heart attack, and now his old friend gone. "Do you think he would want his ashes to be here, among the flowers, shaded by his favorite mango and avocado trees?"

"Yes," he murmured, and continued almost haltingly, "This place was special to him." Dreamily, like an old man who isn't certain if he is repeating himself, he looked around. "Did I tell you? Yoriko and I came here, and selected the same spot."

"No, dear," she said patiently. "You didn't tell me, but that's a perfect place." Duff seemed to be examining the entire yard, perhaps wondering where he would want to be when he died. "There are only a few people to include at the memorial," she continued as she watched him. "Yoriko. Gio, Masao and the children. Malia will want to say a few words about her favorite uncle. Teo will too, if he can get here."

Will he come? It was nearly five years since he graduated into the war, and she didn't even know how long

Teo wanted to serve. Would he stay in the military? "Duff. Dear. Did you contact the command people at Kaneohe?"

"Not yet. I plan to call them this afternoon." He eased onto the wooden bench, next to the yellow hibiscus, slowly rotating his ankle, as he seemed to do more often. "It's interesting, isn't it? So many of our friends are gone now. My brother. Lloyd and Alita, of course. They were not so young when we met them. Ariyoshi-san. I guess Bergen didn't know Paul Chen very well. Ah, and my old boss, Commodore Patterson."

"They were good friends, Duff. And except for Paul, they all lived full lives." Then, gently, "Why don't you try the Marines to see if Teo might get emergency leave?"

Chu Lai, 1970

"Riles, I'm tired of talking about it, man. My mind's made up, and I'm not extending. This shit is not right, and I'm tired of the lies. The CO just told me I got leave. My folks need me home for a funeral. Then I'm getting out."

"Teo," Riley throws his wadded shirt onto he bunk and closes the tent flap to keep out the sun, "They're offering you PG school, man. Then you can write your own ticket. With your rating, you'll be a light colonel in three more years."

"I'm not going to Monterey, and I'm not extending. We read about My Lai last year and I couldn't leave with another year to go. My Lai happened in '68, and it took almost two fuckin' years before the Army admitted it. Now this!" He slides the wrinkled newspaper across the bunk. "Now they're killing college kids."

Donald McPhail

"They were protesting the war, man. It turned ugly and the cops panicked. You know how those hippies hate us."

"They don't hate us, Riles. They hate the war. They hate the lies that Johnson and Kissinger and all those so-called leaders are hiding behind. So, I'm taking leave. The orders came through, that I need to get to a funeral next week. Then I got thirty days, and I'm putting in the resignation papers. I'm half-way tempted to fly to Kent State and join those protests."

"Jesus, Teo. Get a grip. Don't burn your fuckin' bridges with the brass."

Teo looks over, with a grim smile that makes Riley nervous.

"That's right, Riles. I won't burn any bridges, or piss anyone off. Not just yet. My required time is nearly over. Any military honors I've earned will help me tell the story."

Teo arrived in Hawaii after midnight. He rode in the second seat of an F-4 that was being ferried back to Hawaii, then grabbed a taxi home. The $100 ride didn't phase him. He was just glad to be out of 'Nam. It didn't matter much where he was. Just out of the war, is all. As he rode along familiar streets, he realized he is not really out of this war.

The absurdity won't go away. You grow up in a peaceful country, the best in the world. Live in a place like Oahu, go to a good school. You're taught ideals, like loving your neighbor as yourself, and you learn how to get along with people of all kinds. Not just Filipinos or Potaguis or

*Japanese. But tough blalahs from Waimanalo and Wa-
ianae. Kids raised in Kaka'ako. But you learn to get along
with tough guys and old people and little kids, because living this life in Hawaii is pretty nice.*

*But what happened? Riley and I got through the
petty distraction of plebe year, and still had those naive,
idealistic feelings. More of them, in fact, because the
school songs, the camaraderie, the shared competition
turned into big pride. We were proud to be members of the
Brigade that began back in 1845.*

*Then the war came on. Small incidents exploded
into attacks and bomb-shelters and dead bodies. Instead
of kicking their asses, we bogged down. The grunts killed
the Charlies in the jungles, or along the rivers. Jet jockeys
killed them in tunnels and small villages, where the VC
kept women and children so close that we burned them all
up together. And they were killing us.*

*When did American ideals turn into murder? When
did strategies turn into knee-jerk reactions and pay-back.
When did pay-back turn into brutal stabbing of naked babies, and wanton raping of helpless mothers? So much for
ideals. But what about naive?*

*Am I still naive, to think I can join those hippie pro-
testers and change anything? Is this just another knee-jerk
reaction? Does it matter right now? I have to do something,
and it sure as shit isn't going to be sitting in the sun, sipping mai-tais.*

"Welcome home, dear Teo," Christy exclaimed,
hugging her exhausted son, wiped-out from the flight and

lack of sleep. She couldn't stop shaking her head, and touching him to be sure he was real. "I'll fix something to eat, while you two get to know each other again."

Still in his khaki uniform, wrinkled from the flight, and in need of sleep, Teo sensed his dad approaching.

"More hugs, son," Duff reached up and put his arm around Teo. "You know how it is here in Hawaii."

Rubbing his stubbled face and with eyes moistening, Teo allowed himself to be welcomed and appreciated. "Glad to be here, dad. I'm sorry about Uncle Bergen."

"We're glad you wanted to come. And don't be sorry for Bergen. He told me many times, he was ready to go. Like me, he believed in a better place, when it's time."

Teo nods, but doesn't respond.

"I know you just got home, there is something I'd like you to do, son, if you're up to it. There's a time factor." Duff cautioned, "And I want you to think a moment before you answer."

"I don't understand, dad," Teo laughed abruptly, "It's just a memorial. I'll be glad to give a little talk about him. I loved Uncle Bergen."

"It's more than that, Teo. Come with me a minute," Duff stood and walked back toward the small house, motioning him to follow. "Yoriko, are you inside or out?"

"Out here in the garden. Out in Bergen-san's corner."

Teo reached down and hugged Yoriko, lifting her off the ground slightly. "Ah, Yoriko, I am so sorry about Uncle Bergen."

Looking confused, "Oh no, Teo. Please don't be sorry. Bergen-san lived a full life, much of it quite beautiful. He talked about you many times."

"I didn't mean..." Teo stammered.

"No. Please. He is very happy now. He and his friend Ariyoshi-san will be laughing together again, and will be very glad to see each other."

Gently, Duff said, "Yoriko, I believe you were going to ask Teo to help you, as a tribute to his uncle."

"Would you please come with me to the little house now, and help me with the washing ceremony? Bergen-san needs to be prepared for his next place."

"Of course I will help you," he hesitated, "if that's what is needed."

Teo followed Yoriko into the darkened front room, where drapes were drawn and candles provided the only light.

As she shut the front door, "Teo, do you know about the cleansing?"

"I don't, but if you tell me I will do my best."

CHAPTER THIRTY-FIVE
Cleansing Ritual

"We will take these damp cloths and carefully wash Bergen-san. We can rinse them in those bowls. Then we take that soft material over there and fill each place on his body, his openings. I think you say 'oh-ri-fis'." She gestured to a white silken gown, "We will dress him in that kimono, and then he will be cremated." She asked gently, "Can you do this?"

Dutifully, Teo nodded and rolled up his sleeves.

At first he was afraid to touch the cold, dead body of his aged friend. *I don't want to do this.* Given no choice but to keep his word and help her, Teo concentrated on the task itself.

He gently touched the cloth to Bergen's ankle, badly scarred from heavy blows. He took a deep breath and moved to the feet, washing them the way a father might bathe his infant son for the very first time, spreading the toes, then wiping around the ankles and calf. Bone-thin legs bore harsh scars, where lashes must have cut him. Batons or cudgels must have smashed the tibia and shin. Teo diligently rinsed the cloth and resumed, behind the knee to the bend in back, moving to the thigh, around the back to the withered front. Then the decision, how to wash his genitals. Do I skip them and move further up, as Yoriko moves down from the shoulders and chest?

Like a parent, Teo knew this was real, and anything but disgusting. It was a responsibility. It was also a tribute to his Uncle Bergen.

"I can do this," he told himself. He dipped the cloth again into the warm water, squeezed it nearly dry and carefully took Bergen's shriveled penis and wiped it, moved to the fold of the buttocks and cleaned gently and thoroughly. This is where Yoriko would place the ritual cloth.

This led him up the spine to the small of the back, until his hand met Yoriko's and they bumped softly, each looking up, gently startled from concentration, or meditation, or wisps of thoughts about where our inner person goes. *Where does it go? Will mine go there? How is there room for so many souls? Yoriko mentioned "crossing the river". What does this mean?*

It was barely daylight, and Teo paced like a cat, carrying a heavy floral mug with him along the lanai, following the rails from one end to the other. He had slept for four hours, but was too hyped to stay in bed. Duff, awake earlier than usual, sat still, his eyes following his son's nervous path. Two days home, and Teo still couldn't let it go.

"You want to talk about it?"

"No, dad. I don't. Not yet."

"Just tell me if it's something I should worry about. Is it us? Is it your health?"

Donald McPhail

"It's not you or mom, and I'm healthy dad. You can quit worrying."

"All right. Let me say just this. Whatever it is that's bothering you, if it is not us, please don't take it out on us. At least be civil to your mother. We're both very worried about you."

Teo rubbed his eyes and turned away. "I'm sorry, dad. I get angry now, for no reason. At least none that I can talk about. I don't mean to take it out on you and mom. There are things about this war I can't tell you about. About me. But I plan to do something about it." Then he started, "Dad, why are we killing them? Why are we destroying their countries? Vietnam, Cambodia, Laos. Who knows where else? And why are politicians lying to us? Burying the truth. Is it because we're pissed off at Russia? Or China? Or are politicians simply trying to keep American voters afraid enough to reelect them?"

This is what worried Duff. The intensity, the absolute certainty. Teo had always been an idealist, most of all when he was at Annapolis. As a Marine pilot his ideals were even narrower and stronger. But what had the war done to him? These opinions were truly angry, and would get him in serious trouble with his commanders.

"What about here in America?" Teo said. "Two days ago I read about killing those kids at Kent State, and it made me want to puke. That's why I'm leaving. My time is up and I already resigned my commission. I'm going to San Francisco. I can see what is happening with the protests, talk to people, tell them that not all of us are killers. Help them find some peace."

Duff accepted the anger, even if he couldn't begin to imagine what his son had seen and done. He had that look in his eyes, wild and distant, same as the kids on R&R over on Kalakaua Avenue. He wondered about drugs. He wanted to prevent Teo from leaving again, joining the protesters. But he didn't disagree with his intentions.

"You know, dad. I'm really not crazy. Not yet," Teo said, and relaxed, leaning back against the rail. "When I read about these things, the dots have to connect, you know?"

"I'm not sure I'm following you. Go on."

"Let's look at it. Uncle Bergen, an American from Germany, was tortured by the Japanese. Uncle Masao, a Japanese-American, was imprisoned by the Americans for being Japanese. China was bombed and citizens raped and killed by the Japanese. Uncle Gio, an Italian-American was threatened and followed by the Americans, for being Italian. When you visited Johannesburg, you saw how twelve million people with white skin controlled twenty-five million people who had black or brown skin. They still do. And America has been bombing and killing in Vietnam for nearly ten years. Why are we doing all this?"

"I don't know, son. I understand your examples. I see the dots, and there may be some common link. I just don't know what it is."

"A common denominator, dad. I wish I knew what it was. The theme running through all of these killings. It isn't skin color, and it isn't national culture, or political and economic systems. Our people killing those Asians are every color, with way too many of our soldiers poor and black or brown. The Japanese and Chinese who killed each other in Nanking are technically Asian Same color, according to most people, but of different cultures and races, and with different political systems.

"Our mainly-white country imprisoned Japanese-Americans during World War II as if they were enemies, as we once imprisoned or killed native Americans. But we also imprisoned Germans and Italians, who are mostly white. In South Africa it's whites divided against anyone who is not.

"There's plenty of evidence that every country in the world has bad people, and good ones. Black despots like Kaunda and Nkrumah, white ones like Hitler and Stalin and Mussolini. Asians like Mao and Tojo."

Teo stopped for a moment, then went on, nodding his head slowly as he reached some important conclusions. "You know what? I'm convinced that the common denominator is male dominance. In business, government, the military. Men making the decisions. Every one of these damned wars and prisons and atrocities was decided by men. Implemented by men. That's the common denominator."

Duff waited to see if there was more, then he said, "Oh, it's one common denominator, but there could be others, son."

Teo remained quiet, so Duff continued, "I suspect that most of the people in power, the ones financing political leaders, were also wealthy. Germany, Japan, China, Italy, Russia. Even America. The elite. The wealthy and the military together can make some very bad decisions. And while it is more an effect than a cause, it seems to me that another common denominator is 'civilized people doing uncivilized things', because they believe the propaganda that justifies it. Is there such a thing as a just war?"

Teo hesitates, "There is no such thing as a just war, dad. There hasn't been one, except maybe World War II. It's all about power. Money. Land. The Japanese leaders justified going into Manchuria, because they were more technically advanced than the Chinese. Japan needed land for their millions of people pressed into a small space. Germans were technologically advanced and Hitler needed *Liebensraum*, space, in Poland and Czechoslovakia and Latvia for his millions. Japan and Germany also wanted the natural resources for their war industries. But America is also technologically advanced, and here's where it falls apart. Why did Americans attack the North Vietnamese? Land? Minerals? Religion? We're told it was to hold back communism coming from the USSR and China. But how can any of this justify such brutality?"

"Let's thank God, Teo, that civilized people do civilized things, too. You know that. It's what you're doing now. Standing up and protesting against powerful people who are lying, or inhumane, or selfish. That's civilized, to me. It's what those kids were doing at Kent State and Berkeley and so many campuses. Or what that singer Joan Baez, that boxer Cassius Clay, are doing. What Pete Seeger, Ghandi, Jesus were doing. Protesting wars and advocating peace." Duff lifted his hand, to add a final thought. "I can't begin to understand what you've done, and what you've

Donald McPhail

been through. Obviously, you are struggling. I respect that. But please don't do anything foolish."

"It's something I have to do, dad. I'm staying here for three more nights, until after Uncle Bergen's memorial. Then I have a job to do over on the mainland. I'll be gone a month or two. I should have things figured out by then."

"Have you told your mom?"

"No, dad. I was hoping you'd do it for me."

"Come here, son." Duff moved toward Teo. "I know you're too old for so many hugs, but I need one anyway."

Teo stood still, arms at his side, then turned and accepted the embrace, letting Duff wrap his arms around him. "It's okay, dad. I have a plan, and I won't hurt anyone."

"I'll tell your mom. Tonight. Then she'll want some hugs, too."

"Welcome, dear friends, to this remembrance of our friend, a beloved member of our family, Werner Bergen." Duff stood at the edge of the lawn, with his back to the garden where the red hibiscus and bright yellow ilima provided a regal background. In front of him were just seven other people, seated in two casual rows.

"Bergen passed away a week ago and I think we all feel he is with us here in spirit." He glanced toward the corner of the yard, at the white pedestal containing a white porcelain urn. Next to it was a framed black-and-white photo of Bergen, smiling confidently, perched atop a camel with the Sphinx clearly shown behind them. "Thank you, Yoriko, for creating this memorial, and for your extraordinary love for Bergen-san.

"It's just the eight of us here today, Bergen's dear friends. We constitute his remaining family, really. Along with a handful of colleagues in remote parts of the world, we are his only living family."

Duff looked up and smiled his gentle smile, as he looked at Christy, then Malia and Teo. He nodded at Yoriko, then Sorvini, Masao and de Villiers. "Mr. Ozawa could not join us, as he is unable to leave his house these days. But he knows this garden better than any of us, and he sends his love and respects to us all, most especially to Bergen.

"We are blessed to be surrounded by Bergen's beautiful things here. These are his houses, and we're seated in his lovely gardens beneath his favorite mango and avocado trees. His ashes will remain here. Typical of our friend, he has given all of this to us, to keep and enjoy, and to share with one another.

"Now Yoriko would like to say something. She was Bergen's closest friend. He often told me that she was the daughter he always wanted."

Yoriko rose slowly, briefly straightening her white kimono, then raised her chin and strode to the front, calmly facing her friends. "I am honored to be here with you, to remember our wonderful Bergen-san. Most of you already know he was a father to me. I must tell you, my first father was not a kind man. Not educated. A hard worker, but very cruel. Bergen knew this, and for nearly twenty years he was my kind father. Very loving and generous. He taught me to be more open and to speak what I mean. He helped me to read English books, and to write. He worked with me in the garden. He also taught me how important it is to love others, even our enemies. He taught me how to survive, after they took my brother Koji into the army to die in China.

"Bergen was taken from us in 1942, from the home he shared with Ariyoshi-san and me. They took him to Omori prison camp and beat him. But Bergen was strong in his spirit. When he was rescued and brought to us, he was crippled and almost dead. But we hid him and fed him, and he became healthy again. After the war, when he was rescued, he became my father. He insisted they bring me to care for him on the ship. People were not nice to me, a Japanese. But he was strong with them. By the end of our journey to Hawaii, all people were nice to me.

"Now the Malones make me part of this family. My father Bergen changed my life. He made me happy and good. I will miss him. But I know he is crossing the river, and is in a happy place, with Ariyoshi-san and many other friends. Thank you."

Donald McPhail

CHAPTER THIRTY-SIX

A Troubled Mind

Teo was troubled after Bergen's ceremony. Bergen had been a thoughtful man, a man of principle. The Japanese had brutalized him because America fought back against their country, and for being a *gaijin*. But he held no grudges. In fact he loved the Japanese culture, and the people he knew there. Uncle Bergen was able to distinguish the soldiers who nearly killed him, from other Japanese.

Teo had a plan, and it felt right. If he joined the anti-war movement, he could make a difference. Dad and mom might not understand it, but Bergen would. So would Malia, and her support was important to Teo.

This powerful anger that he carried with him from Vietnam had been eating at him for nearly two years. It was directed at the lies and assumptions that got America into the war. The lie that told America that our troops should fight this enemy. The lie that said it was winnable. There were so many lies and inconsistencies, back to when we sided with the French when they tried to take back their colony. It made no sense that our tax money backed invading colonists, not the Vietnam nationalists. Now our leaders refuse to admit we are bombing Laos and

Cambodia, aiming for the Ho Chi Minh Trail and killing un-armed civilians.

He was angry about the endless, indiscriminate killing — the napalm and explosives that he and his buddies were showering on real people, resulting in thousands of painful deaths.

As a pilot, he didn't know how many people he killed. He could hardly witness them, but he knew what he had done. As for his country, he had read the body counts and knew the figures were fabricated to mislead the public; and about that horrible massacre in My Lai. What other brutalities had been inflicted and never become known? The enemy had killed and maimed, and there was no attempt to overlook this. But they would not be killing our people if we hadn't invaded their land.

For the first time, as he assisted Yoriko with the bathing ritual, Teo had been intimate with an actual death and it troubled him. How many had he killed? Death had become personal, something that deserved introspection. By cleansing an aged and withered body, he honored the cycle of life and death. This awareness made the desecration of exploding, burning bodies, young innocent bodies, even more horrible and real.

Unlike his isolation in Chu Lai, where news was scarce and always many days old, Hawaii was filled with instant coverage of the war. Teo now felt buried by an avalanche of news from multiple Honolulu television stations, and multiple newspapers. Photos and articles exploded with descriptions of violence all over America. Following Kent State, two Jackson State students were killed, two days after that, four more at Buffalo. Students against cops. Blacks, browns and whites against angry uniformed enforcers of all colors. Pro-war politicians against students, and anti-war politicians arguing back.

The Kent State story stayed in every edition, always carrying the startling photo of student Mary Vecchio, with her unforgettable, silent scream, and arms stretched over the dead body of young Jeffrey Miller.

He read the cruel remarks from president Nixon, calling the student protesters "bums". The article continued with moving words from the father of another dead Kent State student, Alison Krause, whose body he had just identified at the morgue, "My daughter was not a bum. She felt that our crossing into Cambodia was wrong. Is this dissent a crime? Is this a reason for killing her? Have we come to such a state in this country that a young girl has to be shot because she disagrees deeply with the actions of her government?"

It comes down to leadership, and my leader is gone. Without King and Robert Kennedy, where are the leaders? Certainly not Nixon. Eugene McCarthy? McGovern? Who else? King and the Kennedys were leaders. They made sense to people, especially young ones.

Teo knew he had to get somewhere and act. For him "somewhere" was San Francisco, with activist schools like Cal nearby, and San Francisco State. Even at conservative Stanford, students had occupied the research institute and overthrown the university's president.

Everyone knew Mario Savio's name, and Jerry Rubin's, from early in the war, but they had left Berkeley a few years ago and seemed to have dropped out. Was Teo too late to join the the peace movement?

He heard that San Francisco State had a militant campus. It was known as an anti-war, pro-civil rights school, but without the kind of crazed and violent protesters he would find in Berkeley. That's where he would start. But first he needed to deal with his parents.

Donald McPhail

CHAPTER THIRTY-SEVEN
Off The Pigs!

Teo trudged from the United red-eye at six in the morning San Francisco time. Usually sharply dressed and tucked-in, even in the heat and dust of Vietnam, he felt like a mess in the rumpled jeans and denim shirt that he slept in all night in his narrow airplane seat. He wanted to look like a student or an activist of some sort, to lessen the likelihood of confrontations with kids who hated the military. Military guys can be easy to spot with their short hair and straight clothes, and he knew people made visual judgments. Protesters are no different from cops in that way.

By now his hair had grown out some, and he hadn't shaved since Bergen's memorial. His Academy teammate Frank Wikman had flown in from Cleveland a week earlier, and in a hurried phone call he said he would be crashing at a pad in the Haight. Teo had written down the address and stuffed the note into his jeans pocket.

He located the baggage area and grabbed his dad's old leather suitcase, with faded cruise ship stickers on it. It looked like a relic that he might have bought for himself at a flea market. Then Teo waved a taxi from the queue. When he handed the portly driver the address over on Clayton Street, he handed it back, "Sorry son. No free rides for hippies today. Especially into that war zone."

"Who asked for a free ride? And what's this about a war zone? I just arrived from 'Nam. That's a war zone."

"Sorry, son," the driver warmed a little. "You don't look like a soldier, but I'll take your word. Lots of hippies coming in for the protest. I took three of them into the Haight two days ago and they stiffed me. You got dough? I'll take you if you pay up front, thirty bucks, and that's a deal."

Tossing his bag into the open trunk, Teo handed the driver three bills and got into the back seat, hoping he wasn't too late to get involved.

They had driven in silence for twenty minutes, and as the driver slowed for traffic he sneered, "Look at those bums," pointing at dozens of bodies lying on cardboard and mats along the Haight Street sidewalk. Shops were closed, except for a rundown diner where bearded youngsters were filing in. Teo had eaten breakfast on the plane, but he would remember this place if he needed coffee.

"Another block, son. There, on the right side."

The taxi pulled over and Teo slid out, hoisting his suitcase from the open trunk to save the driver the trouble.

There weren't any sidewalk sleepers in front of the dingy apartment house. Once a faded salmon color, the building was chipped and peeled in patches to the white undercoat, and spray-painted with childish graffiti. "FUK U PIG!" it said with what looked like a middle finger extending from a sort of fist. "Not very peaceful," he murmured.

Pushing the speaker-button as Wikman had instructed, he got no response and pushed again. Then a growling voice, "Shit man. You know what time it is? What the fuck you want?"

"Teo Malone for Frank Wikman. He told me to come here."

Teo heard a light buzzing sound and quickly grabbed the door knob and pushed. Fortunately the heavy door opened and he walked into the filthy entry way. As he looked around the space, he saw what once had been ornate wood sconces and wainscoting. The dirty beveled glass windows had been elegant, and the wooded stairway, now marred and stained, looked as if it had once displayed debutantes. Now the walls were discolored and wall paper was torn off in large sections. It smelled like an old urinal.

"What is it, man?" He heard a tired whiskey-voice from the top of the stairway.

"Sorry to disturb you, but Frank Wikman said I should ask for him here."

"Wikkie? Sure, come on up. He's here."

Surprised by the good-natured response, Teo hoisted his suitcase up the steep stairway.

"You another one of them renegade soldiers, man?"

He looked up at the red-bearded man in a blue headband and smiled, "You got it."

Red-beard smiled back, "Welcome, then brother. We can use all the help we can get." He led Teo down a long corridor, with doorless rooms where he was surprised to see groups of people. One candle-lit room looked like a

seance was going on, with a heavy-lidded woman in rim-
less glasses facing an audience of unkempt listeners, sitting on the floor in silence. Another room was dark, except
for a single candle surrounded by cross-legged participants
chanting quietly. Finally, they arrived at what must have
been a ballroom once, and was now filled with clumps of
people. The walls were covered with ragged posters with
fantasy designs and fading colors. It was nine in the morning and there wasn't much movement here. Red pointed
off to the left, "Wikkie's over there, I think. There in the corner."

"Thanks, man." Unsure of the protocol, and remembering how new arrivals in Vietnam were given a similar unceremonious welcome. He toted his case over to the
corner and looked for his friend. At the farthest end he
found a threesome. Two seemed to be girls, one blonde
and the other with blue hair. They were wrapped around
someone with a dark beard and lank, dirty locks. He
leaned down so he didn't have to speak loudly, "Frank
Wikman. Anybody here know Frank?"

The bearded man opened his eyes, "Who wants to
know?"

"Tell him Teo wants to know."

"Teo, man, is that you?" He smiled broadly and
gently rolled the girls away, covering their naked rear-ends
with his thin blanket. Standing in gray tee shirt and military
skivs, he reached over and hugged Teo.

"Yes Frank, it's me," in an even tone. "I just flew all
night from Hawaii, and here I am. You said you had a
plan." Teo wasn't sure that Frank heard the edge, as Teo

was growing increasingly impatient with the mess around him.

The blue-haired girl said in a dusky voice, "Look at that, Dreamgirl, it's a new recruit."

As the blonde wakened and tried to focus, Frank said, "It's Wikkie now, man. The family here knows me as Wikkie. I been here six days, and they've welcomed me to the cause."

"And so they have, Frank. I'm beat and I thought you said you had a place to stay, a place for me to stay."

"I do, man. Look around. There's a spot here for you. I told King Saul over there, and he said it was cool."

"That's the guy in the red beard?" asked Teo.

"He's The Man here, King Saul."

"Here's the thing, ah, Wikkie. I'm here to join the protest. I'm here to help end the fucking war. This isn't the kind of scene I expected."

Eyes clearing, and sensing Teo's growing anger, "Teo. This *is* the scene now. This is how the movement works. It may not look like it, but these people are going to put their lives on the line today. Give us two hours, and we're heading out to campus for a happening."

"I hear you, Frank. I'm just a little beat right now, and I could use a place to sleep. Other than that classroom down the hall, I don't see any seriousness or preparation. All I see is scruffy people crapped out on the floor." Teo caught himself, "Okay, Frank. I'm a little tired is all. Let me catch some sleep — an hour or so, and I'll get with the program."

"Over here, big man," said the blonde with a sleepy voice, but more awake. "Settle in next to me, and you can sleep if you like. There might be some other things you like, too."

Teo wakened and the girl was gone. He had zonked in two seconds. When he looked around, the mats and mattresses were empty, and only a few people remained. The ones he saw looked ready for combat. They wore old military fatigues and jeans with holes in them. Some had tie-dyed shirts, with denim vests. There were woolen caps pulled down over dirty hair. He looked further to see Frank was striding toward him. "Come on, Teo. The bus is here and we're headed to State. The signs are loaded up, and you have ten minutes to pee and clean up. Bring a jacket, cause it's usually cold out there."

Teo scrambled to locate his shoes and stash his case against the wall. If he decided to find a hotel, he would do it after the protest. Meantime, the only valuables were his ID and some cash, and these were in his pockets.

Frank pointed him to a yellow school bus, spray painted with "City of New Orleans" along the side, and covered in psychedelic posters. Flags covered the windows, and Teo recognized the "Don't Tread on Me" union jack. Then he felt himself getting riled, seeing a Cuban flag in one window next to the American flag with a peace symbol where the stars should be.

"Cool it, Teo," Frank urged. "They want peace, and they want to draw attention. That's what it takes now. You get the message out about no more wars, and no-one listens any more. You attach it to the flag and create some shit, and people respond. You may not like it, but it grabs their attention."

Teo knew there was a time to shut up and learn, so he kept his reactions to himself as he sat down next to a black-haired girl in jeans and a poncho. She was attractive in a unique way, with brown skin and short-cropped hair, almost a man's haircut. She nodded as he sat, then looked out the window, seeming to prefer her private thoughts to anything going on around her.

During the short ride through Golden Gate Park over to 19th Avenue, Teo smelled the same sweet reefer smell he knew from Vietnam. He heard a familiar song, sung by a few of the folks in back, about peace and treason, love and reason, "But I ain't marching anymore...." His hopes lifted when they began, "We shall overcome..." and everyone seemed to join in. He hadn't yet come across any serious talk about why they were protesting, so this was a promising tone. The peace song animated the girl next to him. She had a clear and confident voice, with what seemed like a British accent. From India, maybe.

As the song ended, the bus quieted and Teo nodded to her. "That's a hopeful song. You sing it well."

She nodded back, "Thank you. It's the one we need now. Today needs to be about non-violence."

"Peace. Non-violence. What's the difference?" He asked.

She looked at him, her face without expression, then turned away again for a few seconds, then looked back. "I apologize. You're serious, aren't you? For a moment I thought you were being sarcastic. You really *don't* know what is happening now."

"There's a lot I don't know, I guess. I've been away." He was getting confused. "Why are we here, then, if it isn't to demand peace."

Shaking her head, "Where were you during the Chicago riots? The Democratic Convention? The yippies? the Days of Rage? Those and these killings on campus. The landscape has changed. Peaceful protests are considered quaint or naive these days."

"But that's just wrong. I've been bombing Viet Cong for two years now, and it has to stop. It's not quaint. It's insane."

She looked at him, shaking her head, then held up her hand, "I agree with you, friend, it is insane. But look around us. These people are angry, and it's going in the wrong direction. That's why I join these protests, sitting in those little rooms and trying to teach these kids the difference between nonviolent protest and pointless anger. We know you can't have peace through angry demands. We can't stop violence through fighting and acting up. People just respond with more violence. I spent the past three days holding sessions with them, reminding them, trying to refocus. Most of them are not interested. So many are here simply to fight authority. Some are agitating for their drugs, others for black power, some for free love. A few are just angry and want to vent. So many people are looking for a fight."

"But they're angry. I'm angry. About the war and the killing…"

Donald McPhail

"Hold your thought. We're almost there, and I have some work to do at the site. Look for me later. My name is Donya. People will know me." She squeezed past him and moved toward the front, then took his hand and pulled him with her. "We'll get separated out there, but it we have more to talk about. Watch out for yourself, new boy. Some of these people are dangerous."

They were crowding toward the door and he didn't know what to say, "Yeah, great. Look for me, too," he stammered. "I'm Teo, or Theo. Find me through Frank Wikman…er Wikkie."

The bus arrived at 19th and Holloway and dropped them off at the wide concrete corner. He followed Donya in the flow of people funneling down the walkway to the grassy center of campus, directly in front of the student union. People of all kinds and ages milled around, a few in chinos and Pendleton shirts, others in jeans and sweatshirts. There were even a few men in suits and neckties, and a woman in a yellow dress, fur jacket and high heels.

Teo and Donya moved along with the hippies into the center lawn area, where he was elbow-to-elbow with clean-cut college girls and boys, holding peace signs and chatting amiably, next to scruffy men and women in their worn denim garb. Standing firm around them was an ominous semi-circle of police officers wearing full battle dress, holding large defensive shields, and wearing opaque plexiglass visors and black hard hats. Behind them was an intimidating line of armed police, mounted atop well-groomed horses that looked nervous and powerful.

Teo was startled to see another ring of people, a sizable crowd of students, just standing and observing, like they were waiting for a parade. The mood was congenial, and he wondered what the armed police presence was about.

He looked up to the flat roof of the student union and saw a crowd of what must have been press people. There were microphones and television cameras on tripods, that must have been set-up for a while. Then as if on cue, red lights glowed on the television cameras and somebody shouted, "Go for it!"

Immediately the crowd around Teo surged toward the police in riot gear, and he lost track of Donya. The chants started as rough shouts. "Off the pigs, man!", "Fuck the pigs!", "No more war!" "Hey, Hey USA, how many gooks did you kill today!" Where was the supervision? Who was in charge?

Teo watched a baseball-sized rock thunk off one of the shields, then a bigger one. They came from someplace in his group. Then the police edged confidently toward the protesters in a solid line, shields up. He was being pushed to the front, toward them, and couldn't go any other direction. The crowd was too tight.

Now in the front row, he was within six feet of the riot police. He saw the anger and determination in their narrow eyes. He also saw hatred, as the "kill the pigs" chants continued. Suddenly, half a brick hit one of the riot police on the side of his head just below his helmet, knocking him down. Without thinking, Teo darted from the group and moved to the downed cop, dabbing blood with his handkerchief, trying to help him. He edged the man as gently as he could, toward the police line, getting him through embattled cops and safely past the horses' legs.

As Teo looked around for help, two uniformed officers grabbed his arms and pinned him to the ground, guns aimed at his face. They jerked him onto his back and dragged him by the arms, butt skidding along the ground. He saw the crowd of protesters and cops getting smaller as he was forced away, into a grove near the gymnasium.

They pinned his arms and knelt on his chest, reaching for handcuffs, as Teo croaked. "Officer. What the hell?"

The meaty cop hissed, "Shut the fuck up, scumbag. Don't say a fucking word. Or I'll beat the piss out of you."

Teo said nothing and lay still while they cuffed his hands behind him. They jerked him to his feet and shouldered him toward a van near the gym. Suddenly the two cops stopped and turned, looking at a heavy-set black man with a deep voice. "What's that Lieutenant?"

"I said stop hassling that man, Carlo. You and Connelly knock it off. He just saved sergeant Wilson's life back there."

"What're you talking about, Jackson? I'm taking this punk to the van."

"Officer Brito, I'm ordering you to back off. Remove those cuffs. This man helped get Wilson out of the battle. He was hit with a brick, I saw it. This man crawled over and helped loosen Wilson's chin strap and stop the blood, then he pulled him back to where you found them. You could have cost a life, leaving Wilson there like that."

Teo could taste blood in his mouth, where he must have been punched, or ground into the cement walk. Then he felt his wrists and arms released, and flexed his arms to get them working. He approached Lieutenant Jackson, "Thanks, officer. I don't know how to thank you. Last week I was in 'Nam, and I felt safer there than I do here."

"It's okay, son. I'm glad that my partner and I saw what happened. I don't know what you mean about being in 'Nam, but the cop that was busting you is a good man. He lost a boy over there last year. He sees you protesters as the enemy, and I can't say I blame him." He took Teo's elbow and guided him to the steps of the gym. Sit here and get your bearings. We'll take your name and get you back to your friends after this little skirmish is over."

"Thanks, Lieutenant. But I'm not rejoining that crowd. This senseless shit isn't what I signed up for. Where's the peaceful protest? Where's the debate?" Teo removed his military ID card and handed it to the officer."

Raising his eyebrows, he handed it back. "Welcome home, son. It ain't here, not these days. I've been working protests at State since they started a few years back. Something's gone wrong since the Chicago and DC riots. In the beginning the kids were all peaceful and wanting to end the war, like a lot of us. We'd book 'em and let 'em loose. It was a kind of dance we were all doing. But now we hear 'Kill the cops!' and most of them are stoned and smart-ass. Why did that happen? That's not right. Throwing rocks and bricks. Maybe the peaceful ones got tired, or turned cynical."

Donald McPhail

"I didn't expect this. How it is now. I just know we need to end this war. It's killing us. But I came for peace, not more killing."

"I really don't know why you're here, son. But these protests aren't helping the cause, at least not with anybody I know. I still see some good kids when we're booking them, but there are serious psychos, too. Like the guy who threw the brick."

Teo watched the injured cop placed on a stretcher and loaded into the ambulance that had been positioned nearby. The Lieutenant walked him over to a squad car and said, "Mackey, take this man over near the Haight and drop him off." Nodding at Teo, "He's on our side, doing some undercover work. He needs to get his stuff and move on."

Donald McPhail

CHAPTER THIRTY-EIGHT

Next Steps

De Villiers sat across from Duff, with Christy at his left. They were at The Willows, admiring the lava rock fire pit and sipping cocktails. Duff nursed his glass of chablis while they listened attentively to the traditional Hawaiian music from a local trio, a petite guitarist called Lena, with black hair and a lively smile, next to a large, dignified woman of middle age, Auntie Harriett, who played the standup bass. They were accompanied on guitar by a handsome young man known simply as Brickwood, who had been introduced as, "a local boy from Kakaako."

As the music ended, they joined in the applause, then settled into their conversation during the break. He activated the recorder.

"I have plenty of information to finish the article, and as you warned in the beginning, my book is far more complicated than just the Pan Am story. But there is one question that we haven't discussed. Duff, you retired a year or two before people expected. Pan Am seems to be in good financial shape, and is considered one of the world's leading airlines. Does your retirement suggest anything I would want to be aware of?"

Duff smiled that quiet smile, thought for a moment and responded, "For the record, I see Pan Am as the world's greatest airline. Better than any of us could have imagined back in 1934. I'm biased, of course, but recent financial results reinforce this claim. So do our customer surveys about services, and look at our passenger loads. I look at the early days, at the risks we took, and the many new aircraft we introduced, the innovations. I see an incredible achievement, and it all began with my old boss, Juan Trippe."

Then Duff reached down and pressed the off-button. De Villiers began to object, then he sat back to see what Duff had in mind.

"Off the record, Marcus. Things have changed. The industry has, and so have technology, attitudes, standards. And the standards are not necessarily better, just more measurable. Everything is more analytical, but attitudes and personal service can't always be quantified.

"Management has certainly changed. Juan Trippe resigned two years ago, and we have become a company of report-writers. There are operational memos, self-awareness training courses, stringent targets for on-time departures, crew accountability reports, all these institutional changes. There are many days when I feel like a very sophisticated pencil-pusher.

"I'm a man who enjoys people and personal trust. I enjoy conversations and genuine friendships among our employees, whether they are union or non-union. I don't want to limit these relationships to just my management team. Without a cooperative, supportive atmosphere, I'm pleased to retire while my airline is at the top."

"I could act surprised, Duff, but I'm not, really," de Villiers responded. "I've heard these kinds of things from others around Pan Am's system. So your assessment doesn't startle me. Things change, and not always for the better. And they are often hardest on longtime employees. I'm curious. Why did you carefully make these comments off the record? What more is going on?"

"I'm concerned, Marcus. Before he retired, Mr. Trippe committed to purchase forty-five new 747s from Boeing. This is a huge order for very expensive planes, and their limited range doesn't seem to suit our longest routes, so we will put them in less productive places. While our financials look very good today, things will look quite different when these planes are operating and the payments come due.

"Then there are the expensive distractions. The Pan Am Building, Intercontinental Hotels, and a new division for business jets. Real estate, hotels and small plane charters are not my idea of Pan Am. At the same time, we receive petty memos about conserving paper in the copy machines, fewer pens and pencils, limiting overtime, enforcing the vacation-time rules so the books are clean. We are a worldwide airline, and a damned good one. But these are the signs of a struggling company whose values are different from mine. So retirement with a certain amount of dignity is the best step."

Again Duff reached down, this time to press the on-button. "So I am happy with my decision, Marcus, and I look forward to my next phase." Turning to nod at Christy, he continued, "That is, my next phase after I have regained my health."

For the first time, Christy added her thoughts. "We're all looking forward to our new life, starting with a healthy Duff Malone. We will be busy, that's for certain. Marcus, you probably know that Teo came back early from San Francisco. It seems that he found what he wanted to learn more quickly than expected, and it's more complicated than he thought."

"In what way?" Marcus asked.

"The strangest thing. A young woman came back with him. She's an activist of some kind, an extremely smart, very independent girl that he met at the protest gathering. She's staying with us for a few days. Apparently she tracked him down through a mutual friend and caught up with Teo at the airport. She was with a man from her organization, who was like a professor. They spoke with Teo for an hour or so, interviewing him I think. They work for an organization that specializes in nonviolence. Next thing you know, she bought a ticket and traveled here with him."

"They must have some money, to pay for a ticket at the last minute. Think they're legitimate?"

"She does seem to have money enough. She is nicely dressed and is quite professional. Last night she told us she was raised in Iran, and her parents are teachers at Stanford. She's a musician of some sort, who works at this peace institute near Monterey."

"How do you feel about bringing her into your home?"

Duff interjected, "You know, it is quite refreshing. Donya's a smart and polite young lady. She seems quite professional, as Christy said."

"I believe Marcus is referring to the romantic side of things, Duff."

"Ah, that. Well, as I said, they seem to prefer separate rooms."

Christy responded quickly, "I truly think she wants to help him. Donya sees something in Teo, maybe at the Institute. Perhaps she's just protective. We all see how idealistic he is, and not much aware of life outside the military. But they find something in Teo that impresses them. As a Marine who is against the war, his message is certainly unique. But she says it's more than being against this war, or peace at the end of a rifle. It's about nonviolence. Maybe the Institute can help him understand the nonviolent movement; help him channel his feelings into something more productive than the protest marches do. He's smart, and his military experience didn't exactly provide a balanced view."

"They aren't likely to be balanced either," added Duff. "But they are certainly well informed."

"Where's Teo now?" asked de Villiers.

"They must be home by now. He and Donya were over at Iolani Palace this morning," said Christy, "checking the rally site. It's amazing what Donya knows about these things. She said she has been with the Institute since the late sixties, and she knows what it takes to make an event work."

"We're glad Malia volunteered to help. She seems very impressed with Donya," said Duff. "Through friends at the University, they got permission to use the main steps and the grounds at the palace, and local newspapers and television stations will cover it. They are stressing to UH students and everyone else, that this is to be a peaceful event, and not a place to raise hell with the system."

Donald McPhail

CHAPTER THIRTY-NINE
Teo's Protest

Honolulu weather was unusually hot and humid, and Teo was worried that the Kona winds might rain-out the peace event. He was edgy from all the traveling and from trying to pull this political rally together with so little preparation time. He didn't even know if there were activists in Hawaii, and was relying on gut instincts. He was wary about his experience in San Francisco, but intent on doing what he could to change the world.

He had relied on Malia to interpret Honolulu politics and local attitudes, because she knew this place way better than he did. Counting college and Vietnam, he had been away for nearly ten years, and the islands had changed. So many new people had moved in from the mainland, especially from Asia, Canada and California. And the place had grown. It was hard to believe, despite the ongoing war and political turmoil, over two million people visited Hawaii this year.

Malia cautioned him about his appearance. "Don't look like some tourist, or a hippie, or a guy in the military. You need to look local, but in a way that goes over with ordinary working people." Since the event could hit the television news, this meant clean golf shorts and a nice aloha shirt, clean-shaven and presentable to middle-aged viewers.

Donya stressed that they needed mainstream support if the peace message was going to be taken seriously. It couldn't have a hint of violence or drugs. Malia told them there were campus protesters in Hawaii, as there were across the mainland, but there had been no successful anti-war traction here. Much of the population was from the military or held government jobs, and it was clear from the newspapers and television that most public symbols about protests were designed to look like hippies or angry native Hawaiians.

Local anti-war efforts had centered on the UH campus at Manoa or outside military gates, but they were seriously fragmented. One professor led his radical group toward Marxism, siding with the Viet Cong, and that created a nasty public backlash. The native Hawaiian activists appealed to an entirely different group, advocating for peace, but concentrating their messages around longstanding injustice for native Hawaiians, promoting Hawaiian independence from the U.S. There were natural pockets of support, but the sovereignty talk alienated people, including many local Hawaiians, and it further fragmented the anti-war message.

Sitting with Teo at Kapiolani Park, Donya's dark skin and black hair made her look more like a local girl from Manoa than a Stanford grad from Iran. They were at one of his favorite spots near the tennis courts. This was

Donald McPhail

the place where he first threw a football with Duff as a little
kid, and where he often went when he needed to think.

Teo had watched Donya and Malia work together at
the palace, discussing the seating and exchanging ways
that Malia's recruits could help with security. Donya was
observant. She watched and listened, and didn't waste
words, but always seemed reassuring. When she offered
an opinion, it was well considered and not combative.

Donya emphasized to Malia that nonviolence didn't
mean being pushed around or caving-in when you disagreed. There were strategies to deal with any of the participants who got too aggressive. She shared suggestions
about de-escalating flareups through friendliness, cooperation and understanding, and not combativeness. Her guidance obviously came from experience. Malia immediately
took to her, appreciating another strong-minded woman.

They had left Malia and her team of volunteers to
finish the setup, so they could get away and talk about his
speech. Teo wanted feedback on his presentation, knowing
that Donya wrote speeches for her board members, and
for organizers of all kinds.

Donya leaned against the picnic table while Teo
paced on the lawn and briefed her, "We begin with a local
TV newscaster, Mona Tang, who is recognized as an activist and a voice of reason. She'll draw a supportive
crowd. Then she'll introduce our senior US senator Tom
Ito. He's popular here, and was a member of the 442nd
Division, the all-Japanese unit that fought in Europe. He's
a war hero, but very outspoken against Vietnam."

"I read about the 442nd. Most of them came from those prison camps, didn't they?"

"Internment camps, they were called. And yes, Tom was at Manzanar for a year before enlisting."

"So there are two of you ex-military heroes who will be advocating for nonviolence? One is from an internment camp, and the other from America's Naval Academy — sort of polar opposites. It's unusual for politicians or military officers to stand up for nonviolence. Joan would smile at that."

"Who is Joan?"

"She's the one who founded our organization, the Institute For The Study of Nonviolence. You've heard of Joan Baez?"

"I've heard of her, sure. Everyone has. I thought the man I met at the airport was in charge of your institute. What was his name, Ira?'

"Yes. Ira Sandperl. They both founded it, and they both teach there."

"How will they feel when they learn you're helping a politician and an ex-marine? When we talked, Ira didn't seem to object, but I've read that Joan doesn't seem to think much of the military or politicians."

Smiling patiently, Donya said, "That's not entirely true. She's against violence and killing, whoever is doing it, or causing it. But you can't end violence through more violence. She doesn't want you and other soldiers to die, or to kill. She's against politicians who create and encourage wars. That's why she met with Dr. King a few years ago, and tried to convince him to run for president."

Donald McPhail

"I didn't know that. A man like him as our president? Wouldn't that have been something?" He shook his head, "She sounds pretty wise to me. Why does she have such a bad rap in the newspapers?"

"It's an old tactic, Teo. Politicians try to discredit people who disagree with them, and turn the public against them. As for soldiers, Joan doesn't want them killed, or killing others. That's why she protests at draft boards, and supports anti-war actions. She's gone to jail for it more than once. It's frustrating and sad, that a farmer in Lincoln, Nebraska will automatically dislike her, even though she's trying to save his son from being drafted and killed. She is certainly not against America. Look how she works for peace, and for peaceful protest, with men like Dr. King, Cesar Chavez, Pete Seeger. She's against this and every other terrible and illogical war." She looks up, "Now why are you smiling?"

"Just remembering," he nodded. "We loved her at the Academy, back in 1961 when I was a plebe. Her first album was the most popular one with nearly all of us. We used to listen to it in some of the upperclassmen's rooms."

"Joan has a great sense of irony, believe it or not, and she will appreciate your memory of that simpler time." Donya pointed at his notes, "But back to your presentation. I'd like to hear what you plan to say."

Teo unfolded a piece of lined paper that had been stashed in his shorts. "I was blown away by Bobby Kennedy's announcement two years ago to run for president, and I was crushed when he was killed. Every time I think about it, I get angry all over again. He told us straight-

out what's wrong, why the war is wrong, and how to fix it."
He scanned the page, "So here it is. I start with his words
as a quotation. No intro.

" 'You can change these disastrous, divisive policies only by changing the men who are now making
them'." He paused, then continued slowly, " 'It is now unmistakably clear,' Senator Kennedy said in 1968, just forty-
two days after the assassination of Martin Luther King, and
seventy-five days before he himself was killed, 'that you
can change these disastrous, divisive policies only by
changing the men who are now making them.' " He looked
up. "I'd like to lead with that, to repeat his words so no-one
misses them."

"Go on," she said.

"I believe we all need heroes. Not just for our kids
or our grandchildren, but for ourselves. Right now. We
need them for hope. For inspiration. To help us know who
we are, and who we can become. I'm twenty-eight now,
and my generation was once idealistic, naive, probably a
little cocky. We were going to change the world for the better. We were ready to be inspired. We were ready for heroes."

His eyes are fixed on Donya's, "I had three true heroes in my life: John Kennedy, Dr. King and Robert
Kennedy. My three heroes are dead now. Why is this? Why
do we kill our heroes? Why do we allow it?"

"Teo, are you asking me this? Or is this your presentation?"

"My speech."

She nods, "Please, go on."

Donald McPhail

"So why are we killing our heroes? Is it is for politics? For money? I met President Kennedy in 1962, at Navy football practice at Quonset Point, Rhode Island. It was an unexpected meeting. We were idealistic young midshipmen, shaking hands with the President of the United States. That experience changed my life. Here was this young president who talked to us about values, ideals, about reaching for the stars. About what we could do for others.

"So now that these three heroes are dead, do we abandon the ideals, and stop believing in possibilities? Do we become cynics and tear down the system? Do we drug ourselves stupid and shut things out? Or do we get angry enough to do something about this world we have created?"

He smiles slightly, "Another of my heroes told me a long time ago, that we shouldn't mistake frustration for anger. That frustration occurs when we expect one thing, and we get another. Frustrations are fixable. We can either change our expectations, or change the results, the outcome.

"I say, let's change the results. But if the results take too much time to change, I say that anger is the next step — if that's what it takes to change these men who are creating these disastrous, divisive policies.

"Robert Kennedy's words inspire me to action. This is about more than just the Vietnam War. It's about our political system. We need to shine the light on the rest of his message. He said, 'I run to seek new policies. Policies to end the bloodshed in Vietnam and in our cities, policies to close the gaps that now exist between black and white, between rich and poor, between young and old, in this country and around the rest of the world. I run because I want the United States of America to stand for hope instead of despair, for reconciliation of men instead of the growing risk of world war.'

"And then I repeat Senator Kennedy's unwavering conclusion, '…it is now unmistakably clear that we can change these disastrous, divisive policies only by changing the men who are now making them. For the reality of recent events in Vietnam has been glossed over with illusions. The Report of the Riot Commission has been largely ignored. The crisis in gold, the crisis in our cities, the crisis in our farms and in our ghettos have all been met with too little and too late.'

"Friends, we need to help each other to embrace Senator Kennedy's words. You will read and hear about our new peace movement in the next days and weeks. I ask you to join our movement to end the war in Vietnam. To end the killing." Looking up, his eyes were moist and his fists were clenched. Then he relaxed them and gave a small grin, like a little boy, "What do you think?"

Donya smiled and applauded lightly, "That was quite inspiring. Beautiful, really." She reached and took his hand and asked quietly, "Would you mind a suggestion?"

Shyly, unprepared for her touch, "Sure. That's why I wanted you to hear it."

She withdrew her hand and spoke carefully, "Those are inspiring words, Teo. And you have a powerful message. Several messages. But for this audience, people

who may not know you yet, the best part is your own
words. Persuade people yourself. Connect Robert
Kennedy to your own reality, so that everyone in the audience understands and takes your message personally."

"And how can I do that? His words seem more be-
lievable."

"For me, Teo, your words mean more because they
are your own. When I first met you on that bus I could see
your intensity, your absolute commitment. Up close, you
are very easy to read." Laughing at his embarrassment,
"No, Teo. No, that's a good thing. A rare thing. It's your
honesty. The audience needs to feel that. But they won't
be up next to you. Out there, they need to hear your
thoughts. Your conclusions, based on your own unique experiences, and your beliefs. I'm inspired by Robert
Kennedy because you are. But this is an opportunity for
people to know your own clear-eyed, soldier's reasons for
wanting to end the war. To end the killing, and to choose
peace."

She motioned to the bench next to her, as she continued. "I'm drawn to the part about heroes and about
meeting President Kennedy. If we'd known each other
longer, you would know all about another hero, someone
that Dr. King and our-Joan admired, Mahatma Ghandi. But
use your experiences. Use those, and reduce the actual
Kennedy speech. Use just enough to win their support.
Leave them wanting more, not less."

Teo's eyes narrowed and he rubbed his forehead,
and Donya wasn't sure if she had made him angry, or hurt
his feelings.

Then he said, "I need to regroup a little. I feel ready with the version you heard. I expected that you'd suggest getting rid of my personal stuff, not the speeches." Then smiling, he added, "But I agree about the personal part, too. I added the Kennedy speech because he was a great man, and his words mean so much to me. I was sort of depending on them. But, sure, I can use just the beginning quote, and repeat it at the end. For most of it, I'll try to use my own words."

The peace-protest at Iolani Palace was set for 4 o'clock and it was likely to tie-up traffic throughout the downtown streets, with backups spreading in both directions all the way to the main highways. Organizers knew the timing would delay workers on their commute and keep unsuspecting tourists from reaching their departure flights, but the inconvenience was for an important cause, and it would raise awareness for their message.

Spectators were gathered out on the palace grounds, filling the spacious lawn, including his favorite grassy area beneath that large banyan, where he had sat as a ten-year-old, listening to Hawaiian elders, *kupuna*, describe the brave, often tragic history of the Hawaiian people.

Scanning the crowd, it looked eerily similar to his San Francisco experience, and it worried him. Demonstrators were surrounded by burly Honolulu police officers dressed in battle garb. Circling them were onlookers and counter-protesters, safely hidden behind the cops.

Teo was disappointed how the authorities always assumed that war protesters were enemies who should be surrounded by police. The protesters were not nearly as dangerous as the politicians who led us into war, yet the police took the politician's side. He was also disappointed at some of the protesters, when he heard them calling the cops pigs. Today, this was a protest for peace and hope, and he had to make it happen.

At this peace-event, they had to prevent random provocateurs from shouting down speakers and creating chaos. He felt the Hawaii crowd wasn't going to be as negative as the hard-core activists in Chicago or the Bay Area, and that his mix of carefullyselected off-duty military and cooperative UH students would mingle and calm outbursts, using some of the peaceful words and tactics that Donya had suggested.

Clean shaven now, and with his hair grown out, Teo looked like a young politician and he felt confident of his message. Donya stood with his family on the stately porch, standing off to the side, where they could see him and observe the crowd. Yoriko was there alongside Malia, Christy and Duff, with Donya and de Villiers standing with them. Their friend Bully stood quietly with his guitar, anticipating a traditional ending to the gathering.

Teo shut his eyes and tried to channel the anger he felt about My Lai and Kent State. He needed to have that edginess, the way he did before his football games. At the same time, he wanted to maintain control, and communicate that peace was the outcome they wanted, not more conflict.

Mona Tang's opening was energetic and bright, with the kind of clarity and hope that attracted her large television news audience. He wouldn't be surprised to see her run for mayor or state senator soon.

As she introduced Senator Ito, the audience rose and welcomed him warmly, except for the small group of hippies who dominated the banyan area. They stayed seated. Teo was worried about their belligerence.

In his brief comments, Senator Ito reminded the audience of his childhood in Hawaii, his difficult encampment at Manzanar, his belief in America and our heroic actions in World War Two after the Japanese military attacked Hawaii. He praised the efforts of heroic leaders like Daniel Inouye and Eugene McCarthy, affirming his support for leaders who promoted peaceful solutions, and a swift end to the pointless war in Vietnam. Even the hippies were drawn to his words.

He emphasized his Hawaii roots when he introduced Teo. "I must say," began the senator, "that our next speaker's name is well known to me, although I have never actually met Teo Malone. Like most Hawaiians, I followed his football career at St. Louis High School." He paused for the inevitable cheers from St. Louis alumni scattered around the audience. "I also followed his stellar career at Annapolis. Not so much for his football exploits," prompting kind laughter from knowledgeable participants, and a large smile from Teo, who stood in plain sight, wearing his floral shirt and shorts.

"Since we all know he picked the wrong four years to be a quarterback at Navy. Somehow another fellow was ahead of him on the depth charts." Amidst polite laughter, the senator concluded, "I'm proud to welcome one of our own heroes home to Hawaii following a distinguished military career." An unhappy buzz began in response to mention of his military career.

He raised a gentle hand. "But please, listen while I finish. Teo Malone has a particular right to talk about peace and war, because like me, he has experienced both. And like me, he has clearly chosen the side of peace." As the audience applauded respectfully, the senator concluded. "I'm proud to introduce one of my own personal heroes, a man of peace and integrity, former U.S. Marine and a new leader of the peace movement in Hawaii, Mr. Teo Malone."

As the applause continued, Teo stepped to the microphone and waited. Because of his silence, they began to quiet down, until a challenging chant started from the banyan tree crowd. But it went nowhere, as a few of the university kids and some of the hippies raised their arms to quiet their own.

Teo then spoke into the microphone, low enough that people had to stop the murmuring in order to hear. The sound system was powerful, and he spoke just loud enough to be audible. "You can change these disastrous, divisive policies," he began, "only by changing the men who are now making them."

Louder now, and fully audible, "These are the inspired words of the late Robert F. Kennedy, when he announced that he would run for President." Teo continued without notes, using his own clear words.

"We all need heroes. Not just for our kids or our grandchildren, but for ourselves. Right now. We need them for hope. For inspiration. To help us know who we are, and who we can become."

Slowly, patiently he scanned the crowd, looking individuals directly in their eyes and challenging them to look at him. "I'm twenty-eight now, and my generation was once idealistic, naive, cocky. We were going to change the world for the better. We were ready to be inspired. We were ready for heroes.

"I had three true heroes in my life: John Kennedy, Martin Luther King and Robert Kennedy. My three heroes are dead now, and we are mired in an endless and futile war. Why is this? Why do we kill our heroes? Why do we allow it?

"Were they not patriots?" He paused. "But not all patriots are leaders. Remember this when failed leaders tell you how much they love their country.

"Why are we killing our heroes? Is it is for politics? For money?

"Another of my heroes told me a long time ago, that we shouldn't mistake frustration for anger." He turned his head and smiled over at his father. "That frustration occurs when we expect one thing, and we get another. Frustrations are fixable. We can either change our expectations, or change the results, the outcome.

"I say, let's change the results. But if the results take too much time to change, I say that anger is the next step — if that's what it takes to change these men who are creating these disastrous, divisive policies." Teo heard

Donald McPhail

whistles and applause from the protesters. "But our anger must be non-violent, or it will make things worse. Violence causes violence. We need to vote for people of peace, and we need to hold them accountable. We need to change the men who lead us into these terrible wars.

"Now I speak to you here in Honolulu, on the historic steps of Iolani Palace, where generations ago monarchs spoke to the people of their islands. I am announcing a peaceful protest against these disastrous, divisive policies. I am asking all of you here — Honolulu Police Department, National Guard, students, hippies, surfers and *blalahs*; Hawaiians, Samoans, Japanese, Chinese, Koreans, *kama'ainas*, *ha'oles* — everyone here tonight. Stand together to protest four clear and specific things about this war, and the men who make the policies.

"First, stop the war. America's young men and women — and hundreds of thousands of Southeast Asians — are being killed in a senseless war created by misguided leaders, and this must stop." Another burst of applause, mostly from the protesters.

"Second, stop the lies. These leaders continue to lie about secret bombing of Laos and Cambodia, that everyone seems to know about. Both the bombing and the lying must stop." The applause grew and again subsided as he raised his hand.

"Third, stop the murder. Our government has hidden shameful truths about our own troops' brutal rape and slaughter of defenseless women and children, in My Lai and who knows where else? This brutality and coverup must stop." A loud and lengthy applause interrupted him for

several minutes, with a handful of uniformed officers joining the protesters.

"And finally, stop the college massacres. Through
his callous words and attitude, our own president has encouraged the killing of innocent protesters at Kent State
and Jackson State and Buffalo University. At the same
time, protesters have to be true to the cause of the peace
they are demanding. They can't waste their energies and
lives, simply overthrowing the university presidents and
provoking cops.

Teo pauses to emphasize these words, "For us to
survive, freedom and democracy must survive. Censorship
and violence must stop." The applause was now deafen-
ing, and Teo stood back from the podium and allowed it to
continue. The crowd quieted again as he approached the
microphone.

"There is too much killing, too much senseless
killing in this world. It has to stop. I was raised here, and I
learned about racism here. I learned that race does not
justify conflict, nor does it create attitudes. Ignorance does.
Education, motivation, clear thinking and compassion create informed attitudes and prevent ignorance. They prevent conflict.

"It is not a nation that creates wars and imprisons
people. It is the leaders of those nations who make those
calculated decisions. It is not someone's race that makes
them aggressive, or bigoted or unfair. It is ignorance and
fear and propaganda that cause people to believe the lies
about those 'other people.'

Donald McPhail

"And let's never assume there is anything about America that gives us a free pass when it comes to unfairness and brutality.

"Two months ago I was stationed in Vietnam, following orders and carrying out bombing raids against people I didn't know and do not hate. As a former United States Marine, I stand here to tell you that I will no longer stand by and say nothing. We must all act for peace, and we must act now. Protests are not parties, or gang violence, or open season on the police. We're in this together.

"Let's pick up the torch that fell from the hands of heroes like Bobby Kennedy, as he picked it up from his brother John, and from Martin Luther King. We need to remember Senator Kennedy's words and act on his pledge, and we will make it our own.

"Because 'it is now unmistakably clear that you can change these disastrous, divisive policies only by changing the men who are now making them.'

"Thank you. Aloha, friends. And let us end this peaceful afternoon the way we end all of our family occasions, with our anthem, 'Hawaii Aloha'. "

As their friend Bully walked over and stood beside Teo, strumming his guitar, Malia joined hands with her mother and father, leading them over next to Bully. Raising his right arm, Teo began the familiar words,"E Hawai`i e ku`u..." that means, "Oh Hawaii, sands of my birth..." and others immediately joined in. Old Hawaiian men seated on folding chairs beneath the nearby banyan tree stood with their wives and grandchildren, singing this special song they all knew so well. Masao, Gio and Yoriko joined Christy and Duff. Malia took Donya by one hand and Marcus by the other, and encouraged them to hum along with the Hawaiian words and join the powerful refrain, " 'Oli e!, 'Oli e! ", meaning, "rejoice, rejoice".

Teo watched as brown-skinned HPD officers re-moved their helmets and put down their batons, joining hands with local girls and boys, who set their peace signs down and joined hands with Asian boys and black girls in tee-shirts and shorts. Soon everyone in the crowd had linked hands, swaying in massive concentric circles, like a human mandala, browns skins and black, asian and white. Uniformed soldiers on crutches were helped to their feet by young men with beards, and girls with red bandannas around their heads. No longer a protest, but a peaceful celebration of hope, the powerful moment continued for another twenty minutes before the crowd finally departed through the historic gates.

Donald McPhail

CHAPTER FORTY
Duff's Decision

Christy rode with Duff in the back seat of de Villiers' rental car, while Malia sat in front with Marcus. Teo and Donya stayed back at the palace to field questions from the media and do follow-up interviews.

Still stimulated by the moving and peaceful climax to the rally, Duff asked Christy, "Are you as proud as I am, of our son?"

"More than proud, is what I am."

"And you, Malia," he spoke over the seat-back. What are your thoughts?"

"Proud, dad. And not just with Teo. He was amazing. I'm proud of Hawaii today. Did you see how moved they all were, and peaceful through all of it? I've seen rowdy fans at Diamond Head festivals act-out, and those crowds aren't anti-anything. But standing up for peace and ending the war. So yes, I'm very proud."

"And you, Marcus?" asks Christy. "You have seen wars and protests in many parts of the world. How do you feel?"

"I'm impressed, naturally. Teo's words and the crowds' reaction were very powerful. And I think it is a small first step."

"How can you say that," challenged Malia. "There must have been a thousand people there."

"I don't mean to sound unimpressed, truly. But I see Teo leading a much larger movement than this, whether he speaks, or organizes, or goes into national politics. So I see it as a small, powerful, necessary first step."

Christy patted Malia's shoulder and said, "We haven't been able to talk to you about Teo's opportunity, if it happens. But I believe that is what Marcus is referring to."

"What are you talking about? Why didn't you tell me? I was about to ask Marcus to let me out of the car."

"Donya asked Teo to join the Institute for Nonviolence, in California. It won't pay much, but he will learn from leading teachers and thinkers from around the world, and he may eventually influence American leaders on a personal level, and not just at public rallies."

"That's quite a step up, mom. But I suspect that he can hold his own with politicians. Senator Ito will certainly introduce him to his colleagues in DC. Located in California, the Institute may not exactly be 'inside the system', but it has global visibility and respect. You are forgiven, Marcus. But let me know next time. I almost said something I would have regretted."

It was still daylight when they arrived at the house. As Malia and Christy went inside to wait for Teo and Donya, Duff announced his nightly walk around the park.

Donald McPhail

"Hold up a moment and I'll join you, Duff. There's something I need to discuss with you."

"So Duff," began de Villiers, as the two men strode across the lawn past the tennis courts, driven by Duff's new exercise tempo. "I need to level with you, and this seems the right time to do it."

"What do you mean, level with me, Marcus?"

"I'm something more than a writer, Duff. You remember when we first met, I told you I had been a journalist in South Africa, writing political articles that nobody would publish? That when I asked for this assignment, I emphasized that you are also from South Africa? I have a private reason, as well. I want to offer you an assignment, if you think you're up to it."

"You're offering me an assignment?"

De Villiers led them to a bench so they could sit and talk. "We needed to be sure you are the right man. We believe you are, but a lot depends on your health. People I work with would like your help. They are an association of South African business men and women who are looking for peaceful solutions. They know apartheid is killing our country. It's wrong and it must change. We want it to change without bloodshed.

"We're in discussions with leaders of the freedom fighters, the ANC. You heard about them from Cebo when you saw him in Johannesburg."

"Yes, I know of them, and I remember Cebo said something about using our family money to help support them. But Cebo is in prison, you said. On Robben Island."

"He and Mandela are both there still. That is part of the challenge."

"Go on," said Duff.

"These business leaders have genuine financial power in South Africa, and we know the government wants to keep them from speaking out. But the business people are organized, and they are committed. They operate our gold and diamond mines, and they are automobile manufacturers, educators, religious leaders. There is a former commando, the leader of an ex-soldiers movement who is now an equal rights attorney."

"And do these people have names, Marcus?"

"You will know them if you decide to meet with them, Duff. For now, you should simply know that they represent Anglo American, General Motors and Ford, many familiar companies that influence the country. They realize apartheid and racial division are wrong for South Africa, or for anywhere. Our system is wrong, and it doesn't work. South Africa has turned into a police state, finances are threatened because of the world sanctions, and it cannot end well unless someone acts. It is very much as Teo quoted from your Robert Kennedy, we truly have to change the men who are making these disastrous decisions.

"The economic sanctions from America and countries around the world are certainly hurting supporters of apartheid, but they're hurting anti-apartheid activists and millions of poor people, as well, of all races. We need to take action, if apartheid is ever going to end."

"Are you working with the Prime Minister?"

"No, not Vorster. We put out feelers, but he would never meet with us."

"Are you advocating a war?"

"Just the opposite. We know what a war would be like. It would be a bloodbath, worse than the *Mau-Mau* in Kenya a decade ago. Millions would be killed; not just hundreds of thousands. South Africans must have a nonviolent resolution if our country is to survive. But we also need a contingency plan."

Duff looked as if he finally understood what de Villiers was proposing. "Obviously, you aren't asking me to lead this group, or do the negotiating. You want my experience with evacuating injured victims from war zones, and bringing in supplies? As I did in Korea and now in Vietnam.

"That's the main goal, Duff." De Villiers stood and paced. "You have unusual skills, and you care about South Africa. There are hundreds of airline people who know logistics, probably dozens who know how to operate in war zones. But my South African military and airline contacts need someone who also knows the country, who understands the importance of saving millions of lives. Someone who cares about what happens next."

"I'm not a young man, Marcus. I have just had a heart attack."

"We know this Duff, and that nearly ended any consideration that you might be our man. But you're healthier than we realized, according to Christy and Dr. Chen. And if we take precautions, here and in England, they think the risk is manageable. It would mean two or three months for you in London."

"I would be an advisor, it seems. But I agree with Teo. I'm a peaceful man, Marcus. If this blows up, I won't work in another Vietnam."

"We don't want a war, either. None of us does. And the way you operate, you work well with differing views. You could help us to create a peace plan. We want to convince white leaders that there are other ways. That they must share power, or risk a bloody war. But only if you feel strong enough, Duff. And if you want to be a part of saving lives."

They completed the walk in silence, as Duff sorted through Marcus's offer. What sort of physical or personal tolls would it take on him, and on Christy, if he were to spend time overseas? He knew now how she felt about his long absences, and he wouldn't put her through another one.

But she could go with him. Duff would be in meetings, of course, and he would certainly not be flying to South Africa. None of them would be allowed in the country. Not if they were part of this rogue band of business people. Simply recognizing the ANC as an official political organization was against South African law, and any of them would be jailed there.

A peacekeeping force would need a plan to save lives by ferrying troops and equipment into South Africa, in the event it became a war zone; and ferrying people out under hazardous conditions. These would be citizens of all colors escaping to safety, away from the powerful government forces, with jet fighters strafing and bombing civilians and ANC fighters. The terrain would be like Vietnam in some respects. South Africa is a country with major urban centers, that are built up like Saigon, but with vast farm-lands and tribal village areas in between. The game pre-serves would complicate matters, protecting animals in the wild. The peacekeeping force would need to mobilize South African Airways, if they cooperated, as well as Pan Am, BOAC and others if they were willing.

They would need to use neighboring countries for trucks and busses. The plan would depend upon whether an orderly traditional war was underway, or unpredictable, uncontrollable massacres by armed tribal fighters, as it was with the Mau-mau in Kenya.

He was tempted to accept de Villiers' offer, but would Christy agree? Would she join him in England?

By the time they made their way through the gar-den and onto the lanai, Duff had sorted things out. He was preparing to talk about it with Christy. As he looked over at de Villiers, he sensed some discomfort.

"There is something else you aren't telling me, isn't there Marcus? I can see it."

Grinning slightly, "There is something, Duff. And I hope you will approve."

They sat, as usual, on their familiar chairs.

"How do you mean, approve? Have you spoken with Christy already?"

"I have, as a matter of fact." He looked sheepish.

"And does she approve of your offer to me?"

"She has reservations about your health, but she knows you are much stronger now. She also knows how passionate you are about making a difference to people.

You have always taken on difficult business assignments. This time it's for a cause that you believe in. You can prevent another Vietnam. Plus, you will have two nurses with you at all times."

"Two nurses? Is one of them my wife?"

"One is your wife."

"And the other?"

"Your daughter, Duff," de Villiers appeared nervous. "She agreed to accompany us, as well. We have been seeing each other, you see."

"Seeing each other? Is that what you call it?" Duff seemed surprisingly good-humored, and Marcus relaxed slightly.

"An old-fashioned sort of man might call it 'courtship'," offered de Villiers. "After you introduced us at dinner, we have been seeing each other for drinks after work, over at the Halekulani. Last Sunday she took me out on a surfboard with her friend Bully. He was very patient with me, I must say. And she allowed him to be the teacher, even though I could see she wanted to interrupt and make suggestions several different times. Malia is quite a strong-willed young lady."

"Much like her mother, I should say. So that's why you look uncomfortable. And why she reacted toward you the other evening in the car. I knew you were dead serious about the South Africa situation, so it wasn't likely that. So it is my daughter that is making you nervous."

"Not so much Malia, but the fact that we were seeing each other without your knowledge. That was bothering us both."

Donald McPhail

"Well, you can put that behind you. As far as I'm concerned, you are both good people, and you are mature enough to know what you want. Besides, if Christy and Bully accept your relationship, you are passing the sternest tests I know.

Donald McPhail

CHAPTER FORTY-ONE
Hana Hou

Christy stops at the bar to chat with Bully, leaving Duff to welcome arriving friends from a prominent seat at the greeter's table near the front entry. With Duff's consent, Christy decided to "hana hou", to "do it again" with Duff's retirement party at the club. She and Bully remember the panic they shared when Duff had his angina attack. With Duff back on his feet, they look relaxed, talking about Malia and her new writer-friend, and about Teo and Donya and their work at the Institute.

After a time, Duff is released from his responsibilities as a greeter. He clearly loves seeing old friends, some of whom are here from Asia and many from the mainland. Naturally, there are dozens of Pan Am colleagues from around the world, as well as his Honolulu offices. Most everyone is gathered now, each with a glass in hand, as Duff enters the main room and looks around for his favorite wine steward.

Just as on the first occasion, there is a gentle ukulele fanfare and the music celebration begins. Auntie Irmgard agreed to start with " 'E Maliu Mai", as she had done at the first party. This time her son Nane accompanies on ukulele and takes the lead for the first verse, gently singing the inviting words of love, as his sisters and his cousin provide the melodic chorus. Surprisingly, Nane is also an airline man like Duff, though thirty years younger. He works for Masao at Hawaiian Airlines, and is quite a singer himself.

Duff looks around to take in his guests. The young hotel people are over at the bar, holding lively conversations. They are young and fun, and smart as can be, thinks Duff, as the ladies laugh and point accusatory fingers at two of the men from the Hawaii Visitors Bureau. These are Hawaii's next travel industry leaders. The old guard are here too, fine hotel managers and motor coach owners, directors from the Bishop Museum and Sea Life Park.

Andy Cummings approaches the microphone with his longtime friend and one of Hawaii's beloved artists, Uncle Moke Ka'aihue, to perform "Waikiki". Andy acts like a crusty old man sometimes, yet he wrote this gentle love song to his favorite place in Hawaii.

The next artist is lovely Marlene Sai, singing a tribute to Queen Lili'uokalani, the Queen's own composition "Aloha O'e", accompanied on the piano by Mahi Beamer. Then his cousins, the young Beamer brothers, sing and play guitars in a tribute to their great grandmother, herself a beloved singer and dancer.

Duff loves Hawaii's extraordinary music and classic hula, and he knows how rare it is to be honored by Hawaii's most respected musicians and dancers. He also knows he has to gather his thoughts for the presentations. He will be expected to speak, and he wants to express himself coherently. As he observes Don Ho approaching

Donald McPhail

the stage to introduce him, Duff decides to simply relax and speak from the heart.

"Ladies and gentlemen, kanakas and titas, uncles and aunties," Ho begins with his comfortable style. "I have the honor of introducing one of Hawaii's industry leaders, our friend and a man with a true Hawaiian heart. You all know him, Mr. Duff Malone."

Ho greets him with a hug, and Duff approaches the microphone. "Thank you, Don, and thank you friends. As I look around this evening, at all of the good people gathered here, the first word that comes to my mind is 'ohana, for you are truly my family. I am very touched, and keenly aware of how fortunate I am to be alive and well, and here with you. I must say that my heart attack frightened me at first, but I have received love and care from Christy and our children, and from many dear friends. I have also learned some surprising lessons about life. I am not a religious man, but I do believe there is another life after death. While I am not afraid of dying, I worry that it could happen before my real work is done. I will speak of this in a moment.

"Christy and both of our children are with us now, for the first time in many years. You all know Christy."

As she stands, friends cheer and whistle, knowing her fun-loving nature, as slim, suave Bones Johnston, a close friend from Hilo, leans down and presents her with a delicate pikake lei, and a kiss on her cheek.

"And our incredible daughter Malia." Solid applause, as she, too, stands and Masao presents her with a

haku lei of white orchids, her favorite, to be worn on her head like a floral crown.

"And our brave son Teo, back from Vietnam, and soon to work for peace in Vietnam and elsewhere, with some of the world's brightest minds." Scrappy presents him with a lush ginger lei. She whispers something during their kiss, and Teo looks pleasantly embarrassed.

Before Duff can continue, Christy approaches him with a regal Maile lei, stretching high onto her tiptoes and placing it around his neck, adding a long kiss on the lips, while Masao and Gio lead a kindly commentary about their public display of affection.

As Christy leaves him to return to her chair, and guests sit again, Duff continues. "Let me extend my use of 'ohana, friends, because all of us here are family, indeed. I raise my glass to you, my only glass of wine allowed tonight," drawing nods of understanding.

"Christy and I arrived in Hawaii in 1934, not the way the missionaries did, thank goodness. And we didn't come here to change Hawaii as they did, but to become part of this unique and loving community. But as we all know, the airlines did change these islands, just as air travel changed much of the world. Back then, visitors came via steamships, and numbered in the thousands. This year, over two million people visited Hawaii. We did change these islands quite substantially, and not always for the better.

"I hope you don't mind that I'm speaking seriously tonight, but since we are family I will risk turning an evening of love and friendship into a moment for serious

Donald McPhail

issues, such as those young military men and women we see each day around Waikiki, trying to enjoy their lives a little before returning to a devastating war. If you bear with me, I believe you will find that my serious thoughts are prompted by feelings of love and friendship.

"As airlines, Pan American, United, Hawaiian, Aloha and others in our industry have brought jobs and a certain amount of community pride to Hawaii, and a good life for many. For many more, however, our industry has dramatically raised the cost of living here, to the point where families have to work far too hard, both moms and dads, many with more than one job so they can pay for their children to go to good schools and live in decent homes. At the same time, we brought visitors here, who learned about our islands and fell in love with our cultures. Unfortunately, we also transported other kinds of visitors, who sometimes usurped our culture, abused our hospitality and damaged our local communities.

"Overall, I believe that travel and tourism are healthy things, for education and human relationships here and around the world. The more we know about other places and cultures, the more likely we are to understand and engage with them. This is good. People who have not traveled can be easily frightened about 'those others' who don't look or act like them. Our son Teo recently returned from a long and difficult tour of duty in Vietnam, a country that many of us don't know at all. If we did, I believe we would be unlikely to carry out our current destructive, terrible war there. In his new job, Teo will work hard to eliminate violence and wars.

"On the subject of peace, I'm afraid my retirement will be brief. I've accepted a new assignment, and Christy and I will work for peace too, in a different part of the world. We'll be in London for a while, helping to prevent massive bloodshed in a troubled South Africa.

"South Africa is the place where I was raised. It is quite far away, and it is a beautiful country, filled with many of the very same lovely flowers and trees that surround us in Hawaii. Its major cities are large and sophisticated, yet most of the population is under-educated and unrepresented.

"You may not know it, but South Africa is on the precipice of a violent and bloody revolution. It is currently a place where citizens' personal rights are defined strictly by race, not by education or accomplishments. There are laws that legally separate black and brown-skinned people from white ones. They cannot marry, or hold hands, or even socialize together. Some twelve million white people govern the lives of more than twenty-five million non-whites. This is wrong, and it will lead to a bloody war if it is not changed. Many of us know that millions of people will be killed if something triggers this civil war.

"So you can see why I am serious here tonight. After all my years in a commercial business, I have an opportunity to make an important difference in this world. I have agreed to do a small part to prevent violence in South Africa. My role will be limited, and I will need to look after my health, but this is something I feel I must do.

"I'm now an American citizen, but like many here in this room, my roots are overseas. I still hold surprisingly

Donald McPhail

*strong feelings for my home country. Some of my work will
be done in London, not so far away from Africa, a place
where leaders can meet and plan without interference from
the South African government. Though our true home remains here in Honolulu, Christy, Malia and I will spend time
in England, working for this crucial peace.*

*"I want you all to know that my heart attack was a
blessing for me. I nearly died, and that captured my attention. As I recuperated, I learned some facts of life that startled me. I learned that my closest friends had faced near-
death experiences themselves, and I never knew it. That I
had allowed my job to become more important than my
family, and I hadn't seen it. I also learned that I still have a
chance to help make this world a little better, and that's
what Christy and I are going to do, together.*

*"And so back to this lovely evening, we are friends
and family here in this room. The music will continue, and
we should all enjoy ourselves. But as family, we need to
appreciate the peace and joy that we share here, without
forgetting the work that remains to be done in places like
Vietnam and South Africa. That work involves each of us,
and the responsibility extends to our leaders here in
Hawaii, as well as in Washington, Hanoi, London and Johannesburg.*

*"I thank you for your friendship and your love. As
we end our evening, let us join hands, as we always do,
working for peace and sharing our lovely anthem, 'Hawaii
Aloha' ".*

THE END

Author's Note

Many of the events in this novel did happen, although the main characters and their experiences are entirely fictitious.

Pan Am did become America's flagship airline. It did establish its worldwide service using those pivotal facilities on remote atolls of Midway and Wake, constructing essential fueling stations with the unofficial help of the U.S. Navy. Pan Am's evolution from government airmail contracts to commercial passenger flights did take place, and Juan Trippe was a masterful and daring strategist, parlaying finances, aircraft purchases, board members and government alliances into advantageous positions for himself and his airline.

While 1934 Honolulu would have been an unlikely headquarters for Pan Am's Pacific division, current world events and the emergence of Honolulu as a sophisticated commercial hub would make it an ideal choice today.

Duff Malone is entirely fictitious, though he looks and acts a lot like my dad might have if he had lived the life I created for him. My father began with American Express and was a successful cruise director before joining Pan American, where he was a station manager in New York when he died in 1944, at the age of 43. I grew up in California with his silver-framed image prominently displayed, wearing a Pan Am pin on his lapel. So Pan Am was larger-than-life to me.

For the early days of Pan American Airways and affiliated China National Aviation Corporation, I consulted Max Watson's "The Man Who Made Pan Am" and Gregory Crouch's "China's Wings: War, Intrigue, Romance and Adventure in the Middle Kingdom during the Golden Age of Flight." Both books are meticulously researched and beautifully written, with valuable insights as to the character and human frailties of figures like Juan Trippe and CNAC's William Langhorne Bond, as well as Generalissimo and Madame Chiang Kai-shek.

Donald McPhail

Also informative and helpful were web sites created and maintained by former Pan Am employees of all job levels and departments. The sites radiate with the ongoing pride, sophistication and love of their Pan Am roots. Their pain at the loss of this once-great airline is clear and deeply expressed. Some of the sites include clipperpioneers.com, panam.org, and panamair.org.

My settings and characters in Hawaii were observed and nurtured during more than fifty years of visits to those unique and beautiful islands, as a visitor, writer, and an employee with airlines, resorts and travel companies. I was blessed to know many of Hawaii's most talented and respected travel industry people. I was also fortunate to know many of the islands' extraordinary musicians and dancers, as I accompanied them to performances throughout the mainland during my stint at Hawaiian Airlines. These artists shared their pride, knowledge and Hawaiian hearts in ways I appreciate even more as I grow older.

Acknowledgements

Factual information about old Hawaii and beachboy characters came from the Scrappy Lipton Collection of books and music. Distinguished local organizations like *Hui Nalu* and the Outrigger Canoe Club do exist, though my references to them are entirely fictitious. "The View From Diamond Head" by Dan Hubbard and David Franzen, and "Waikiki Beachboy" by Grady Timmons were especially helpful in understanding early Waikiki and its unique characters.

Understanding of Hawaiian pride and culture came from my own good fortune of meeting extraordinary people, including Nane Aluli, Mas Takano, Bones Johnston, Kealoha Chang, Marlene Sai, Dr. George Kanahele, George Manu and many others.

My character Ke'alii was inspired by the late George Helm, an inspired leader of the Protect Kaho'olawe 'Ohana. In 1977, Helm and his friend Kimo Mitchell were lost in the waters off of Kaho'olawe.

Malia's strength of character, spiritual awareness and surfing prowess were prompted by stories about the late Rell Sunn, and enhanced by a respected friend and colleague on the island of Kauai, Malana DeSilva.

I acknowledge and credit Mas Takano, my boss at Hawaiian Airlines and a dear friend, before, during and after those great airline days, and his beloved sister Cookie Takano Takeshita, for the beautifully told, painful stories of growing up as youngsters in Amache internment camp. Over 150,000 Japanese-Americans were imprisoned at Amache, Manzanar and multiple other camps during the first years of WWII. Their touching and important stories still need telling and understanding.

The source of my 1937 eyewitness scenes of Japan's attack on Shanghai, where Chinese planes bombed thousands of their own people, came from actual letters written during and following those devastating events, from Jean McClellan to her mother in America. These and actual 1937 periodicals "Oriental Affairs", "China Journal" and

Donald McPhail

"Shanghai Evening Post & Mercury" provided first-hand reports and photos to help describe those horrific scenes. I thank my oldest childhood friend and extraordinary sculptor and scrum-half, Michael T. McClellan for loaning me his family's treasures.

Special thanks to my patient and insightful "editorial board and beta-readers": my loving wife Gretchen, who bears an uncanny resemblance to Christy Malone, and dear friends Sue Mellberg, Alison Mellberg, Anne Rothwell Carr, Wade & Phyllis Meyercord, Steve Lovette, Kevin Carroll, Steve Grosvold, and old ball-playing buddies, Roger Baer, Dick Fregulia and author D.W. Buffa. I also thank historian Rick Helin, the "Kailua Kid", who helped me to realize the importance of careful research and to appreciate the real *Malolo* cruise and its passengers.

Vietnam Fighter information came from "Memories of Chu Lai", written by Annapolis graduate Dave Hunter. His was a powerful personal story within the 2002 book entitled, "There I Was…", created from wartime memories written by active duty graduates of the US Naval Academy Class of 1965, who were also my classmates.

I thank my favorite Hawaiian singing duo, Cecilio & Kapono (Cecilio Rodriguez and Henry Kapono) for their original, melodic and inspiring songs that reflect, to me, the wild and free flowing atmosphere of young Hawaii in the seventies. "Sunflower" was written by Cecilio Rodriguez, and is as refreshing today as it was for me back then. As for my character Ke's *aumakua*, the owl, I thank Keola Beamer's "Old Man Pueo" for the inspiration for this revered creature.

Finally a personal thanks to old friend and travel industry colleague Nane Aluli, for the use of his mother's song, "E Maliu Mai", and her family singing group, "Puamana", to open and close my story. Nane was a Vietnam veteran, injured in the war, and is one of he most serene, hospitable, committed and inspiring people I know. His mom, Irmgard Farden Aluli, was a beautiful soul, whose poetry, songs, music and dance made her a "living treasure of Hawaii". She died in 2001.

A special thanks to old friend Joan Baez, an inspiration and hero of mine for more than sixty years, for generously allowing the use of her name, her work and her quote on my book. She is a global treasure for her tireless work on behalf of peace and freedom, and for making a difference in the lives of poor and disenfranchised throughout the world. She has improved all of our lives as an example of integrity and real toughness in an unnecessarily cruel world. Thanks to her associate and my friend, Jeanne Triolo Murphy, for her valuable support.

There are many who have helped me, whose names are not included. If I missed someone, I apologize.

Donald McPhail
Mountain View, California

Further Acknowledgements

Amache Japanese Internment Camp, from Mas Takano & Cookie Takano Takeshita articles and video clips:
https://www.youtube.com/watch?v=WyOsdesOVyg,
https://fpdl.vimeocdn.com/vimeo-prod-skyfire-std-us/
01/2981/6/164909514/523763408.mp4?
token=1511388274-0x686d9c4b982a227b87de48a5cd6a8
eccd661e451

Hawaii history from the Scrappy Lipton collection:
"Hawaii Looking Back" by Glen Grant and Bennett Hymerand the Bishop Museum Archives, Mutual Publishing, November 2000.
"Then There Were None", by Martha H.Noyes, Bess Press, 2003.
"The View From Diamond Head" by Dan Hubbard and David Franzen, Editions Limited, Wilcox and Rick, November 1986.
"Waikiki Beachboy" by Grady Timmons, by Royal Editions Limited, Wilcox and Rick and Lambert, October 1989.

Shanghai and China information from the Michael T. McClellan Asian Collection:
Correspondence, Jean McClellan, August, 1937
"Oriental Affairs" by H.G.W. Woodhead, CBE, Vol. VIII. No. 3, September, 1937.
"The Shanghai Evening Post & Mercury" special edition
"Pictorial Review of Shanghai Hostilities, Vol. 1, Number 2, September 10, 1937.
"The China Journal", Vol. XVII No.3, September, 1937

History of Pan American World Airways and China National Aviation Corporation:
"The Man Who Made Pan Am", by Max Watson, New Word City, Inc., October, 2011
"China's Wings: War, Intrigue, by Gregory Crouch, Bantam Books, February 2012.

My Lai Massacre Article:
My Lai Massacre: Cameraman Saw GIs Slay 100 Villagers By JOSEPH ESZTERHAS. (c) Thursday, Nov. 20, 1969, The Plain Dealer

Pan Am History from Various Web Sites, including:
http://www.aviation.hawaii.gov
http://www.centennialofflight.net
http://clipperpioneers.com
http://hawaii.gov/
https://huinalu.org
https://www.outriggercanoeclub.com
http://www.panam.org
http://www.panamair.org

Vietnam Fighter information from:
"Memories of Chu Lai" by Dave Hunter, within the book, "There I Was…", Gateway Press, Baltimore, MD 2002, US Naval Academy Class of 1965

Sound and Music From:
"E Maliu Mai" by Irmgard Farden Aluli, 1958, 59, 87 Criterion Music Corp.
"Sunflower" by Cecilio Rodriguez, 1974, made popular by Cecilio & Kapono, August 2, 1988, 1974 Sony Music Entertainment Inc.

Donald McPhail

Author Donald McPhail

The Guest From Johannesburg is Donald McPhail's second novel, a sequel to his popular The Millionaires Cruise: Sailing Toward Black Tuesday *(isbn13: 978-0-692-36611-0). A longtime freelance writer and travel industry executive, his fiction career began in 2007.*

Born in Chile and educated in the United States, McPhail sang with Joan Baez, trained and coached with Olympic decathlon champion Bill Toomey, and served as the backup to Hall of Fame quarterback Roger Staubach as a midshipman at Annapolis. He lettered in football and baseball at Navy.

His first love was athletics and he entered the travel industry by chance, but a travel career was definitely in his blood. His father was a manager for American Express Travel before joining Pan American Airways in New York, where he passed away at the age of 43. His mother was a registered nurse, who moved to California, where she raised McPhail and his brother Bill, while working overnight shifts at Palo Alto Hospital. These events had a profound effect on McPhail, and influenced his writing.

At nineteen he made the first of nine trips to South Africa, his father's country of origin. At twenty-five he joined United Airlines in San Francisco while earning his degree in international relations and world literature at San Francisco State University.

At age twenty-seven he was national commercial sales manager at United Airlines' Chicago headquarters; at thirty-seven he was regional manager for Hawaiian Airlines.

Throughout his forties McPhail combined three careers — as a successful high school football coach, a consultant for the state of Oregon, and a writer with articles published in newspapers around the world.

In his fifties he was general manager for a luxury resort on Maui, and helped reopen a Kauai resort that had been destroyed by hurricane Iniki. Today in his late seventies, he is a productive novelist and volunteer organizer for his old high school and college athletic programs. He lives in Northern California with his wife Gretchen. His sons Scott and Jack live in Berkeley and Anchorage.

Donald McPhail

www.ingramcontent.com/pod-product-compliance
Lightning Source LLC
Chambersburg PA
CBHW070201120726
47909CB00001B/209